KT-494-670

THE ENLIGHTENMENT PROJECT

THE ENLIGHTENMENT PROJECT

Lynn Hightower

SEVERN
HOUSE

First world edition published in Great Britain in 2021 and the USA in 2022
by Severn House, an imprint of Canongate Books Ltd,
14 High Street, Edinburgh EH1 1TE.

Trade paperback edition first published in Great Britain and the USA in 2022
by Severn House, an imprint of Canongate Books Ltd.

severnhouse.com

Copyright © Lynn Hightower, 2021

All rights reserved including the right of
reproduction in whole or in part in any form.
The right of Lynn Hightower to be identified
as the author of this work has been asserted
in accordance with the Copyright,
Designs & Patents Act 1988.

British Library Cataloguing-in-Publication Data
A CIP catalogue record for this title is available from the British Library.

ISBN-13: 978-0-7278-5088-1 (cased)
ISBN-13: 978-1-4483-0719-7 (trade paper)
ISBN-13: 978-1-4483-0718-0 (e-book)

This is a work of fiction. Names, characters, places and incidents
are either the product of the author's imagination or are used fictitiously.
Except where actual historical events and characters are being described
for the storyline of this novel, all situations in this publication are
fictitious and any resemblance to actual persons, living or dead,
business establishments, events or locales is purely coincidental.

All Severn House titles are printed on acid-free paper.

Typeset by Palimpsest Book Production Ltd.,
Falkirk, Stirlingshire, Scotland.
Printed and bound in Great Britain by
TJ Books, Padstow, Cornwall.

For Robert. Je t'aime toujours.

ACKNOWLEDGMENTS

My heartfelt thanks to Dr Alessia de Paola Gottlieb, specialist in pediatric psychiatry, for reading and insights. Much gratitude to Carl Moses, LCSW, because sometimes my characters need a therapist. To Laurel, Rachel and Alan, and Sheila Williams for plotting discussions, and to all of my beautiful family. To my publisher, Kate Lyall Grant, and editor, Rachel Slatter, and my agent Matt Bialer, Bailey Tamayo and Stefanie Diaz of Sanford J. Greenburger. Many thanks to my amazing publicist, Kim Dower, of Kim-From-LA. And to my pup, Leah, who is a Very Good Girl.

AUTHOR'S NOTE

The Chapel of Disciples exists only in the imagination of the author, as does Ward Five at Eastern State Hospital.

ONE

That night, late in the OR, exhausted after hours on my feet, topped off with a late-night emergency surgery, I was removing the octopus tentacles of a medulloblastoma from the brain of a fourteen-year-old girl who wanted to work for NASA when she grew up . . . and I felt the presence.

It had been there since I was eleven, like a shadow in my peripheral vision, but tonight . . . tonight there was some kind of shift, like a sudden change in air pressure, and it broke my concentration.

Nothing broke my concentration when I was operating. I would only be aware, after it was all over, of the pain in the small of my back, that my feet were on fire, that I needed to piss, but I was not conscious of any of this when I was perched on the edge of the cliff making minute incisions or cauterizing the cells of your brain.

I felt a surge of nausea that brought bile to my mouth, and caught a whiff of something that would make a man with less control gag and turn away.

A quick look at my surgical team – but no one had noticed anything. The anesthesiologist was focused on her computer monitor, sitting heavily on the stool at the head of the table where Olivia Van Owen lay with her brain exposed. She wore black-framed rectangular glasses, Olivia did, and had two long blonde braids. She presented with four months of on-and-off headaches, vomiting, tinnitus and a stiff neck before she was diagnosed. Vigilant mother, good pediatrician. Luck.

My student, Marshall, watched with sweat globules rolling down the side of his face into the beard that was starting to shadow his face at the end of an excruciating shift. My head nurse, a veteran of Iraq, wiped sweat from my forehead, bringing me back into the moment. He was the only one who seemed to feel the prick of something *other* in the room. He gave me a strange look, his combat experience putting him on the alert, for what he likely did not know.

Because like me he had the sense that something here was wrong.

I took another long look at the brain tissue magnified for my viewing pleasure. I had the feeling that something was waiting, wanting, circling my patient, and that I was out of time. I was just on the verge of letting Marshall close, and Marshall knew he was closing, which was why he was sweating. But this thing stirred my warrior energy and my protective instincts for Olivia Van Owen. Something was wrong and I took another look.

I knew exactly where. A small feeling, earlier, looking at the brain stem, though I knew the tumor, burrowing into Olivia's cerebellum, had not reached that far. And yet, something felt off, like a small wrong note of music, and I tilted my head and squinted, well aware of the dangers here; the brain stem was the gatekeeper of the brain, less was safer, always. Still. That small, anvil-shaped bit of tissue near the bone should not really have had a shape, and healthy as it looked, it bulged slightly, which I didn't like to see. I probed ever so gently, and I found it . . . the dirty little handprint of the tumor, hiding away.

Malignant tumors were ambitious. Warriors out to invade and conquer. The enemy. We still don't know what causes them. I did not like not knowing; I do not like uncertainly. I was a neurosurgeon, one of the Gods Of Medicine. But like all of us, I had to live with it.

So I took what was wise, prayed to the gods of radiation to annihilate the rest, and envisioned my patient in twenty years. I pictured myself sitting at my desk, opening an email from Olivia Van Owen, where she told me about her promotion at NASA, and that, yes, all of her kids were doing fine.

I did this with all of my patients.

My recovery stats were extraordinary – for a neurosurgeon. So many of my patients die, or wind up in nursing homes needing twenty-four hour care. I might buy them a year or two before hospice. It made a difference, the doctor, the surgeon you chose. A series of decisions, of instinct, of hands that might heal better than others. There was more mystery in healing than you might think, and I looked for this in my students. Perfect candidates with no sign of this ability were shocked to be passed over in favor of students with more mundane qualifications, but innate ability. Healing hands.

I nodded to Marshall to close, my head nurse gave me another look, and I walked away from the OR, stripping off, taking a racehorse piss, then heading down the corridors that were so quiet here, late-night silence in a hospital, so pregnant in the halls outside the patient's rooms, so empty outside the OR.

Olivia's parents jumped when I came into the room, their faces tight with tension and the tracks of tears. I held their hands and we sat together, and I answered their questions. All of them that could be answered. I didn't rush away, like most surgeons, who are fairly slick at the art of disengaging, which is simpler than it sounds. A quick nod, then you walked away. Instead I sat with them a few minutes, allowing the silence to settle, allowing them to process. It was life or death for their child. I could give them a few minutes.

Olivia's mother looked up at me, holding tight to her husband's hand. 'I'm just . . . scared,' she said.

'I know. It's scary stuff. You have my cell number.'

She nodded.

I stood. Touched her shoulder. Her husband leaped up and shook my hand. And I was off.

The corridors to my office, noisy during the day, were quiet, the thin gray carpet absorbing the tread of my footsteps. I longed for Moira, knowing she would be curled up in a Sherpa blanket on the leather couch, lesson planning or reading a Georgette Heyer Regency. She read them over and over, sneaking chocolate, smiling absently when I came into the room and ignoring me when I buried my face in the rich, chocolate-dark curly hair she hated and I adored. I would have to wait for my kiss until she was at the end of the chapter. This was to keep my surgeon's ego in line; she really couldn't concentrate with me roaming behind her, clattering in the kitchen. Delicate as a dancer in the OR, in my own kitchen I tended to break glasses, knock things over, and make Moira wonder out loud why anyone trusted me to actually open up their head. I was a god in the OR, and the village idiot in my own home.

There was something, a darkness that scurried, like a rat in the corner, right at the edge of my vision. I stopped for a moment, then, wisely, I ignored it. Wisely, I looked away.

When the crossroad comes, you do not recognize it. You do not know it until afterward, looking back. But this is when it began. Again.

Have you ever known anyone who survived being possessed? You do now. You've met me. Like you, I had questions. Why bad things happened, the nature of evil. Was it safe to bring a child into this world?

I headed into my office to get my car keys, make a few notes. My office lights were on, the door opened a crack. I felt the presence before I saw the man on the couch beside my desk. A priest.

TWO

The priest rose when he saw me, and whatever darkness there was behind me melted away.

'What the hell?' I said, our usual greeting, and he grinned. He wore the robes, the collar, the silver cross swaying on his chest. Not Catholic, but Episcopal, the American version of the Anglican Church.

This was not just any priest, this was my priest. My guy. The man who pulled me out of the dark and into the light.

The presence, when it had you. You felt it like a weight in your very bones. It was there, in you, hanging on you, but it was not you, it was wrong, and you wanted it out. Even when you gave up. When the weight, the whispers in your head, the oppression dragged you down and down and down, there was always something in you that wanted it out. It was out of me now, but times like tonight, I felt it, sometimes menacing, sometimes like a sulky child. I kept the barriers up. I would not let it in. But Father Cavanaugh had warned me – I would be vulnerable, always.

I don't like most doctors, but I was one. I was a neurosurgeon, and went into this line of work trying to understand what the hell was in my head and in my soul when I was eleven years old and my life derailed. Enormous research had been done on spirituality and the brain, and I'd spent a major portion of my days and nights mapping out exactly where good and evil is located in the brain, and could pinpoint the primitive parts of your brain where the cells that fuel the spirit will bunch, live, die. It was not just one place. Spirituality was *integrated* throughout the brain.

I had studied the research – Hood's scale of mysticism from way back in the 1970s, scans of the brain activity of Carmelite nuns, meditating Buddhists, evangelists speaking in tongues.

Spiritual activity in the brain happened almost like a net of energy, lighting up some parts, muting others. The frontal lobe, ignited in concentration for the nuns and the monks, the parietal lobe, where we got our sense of self, slowing down, going mute. Generating, perhaps, the loss of the sense of self, creating oneness, unity with God. The activation of the speech centers for the nuns, the visual areas lighting up for the monks. And in strange contrast, the curious decrease in frontal lobe activity and focus for evangelists speaking in tongues. There was a chain of neurological events that triggered spirituality, myriad facets of a complex process. Even forgiveness was a complex neurocognitive process. The very neural architecture of our brains compelled us to see the world in myth, religion, God.

Or – not God. The presence of the Other. Dark things. Ye shall know them by their fruits.

For me it began with the whispering, just out of earshot, voices that made the hair stand on the back of my neck. I was a typical boy, smart for my age, but lazy. I had to be forced to go to church, I watched girls from the corner of my eye and I lived for soccer and science, in that order. I hated taking showers, wanted my own dog, liked to get lost in computer games which my mother fiercely limited: two hours every day for TV or video, and not a minute more. I felt badly used.

I fought that voice, but when my father died of a sudden aneurysm that drowned his brain in blood, and my mother struggled to do what no woman can, which is be a father to a son, I had *the voice* for strength. Comfort my mother gave me in waves. It was strength I craved. Safety. I listened until it had me, alternately making me feel like a superhero, then flooding my mind with stupid thoughts that got mean and nasty – crap in the floor,

kill a bird, tell your mother you're glad your daddy is dead. I
didn't do any of those things. It never got that far. There was a
part of me that knew wrong things when I heard them.

But it would not let me go. It stayed in my head, it kept me
up when I was desperate to sleep, and gave me images I did not
want to see. Dark angels were like vermin, and once they had
strong hold they didn't let go. And that is what it said it was. A
dark angel. Which I took, for the longest time, as just another
stupid thought.

It's the fatigue that gets you. It is a struggle, living with
voices and urges that shame you, then pull you in. I was so
exhausted and so lost I could see no way out but death. I planned
it out, ways that I could die, and believe me, it's not as easy as it
sounds, not when you plan for real, when you worry about who
will find your corpse. Not when you are only eleven years old.

And when I stood looking down into the brown oily waters
of the snaking Green River, one leg over the side of High Bridge,
an old railroad track stretching out a mile and a half over a
narrow band of water and rock, where teenagers liked to hang
out, attracted in equal parts by danger, privacy and a trail of
stories of other kids who had fallen off the bridge or been trapped
on the tracks and shredded by a train, it occurred to me that I
could always die tomorrow, if need be, that it was worth a chance
to ask for help. I knew where the bridge was. My friend Orin
had a big brother who was happy to drive us up there on a
Saturday afternoon, I could come back and die another day.

And help I got. From my mother, who took me seriously when
I needed her to take me seriously. And from Father Cavanaugh,
young enough to be my big brother, an Episcopalian priest from
out of the parish who landed like a bomb in our household – an
avenging angel who told me from the very first meeting that if
indeed I was possessed by a dark angel, as I said I was, the fight
could only be won with everyone on board. He and I, working
side by side, the light of God to guide us and give us strength.
It would be God who did the heavy lifting, Cavanaugh told me.
But we had to do our part.

I was not so sure about God but I kept that to myself. I was
very sure about the dark.

I survived my exorcisms, performed one after the other in ever increasing doses until I felt the dark angel leave me, and it was a physical thing, like being freed from an octopus-like creature that wraps its tentacles around you, in the same way as the malignant tumors I remove. You had to be there to know how strong it was, how bad it smelled, how joyous when the dark went out of the room. I can't explain it. Like so many other things in my life.

I liked to think sometimes that it was the presence of my father, there beside me on the bridge that day, whispering in my ear, telling me not to give up. But what I know is that it was Father Cavanaugh who pulled me back from the edge.

He was up on his feet now, and we embraced, a stocky man, barrel-chested like a German shepherd, fine blond hair streaked dark with gel, combed back away from his face.

'How are the boys? Moira?'

'They're great.' I gave him a second look. Beneath the polite priest facade, the lines in his face looked like they'd been etched in acid, and I wondered if he'd been getting any sleep. But his robes seemed crisp, as always, everything about him starched, precise, like a model out of *PRIEST GQ*. Women had always been mad for Perry, and I had seen him look at them wistfully, as if there was a distance that could not be crossed. It was not his calling – Episcopalian priests could marry, have families. They didn't have to wander around suited up in their robes. At first I thought it was ambition and obsession with work that kept him alone, but over the years it has seemed more like a weight he carried that set him apart. And the robes – a sort of armor.

'I brought you a coffee,' he said. There was a Starbucks cup on my desk. 'Lily let me in, I hope you don't mind.'

He knew I didn't mind. I would give him a key if he asked for it.

I shut the door, slid behind the desk, and grabbed the coffee. Stone cold.

I frowned. 'Been waiting a while?'

'Three hours, give or take.'

'It's two a.m. and you've been here all night? What the fuck, Perry?'

He settled back on the couch, but his back was straight, and he watched me. It was the same kind of watching I did with patients. You could tell a lot looking at patients from visit to visit, though you'd be shocked by the number of doctors who don't look at patients. They just looked at charts, screens, stats.

'Do you remember a patient of yours called Henry Mandeville?'

I settled back in the cracked red leather of the throne Moira had installed behind my desk. She'd researched Italian leather for two weeks. She spent carefully, astounded each month at how our bank account filled.

'Mandeville,' I said. And I knew that name, it came with a whiff of something bad. Terminal. Dismissed from this phase of my research project when an MRI revealed a ravenous tumor in the prefrontal lobes of his brain. 'Oh, right. Yes. I know him.'

'And?'

'I can't discuss patients, Perry, even if they're dead. Come on.'

'He's not dead.' Perry slid to the edge of the couch and we both knew that if pressed I'd spill. I owed this man everything. He reached into the pockets of his robe, patting his side as if he were looking for something, then pulled his fists on his knees and sat forward. 'Then let me tell you. Eighteen months ago, Henry Mandeville was a subject in your ongoing study.'

'The Enlightenment Project.'

He canted his head to one side. 'You actually call it that?'

'It's sexy. Sex sells when you're grubbing for dollars. And . . . we've had breakthroughs, Perry.'

He was not smiling. 'Tell me the worst.'

This was an old argument between us.

'Three years ago, Hilde and I managed to fund our very own MRI. We've rather precisely mapped out what we think is the signature pattern of brain activity – the neurological sequence – that red-lights when the subject is having a spiritual experience.'

'By subject, I assume you mean human.'

'I do.'

'So what, Noah? You wire people up and ask them to pray, or meditate, and when the OM comes, your screen lights up? Other scientists have found the same thing.'

I tapped the side of my desk. 'Actually, it's the other way around. We've refined brain-stimulation techniques—'

'Electric shock?'

'We're talking about a very minute stimulation of the brain cells. Creating novel impulses across . . .'

'Go on, Noah.'

I felt eleven again. 'Why are you so pissed off?'

'In a minute. So you shock the human and then what?'

I placed my hands carefully on the desk. 'We gently and selectively stimulate electrical impulses across and between brain regions for a coordinated outcome.'

'The result?'

'To begin, a strong meditative state. The goal – *Enlightenment*.'

'Artificially?'

'Semantics, Perry. It is what it is. A state of enlightenment. However they get there, they get there.'

He frowned, sat back and crossed his ankle over one knee. 'Really. Why?'

'Why?'

'Because you can? To create . . . *Enlightenment on Demand*?'

'OK. Say it however you want to say it, it's pretty damn cool.'

'Damn cool? Like cable TV? And you think that's a good idea? Can you make a constant orgasm?'

'Fyodor Dostoevsky had ecstatic seizures that put him in a state of enlightenment. He considered it the highest joy of his life.'

'And yet he wrote really depressing novels.'

I paused, and kept my voice steady. 'Consider the effects of meditation. Proven – specific. Lower blood pressure, lower heart rate, decreased anxiety, decreased depression. Think of what enlightenment can bring. Peace of heart. Hope. Optimism. Which could mean breakthrough treatments for chronic depression. Addiction. Mental illness. Despair, Perry. The world stinks of it.'

'Dangerous territory, Noah.'

'*Proven* territory, Perry. The brain has two functions. Self-maintenance and self-transcendence. And, coincidentally, spirituality has the same two functions, don't you see that? Spirituality is like a tool for the brain, spirituality helps a brain function. Our brains are literally set up to use spirituality to survive. A spiritual experience, enlightenment, has two sides. One – the emotional, intellectual manifestation – a mystical experience. Two – the physical trigger – an electrochemical surge firing in the brain.'

'You say spirituality. Not religion.'

'Some people find religion leads to a spiritual state. That's all I'll give you. It's only one path to get there. I'm sure it works for some people.'

'Yourself not included?'

'Myself not included.'

'And what do you consider a normal spiritual experience? What about an abnormal spiritual experience?'

'Why do you think I have spent my life on this when what I had as a boy was the most abnormal of experiences? The most horrible of them. I am looking for a way around it. A way out. A way to be in control, to chart the path. I have had *no choice* but to consider the mind beyond the brain. I have been trained in the brain but the mind . . . the spirit . . . this is something intangible but very real.'

'Yes, exactly, very real. *How can you not see this?* After your own experiences, Noah? Do you not see the danger of pushing a person into a religious experience they are not ready to have?'

'A *religious* experience, Perry? Really? I am not stimulating religious experiences. I am physically putting the brain into a gentle state of meditation. To enhance a sense of well-being. Wherever it leads them.'

Perry winced. 'Enlightenment.'

'Well hell, Perry, that's just a word. Awakening, enlightenment, heaven within, the highest state of brain function and meaning. So many words and such a stew of meanings.'

He cocked his head to one side. 'And what does it mean to you? Personally?'

'To me . . . I like the Japanese Buddhist take of Satori and Kensho. Simply understanding who you are. Knowing your true essence, the true nature of reality. I can't really describe it because I've never felt it. I believe people who say they have. But for me . . . it's dangerous territory. I don't even try to go there. I am only creating a state of meditation, and letting the patient take that where they will. Look, lots of neuropsychiatrists work with patients on learning to meditate to do exactly what I am trying to accomplish here. To heal. To give control. To let go of addiction, to heal from depression, to no longer need to self-medicate to endure just being human in a world where the very nature of being human means you veer from being miserable and suffering, to being happy, to worrying about losing everything and everyone you love. Meditation is a pathway to healing on physical, mental and spiritual levels.

'But helping people learn the technique – I mean look at the instructions out there. *Think of nothing. Count your breaths. Go inward. Go to a place where you do not exist.* How does that help anybody at the end of a long hard day, much less someone with their back to the wall? That kind of advice is often useless and always frustrating. All it does is put people in the position of wrestling with their brain, which is the opposite of what they need to do. I would like to take the word *mindfulness* and blow it the fuck up.'

Perry's smile was slow and reluctant. 'Can I put that on a tee shirt?'

I leaned back. Tapped my fingers on the arm of the chair. 'You know what some of my patients tell me? That for the first time they feel *free*. Just quietly OK in the world. Really simple things, mundane things, make them happy. That their wisdom, their spirituality – their religion even – is within, and they rely on themselves for guidance. And it shows up physically in the MRIs. Their prefrontal cortex is measurably thicker, which means increased awareness, concentration and decision-making. There is increased neuroplasticity, we've measured the changes in cerebral blood flow, and that means an uptick in positive thoughts and emotions that help people navigate the negative ones. Which means they are healing. They are getting better. It's actually quite fucking phenomenal. And what, by the way, is the purpose of a sermon, since you're talking religion?'

'Gentle guidance.'

Our age-old argument. 'It's time, Perry. Spirituality, religion, mystical experiences – they got split into two camps when Galileo and the church and science went their separate ways. Yes, of course I see the danger. But the risk is worth the gain. The world needs all the help it can get. There is progress out there in the hinterlands of science – possession is in the *Diagnostic and Statistical Manual of Mental Disorders*. It's official now. *Dissociative disorder slash demonic possession*. Time to bring science and spirituality together again, the one does not preclude the other. And the main angle for me? Let's keep it simple, OK? I want to find out where things go wrong in the brain when someone is possessed and I want to . . . to fix it.'

'You going to do that all by yourself?'

I lifted my chin and gave him a mean smile. 'You always tell me I'm special.'

He nodded at me suddenly, and I felt easy again, and leaned back in my chair.

'How's it going? Your study?'

'Can I swear you to secrecy?'

'On my vows, brat.'

'I'm just kidding. Perry, I'm encouraged. My patients are doing well, that's all I can say.' I admit I was smug, picturing my favorite *subject*, Abby. The difference in her now that the moderate depression was gone. Next up, people with chronic, debilitating depression. Schizophrenics. We would help them too.

'They may not be doing as well as you think.'

It took a beat for this to sink in. 'Mandeville? What's his deal?'

'Other than not being dead?'

'Look, if he's still alive, I'm glad for him. But I'm surprised.'

'He tells me you referred him to an oncologist, gave him a pat on the back and six weeks to live.'

'At the outside,' I muttered. 'But he's still alive?'

Perry nodded.

'It's a hard way to go.'

'Except he didn't go.'

'Perry. It's after two in the morning, I'm hungry, and I'm tired.'

'So am I. Here's the thing, Noah. Mandeville has come to me because he believes the tumor is gone, but that there is a demon in his head.'

'He thinks he's possessed?'

'Yes. He went to the archbishop and was referred to me. He has influential friends.'

I rubbed my chin. 'He's not possessed, Perry. It's the tumor talking.'

'Doctors say otherwise. His latest MRI is clear.'

'Impossible. Have him retested.'

'He says the demon got rid of the tumor for him, with his consent, but he's changed his mind. He wants me to exorcise him. He is convinced that once that happens, the tumor will come back, but he's ready for that. He's ready to die.'

'I don't believe it. Do you?'

'On the fence. That's why I'm here.'

I nodded. Perry came to me only for the tough ones, when he simply wasn't sure. Takes one to know one, and all that. And it was not that easy to find doctors willing to play medic on the exorcism team. Getting rid of demons takes a village.

'Will you consult? Another one for your case files?'

Perry knew about my little sideline research. MRIs for genuinely possessed people. There are definitive, consistent physical signs – most striking, a significant reduction in brain asymmetry. Women are more prone to reductions in asymmetry, as are people with OCD.

The bottom line? The reduction makes it harder for the subject to control manic chains of thoughts, delusions, nightmares. It disrupts sleep, can move the nightmare, dream state to a sort of waking consciousness, and leaves them open to losing a sense of self, opening them up to invasion and mind control.

Or so the theory goes.

Whether or not it was a preexisting condition, or came after the possession, was hard to tell. I would have to have benchmark MRIs from before the possession, and those I didn't have. Except with Mandeville. If he was possessed, which I doubted, I'll have a 'before' and 'after'.

'Hell, yeah, I'm in.'

'It means the usual risks, Noah.'

'Don't be a mamacita.'

'Good then. We need to do this soon.'

'How soon?'

'Tomorrow.'

I frowned. That was going to seriously fuck up my day, but I wanted another look inside this guy's head. 'Early then.'

Perry was quiet a moment and gave me a dark frown. 'I never realized you felt that way. That Enlightenment was a forbidden place for you.'

'I have beer.'

Perry gave me his lopsided smile and motioned me up. 'Walk me out? Too bad The Goose is shut for the night. I could use a beer myself, and a thin-crust pizza.'

I took the car keys out of my desk drawer. 'And I'd like a Makers and a fat cigar.'

Something in my tone caught him. 'Something you want to talk about, Noah?'

He knew me too well. And, for a moment, I was tempted to mention that feeling I got, tonight in the OR. But if I fessed up, he'd shut this down. He wouldn't let me within a mile of Henry Mandeville. He protected me like a big brother.

'Long day, that's all.'

And the opportunity was gone. It was the small moments, just like this one, that changed a life.

THREE

I sat in the driveway in front of my house in Ashland Park, almost too tired to get out of the car. Watchful. My last peaceful moment, though I didn't know that then.

We lived, Moira, the fellas, and Tash, a dog who was a Very Good Girl, in a dark-red-brick foursquare, built in the 1920s, and there were four mocha rattan rocking chairs – two regular size, two tiny – on the front porch that ran the length of the house. I took out a mortgage for $489,000 for this house eight years ago. Houses on my street, Fincastle, brought these sums and higher very easily before the economy nosedived in the last depression – or whatever they were calling it, those financial predators who like to spin. And now the housing market was alive here again, and we were no longer upside down in our mortgage, which was a moot point now because we just paid it off. Houses here usually brought in multiple offers. Moira worried about these things but I didn't. This was my home. I was staying. The market could take care of itself.

But the healthcare woes that fuel the economy – people in charge getting rich, patients going bankrupt – that wasn't getting any better, it was getting worse. That was where I put my worry time in. Our pirate economy meant my patients didn't come to me until their symptoms were desperate enough to justify the financial ruin that would come with their medical bills, their finances falling like dominos, another side effect of what passed for healthcare these days. If Olivia Van Owen made it to NASA, she would likely have a load of student debt on her shoulders – any money her parents set aside for her education would be sucked up by her medical bills. They might lose their house. Their cars. Of course, if her parents lost their jobs, there was a good chance she won't get any medical care at all.

I tried not to think about it.

Moira and I had fared well. Very well, actually. The worse the economy, the sicker people got. It is always boom time for doctors.

I watched the house for a while but I saw nothing worrisome, just the comfort of lights behind the sheers, coming from the kitchen great room where my wife would likely have left my dinner on the stove. Upstairs I saw the glow of a nightlight from the bedroom where our boys – our fellas, as Moira and I like to say – slept in the same bed.

They could each have a bed, and a room to themselves. But they were brothers from a mysterious but hard life I know nothing about – our foster children until their mother agreed to let them go to adoption. Moira and I cannot seem to conceive, and these boys came to us through Episcopal Charities. Perry, coming to my rescue for the second time in my life, told me the social worker's story: how she went to the police station to pick up two little brothers who sat together in the same plastic chair, holding the sum total of their possessions in a plastic grocery bag – thirty-eight cents, a mouse puppet, worn and chewed by either a puppy or a teething child, and two plastic cars that were scratched, stained, and well loved. They were four and two when they came to us, and they insisted on sleeping together in a twin bed with a plaid bedspread that Moira picked out. They used the second bed to house stuffed animals.

I shut the car door softly, and it was then that the security light from the side yard flashed suddenly, filtering through the lacework of waxy green leaves and heavy white blossoms on the line of magnolia trees bordering the yard. I jogged toward the light, a thread of tense muscles tingling at the base of my spine. It could be anything. Raccoon, possum, our dog Tash out for a late-night pee. She regularly opens the back gate when she has something to investigate.

But it wasn't just anything, it was my son, Vaughn, just turned seven. He had on soft plaid PJs, like a tiny old man, and his feet were bare. He was staring off to the right, near the far corner of our yard, and he had his chin tucked down like he did when his feelings were hurt or he was scared.

'Vaughn?' I said.

He did not react. He was still enough to make me wonder if he was sleepwalking. He had never done so – that I knew of – though, like all children, he had bad dreams. I spoke softly, gentling my voice.

'Vaughn, hey buddy. What you doing out so late?'

He turned at my voice. His face was chalk white under the yellow light, eyes wide. He turned back to the corner of the yard and pointed.

And I saw him. A man in the shadows, facing us, just out of the spill of light. I was aware of Tash barking madly from inside the house. Lights going on behind me. There was something familiar about this man, and I grabbed Vaughn and scooped him into my arms.

Vaughn's voice was high pitched. 'He's going to do it again, Daddy. Make him stop.'

'Who's out there?' I said, in my tough-guy voice.

I expected the man to run like hell, the house was awake, he was busted, but he stepped forward, closer to the light. Which was odd behavior. Unnerving, how he held his ground.

Something inside me recognized him before my brain caught up.

A physical memory, an instantaneous somatic trigger, and I froze in place. Childhood trauma did not go away. You were never free of it. It was a feeling all through your body. I willed myself to take a step forward, but somehow, I couldn't. I was eleven again, and helpless.

My arms were an iron band around my son, holding him so tight that I worried I was hurting him but, like me, he was unaware of pain, and in truth I could not loosen my grip.

I could not catch my breath, either. Air hunger gave me a cold flutter of panic. I tried to steady my breath, inhaling, exhaling in rhythm, which helped a little, but I somehow could not get enough oxygen into my lungs.

I had studied this. I knew, intellectually, what was happening to me. I was once again that frightened child, locked into a state of being hyper-alert and hyper-vigilant.

My heart was beating hard and fast and my hands and feet were cold and tingly.

My brain, trying to keep me safe, had triggered a warning system. It was like the aura of a migraine, this knowledge that the terrible things were going to happen again.

My voice was tight, terse, forced. I took the cell phone out of my pocket. 'Calling the cops,' I said.

'There's no need for that, sir. I mean you and your son no harm.' He stepped closer, fully under the light now, cupping something between his hands.

The red-haired man.

And the memories came back in a flood.

Tonight he wore a white priest's collar and a black button-up shirt, perfectly creased blue jeans, new-looking desert boots.

Lean into the fear, don't hide from it. Like Perry told me. Like he coached me all those years ago. I did it then. I could do it now.

I set Vaughn down. 'Stay put,' I whispered. My son nodded, but did not look at me. He was mesmerized by the red-haired man. I positioned myself in front of Vaughn, blocked him from the red-haired man's view, and moved closer to the end of the yard, but the red-haired man did not give ground. He even smiled a little, like the closer I came, the happier he got.

He had freckles, pale, pale skin, oddly creased and wrinkled, old man skin and a young man's face. His hair was collar length, straight silky red-brown hair. His eyes were black and fathomless, they sucked me in. I had tried not to think of him, the memory had faded in the last thirty-five years. But I remembered him now. The feeling he evoked. The sucker punch of pure merciless malevolence that emanated from him in waves.

'I know you,' he said.

'And I know you.' Perry had explained it to me years ago –
that the church draws evil as strongly as good. What had Perry
called him? *The Inciter.* He was not really human. Not really.
'What are you calling yourself these days? Brother Gladhand of
the Peckerwood Baptist Church?'

'I am the Reverend Travis Smallwood of the Chapel of
Disciples.'

'And you're trespassing.' I willed myself to dial 911 on my
phone, letting myself hope that a patrol car of uniformed officers
could simply remove this vermin from my home.

But I knew better, and there was dread in the pit of my stomach,
because trouble was coming with this red-haired man. What it
would be and how it would hit, I did not yet know. I had had
years of peace. A lot of happiness. Work that obsessed me and
a family I lived for. I was not letting go of any of it.

The memories kept coming, flashes and fragments. How he
stood at the end of High Bridge, all those years ago, watching.
Nodding his head to encourage me. Walking closer and closer
as he did right now.

And I was back up on that bridge, my stomach jumping because
it was so high up, and it was the red-haired man who held my
arm, urging me on with a twisty sideways smile as I put one foot
over the rail.

I felt Vaughn grab my leg and hold it tight. Smallwood smiled
at me now, at me and my son, ever so gently, and he was doing
some kind of chewing thing, maybe grinding his teeth, and I
knew what he was hiding in those twitchy, pallid hands, I knew
from before, looking down from my bedroom window all those
years ago on those nights when he would appear in my backyard
looking up at me, the body of a small bird crushed in his hands.
How he held them up, those hands, long slim fingers with white
parchment skin. Showing me.

'Don't let him do it, Daddy.' Vaughn ran toward the man, and
I felt a flash of pride and panic as I lunged forward and grabbed
Vaughn by the waist, aware, as I hoisted him up, that the back
door had opened. The screen door slammed and Moira and Tash
were both out of the house, Tash scrabbling at the gate and
snarling.

Moira took it all in, looking at us over the two-and-a-half-foot white picket fence, and tonight the fence seemed silly. Suburban. Cute.

'What's going on out here, Noah? Is everything OK?' Moira's voice quavered but she held her right hand down by her side and I had no doubt she had taken her Glock out of the gun safe and loaded it. Her dark curly hair was loose on her shoulders, and she was wearing one of my worn white button-down shirts, which told me that – though she looked wide awake now – she had likely been deeply asleep.

'We have a prowler. I've called the cops.'

'Hello, missis.' The man opened his hands and I saw the bird, tiny tiny bones crushed. It fluttered and was still.

Vaughn wailed and I turned his face into my chest.

'What the fuck?' Moira said.

God, I loved that woman.

Smallwood dropped the bird, and dusted off his hands. 'That's for you and your brother, Vaughn. I'll be back.'

Moira started to open the gate to let a snarling, foamy-mouthed Tash into the yard.

'*Don't*,' I said. Tash was very old. I don't want her anywhere near Smallwood, who was backing away into the dark.

Moira touched my arm. 'Get in the house, Noah. Come on.'

But I was rooted to the spot. It was a strange thing not to be able to move forward. To be unable to walk.

Moira, puzzled, put a gentle hand on my shoulder. 'Noah? What is it? Are you OK?' She took Vaughn out of my arms and he burrowed his face into her shoulder. Moira is so little. She only comes to just beneath my shoulder.

My phone hit the ground and she waited for me to pick it up. An impossible thing. She bent down awkwardly with Vaughn in her arms, and scooped it up. 'Noah?'

'I can't breathe.'

She nodded. 'Tell me about it.'

My wife settled Vaughn on her hip, and took my arm, dragging me forward, leading me back in. She looked from me to Vaughn, her face tight, shoulders tense.

'I can't breathe, Moira.'

She nodded and kept pulling me along and I realized that my wife thought this was an existential issue, not a matter of too little oxygen in the lungs. I could not find the words to explain.

I was halfway through the French doors when the cruiser pulled up, the flashing blue pulse, lighting up the front of our house. The police had arrived.

FOUR

I was in the den with two cops, when Moira thumped softly down the stairs and into the room. She had put the boys in our bed, with Tash, and the lights on, promising to come back as soon as she could. She'd taken the time to put on yoga pants and a bra under the shirt, and slip-on ballet shoes. Her hair, untamable in the best of times, curled loosely down her shoulders, and she pulled it back and fastened it with a dark black stretchy thing. It was clearly time for business.

No doubt she'd put the gun away.

I saw the cops noticing her. Moira was tiny, four foot eleven, curvaceous, large breasted. She binge-dieted occasionally but luckily it had no effect on the lush curves. Both of the cops were young, one with a blond crew, the other with close-cropped black hair. They had searched the yard with a wary but eager excitement, but Smallwood was long gone.

'I talked to my sons,' Moira said. 'That guy, he's been here, out in the yard, late at night, once before, maybe twice. That's how Vaughn knew what he was going to do. He holds up a little bird and smashes it while they watch.' She and I exchanged looks. I wondered how long this had been going on.

The cop with the blond crew, Halloran, colored a deep red. 'Do you know him, ma'am? Your husband says he's a complete stranger.'

Moira gave me an odd look and both cops noticed. 'I actually recognized him.'

I took a breath. *She* recognized him?

'Saw him under the security lights?' The one with baby-fine black hair asked. He'd been out searching in my yard, so he knew about our suburban security.

'Hang on, I'll show you.'

Moira went to the kitchen, which was separated from the den by an island that housed a provincial blue La Cornue stove that Moira loved more than me. She burrowed through a stack of bills and advertising fliers that were piled next to a stack of worn schoolbooks – Moira's. She taught high-school English and was the drama coach.

'Yep,' she said, bringing over a creased, cheap yellow flier that invited us to the Chapel of Disciples, though oddly did not give any address or times for services. An amateurish photo showed that smiling face, identified as the Reverend Travis Smallwood. 'I can't believe this guy is a preacher.'

The dark-haired cop took the flier and studied the face smiling back. He grimaced, hoisted the heavy belt of equipment on his hips and looked steadily at Halloran, and there was an air of tension between the two of them.

'You know this guy,' I said.

Halloran looked at the perfectly distressed leather of my man couch. 'Do you mind if we sit down?'

Moira waved them over. 'I'll make coffee.'

'What do you know about this Reverend Smallwood?' I asked. 'Does he have some kind of a record?'

'He's been in the middle of some trouble,' Halloran said.

Moira was cuddled next to me, holding her second favorite lavender mug, feet tucked up like a cat. I had my arm around her, so I was the only one in the room who was aware of the slight trembling in her shoulders.

I admit I felt a certain relief that the red-haired man seemed to be causing trouble for people who were not me. Maybe this wasn't about me at all.

The dark-haired cop took a big gulp of coffee. 'There have been complaints about this guy. About his congregation.'

'Where is this church anyway?' Moira asked. 'Out in the boonies somewhere?'

'No, it's close. Around Euclid, where all those little bungalows are.'

The neighborhood he meant was called Hollywood, for some reason I've never understood. Pricey little bungalows built in the 1920s, 30s and 40s, no more than a mile or two from our home.

'Where exactly?'

'Remember that old church on Tremont?' Halloran asked.

'The one that's been for sale forever?' Moira said.

It was a tiny sanctuary, long ago outgrown by a congregation that built a mega-church off Harrodsburg Road. Everyone assumed some trendy millennials would buy the little church and make it into a cool home. Unfortunately, no trendy millennials could afford the price – second-tier prime in the heart of Lexington's preferred 40502.

'This Smallwood guy, he's pretty aggressive,' the dark-haired cop said. 'Bothering people, knocking on doors late at night. Says he wants to catch people home after their dinner.'

'Does he kill a bird for every house he goes to?' Moira asked.

I made a note to go out and get rid of the dead bird before the boys woke up in the morning. I wondered if they'd been able to fall asleep.

'That's the first I've heard of the bird thing.' Halloran sat his coffee cup down. 'Most of the complaints we get are about parking.'

I watched the two cops exchange looks. There was something more here than parking.

'The church lot would fill up and the congregation was parking up and down the streets; you know how narrow those streets are over there, and they only had a tiny parking lot. People were blocking driveways, sometimes parking *in* driveways. We started getting a lot of calls, complaints. They have a lot of services late, dinner time and after dark, and people were getting snarled up trying to get to their houses after work. Wasn't long before things kind of escalated. Vandalism and missing pets for any of the neighbors who complained.'

'Missing pets?' Moira said.

I thought of Tash, glad I kept her gated up.

'That's not all, is it?' I said. I felt Moira tensing beside me.

The cops exchanged looks.

'There was an odd incident about three days ago,' Halloran said. 'I'm not trying to scare you. But if this guy has been at your house more than one time, that doesn't feel random to me. You sure you don't know him?' Halloran looked at me.

'We don't know him,' Moira said. 'Tell us about the incident.'

'One of the neighbors came home late, he'd been traveling for business, and he finds somebody has parked in his driveway, blocked him out, he can't even get close to the house there are so many cars. He's tired, he's had enough. His wife said he wasn't any kind of hothead, pretty reasonable guy, he went over there just to ask whoever it was parking in his driveway to move their car. And some woman comes out, moves the car, apologizes, the wife says it was all really polite. Husband gets something to eat, the two of them go to bed.

'They'd been asleep awhile, then they got woken up, some noise outside on their back porch. The wife, she watched out the kitchen window, but she didn't see anybody. Her husband just planned to do a quick perimeter check, you know, and if he saw anything call the police. Of course, the smart thing would have been to call us and let us do the perimeter check, but people most often don't do that. Don't want to look silly. Next thing she knows, she heard him scream.'

I found it interesting that the cop used the term 'scream'. My stomach went tight.

'She found him outside, they had one of those outdoor cellars, and he'd fallen down the steps. He was dying when she got to him, couldn't breathe.'

'Broke his neck?' I said.

The cops looked at each other. 'It's an ongoing investigation. We really can't say.'

Moira leaned forward. 'You can't say? This guy has been in my backyard looking up at my kids' bedroom window. Please.'

'Crushed,' the black-haired cop said. 'All his muscles were crushed. Heart too, diaphragm.'

'That makes no medical sense,' I said.

'No.' Halloran shook his head. 'It doesn't.'

FIVE

Moira offered me dinner but I shook my head. She frowned then poured a nice slug of whiskey over ice for me, and a large glass of red wine for herself. I gave the glass of Jack Daniel's a wistful look and set it to one side. Moira had given me a generous pour, but I could no more drink or eat than I could fly. My brain sent the flow of blood to where it was needed, and stopped my stomach cold.

'Boys asleep?' she asked, as I slid off my shoes and settled back onto the couch.

'Sound asleep. I carried them to their own bed and they barely peeped.'

Tash had followed me back downstairs and lay on her belly, a tennis ball between her paws. She was alert, as if this was a conversation she needed to be in on. Tash was a yellow lab, big paws, seventy-five pounds, with white around her muzzle.

'This Smallwood,' I said. Feeling odd to have an actual name for him. 'The boys have seen him before?'

'It's hard to get a straight story out of a seven-year-old, but that's the impression I got. Marcus came and got me. He was pointing out the window and saying *back again back again*.' Moira pulled a blanket out of the antique stagecoach trunk we used as a coffee table, but evidently there were to be no cuddles on the couch. She curled up in a chair, facing me. 'What did Smallwood mean when he said he knew you and you knew him.'

I stared at my whiskey. The ice was just starting to melt.

So she heard.

Moira did not know about me, about those dark days as a child. I didn't confide that in anybody. My mother knew. Perry, of course. No one else. I didn't want to be judged by it. I didn't want it to define me. I didn't want to give it presence in my life. I boxed it away years ago and put it up on a shelf.

'You look like a man trying to come up with a story, Noah.'

I looked up at my wife. 'It's annoying, sometimes, Moira.

How damn smart you are.' But my voice was gentle and kind, because I love how smart my wife is.

She pulled her knees up to her chin and her eyes were big, her shoulders high and tight.

'It's something private,' I said. 'It has nothing to do with you or the kids. And it's something I don't want to talk about. To burden you with.' I knew I sounded guilty. I felt guilty too.

'You can call it a private burden and then not tell me?' She looked at me sideways. 'Does it have anything to do with another woman?'

'God no. Only you, my love. Only you.'

She smiled her big smile that always spread slowly across her face. 'Well then, Noah, let me put it to you this way.' She was going the reasonable route, which showed serious restraint after the night we'd had. I felt sorry for her. Though I was well aware that if the reasonable route did not work, she'd eventually move into phase two. I am not sure how many phases she has in her repertoire. I never last past two.

'Are you even listening, Noah?'

'Yes.'

'If you don't tell me, it creates a distance in our marriage. On the other hand, we're not joined at the hip and everybody needs some privacy in their life.'

'Even married people?' I gave her the smile she rarely resists.

'Especially married people.'

She said this so seriously I gave her a second look. Did Moira have secrets too? I couldn't read her. But who doesn't?

'Come on, Noah. This guy, this creep, he's in our yard. Vaughn, for some reason, is down there with him, and, God, how did that little scene even come about?'

'I'll talk to Vaughn and Marcus tomorrow.'

'*We'll* talk to them. This is scary. I feel like my sons are at risk and I can't see what it's about. What's coming. But I can imagine a whole lot of things. So can you tell me in all honesty that your *burden* or your history with this dude – no, don't even try to tell me you don't know him, there was something going on between the two of you. I'm not stupid, Noah. Can you tell me whatever this is poses no danger in any way to our sons? To our family?'

I was backed into a corner here. I always thought I could keep this secret. How do you tell the woman you love that way-back-when you were possessed by demons? At best she'd think I was crazy. I would not believe it myself if I had not lived it. Perry had told me to tell her. Time and again, he had told me. No secrets in your marriage, he'd said, not with the kind of connection you and Moira have. But I had honestly thought this day would never come.

In truth I had thought of telling her off and on for years. In my own time and my own way. Which I admit would likely have been never. The urge to confide never made it past my instinct to protect. The less she knew, the better. And maybe I didn't want to test her. Maybe I didn't want her to look at me like I'd lost my mind.

And talking about it gave it power. Made it real.

I took a breath. Cocked my head to one side. 'No, Moira, just the opposite. I think this Smallwood guy is trouble.'

She nodded and folded her arms. Maybe a little surprised to convince me so quickly. But ready for something terrible, by the looks of her. And yet I was well aware that she had no idea what was coming.

My wife and I were going to have to have the talk. And I knew that things were going to change between us, once she knew my secret. And it wouldn't be a change for the good.

So I told her everything. The death of my father, the onslaught of compulsions, voices. Not that day on High Bridge, not even Perry or my mother knew about that. My voice was soft and steady, the tone I used to reassure patients, but the magic wasn't working, my wife was clenching and unclenching a tuft of blanket in her fist.

She sat across from me, curled in a tense little ball, lips parted, eyes intense, and the look on her face – fear of me? Concern? Disbelief? A suspicion that her husband had lost his mind? Perhaps an unholy mix. I could not read her like I usually can.

But it was too late to stop, and I was awash with the release of confession, mingling with the prick of shame.

Moira was thoughtful as I trailed off, and I waited for her

reaction. She was frowning, looking away at nothing, finger tapping the side of the chair, which told me she was thinking and thinking hard. She looked at me abruptly, checked my glass, saw that I had not touched my drink.

Tash moved to lie near me, muzzle on my feet. I touched the top of her head, felt her warm breath on my fingers.

'Is that why you went into neurology?' Moira stood up, refilled her glass of wine with a generous hand. I did not blame her for wanting a comforting haze of alcohol, but she put the glass down and did not drink.

I patted the side of the couch. 'Come sit beside me.'

She shook her head, and moved restlessly to the window, looking out into the yard. It was dark. She would see nothing but her own reflection in the glass.

'Noah, I don't believe in this stuff. It shakes me up that you actually seem to.'

My stomach knotted and I went cold. I tried to smile. 'You believe in God.'

Moira was the reason for our occasional attendance at the Episcopal church, though most Sunday mornings, when I was here at home, we preferred a lazy breakfast in the sunroom. Moira came from a family of dignified Presbyterians, and she liked the idea of religion more than the actual practice.

Moira put her hands on her hips. 'Of course I believe in God. Don't you?'

'But you don't believe in demons. Satan. The dark side.'

'No. That kind of thing . . . it's just made up to scare people. To manipulate them. It's one of the things I hate the most about organized religion. The patriarchy. The cruel side. Judging people, threatening them with hellfire. That's not my kind of God. That, to me, is man sticking his foot in it, contaminating things.' She sat on the arm of the couch looking down at me. She was so close I could touch her. But something told me not to. 'Do you really believe in it, Noah? For real? You're a neurosurgeon, I mean, didn't you have some patient with a brain tumor who thought he was possessed by demons?'

Funny she'd bring that up.

'Several. But they *had* brain tumors. And there were no inexplicable manifestations of demonic possession, no . . . no red-haired man. You saw him, there in our backyard. In the actual flesh.'

Moira stood up and moved back to her chair. I wanted her to come to me. To put her arms around me. To say she loved me no matter what. Not to look at me with that distant coldness, the way women look at men who let them down. Men who failed.

Men who lied.

'Who is that guy anyway, that red-haired man, Smallwood? Why did he come *here* to *you*?'

She'd nailed it. My greatest fear. That I would somehow bring dark things to my family, that I would somehow infect them. But I'm not sure she'd really added all this up. Yet.

'I don't know why me. Why now.'

'Are you telling me you don't think he is dangerous?'

'No. I told you already he is trouble. I'm telling you I think he *is* a threat. To you, to me . . . to our sons. That's why we're talking. That's why I've been telling you my deepest, darkest secret.'

'Who else knows?'

'My mother. Perry, of course. And you. And I expect us to keep it that way. Please.'

She swallowed. 'I'm scared of him, Smallwood, but I don't really know why. There's something disturbing about him. I admit . . . when I look at him, I could believe in really bad things. He has that effect.'

'Yes. I know. And I will kill him before I let him hurt you or the boys.' If he could be killed. But I didn't tell her that.

Moira gave me a sideways look.

'If there's any shooting to be done, I'll leave it to you, sweetheart. I'm pretty good with a scalpel.'

I got a small smile, for which I was pathetically grateful. Moira looked at my drink, the ice melted, the liquid growing warm.

'So this. This is a reality shift for me, Noah.'

I nodded.

'Not because of the crazy demon stuff. But that's bad enough. What I can't wrap my mind around is for all these years . . . You've lied to me.'

The way she said it made me worry.

I knew better than to argue with her. A lie of omission was still a lie. In the kind of marriage we had. The kind of closeness that I had been so very unwisely taking for granted. There was a cold knot forming in the pit of my stomach.

'Whatever this was . . . it shook you to the core. You were . . . you looked like you were in shock out there. I've never seen you like that, Noah, never. And . . . I've told you *everything.* About my dad. All the debt collectors who called us night and day when he got sick. When he lost his job. No one cared about us. My family. No one helped us, no one came, we were all alone. And I thought when I met you, I'd never be alone like that again. I'd be safe. And now I don't feel safe anymore. I feel like I did back . . . back when there was only me, a checked-out grieving mom, and my baby brother.' Her voice broke. 'I'm sorry, Noah, I'm not trying to make this about me.'

'Of course it's about you, Moira. I'm just so sorry. To put you through this. That I didn't tell you. I didn't think about it that way. About how you'd be so hurt. All I could imagine . . .' I rubbed the back of my neck. 'All I could imagine was that you'd think I was fucking nuts.'

'Because you did not trust me. Like I trusted you.'

'Moira, this thing I went through. It . . . I was so scared back then. And when it stopped, when Perry came and took me through the exorcisms—'

'Exorcisms.'

'That's the word,' I said. 'Exorcisms. Possession. *He saved me.* And afterward I didn't want to think about it. *Ever.* I didn't want to give it power. I compartmentalized it and I thought I would never have to think about it again.'

'But Perry knew. Of course. And your mother knows. And you didn't tell *me.*' She looked away, out the window again. 'Remember Mr Timothy?'

'The kitty you lost when you moved?' Mr Timothy had been eight months old, with soft fur and tiger stripes and had slept on her head at night. And he'd slipped out the door when the movers came early – right after their house was repossessed. And she'd never seen him again.

'It devastated me.'

'I know, sweetheart.'

'But I never told anybody but you. My brother knows, of course. My mom knew. And you. I told you.'

'I'd have never stopped looking for him, Moira. If I'd known you then. I'd have found him.'

She shook her head and the tears came fast and furious. 'That's not the point. This is not about me, this is about *us*. Our marriage. Our connection. Our *trust*. What else haven't you told me? What else have you lied about?'

'Nothing, Moira. Nothing, I swear.'

'But how can I know that now?'

I had no answer.

'Don't you see this makes me . . . it makes me rethink every-thing. I feel like our whole marriage, our whole life together . . . was never real. I don't even know you anymore. I don't know who you are.'

She sat down hard, cross-legged on the floor. 'I have to know why you kept this a secret. Why you didn't trust me. Why I wasn't good enough . . . for you to tell. If it was something about me or if you're just a liar. Because what I feel, deep in my gut, is you don't love me. You don't love me enough to tell me this thing. It's like . . . I thought I was this special person in your life. But turns out . . . I'm just not.'

'Oh God, Moira. You are.'

'I'm supposed to believe that how?'

'Because that's not how it was, Moira. That's not how it works. I love you and the boys and the life we have more than anything.'

'Why would I believe that? You're a stranger, Noah.'

'I *couldn't* tell you. I couldn't tell you because it was *dangerous*.'

'Dangerous how?'

'To speak of it. To even *think* about it, *gives it power*. I've spent my life walking a tightrope. Eyes forward, step by step. That's the only way to *contain* it. The only way to stay safe. If I don't see it, if I don't look at it, if I don't think about it . . . it's not real.'

'But if this has been a weight on you, Noah, if it's been drag-ging you down, and you've been *pretending* you're OK—'

'*Not* pretending. I *have* been OK. I compartmentalize. People act like compartmentalizing your life is unhealthy, but it's *not*, Moira. It's a skill. It's a skill that's kept me safe.'

Moira, she was listening hard to every word I said, and the tears were rolling down her cheeks, and her arms were wrapped tight around her stomach, and she was rocking gently, rocking. I saw her do this only once before, late into the morning, sitting by her mother's bedside, moments after she died. I remember that morning so well. How still Moira's mother was, how Moira held her mother's hand while she rocked, how the sun was so bright in the room, throwing stripes of light across the bed.

And I knew now, with a cold knot in the pit of my stomach, that Moira and I . . . We might not get through this. My hands trembled because at best we had a long road ahead. I realized what I would have thought was impossible this morning when I woke up. That I might not get Moira back. That we could lose each other. And it would be entirely my fault.

'And this is why you became a neurosurgeon? Isn't it?' She stood up and stood over me. I could smell the sweet scent of the lotion she used at night. Sugar and pastille. 'You look so tired, Noah.'

'I'm fine, Moira.'

'What a terrible thing for you to go through. Don't you think it might have been some kind of a grief reaction, to losing your dad? You say that's when it all started up.'

'That's what made me vulnerable, of course.' I grabbed her hand but she pulled it away. 'The possession was real, Moira, though I get how comforting it would be to just explain it away. And if that gets you through the night, that is fine with me. I don't blame you for doubting me. If it hadn't *happened* to me, I would doubt too. But it *did* happen to me.

'And yes, Moira, I have scanned my brain, peered inside my skull in every way I can, and researched, and theorized, and looked into the spiritual areas of brain function—'

'Spiritual, not delusional?' she said.

I put my palms flat on my thighs and pressed down hard. 'Both, because you know, anything is possible. I could be out of my mind. I've had years, Moira. *Years*. To think it through, to doubt, to run tests.'

'That's why you're doing the research study? The Enlightenment Project?'

'Yes. To help people. People like me.'

She gave me a small smile. 'I have always wondered why you are the only neurosurgeon I've ever met who is not a son of a bitch. Whatever happened to you, Noah. It gives you great compassion.'

'Because every patient could be me.'

She nodded. 'This at least I do believe. I do think you're a good man, Noah. I do think you help people. I think you're trying. To do good.'

'I'm sorry, Moira. Sorry I brought this into your life. I love you, and I love the boys. More than anything.'

'Yeah. That's what makes this hard.'

I reached for her but she backed away.

'The thing is, Noah? I'm never going to trust you again.'

SIX

At Moira's request, I moved into the guest bedroom that night. I did not get much in the way of sleep. I was up early, way before Moira and the boys would even stir. I scooped the dead bird into the garbage can outside, in the glare of the porchlight, so early in the morning it was chilly and pitch dark. I trudged out of the house without coffee and headed into work.

I did not for one moment believe that Henry Mandeville's Stage IV glioblastoma had disappeared, and I was in my office early, as Perry and I had arranged.

While Mandeville was waiting to be prepped for his tests, I had a good hard talk with Macy, my very best tech. Macy was something of a hospital cocksman, floppy blond hair, brown eyes, and attention to nuance – with women and with work. He would make damn sure it really was Mandeville being scanned for that MRI, and would pay close attention to the details – no pacemakers, no shrapnel, no brain clips, nothing metallic in the body that might skew the results. And he would do a quick visual for new surgical scars on the skull as well.

Mandeville would not be possessed. He would be suffering

from the delusions and personality changes that are all too sadly common in my patients. It would be the work of the tumor, not the devil. I had the utmost respect for Perry, and his instincts, but on the other hand when you spend your life looking for something, you are bound to find it. So Perry's concerns would be set aside for now. And even he had his doubts.

Macy called me in before lunch, and he had two scans up on the board. The before, dated six months ago, illuminated on the left, and the after, on the right, done first thing this morning.

I studied the images. Took a breath, and said fuck three times under my breath. Macy gave me a sideways look.

Henry Mandeville's brain had undergone astonishing changes.

And the tumor was gone all right. No trace that I could see.

I hit the pager on my belt to summon Hilde, my research partner and fellow surgeon. She was the one who'd actually found the initial tumor.

Hilde was so shy that she stared at the floor when talking to colleagues, never spoke in meetings, and generally stood with her back to the wall, head down, hands balled into fists and crammed into the pockets of her white coat. I had never known Hilde to date, though she seemed to prefer men rather than women as colleagues. She told me once after one-and-a-half girlie cocktails that she thought women were mean.

Hilde arrived breathless and wary, with the whoosh of energy that seemed always to surround her, and the minute she saw Macy, who was leaning against the desk with his rock-star slouch, her head went down and she stared at the floor. She had a formidable crush on Macy.

The overhead light popped and went out, and Macy looked at me and rolled his eyes, because Hilde in a room meant computers got wonky and lights popped out. One frozen February night we both witnessed three streetlights blow in Hilde's wake when she was crossing a street, with nothing more on her mind than the usual genius-level hum. My diagnosis was kinetic energy.

'What do you *want*, Noah?' I was the only one in the world she talked to with such offhand comfort, and I cultivated this from the moment we met when I exasperated her by stealing a pumpkin muffin she had been saving, and only giving her half. She trailed the scent of Nivea moisturizer. Her hair, heavy and ropelike, was tied and twisted and tortured into some kind of ponytail, and looked like she slept on it that way. She had a nose that I found interesting and attractive, and it was certainly a presence. Her eyes were dark and laden with heavy makeup, inexpertly applied, her eyebrows needed a trim, and she was wearing one exquisite pink pearl earring, the other likely forgotten on the side of some bathroom sink. I found her glorious.

I pointed at the scans, but she was already studying them. She ran a finger over the image of the scan on the left. She was a tactile woman, unconsciously sensual. I wished the right man would notice this. Not Macy, who *had* noticed. Macy noticed everything. He touched her shoulder on his way out the door, and I glared at him. Hilde shut her eyes tight till he was gone, then her attention was on the scans.

'Mandeville, XAR277748921Z.' Her eyes narrowed. 'Holy crap. Is this even the same brain?' She traced some signature, subtle anomaly in the scan on the right that only she could see. 'When was this taken?'

'This morning,' I said.

'Stop fooling around. I was on my way to the *lab, Noah*.'

'This *morning*, Hilde.'

Her voice dropped to a whisper. 'How?'

I shrugged.

She bounced on her toes, oblivious, as usual, to how odd it is for a grown woman to hop, no matter how excited. 'His tumor is gone. But the orbitofrontal cortex, amygdala, and the anterior and posterior cingulate and adjacent paralimbic structures . . . all of them are smaller.'

'Yeah. His brain has shrunk.'

'I've never seen a change like this. He's had radiation treatments? Chemo? Some new experimental drug? What does his oncologist say? I sent him to Dr Jacobs. Jacobs is good.'

'None. No chemo. No surgery. No treatments, no drugs, I talked to Jacobs already. Chances of recovery were slim to none with a heavy dose of suffering and a severe burden of caretaking for the family. Henry didn't want to go through it. Jacobs sent him to hospice.'

Hilde's cheeks were flushed. 'You know what this looks like.'

'Yes. Classic implications of psychopathology.'

'Our treatments didn't do that. That last MRI we did proves that. He had a tumor but . . . not this.'

'Exactly.'

'So what the hell happened to this guy?'

I glanced out into the hallway to make sure Macy was gone, then shut the door. 'Actually, Mandeville credits his cure to demonic possession,' I told her. 'The devil cured him in exchange for his soul.'

She rolled her eyes. 'He's delusional, Noah. You know that.'

'Yes. Except, of course, the tumor is gone, Hilde. So what is causing the delusions? Because the tumor *is gone.* And his brain is fucked up.'

Hilde gave me a hard look, opened her mouth, then began to pace, her white coat rustling, the rubber soles of her shoes squeaking. 'Oh, I *knew* it, I *knew* something bad was going on when I saw him.'

'Who?'

'That priest. I saw him this morning. He hasn't been here, in what, eighteen months? I thought that phase was *over* . . . that our project would be enough to satisfy your curiosity about these kinds of things. *What is he doing here, Noah?*'

'We have a meeting in, oh, about ten minutes ago.' I put my hands on her shoulders to slow her down. 'Hilde, be still. Mandeville went to the priest. They came to me.'

'I won't be a part of this. You *know* how I feel about your work with him.'

'I check out patients for neurological issues. That's all. You know that.'

'I know that priest has a reputation. I told you I don't want anything to do with that kind of Catholic stuff.'

Perry is Episcopal, but I didn't bother to correct her. Her cheeks were burning and she wouldn't look at me. She was raised by her mother in the Greek Orthodox Church, with a bit of her father's Presbyterianism thrown in, and that somehow turned out a diehard atheist.

'You disgrace the hospital, Noah, and you disgrace yourself.'

'*Hilde.*' My stomach went tight. 'Possession is officially part of the DSM. And like it or not, Mandeville was part of our project, and we can't turn our backs on this.'

But that is exactly what she did. She was out the door in a heartbeat and I leaned back against the desk and gripped the edges. I could not believe I was feeling that rush of shame and humiliation that dogged me as a child when I began to hear the voices. And at the hands of Hilde Sweetwater no less.

But I got what I needed. Total confirmation. However it happened, the Mandeville tumor was gone, and Henry Mandeville was in the grips of something very dark.

SEVEN

There was a side door into my office, so I could enter without going past the waiting room, anxious patients, hospital staff. I was in a hurry to talk to Mandeville face to face. I leaned over the side of my desk and pushed the intercom buzzer on my phone, but then I hesitated, catching sight of the pictures on the edge of my desk. Moira and I, formally posed and elegant at our wedding, the glow of happiness unmistakable. Moira and our boys rassling with Tash, scattering the pile of leaves I had just raked up in our backyard.

I looked at those pictures every day of my life, and I *saw* them. I walked with my patients in the valley of the shadow of death, so I knew every day how lucky I was.

I took the picture frames and laid them gently in my middle desk drawer, because I did not want Mandeville to see them. As if such a small thing could keep my family safe.

I picked up the phone and waited for Lil to pick up. 'Are Father Cavanaugh and Henry Mandeville ready to come in?'

'Yes, they're ready.' She said it with a hint of tension in her voice. Lil was old enough to be my grandmother, and she kept me remarkably free of pushy pharmaceutical reps, hospital politics, and the torturous machinations of insurance companies that permeate the medical profession like robber baron bedbugs: obnoxious, toxic and impossible to get rid of. Something in the very steady gaze of Lil's blue blue eyes reminded me of my mother. And Lil did not like it when I kept patients waiting, particularly when one of them was Father Perry Cavanaugh, whom she adored, and though I will admit it to no one, I did not like upsetting Lil.

'I'll send them in,' she said, hanging up.

First Hilde, now Lil. Working with judgmental colleagues was exhausting.

Henry Mandeville wore a charcoal suit and white shirt, the knot of his tie loose around his neck. He was rumpled by the joys of hospital testing, and clearly would be on his way to work after our talk. I tried to remember what he did for a living, something in banking – which bank, I didn't remember. He was darkly handsome. Brown hair, short on the sides but longish enough at the back to graze the expensive collar of his shirt. Brown eyes, heavy brows. A shadow of beard growth already, though clearly clean shaven when he left the house. A ski-slope nose that was pudgy at the end, broad cheekbones. Connecticut. That's right. Born and raised, father commuting daily into Manhattan, disappearing just before retirement into blood-soaked dust and debris, pulverized, as the Twin Towers crumpled to their knees.

Perry nodded at Henry and at me, and sat to one side, his fingers grazing the silver cross that hung beneath his robe. Moira called him a dress-up priest and longed to see him in sweatpants.

Perry slid to the edge of his seat, watching both of us. I saw him notice the pictures missing on my desk. He made a fist with his left hand, rubbing a thumb and finger in constant circles. An unconscious habit when he was agitated.

Mandeville leaned forward. 'I brought you the two MRIs Dr Jacobs did, you've got his report, I've been grilled by your tech nurse, and I assume those are the results of this morning's MRI on your computer screen there. So, gentlemen, can we all agree that the tumor is gone and get on with this?'

'Noah?' Perry asked. His voice was matter of fact, but he was tense and watchful. I had seen him like this before. With me. Years and years ago.

'You're right about one thing, Henry, your tumor is gone. Dr Sweetwater and I both looked at the MRI. You're clear as far as the imaging shows.'

This was not news to Mandeville.

He smiled gently. 'How is Dr Sweetwater?'

There was something sad in that smile, like a man nostalgic for the good old days. His face was newly lined, he had aged since the last time I'd seen him, sitting dazed but frantic in the same chair he occupied right now, soaking in the news that his forty-fifth birthday would be his last. His cheeks were caved in, and I noticed the suit hung loosely. He had lost weight and muscle tone in the last six months. He had lost something else too, and it took me a moment to figure it out. Hope. He'd lost hope. Henry Mandeville might be here in this office looking for help, but this was a man who had given up. And yet, the tumor was gone.

'Dr Sweetwater wants to know what Dr Jacobs thinks about all of this. What kind of treatment you had.'

'I did see Dr Jacobs. An honest man, is Dr Jacobs. He gave me the odds. The treatment options. If that's what you want to call them. He wouldn't give me a timeframe like you did, but he said I should have my affairs in order by the end of that *week*. And he didn't argue with me when I said no thanks to the surgeries and treatments, he even said he'd probably do the same. He was good enough to offer to make me comfortable when I needed it. Later, he congratulated me on a spontaneous remission, shook my hand, and told me to make a follow-up appointment so we could keep an eye on things, was how he put it.'

'And here you are,' I said.

Mandeville closed his eyes tight, then looked at Perry for help. 'Do we have to do this dance here? Can't we just cut to the chase? Surely you guys have been talking about me, right?' He looked at his wrist, like a man checking a watch, but he was not wearing one.

The blinds on my office window rippled, and the noise they made stopped all conversation. The window had a view of the parking lot, but it was not open. There was no reason for those blinds to move.

Perry looked at me, and I was reassured by his steady gaze. 'How they love to show off,' Perry said, giving me a half-smile. I dragged the chair from behind my desk and placed it so that I could sit inches from Mandeville, so I could talk to him literally face to face.

Mandeville shrank back into his chair, and stared at the blinds, and clasped his hands together in his lap.

'Sleeping much?' I asked him.

'Almost never,' he said, and I believed him. He looked at me. 'You know I'm not sleeping. *You know.*' His tone was hard. Then he leaned forward, both feet flat on the floor. 'And how is your *family*, Noah?' His voice was different now, with a singsong cadence. Perry stood up, and moved closer. I could sense him, standing right beside me.

Perry and I exchanged looks. And I couldn't help but give him a sort of sideways grin. He is only supposed to bring me in for the tough ones, but Mandeville reeked. I saw it in the eyes, red rimmed, clear sometimes, then dull, confused and fatigued, and just now – as he looked at me – something *other* and hard. And that is the elusive presence that I saw like a neon sign. Mandeville was not himself. Literally. There was something, some presence, that revealed itself like a shimmer of heat in the desert, a vibration around him that left no doubt in my mind. And it had literally changed the matter in his brain.

Henry Mandeville was a prime candidate for exorcism, suicide, debilitating illness. Whichever route he took.

'How is *your* family, Henry?'

He jerked backward and his eyelids fluttered, and he made a snorting noise like an angry cat, and then he looked at me, gaze steady and clear. 'I am having bad dreams about my family. You've met them, Dr Archer. My slim, beautiful wife isn't sleeping much either, she is watching me, and she is aging right before my eyes. And my little girl avoids me. She doesn't want me to come watch her soccer games anymore. She won't tell me that to my face, she's afraid she's going to hurt my feelings. But she and Mommy are very understanding about how I should work, or rest, or do anything but be anywhere near them. And I don't blame them, I don't. They sense it. I'm going to do something bad to them and they know it.'

'What are you going to do to them, Henry?' I asked.

Perry shook his head at me, but Mandeville answered, sounding oddly casual.

'Crush them.' He opened his hand, then made a fist.

'Did you have these thoughts, these dreams, when you had the tumor?'

Mandeville stopped and frowned. 'No. Not then. This is new. And it happens to both of them. They are crushed, every muscle, every bone. I can hear screaming . . . my daughter. In my dreams my daughter screams, and in my dreams I don't mind. *I like it.* This is not me. This is not who I am.' Sweat rolled down his temples but his voice was oddly calm. 'I would rather be dead than have these thoughts. I would rather be dead. And I will do it, I will take my own life if you can't or won't help me.'

'That's what it wants,' I said.

Perry was up and on his feet, and the interview, clearly, was at an end. 'Dr Archer is right, Henry, that's exactly what it wants. But it's not going to happen. You're going to hold on, you don't give in.'

'He wants to send them away. But we won't let him.' The voice was Henry's, but this was not Mandeville, who talked to me so softly, with a steely but snide tone that was not like Mandeville at all.

Like Perry says, it takes one to know one. You could say that I bring out the worst in people.

'Dr Archer pretends he does not see us,' Mandeville said. 'You should have done it, Noah. Sent *your* family away. You had your warning last night in the OR. You could have done it then, but you let it slip away.'

I felt Perry's hand on my shoulder. 'Seen enough?'

The very air in the room felt heavy now, making me tired, making me slow. My stomach was knotting up and I looked at Mandeville and saw the man, not the presence, which was surely there, but what I saw was the exhausted man who craved release and was losing ground.

'He is barely hanging on,' I said to Perry.

'We'll talk later.'

'We need to move fast,' I told him.

'There is not going to be any *we*,' Perry said, and he held out a hand to Mandeville. 'Let's go, now, Henry. This was it, the final hurdle. I'll put a team together and, until then, you'll have to hold tight.'

'And you.' Mandeville looked at me steadily, and he seemed

full of energy now. 'You'll be there? It's not going to work without you, Noah. Do an MRI during the exorcism. Record it all on your machine. You know you want to. You've always wanted to. I'll be your dream come true.'

How did he know how badly I wanted to do an exorcism with an MRI tabulating the neural dance? Something he assumed because it was logical . . . or something *it* knew. That thing inside him.

He held out a hand for me to shake, to seal the deal, three men with a mission. Only we were not three men. There were others in the room.

I put out my hand, but Perry batted it away, standing between us. 'No. I appreciate the confirmation, Noah, I'll take it from here.'

I rolled back in my chair. 'Fine then, Perry. Not sure why you needed me on this one. Or.' I looked at him over my shoulder.

'It's been hiding till now.' He tilted his head to one side, studying Henry Mandeville.

Mandeville's voice took on that singsong cadence. 'It's not going to work without Nooooah. We wants Noah at the party, Priest.'

Perry's grip on my shoulder hurt. 'Don't engage it.'

Mandeville smiled like a man who had sprung a trap. He stood suddenly, pacing, and sweat rolled down his face, and soaked into the shirt collar, making the crisp white go gray. And his voice was different. Soft. Attractive. Oddly compelling. And I felt somehow compelled. 'Don't overthink this, gentlemen. Do it *now*. The other one is coming. This one is bad enough, but the other one—'

'My schedule, not yours,' Perry said, and he sounded confident, but I was not so sure. I looked at Mandeville and I knew. I had lived those sleepless nights. Time was running out.

'Let's go on and do it,' I told Perry. 'Let me help on this one.'

'Absolutely not,' Perry said, and he seemed larger now, strong. 'You've done your bit, now let me do my job.'

'Mistake,' Mandeville said, choking it out. Then he stopped pacing, one foot still in the air. He turned his back to us, and his head slumped forward, as if he had lost the strength to hold it up. He looked at me sideways. 'Please. Help me. Please just be there.'

Unseen by Henry Mandeville, Perry put a finger to his lips. He shook his head no and I was ashamed by the rush of relief, along with a tiny bit of disappointment because I did so very badly want to try to chart an exorcism during an MRI – to follow the activity in a brain while it happened. But I was out of it. Perry might tell me the outcome later, but I was out of the loop. I was grateful to Perry for not giving me a choice.

Perry leaned down to whisper in my ear. 'I'll take it from here, Noah.' He straightened. 'Come on, Henry. Time to go.'

But Mandeville did not move. He was like a puppet, slumped forward, waiting for the puppet master to pull the strings. 'They have a message for Noah.'

'Noah, I hate to ask it, seeing how this is your office, but best you leave. Just for a little while. Long enough for me to get Henry out.'

'Don't you want your message, Noah?'

I did want it, but I knew better. Perry nudged me, and I was up and out of my chair, but I felt slow when I wanted to feel fast, like a deep-sea diver on the ocean floor.

I was at the door, and turned back once, and saw Mandeville straighten. I heard the smile in his tone.

'Don't run away from me, Noah. You need to know the danger. To the one you love the most.'

I opened the office door just as Mandeville spun and crossed the room, and before Perry or I could react, he had me in hand, fists clutching the lapels of my white coat. 'Please for the love of God help me. Please, Dr Archer, I can't be like this. I can't let it take me. You *know*. They showed me. They showed me how you stood on that bridge after your father died, how you had one foot over the side, and I'm closer to lost than you ever were.'

I felt my stomach drop but I didn't look at Perry. I couldn't look at Perry after that.

Mandeville cried like a man does, the tears squeezing out beneath the lids of his eyes. 'The kindest thing you can do is kill me, Dr Archer. I don't care *what you do*, just get me out of this.'

This was the Henry Mandeville I remembered. The Henry Mandeville sentenced to death from a tumor six months ago, the man I could not help then no matter how much I wanted to, asking me once again. I failed him then. Would I fail him now? Me, who knew more than anyone exactly what he was suffering every moment of every day? Isn't that why I had devoted my life to neurology? Wasn't this the entire reason for my work?

Perry grabbed Mandeville from behind, and he was strong, wrapping his arms around Mandeville's thin, muscle-weakened chest, pulling him away. '*Out*,' Perry said.

I took Mandeville's hand, clasping it between both of mine, just like I did with terminal, frightened patients. 'I'll do everything I can to help you, Henry.'

He did not open his eyes, but he smiled. 'It's coming for you, Noah. You and everyone you love. *Your wife will no longer be your wife.*'

I didn't know what he meant by that. I didn't like the sound of it.

'Now do you see why you can't be involved?' Perry said.

'I won't do it without Noah,' Henry balled his hands into fists.

'Let's do it here, in the lab, with Henry in the machine.' I looked at Henry.

'You think the hospital is going to give you permission?' Perry said.

'To run an MRI? Why would I even ask?'

'He could get violent. He could damage—'

'Put me in a straitjacket,' Mandeville said. 'Anything you want. Maybe it will help. Maybe if you see something in my brain. Maybe you can help me somehow. Maybe you can give me a treatment, before we go in. And I'll be able to resist this thing. Get rid of it.'

'No treatments of any kind,' Perry said.

'OK,' Mandeville said. 'You call the shots.'

I nodded. Looked at Perry, and saw him wavering. He was curious, I knew he was; he wanted to know what demonic possession looked like on a brain scan just as much as I did. And I was close enough to smell it. After all this time. I think we had a deal. With Henry, anyway. Perry was going to take some convincing.

EIGHT

That night, Perry agreed to let me buy him dinner at Malone's, and I picked him up outside of his condo at the Wellington Arms, otherwise known as the 'Wellie', a 1930s stone-and-brick jewel in the Woodlands Historic District. It's got location, straddling downtown and Ashland Park, and an architectural flair that suits Perry perfectly. I couldn't imagine him living anywhere else.

Malone's was very much the upscale guy's kind of place that you will find nestled in every city in the south. The crowd is older, the men in short-sleeved knit shirts with designer logos, front pleat chinos, or loose khaki shorts, faces pink with sun from a day on the golf course or at the races at Keeneland. The menu is all about meat and potatoes with a flair of presentation, foodie trends and a genuinely sophisticated sauce. Sophisticated but manly: meat, seafood, carbs. Moira was not a fan. She trends vegetarian.

Inside it was dark with horseshoe leather booths, and walls crowded with pictures of local society wags. Off to one side was Harry's Bar, with a thoroughbred racing theme. The two worlds collide out on the patio where Perry and I sat at a table in a corner, sideways to one of the big-screen TVs.

We both ordered what Moira calls the Dude Salad, which is a cobb salad heavy with chunks of ham and cheese, a scattering of corn chips on top. I ordered the grilled pork chop with bourbon sauce and Perry chose the medallions of beef.

The waiter looked at me. 'You want that with the sweet potato goulash?'

'God, no,' I said. 'Real potatoes. Mashed.'

'The whipped potatoes, yes sir. Got it,' the waiter said, and grinned.

Perry sipped a Beefeater martini, and I had Johnnie Walker Black on ice. Our salads came, with a basket of rolls that were yeasty and warm, and Perry buttered a roll and took a bite. I liked taking Perry out and spending money on him that he wouldn't spend on himself. He was a foodie and did not deny it.

I picked up my fork, then set it down. 'Perry, you've got to let me help you with Mandeville.'

Perry, chewing ham, corn chips, and lettuce, gave me a small frown. 'You know I don't want you involved any further, Noah, and you know why. But, since you're picking up the tab, I'll listen to the pitch.'

'That, at least, is progress.'

'You're not eating,' he said, wiping dressing off the corner of his mouth with a thick black cloth napkin.

But I was drinking. 'In truth I am wound up pretty tight.'

'Mandeville shake you up that much? I know it's disturbing when it gets personal. I didn't like him bringing Moira into this, Noah, but you know better than to listen to anything they have to say. They are always full of threats. Always trying to intimidate. But it's another reason you should step away.'

'You mean when you get a demonic invitation to the feast?'

Perry chewed and swallowed. 'All the more reason for you not to be there, Noah.'

'I would have agreed yesterday, but not after last night.'

Perry cocked his head at me, and our dinners arrived, and I shook my head no to another whisky and moved to water. Perry said yes to a second martini.

I waited for the waiter to leave. 'Last night, when I got home, I saw the red-haired man. Out in my yard. Right there, two a.m., with little Vaughn outside in his PJs looking . . . mesmerized.'

Perry froze, fork in mid-air. He narrowed his eyes and got that very focused look. 'Why didn't you tell me?'

'I'm telling you now.'

'Noah, for God's sake. You should have told me this before I brought Mandeville in this morning.' He tapped a finger on the table, and I knew without looking that his other hand was making a fist on his knee. 'So he's back then. The Inciter.'

'You remember him then?'

'Of course I remember him. Maybe better than you do.'

'The Inciter. That's what you called him.'

'You were very young, then, Noah. There is a lot you likely don't remember and that's not a bad thing.'

'I haven't thought about him in years. And then, when I saw Vaughn, and how scared he was, but – how would you put it? – *entranced* he was. It, he . . . was utterly disturbing. And I've started remembering things.'

'Yes, I'm sure you have.' And his voice reassured me. The kindness, the confidence, the steel. 'So he's targeting you again.'

I flinched.

The waiter brought Perry his drink, and he took a sip, studying me. 'Is this the first time you've seen him? Since before?'

'Yes.'

'That sounds more like yes *but.*'

So I told him about my prickly sense of awareness in the OR.

'And that's not the first time you've sensed a sort of presence, is it? I told you they'd be there.'

'Keeping tabs on me. Trying to find a way back in.'

'Exactly.' He gave me a half-smile and somehow that took away the sting, the guilty feeling that somehow I had called them back to me, that this was in some way my fault.

'So what happened with the Inciter? I don't like it at all that Vaughn was involved.'

'Me and you both. And Moira.'

Perry went very still. He was reading the tone of my voice. 'Tell me about it, Noah.'

I told him everything, and it was curiously reassuring that his appetite was healthy, he kept eating, working the martini slowly, as if this was business as usual. For Perry, I suppose it was.

He gave me a wary look when I told him that Moira knew everything now, and I gave him the details of what she said. He put his fork down, folded his arms.

'I'm sorry, Noah.'

'You always told me I should tell her about it. I just . . . didn't want to give it power in my life and I didn't want her to think I was nuts.'

'How did she react?'

'She was shook. Really shook. She said that I did not trust her, that I lied to her, and that . . . that she'll never trust me again.'

Perry looked away, nodded.

I frowned. 'Do you really think she means that?'

'Do you?'

'She seemed serious. She's different with me now. I'm sleeping in the spare bedroom. How can we get past this? Or am I doomed?' I grimaced. I wanted him to tell me it would pass like a bad storm and my marriage would be OK. But he didn't.

'I see this a lot, Noah, in my counseling. When there is a lie. Adultery, spending money and not telling the spouse. Gambling, drinking. Keeping a job loss secret. Lies of omission and lies of commission.'

'Jesus, Perry, I didn't cheat on her. I didn't gamble away the house. I don't lie to Moira, I never have.'

'Except about this.'

'OK, except about this. But I don't know how to fix *this*. How do I fix it?'

'Patience. Hear her. Do not tell her how she should feel; listen to what she tells you and respect it.' He put a hand on my shoulder. 'If you mansplain her, Noah, you're toast.'

I nodded. Bit the end of my thumb. 'But.'

He looked at me. The sympathy in his face made me wary. It made me think I was in bigger trouble than I thought.

'OK, Perry, but it's like she is looking at everything that has happened in our lives and going over it again like *everything else is all a lie*.'

He nodded. 'The Butterfly Effect. Revisionist history. You lied to her about this. So what else did you lie about? Tumblers in a lock going round and round in her head. She's going to have a lot of questions. She'll be sifting through your marriage like an archaeologist going through every gain of sand.'

'And drawing conclusions.'

'Exactly. What you want is for her to be talking to you about it. Is she talking to you about it? Asking you questions about other things?'

I nodded. 'Some. Is that bad?'

'No, it's a good sign. If she's talking to you, there's a chance for progress. For processing and rebuilding trust. Together. It's when she keeps it to herself that's worrisome. Because she'll come to conclusions without giving you a chance.'

'Look, how could it possibly have made sense to tell her about all of this? She would have thought I was out of my mind. She still doesn't believe me. And with everything going on . . . that makes things more dangerous.'

'Very much so. The upside to that is that she isn't going to be able to deny it that much longer. Because it *is* happening, and odds are good it's going to get worse. She'll have to face it whether she wants to or not. And think about this, Noah. What if she'd believed you immediately, embraced the concept of demons and possession, and told you it all made perfect sense?'

'It would have been nice.'

He laughed out loud. 'No, I don't think so. Because if she had, our conversation would be focused on why she'd taken demonic possession in stride. Instead she came up with a pretty shrewd and compassionate theory. That it was all the complex grief reaction of a child facing the sudden loss of his beloved father.'

'I hate dragging my family into this.'

He frowned. 'About that. What Mandeville said. The threat. Now that I am up to date.' He gave me a look.

'You think my family . . . Moira . . . they are in danger?'

'I do, Noah.'

I swallowed hard.

'The Inciter is trouble. I don't like that your sons and your wife are on his radar.'

'How do I protect them?'

'You can't run away from it, Noah. You know that. They'll find you wherever you are.'

'Maybe I'm the one who should go away. They'll come after me and leave my family alone.'

Perry shook his head. 'It doesn't work that way. Moira and the boys, they are safer with you there. Especially since they have no idea what they are dealing with, and you do. You have to let it play out. And know this. You have navigated the dark things since you were a child. And here you are. Trust yourself to find your way.' He set his fork down. 'We don't wait for them to come after you. They don't want us to help Henry. So that's exactly what we do.'

'So you'll agree then? We can do the exorcism in the lab? Scan Mandeville's brain while you do your thing? I'll be safe behind the partition watching his brain light up.'

Perry frowned, put his fingertips together. 'I'm afraid so. I don't see any other alternative, unless we abandon Henry, and cut and run.'

'That would make us prey.'

'Exactly.'

'So let's be predators.'

He almost smiled and I felt a tingle of excitement at the base of my spine. 'Let's frame it up, Noah. We're going to be working with Mandeville using the same techniques you use in your research project. You know my thinking.'

I nodded. 'You think I caused this. With the treatment protocol.'

He shook his head. 'I think you created an opening that put Henry Mandeville at risk, but he made his own decisions. Still. It's a dangerous thing to do. Now, suppose you realize as we work with Mandeville together, that your project, your study, your brain shocks creating enlightenment on demand, *are* putting your patients at risk. That you are opening the door to darkness. To *evil*, Noah. Will you shut the project down?'

I took a hard breath and let it out slowly. Rubbed my stomach where I felt a sudden sharp pain. I leaned forward. 'Perry, don't you get that I am helping people? That a little risk is worth the incredible gain? I've got patients whose depression is gone, eating obsessions, *gone*, extreme OCD, gone.'

Perry held up his hand. 'And Henry Mandeville, whose very soul is at risk?'

I rubbed a hand over my face. I could agree, but *not* shut the project down. There was no way that Perry could compel me. 'Who decides? Who judges how bad the risk is – that it would be bad enough to shut the project down?'

'You do, Noah.'

I looked at him sideways.

'Obviously I'm going to have an opinion. But I trust you, Noah.' And he looked at me steadily. 'No one knows better than you do what Henry Mandeville is going through. I see you, Noah. I see that you've spent years, and everything you've got, relieving the suffering of the body but compelled by your memories to find a way to cure the body *and* the soul. Stay on the side of the good guys, that's all I ask. How you do that will be *your* call.'

I leaned back in my chair, and folded my arms. He was a step

ahead of me, like always. His trust would tie me tighter than a
contract pounded out by a legion of hot-shit attorneys.

And I saw from the gleam in his eyes that he knew this very
well.

We stayed late, talking. I knew that Perry was immersing himself
as we talked. This was how he prepped, talking it out, thinking
things through, peeling away layers. He has told me he does
not have a master plan when he walks into an exorcism, that the
weight of the work and the guidance is on God. That it is a
wise exorcist who knows his place in the scheme of things. But
he prepped just like I did. Knowing the patient. Testing, thinking,
making ready. He would learn everything he could before he
walked into that room.

'I've been hearing things, about this Chapel of Disciples.
We've actually lost some members of our congregation to them.
But I had no inkling it was on this kind of level.' He stared over
my shoulder, not seeing, thinking.

'What level is that?'

'Oh, pure evil, Noah, pure evil. If Smallwood is an Inciter –
and you recognized him, so we know for sure he is. From what
I know, and I admit it is not as much as I'd like, because these
things are hard to pin down. But they go where the opportunities
are. For instance, they spend a lot of time in hospitals. Swooping
in when a member of the family is terminal, or chronically ill.
Families under enormous stress. You know what people are up
against better than I do.'

I nodded. 'Sure. Death. Grief. Loss. Suffering, and frankly
feeling pretty pissy about the whole thing. Courageous battles
with an illness are words for the obituary. Up until that point
people are kicking and screaming, leaving fingernail marks
on the floor.' And what I don't say is that all of it happens against
the supportive backdrop of a predatory healthcare system, bank-
ruptcy, abandonment by friends and family more often than you'd
believe, and having to deal with asshole doctors like me.

I rattled the ice in my glass. 'So it's simple enough then.
Exorcize Mandeville's demons and find out what the red-haired
man is up to, find out what he wants and—'

Perry leaned forward. 'Noah, we already know what they want.

It's what they always want. Inciting despair, guilt, anxiety. We don't engage. We *exterminate*.'

'Good word.' But my mind was elsewhere.

'What is it?'

'Just . . . thinking of Vaughn, out there with that man. That Smallwood had been there before, at night, and I had no clue what was going on. The main thing for me, Perry, is my family. The boys, and Moira. I can't let them fall into that abyss. I'm doing the right thing, aren't I? Going forward with this? I mean, it's not like I have a choice here anyway. I know you say don't give them attention, but, hell, Perry, they're literally in my backyard.'

'You don't give them attention if you can help it, Noah, but we've passed that threshold, I'm afraid. Because the flip side is that you don't ignore it when it comes. So yes, I'm afraid it's too late now to leave you out of it. If you'd told me last night before . . . but even then, I think it was too late.' Perry frowned and reached under his shirt for the cross that hangs on the chain. 'I never wanted to do this. Use the machines, the science. But now. It does feel as if we're being pushed in this direction.'

I give him a crooked smile. 'You mean like divine intervention?'

'Depends on who is doing the pushing, Noah. But there's no leaving you out of it now, so you may as well be of use. Welcome to Team Mandeville.'

'Is there a tee shirt that comes with this?'

He smiled but his thoughts were elsewhere. 'I'm going to want some time to talk to your sons. If Moira will allow.'

'Of course. And Moira? Will you talk to her?'

'That's up to Moira.'

'Perry, I have to ask this. If I had been smarter, back before. When this first started up. If I had not been so vulnerable; if I had fought this harder—'

Perry shook his head. 'No, that's not it.'

'What do you mean?'

'I have always thought that you were very specifically targeted, Noah. Because of who you are.'

'Meaning I'm trouble?'

'Meaning extraordinary. I am truly wondering if the whole

point of them coming after you when you were so young, and so vulnerable, was to turn you, or destroy you, so we would not be right here, right now. Instead it made you stronger, more determined, and ready when the time came. So, yes, you're trouble. Trouble for them.'

And now it's official. This was all very real. Yet again.

NINE

I t began, as everything seems to these days, with paperwork. Because we were using the MRI lab after hours, I handled that set of forms myself, and Mandeville signed his medical releases with the usual methodical read-through of a man who worked in finance.

The paperwork with Perry went more slowly. Perry said his set of releases were an entirely American angle to exorcism, required by the Church's legal advisors, and done only in the litigious US.

Henry had dressed comfortably on Perry's instructions. Loose Levis, a black cotton tee shirt under a thick-knit white sweater. Slip-on loafers, fine but creased leather the color of cognac. Henry flat-refused the usual hospital gown, but agreed to slip off his shoes, and switch out the jeans with their metal zipper for an old pair of oversized sweats that I had in my office closet.

We met in my office. Me, Perry, Mandeville. Just us three. It was after hours, the only time we could have privacy in the MRI lab. The cleaners had already come and gone, and they'd left the blinds raised, and there was darkness outside the windows, washed in the changing neon colors of traffic lights, streetlights, and the halogen security lamps in the hospital parking lot.

It was quiet in the corridors outside the office. The patients had been served their ridiculously early dinners, the last visitors had trailed out and gone home. A thinned-down staff had completed the shift change initiated at seven p.m., and they moved quickly but quietly in squeaky rubber-soled shoes, sounding oddly like basketball players on the court.

There was a distinctive energy in my office. A tingle at the base of my spine. Henry seemed wary but hopeful, and Perry emanated strength and calm. Once the paperwork was squared away, and Henry was dressed for the mechanics of the MRI, we sat in a circle of chairs that I had placed carefully, all of us facing each other, and, like most men I know, taking care that our knees did not touch.

Perry was freshly shaved, his robes crisply laundered. He handled the purple stole with a quiet reverence, kissing the edges, and draping it around his neck. He looked at both myself and Henry Mandeville, who sat up straight and watched Perry's every move. Perry had an air of gravitas about him, a formidable confidence, and he did not smile.

He looked at Henry, and I could sense the compassion behind the steel, and he began.

'These days, Henry, people come to me with certain expectations based on movies and television. They come with the idea that evil is a great and monstrous power, nearly impossible to beat.

'The truth is, Henry, that exorcism is a journey, a spiritual journey, that you will take, and you will think of me as your spiritual director, to guide you on the way. It is a healing more than anything else. You will recover with the grace of your spiritual connections, forged through prayer and the sacraments. Above all, Henry, this is a journey of discovery, and a journey of faith.'

Henry watched Perry, his shoulders down, as if he were bearing a heavy weight. But he listened to every word.

Perry smiled at him. 'This is our first step on the pathway, and there will be many steps, Henry. You will meet with me regularly. A one-off exorcism can happen, but this is not Hollywood, and you and I will likely come together like this every week for quite some time. We will pray the sacraments and call on the power and the love and the grace of God until you are free.

'You are unlikely to get to liberation in one session, but you will always get some relief. So expect progressive improvement, and think of this as peeling away the layers until you are free. Are you ready to begin?'

'I'm ready,' Henry said, voice thick.

Perry looked at me and I nodded.

Perry rose and we followed. I left the lights on in my office, blinds still up, and locked the door. Perry and Henry followed me to the lab, the heels of our shoes echoing on newly waxed linoleum floors.

I looked over my shoulder, once we got to the lab. The corridor was empty, the fluorescent lights harsh. The key was on my chain and my car keys jingled as I turned the lock.

The lab was empty and cold and seemed different, somehow, this late in the day. Standard hours were from eight a.m. to six p.m., with the techs available from nine to five, at an hourly rate of thirty-five dollars each. I was at home here, and I had been awaiting this moment, literally, for years.

Perry muttered something under his breath, looking at the bulky white floor-to-ceiling monolith, the doughnut-shaped opening, the exam table that slid in and out.

I ran my hand along the side of the machine, cool metal beneath my palm.

Henry began pacing in front of the table. 'So here's the thing.'

'Henry, are you having second thoughts about this?' Perry said.

I clenched my right fist. This could not fall apart right now. Not when I was so close.

'If things go wrong,' Henry said.

Perry put a hand on Henry's shoulder. 'It won't go wrong.'

'But if it does. If I'm worse somehow, or . . . dangerous. Do you get me?'

And I remembered Henry in my office, and a voice – not his – saying, *He wants to send them away but we won't let him.*

I glanced over at Perry and I wondered if he was considering the same thing I was. 'You mean complete possession, Henry.'

'Where there would be no hope.' Mandeville licked his lips and looked at Perry.

'So long as you don't give yourself over to this, Henry, there is always hope. It is always going to be your choice.'

'I know that, I do, but those thoughts I've had. About my wife, my little girl.' Mandeville took a black ink pen out of my pocket and grabbed hold of my hand, his fingers very firm, very strong, icy cold. He wrote a phone number on my wrist, bold thick strokes.

'My wife's cell phone. Right where you can find it, sorry, not trying to be dramatic. But this way I know you've got it. Use your judgment. If you think I am dangerous to my family, call my wife and warn her. She'll be expecting the call. You remember her, Dr Archer? From before?'

I nodded confidently, faking it, trying to summon the memory. A small woman. A gamine Audrey Hepburn type with a large and interesting nose. Stunned by her husband's diagnosis. Clutching and unclutching his hand. Yes. I remembered. 'I'll call her if I need to.'

Henry gave me a small smile, and let his breath out slowly. 'You *do* remember her, I can see that. Thank you.' He frowned and put a hand on my arm. 'Be sure and tell her that Henry said *go now*. She'll be ready, she promised she would be. They have to be safe, my family. They *have* to be safe.'

'Yes, of course they do.' I guided him toward the table. 'I'll call if I think I should.'

'You'll know.'

'We'll all know,' Perry said, putting a hand on Mandeville's shoulder. 'Don't be afraid now, Henry. It's time to begin.'

Henry climbed onto the table. Sat with his leg over one side, and glanced at the small pillow that was placed at the end of the exam table, and gave me a half-smile. 'That should make me comfortable.'

'We'll begin with a prayer, Henry. Repeat after me.'

Henry nodded, his eyes shut tight, voice steady, strong, repeating every word.

'We ask your salvation and grace,' Perry said, and it was a wrap but then Henry stuttered over salvation and stopped.

Perry matter-of-factly wet his fingers from a vial of Holy Water, and touched Henry in the center of his forehead.

Henry's eyes widened and I thought I saw the slightest flinch, but it was too quick, too small, for me to be sure. Perry seemed matter of fact and serene.

'Salvation and grace,' Perry said again.

Henry coughed. 'Salvation and grace,' he stuttered, but he got it out.

Perry motioned me closer. 'Go ahead and get Henry situated, Noah.'

I felt the ball of tightness in my stomach. 'And then we begin.'

Perry flicked a glance at Henry. 'We've already begun.'

And I thought of Henry, stuttering over *salvation* and *grace*.

I settled Henry onto the table. Warned him to lie still. Perry and I had discussed this. That Henry might well become agitated, we might have to take him out of the machine, but I was ready for that, we'd have to play it by ear. The exorcism came before the machine, and I had agreed that this would be Perry's call. I would take what I could get, and Perry knew it.

For the first time since I was a student, my hands shook as I sat behind the partition and played my hands across the keyboard, looking from the screen to Henry to Perry, sitting on the edge of my chair.

I tried to remember if I had locked the lab door, imagining a colleague walking in on this, me, Henry, a priest. Freud and many of my coworkers believed God to be an illusion, but there were plenty of researchers just like me, examining the spiritual experience in the brain. For every one who felt such knowledge was beyond the capability of science, there was another who thought spirituality was a chemical reaction, often brought on by meditation, peyote, or LSD. Johns Hopkins had a lab studying spiritual expression with mushrooms, in the delectable form of psilocybin capsules. And there was always Persinger's God helmet, to make us all look like fools.

I heard Perry begin the prayer of exorcism, familiar, but background noise to me now because my heart was with Henry's brain, images at my fingertips. If he were here for a treatment in my study, he would be hooked up to electrodes that would zing the temporal lobes that house the limbic system which dictates emotion, memory, sensory detail. Spirituality is an orchestral experience, involving myriad parts of the brain.

Most research on spirituality involves the temporal lobe. It is suspected that mystics – Moses, Paul on the road to Damascus, Joan of Arc – were epileptics. Hippocrates called epilepsy the divine disease.

Step one of the treatment involves HORACE – Hilde's nick-name for the high-end hairnet that is threaded with ceramic discs that will zing you gently with a myriad of targeted electrical pulses. This stimulates an orchestration of every part of the brain involved in spirituality – at least those that have been identified so far. Even with the God Helmet, subjects experienced a curious sort of rolling darkness that Persinger called the black or the dark of dark. Many subjects were aware of what Persinger calls a Sensed Presence. Persinger considered this proof God did not exist. And yet . . . could this not be proof of God's trail, arcing across the brain? Just because your temporal lobes fire when you fall in love does not prove that love is not real.

I heard Henry whispering to himself as I shifted in my chair. I couldn't make out his words but the intensity in his voice made me think he was afraid. I remembered this. I too had been afraid, and not really understood *possessed*. I never thought I was possessed. Just going out of my mind, was how I saw it. And I was looking for relief no matter where, no matter how.

As always, Perry's approach was matter of fact, distinguished by what he didn't do as much as by what he did. I sensed his frustration as he tried to position himself so that he could see and touch Henry. The machine was making this awkward. But Perry's voice was strong and it had a rich timbre and soothing quality. His prayer of exorcism was as mild as a prayer of a baptism, and I knew from experience that he would not ask the demonic for a name.

Perry called his methods the green approach to exorcism. The prayer a conduit to God, and that was all that was needed or wanted. Perry's take was that demons lied, talking to them was childish, dangerous, and catered to their flair for the dramatic, and was about as useful as trying to hold a conversation with a cockroach you were in the process of exterminating. He felt talking to them empowered them, and wasted time. He felt it no more useful to talk to a demon than a cancer. That exorcism was a healing more than anything else.

And so Perry began with the Lord's Prayer, asking Henry to repeat the sacred words, and Henry was quiet. Perry said the prayer again, and Henry's prefrontal lobes lit up, meaning he was feeling strong emotion. His voice sounded tinny inside the machine, tinny and forced.

Perry's voice rose. 'Almighty and ever-loving God, you sent your only child into the world to cast out the power of Satan, spirit of evil, to rescue us from the kingdom of darkness and bring us into the kingdom of light. We pray for this child, Henry Mandeville, set him free from original sin, making him a temple of your glory and send your Holy Spirit to dwell with him. We ask this through Christ our Lord.'

Henry coughed again, a choking cough, and he cleared his throat.

'Go forth from Henry, unclean spirit, back to God, unclean spirit, and give place to the Holy Spirit.'

As Perry's voice rose and fell, I noticed something odd on the MRI. Henry's temporal lobes were flaring, but his frontal lobe – where the sense of self resides: the anterior cingulate cortex, insular cortex, medial prefrontal cortex – this had gone dark. Something was there. Something not Henry.

Perry's voice was steel. 'I exorcise thee, unclean spirit, in the name of the Father, and of the Son, and of the Holy Spirit, that thou goest and depart from this servant of God, Henry. For They command thee, accursed one, They who walked upon the sea. Therefore, accursed devil, acknowledge thy sentence and give honor to the living and true God. Give honor to Jesus Christ, and to the Holy Spirit, and depart from the servant of God, Henry, return to God, accursed one. Because God and our Lord Jesus hath vouchsafed to call Henry Mandeville to their holy grace and benediction and to the font of baptism.'

Henry made a gurgling sound and I heard the hum of hydraulics as the gurney slid out of the machine.

'Perry?' I said into the microphone, the sound of my voice echoing in the chamber on the other side of the partition.

He shook his head. '*Not me.*'

I came round the partition just as Henry was out of the machine, quiet except for the twitch of his left hand.

'Begone Satan,' Perry said, 'and cease to trouble this servant of God. In the name of Jesus Christ, Amen. Repeat after me, Henry. Jesus is Lord.'

Henry was silent, very still on the gurney, and Perry opened the lid of Henry's right eye, then the left. Henry's eyes were rolled back, and I could see nothing but white. Perry sprinkled Holy Water on his fingertips and made the sign of the cross on Henry's forehead.

'And oh, this pain is pretty, and I thank you for it, Priest.'

Perry frowned and I felt a chill raise the hair on my arms.

The voice was not Henry's, but it was unexpectedly low and melodic, a handsome voice. Henry sat up, rising with no effort, as if he was being lifted by strong arms.

'I am Elliot. I have waited a literal eternity to talk to you, Priest. You who are descended from The Magdalene.'

Perry looked at Henry, his head cocked to one side, then glanced at me, shook his head, and continued. 'Begone, Satan, and cease to trouble this servant of God. In the name of Jesus Christ, Amen. Henry, repeat with me. Jesus is Lord.'

'Jesus is Lord.' The words came with a caress of the voice and tears streamed down Henry's face. But it was not Henry. Henry was no longer here. Henry was a tool and a conduit for whatever used this honeyed, beguiling voice.

'Shall I sing to you, Priest? Say a prayer? You must free me, you must be the bridge, I long to go home.'

Perry took a step backward and looked away, looked at me, and the uncertainty I saw made me sweat. Perry stepped forward and slapped Henry across the face. I know that slap. The exorcism, for now, was over.

But it was not.

'I am Elliot. I want to go home to God.'

And Perry, at last, was drawn. 'And what do you think that will mean to you, demon?'

'Elliot. Elliot the lost, Elliot the fallen. I want to go home to God and what will happen after that is in God's hands. I want to go home to God, if you please.'

Perry took the Holy Water and wet his finger, making the sign of the cross on Henry's forehead and Henry did not flinch. Perry checked Henry's eyes again. Still rolled back, still white.

'I thank you for your blessing, Priest.'

'Is this some kind of demonic reverse psychology?' And I heard the puzzled humor in Perry's voice, and Henry threw back his head and laughed.

It was infectious. I was smiling too, I could not help it.

'Ask me why I possess this Henry, this servant of God.'

'I know why,' Perry said. 'The reasons are always a variation of the same thing and your name that you have so freely given matters only to God. The details, demon, are simply over my pay grade.'

The voice came louder and harder. 'I have great concern for God's servant, Henry, and you must free both of us, at once, or he will be dragged away, they will take him. They have him close in their grasp, a hair's-breadth away. You have two things you must do, Priest.'

Perry went still. He looked away and drew into himself, as if physically detaching from the voice of Henry, of Elliot, the beguiling voice.

Was it possible? Was Elliot a fallen angel who had changed his mind?

I looked at Henry, who I found, with a chill, was looking very intently at me. 'Ask your question, Noah-son.'

'I just . . . are you guys allowed to change your mind? Is it an option, once you've fallen to hell?'

Perry thumped my shoulder. '*Do not engage it.*'

'Why would you not listen, Priest, Perry-son who is chosen? Why do you turn your heart away, you who said this is a healing. You, Priest, who come to this so differently from the others. You who come to this with compassion and healing in your heart. Your very words are different, different always. I have been listening to you and you say, leave this soul and go to God. Not go back to hell. Go back to God. You have given me hope. You are the bridge and the way, don't turn your heart from the very destiny you were born to, Priest. You have been given the stewardship of Noah-son and he will work with you. You, Perry-son, who are descended from a long line of exorcists, direct from the Magdalene, the wife of Jesus, herself a woman of wisdom, and of the Source. Do you not feel God's will – there is not much time. There is . . .' A sigh. A breath.

Henry screamed.

The room went dark. So dark, so black, I felt dizzy. I held my breath. The heat in the room rose, squeezing us like a vice. My heart pounded and I felt sweat roll down my temples. It was hard to breathe. I heard panting. Perry or Henry, I could not be sure. Henry, I thought.

'Don't be afraid.' Perry's voice, and very close. I felt rather than saw him beside me, and his robes rustled as if he were holding out his hand. I pictured his outstretched palm and the vial of Holy Water.

His voice was strong and confident. 'Lord God of Hosts, before your presence the armies of hell are put to flight. Deliver us from the temptations of the evil one.'

But there was something new in Perry's voice, it was forceful in the way of a man who is plowing forward, following a formula, a man pushing through a doubt. He must have the same question that I did. Could he be chosen to bring a fallen angel back? I had known Perry since I was a child. He had always seemed to me extraordinary. Perhaps he truly was. Perhaps both of us were.

The lights flickered, and I saw, in flashes, Henry get up off the gurney and move toward Perry, with a look of such malevolence in Henry's face that I moved forward to block him, because there was no doubt in my mind that he was going to kill Perry with his bare hands. The light flashed and I saw Perry standing firm, hand outstretched with a cross in his fist.

'Free him from evil, and unclean spirit, begone Satan and cease to trouble this servant of God.'

Another weak flicker of light and I heard a sound like the whine of an engine gearing up, bearing down as Henry lunged toward Perry. I threw myself sideways, hitting Henry at the hip and knees, and it was like slamming into the side of a rock cliff. I was knocked backward, hitting the floor hard enough to knock the wind out of my chest. I heard a deafening crash, the crunch of metal and a cry from Perry. The lights flickered and came on.

The pristine quiet of the room was sudden, like a vacuum had sucked the very sound out of the room. My ears were full and popping. The chill of air conditioning hit me like a wave and my breath fogged the air. Henry sat on the gurney, dazed, rubbing his face, sweating and breathing hard. His face was chalk white. Eyes sunken. The look of a man who had been ill for months.

Perry was crumpled on his back, left arm jammed oddly into his side, and there was blood pouring from his left ear.

'Perry,' I said, touching his shoulder. His left pupil was a pinpoint, the right dilated, and there was a massive swelling, beginning on his left temple and running down the side of his neck. When I ran my hands firmly from neck to ankle, Perry groaned. His breathing caught and was labored. I opened his robes, unbuttoned his shirt, listened to his heart. The swelling, puffy red now, swept down the entire left side of his chest, shoulder, left arm. As if he had been hit with a car, or fallen on his side from a very great height. A killing height. Soft-tissue damage. As if he were crushed. And it made me think of the cop in my living room telling me how the man who had asked the church member to move their car . . . how that night he had been crushed. Mysteriously. How Henry had a fear that he would crush his wife and daughter.

I had no idea what was happening internally with Perry, but I thought of torn blood vessels, trauma to major organs. The left arm triggered the strongest pain reaction, a fracture, and I suspected bruised and maybe broken ribs.

I glanced over my shoulder at Henry, who was off the gurney now and coming close.

'What happened to him? Let me help you—'

'Stay right there,' I told him, and he froze.

'This is my fault, please, let me help.' His voice was low, rich with agony.

'Help by staying where you are,' I said, and he stopped, hands hanging awkwardly at his side. He swayed just a bit.

'Either sit on the floor or get back to the gurney, Henry. If you pass out and hit your head on the floor, you'll be concussed too. Go on, I can't have both of you on my hands.'

Perry groaned and opened his eyes.

'Perry, you are going to be all right.' I raised my voice a bit, my habit with concussed patients. 'Perry, you need x-rays on that arm, you may have cracked or fractured ribs, and you're very seriously concussed.'

He was paying no attention to me, but instead was watching Henry, eyes in slits of agony. He whispered something. I bent close.

'Call her, Noah. Call his wife.'

I could not help a quick look at Henry. He looked shaky, and

I remembered the feeling well. I didn't see whatever it was that Perry saw.

But Perry was my first concern, and I was planning how to orchestrate this. It was a matter of who was on duty tonight, whether or not I could get away with this under the radar. Candice usually worked the night shift, and she might help me cover this up. No way I wanted Perry on his feet. I was just going to have to call for help and come up with a story later.

'Henry,' Perry said, rolling to his side and wincing.

I put a hand on his shoulder. 'Be very still there, Perry.'

He was in denial. Not uncommon. I have seen people seconds from death insist they were fine.

Henry bent over, holding his stomach. 'I'm very sorry, but . . .' His voice faded as he vomited copiously on the floor.

TEN

I lost track of Henry after getting Perry hustled off to the ER and radiology. I'd given the lame excuse of Perry becoming ill while we'd discussed a nonexistent patient right outside the hallway of the MRI lab, me taking him in to sit but him collapsing and falling. Anyone tallying up his injuries would be puzzled, but the truth is that healthcare these days is so fragmented that it was unlikely anyone would be putting all the pieces together. Anyone except me.

I found Henry in my office. He had changed back into his jeans, cleaned the vomit off his expensive loafers. My sweatpants were neatly folded and lay on the office couch. I would send them off to medical waste later. Henry gave me a look over his shoulder. He was white faced, drained of all color, eyes dark with bruised-looking bags beneath. His jeans were baggy. An old worn pair. He'd lost significant weight in the last few months. But there was an energy about him now. He was a different man from the one who had walked into my office tonight. There was no uncertainty, no sign of strain, the burden he had carried was gone now. He was light on his feet.

*   *   *

'Good,' Henry said, taking my arm and looking at the phone number he'd written on my wrist with a sideways smirk.

I jerked my hand away.

'I'm glad I caught you. You won't need to call my wife.' He narrowed his eyes at me. He was almost electric with energy.

'I've already called her.' I glanced at the clock on my wall. 'A good half-hour ago, right after you went to the men's room to clean up.'

'Sorry to mess up your floor, Dr Archer.' I could tell from his look he was not at all sorry.

'You're not the first, and you won't be the last.'

'So you hope.' He smiled at me and it was not a nice smile. 'You didn't call her.' He was confident. Strong. Too strong for a man who had been through what he had been through tonight.

'I did actually. Just like you asked.'

He took a very deliberate step toward me, and stood very close. 'Just like I asked. Just like I asked.' It sounded odd, disturbing, how he repeated this, like a parrot. 'How did she sound. *My wife*.' He smirked and took two more deliberate steps toward me, so close now that I felt his breath on my face, smelled the vomit-tinged odor.

'Back off, Henry.' I kept my voice low and calm, and pointed to the other side of the room. He moved away. I felt my fingertips trembling. 'She sounded shocked. She asked me if I was sure, and I said yes. Very sure.'

He gave me a sideways smile. 'Then call her back. Right now. Tell her you made a mistake. Tell her you spoke to me, and I'm OK.'

'No.'

'No? No?' He walked around me like a man observing art. 'Why not, Dr Archer? You *have* spoken with me. I *am* OK. You see that, don't you?'

'Yes. I see exactly.'

'That I am OK.'

'I see that you are a new man, Henry.'

He clenched his teeth. 'This is *me* talking. Not them. I am . . . complete.'

'Yes.' I felt very tired. 'Yes, I see that, Henry.'

He gave me a rueful smile and his eyes were twinkly but hard. 'You don't sound very happy about it.'

'I'm not. I'm so sorry, Henry.'

'Because you failed?'

'Yes.'

'It was my choice, after all. It feels good. To embrace it. To become it. There's no going back now.'

'No. I'm afraid there's not.' I thought how Perry looked almost old when he talked about the failures. Henry Mandeville could be added to that list. When I fail, a patient dies. When Perry failed it was much worse. Complete and total possession. There would be no coming back from that, for Henry.

'I see you understand. So. There will of course not be any more little sessions with the priest and your lovely little protocols. The treatments helped, you know. Helped to open my mind. I was always sorry to stop those treatments. They will be sadly missed. This would never have happened to me, Dr Archer, without your help.'

I flinched. So Perry was right. Right all along.

'It's too bad. Really too bad. You'll have to shut the whole thing down, end your project that you love like a child. You made a promise, after all.'

How did he know, I wondered? How could he possibly know what Perry and I had discussed quite privately over dinner at Malone's? And why did he want it shut down, if it opened up his mind? If *they* wanted it shut down, that was the last thing I should do.

'And poor Elliot. He tried so hard to get away. Elliot is doomed. He did warn you. But you see now, don't you, Dr Noah Archer?'

'I see that you and Elliot are both—'

'Elliot has nothing to do with *me*, don't you get it? And anyway, it doesn't work like that at this stage of the game. I am Henry. Only Henry. A most devoted Henry, of course. I do not require . . . supervision. You can tell the priest he won't be bothered with Elliot anymore. Elliot will be taken care of. As the priest would say, Elliot is over our pay grade, Dr Archer – yours and mine. But I am OK. I am a whole man now. Admit you would be happy never to see me again.'

The cadences of his speech, the rhythm, was off. Different. The new Henry Mandeville. 'I admit I would be happy never to see you again.' It gave me pleasure to say it.

'Then call my wife right now.'

'No.'

I tensed up, waiting for it, the attack, but he turned abruptly, opened the center drawer of my desk and smiled. 'Last chance. Make the call? No?' He pulled out the photo of Moira, the fellas, and Tash.

He should never have known. That the picture was there.

He held the photo high. 'Going . . . going . . .' He dropped the frame and the glass shattered at his feet. '*Gone.*'

I locked the door once he'd gone, picked up the phone on my desk and called Mandeville's wife.

'Yes?' She answered on the first ring. She sounded breathless. Mandeville was right, she was waiting for my call. 'Dr Archer?'

'Yes. Henry says it's time to go. He said to tell you . . . *go now.*'

She made a little mewling noise. 'OK then. You're . . . sure.'

'Yes, I'm sorry, I'm sure. Go now.'

She was breathing hard, into the phone, and I heard the voice of a child, Mandeville's daughter, she sounded about ten. I heard whispering in a mom tone that held a thread of panic. 'Remember what we talked about, Callie? It's time. Put your kitty in the carrier and go to the car. No, right now. Turn the television off and go.' There were scuffling noises, then she was back on the line. 'Where is he now?'

'He just left the hospital. He's on his way. You don't have very long.'

I hear her choke back a sob just as she broke the connection.

ELEVEN

The first thing I did, after peeling the picture of my family up off the floor, and cleaning up the worst of the broken glass, was call Moira. She sounded tense, though she said everything was fine, and I talked to each of my sons, heard Tash snuffle into the phone when Vaughn insisted that Tash was family and had to say hello too so she wouldn't feel left out. I heard the natter of television in the background, the clatter of dishes, water running, all the mundane and beautiful sounds of my family in the usual evening routine. The dishes were done, boys fresh from their baths, snug in clean, soft pajamas. As soon as we were off the phone they would unplug from all electronic distractions, curl up on the couch beside Moira and she would read them the next chapter of *Redwall*, the story of a brave and militant mouse. On the nights when I was home, I liked to curl up and listen too.

Moira shooed the boys away, told me she had to go, her voice vague with habit and distraction.

'What is it, Moira? Something's bothering you.' She did not pick up on it, how upset *I* was. Which was not like her at all.

'It's Vaughn. I've caught him at it twice, just sitting like he's in a trance, looking out the window in his room down into the backyard. Like he's waiting. For that red-haired man.'

'Waiting or watching?'

'What's the difference, Noah?'

She wouldn't know, she hadn't lived it. They called it oppression and it was the perfect word. The perfect description. Feeling apart, somehow alien to the people you loved, as if you could not quite touch their hand when you wanted to hold them tight. Like having your chest slowly compressed. You can breathe but it gets harder. In the morning you don't want to wake up, the weight like iron filings building up in every cell of your body. That was how it felt. Like being infiltrated.

'His attitude. Moira, I am being honest with you here. This is important. Does he seem afraid or worried the guy will come back? Or hopeful? Like he wants him back.'

'Oh, I see. Yeah, that makes sense. Worried, definitely.'

'That's actually good. Worried is better than hoping. What's he doing right now?'

'Watching television with Marcus. *Boys*. He just took Marcus's Transformer.'

'Good. It's good that he is engaging. With television. Marcus.'

'So it hasn't . . . it's not that strong in him?'

'Exactly. And let's keep it that way.'

'What do I do?'

'Just keep an eye on him. Anything different. Distracted, or not wanting to play or just hanging out alone in his room.'

'Noah, I don't like the sound of this.'

My pager went off.

Moira sighed. 'I heard it. That's OK. We'll talk later.'

'We'll talk now. Something happened today, with Perry. He got hurt, and I'm going to be late home, making sure he's OK.'

'What happened?'

'It's complicated—'

'Yeah, OK.'

'It's complicated for *now*. When I get home tonight, I'm going to tell you everything.'

'Everything?'

'Yes, Moira. Today was complicated and there is a lot to tell.'

She was quiet. 'OK. See you tonight, Noah.'

'Moira? Keep the doors locked tight and the boys and Tash very close.'

'Should I be scared?'

'I love you. And yes, you should be scared. And I'm sorry. I'm so sorry.'

I headed to the ER and Perry. Candice O'Brian found me the minute I was through the swing doors. Candice was the best nurse in the hospital.

Candice was seriously beautiful. Blonde hair like corn silk, brown eyes, generous curves and the kind of firm, rounded breasts men dream about. And ever the target of do-gooders with weight-loss axes to grind who couldn't bear to let her beauty 'go to waste' because, my God, what a pretty face.

It was a slow night, and from what I could see, there was nothing on here but a couple of drunken UK students, and a stabbing.

'Your guy is refusing all treatment until he talks to you – and they want him up in x-ray, but not till he's had something for the pain; they don't want him throwing up or passing out. Can you talk to him?'

'Sure. Thanks for paging me on this.'

She nodded, looked over my shoulder for one moment, fidgeted with the stethoscope around her neck, then touched my arm.

'Look, when you're done – would you have time for a quick talk? Or are you trying to get home?'

'If we could do this tomorrow?'

She bit her bottom lip, nodded. 'I'll be on at noon.'

'Catch up with me around five, would you?' I was already walking away, when I stopped. Too much happening. Too much not quite right. That voice of wisdom that I ignored to my peril was whispering in my ear. I turned around. 'Candice?'

She was still staring after me, the slightest twitch in her left hand. I got the neuro ping but it was probably nothing. Twitches were normal. Lots of people had them.

'Is this about your father?' I asked her. Her dad was a subject in the Enlightenment Project. One of my successes. I hoped that was still true.

'It is.'

'You look worried.'

'I am.'

I nodded. 'Let me see to Perry, then I'll check back in with you.'

Perry was shivering under a thin cotton blanket, on a slab gurney in an ER cubicle. He was white with pain and shock. I snatched another blanket off a cart and draped it over him. His teeth were chattering lightly. I expected him to be relieved to see me. But he frowned the minute he saw me.

'What's up with you refusing the pain meds? Against your religion? You want a bottle of scotch? There's a reason I admitted you to the ER, Perry. You need some looking after, my friend.'

Perry swallowed. 'You called her? Mandeville's wife?'

I lowered my voice. 'I called her. I warned her.'

'Had to make sure.'

'It's OK, Perry. I called her and told her to go.'

'So you saw it? With Mandeville?'

'Later, in my office. I didn't see it right after, like you did – but when he came to my office, he was gone.'

'Failed. I failed.' Perry was gripping the side rail with the arm that wasn't injured. 'Shut it down, Noah. Shut the whole project down.'

I did not pretend I didn't know what he was talking about. 'Perry, you're hurt and you're in pain. Right now you just—'

'*Shut it down, Noah.*' Sweat made his face shiny. 'Henry Mandeville is lost. So be it. And I *know*, Noah. I know the good you've done. I'm sure the good is just as powerful as the bad. But I failed Henry Mandeville and so have you. It is just. Too. Dangerous. I have never seen anything this . . . this strong.' He grabbed my hand. 'Noah, it's got to be the treatments. It's enhanced . . . you *have* to shut this down.'

'What about . . .?'

He closed his eyes. Opened them. 'About?'

'Elliot.'

His eyelids fluttered and he settled back on the pillow. 'I admit it caught me up.' His voice dragged. 'But you know better than to listen.'

'I understand, Perry. Close your eyes. Just rest a second, and I'll see about getting you up to x-ray.' In a perfect world, an orderly would be bustling in right now. But that's not how hospitals worked anymore. When they worked at all. And the days when a hot-shit neurosurgeon could crook a finger and get things done was a legend I heard about when I was in training.

There were things I couldn't explain to Perry right now. Because it was not going to be that easy. Even if I wanted to shut the project down, I had a funded study, and there were protocols for pulling the plug. Could be I should have explained that earlier, when Perry and I made our deal. I don't think I believed that it would actually come to this. And I still had to figure out what *this* was.

The syringe of joy juice that Perry had refused was still on the tray next to his bed, and I picked it up and injected Perry in the bicep of his right arm. He flinched.

'Sorry. I've never had that delicate touch with needles.'

Perry grimaced, but looked at my hands with a hint of a sideways smile. 'Baseball mitts.'

He was right. I didn't have those long delicate tapering fingers the surgeons on television had.

The meds kicked in quickly, and Perry was starting to drift when the curtain opened and the ER doc stuck her head in. She squinted at Perry, looked over at the tray, and nodded. 'Good.

Pain a little better now, Mr—' I saw the quick look at the chart. 'Father? You're getting a little color back, that's good.'

Perry gave her a small smile. The ER doc raised her voice, just like I do when I talked to concussed patients. 'Can you tell me what happened? I understand you were feeling ill and you had a fall? Where were you when you fell?'

Perry looked away and closed his eyes.

She glanced over at me. 'Looks like he's fading. I'll check back in after x-ray is done with him.'

I ducked out of the cubicle right behind her.

'You doing a surgical consult?' she asked.

'He's a friend. But yes. Looks like he got his bell rung.' That was my official diagnosis.

'Okaaaay. Hey, what happened with this guy? That arm is broken and he may have cracked a rib or two. Extensive soft-tissue damage on his left side. Looks like he got hit by a truck. What the hell kind of fall was that? Was he up on a ladder or something?'

I gave her my best neurosurgeon higher-pecking-order patronizing smile. 'Listen, I want you to call Alice Payton in on that arm.'

'She's not the ortho on call.'

'So?'

'OK. Sure.' She muttered something about fucking royalty under her breath.

I headed down the corridor to find Candice. She was not due for a break, but she looked over one shoulder, and beckoned me around the corridor, opening the door to the supply closet, clearly expecting me to follow her inside. 'Look, I know my timing sucks, and you need to get home.'

'It's OK, Candice. Tell me about your dad.' Her father had an unusual name. Fielding.

I hung in the doorway, sort of half in and half out, arms folded. I knew how easily hospital rumors got started.

'Listen. You know how big a deal this project is to Daddy.'

Fielding O'Brian had lost sixty-two pounds in the fourteen months of the project. He did not eat too much, ever in his life. I'd say he often did not eat enough. He had a life of extreme physical activity. He ate wisely. But he gained what I called stress weight, steadily over the years. His life as the owner of a small farm got harder and harder, and he worked harder and harder. From what I saw in my practice, which I admit was a worm's-eye view . . . some farmers commit suicide and some have heart attacks and strokes, and some just pile on the weight. His blood sugar bounced higher than I'd like, but it was steadily lowering, though still on the high end of normal. No insulin required. He quit smoking his beloved cigars in the first three months.'

'Yes, I do know.'

'So OK. I've been trying to get him to talk to you guys and he says he did, but I know he's lying. He hasn't, has he?'

I looked over my shoulder. Ducked inside the supply closet and shut the door. 'Seriously, Candice. You know I can't discuss this with you.'

'He's signed the paperwork, so you can give me access. It's in his file. You can talk to me.'

'I'd have to see it. Got a copy on you?'

'OK, fine, Noah. Then let me talk to you. And if all this is familiar and you and Daddy are on top of this, then you can stop me and I'll go away.'

I was getting a bad feeling about this.

'Daddy's got twenty-seven more pounds he wants to lose and he's not stopping till it's gone. He is also worrying about what's going to happen when the project ends in eight months.'

Eight months, I thought, phase one complete, then, according to the plan, on to phase two. So close and maybe so far. I felt Perry looking over my shoulder.

Candice frowned at me. 'You look really tired.'

'You think? Come on, Candice, spill the rest of it.'

Her face did not crumple. Instead she took on her professional distanced look. 'Sorry.'

'No, *I'm* sorry. I see you're upset, I don't need to be such a jerk.'

'OK. Well, you know Daddy's history with Bonnet syndrome.'

I did know. One accumulates quite a lot of medical history in seventy-two years of life, and O'Brian certainly had. Type Two diabetes, one double bypass, one funky kidney that only proved why God gave us two. And Charles Bonnet syndrome, coming in as it does, fairly rarely, on the heels of significant visual loss due to macular degeneration.

It was an odd syndrome, manifesting in what we call 'Lilliput hallucinations'. O'Brian said it was like looking through to a parallel universe. Tiny people wearing hats. Dancing on the table-top, climbing the drapes. He would sometimes catch sight of them strutting by at the corner of his vision. Strutting. That was the word he used.

When it began, O'Brian had feared it was some form of Irish dementia. He was fully aware the little people were hallucinations – entirely visual. They might sing and dance, but he couldn't hear them.

And, in textbook fashion, the visions disappeared in two years, the average time span eighteen months to three years. The visions had been gone for four years before we interviewed him for the project.

'The little people are back,' Candice said.

I leaned back against the wall and folded my arms. Nope. None of this was familiar. O'Brian hadn't said a word. 'Have you had his vision checked?'

'He won't go. He doesn't want it on any official record. Not till he loses that weight.'

'He has to have it checked out.'

'You think I haven't tried?'

'Make him. Candice, you know better.'

'Listen, Noah. It's different this time. The visions. He doesn't just see them, he hears them. There are smells. He is . . . it's like he's mesmerized by this alternate universe he goes into, and he spends more and more time just zoning out, watching them. He's not sleeping well. He gets up in the middle of the night. And he talks to them now. He says he doesn't, but I've heard him whispering when he thinks I can't hear. And he shuts up the minute he knows I'm in the room. And he knows I'm there, he hears me now. Which is weird.'

I nodded. O'Brian had a significant hereditary cookie-bite hearing loss. It should be getting worse as he aged, not better.

'I asked him about it too, don't think I didn't. He says they tell him when I sneak up. Their words . . . his, I mean. Sneak up. I get this weird feeling. I'm getting paranoid. It's like the little people – like they don't like me. Like they try to influence my dad against me. I get how nuts this sounds.' She put her hands over her face and rubbed hard. 'I think Daddy is going fucking nuts. For real this time.'

'Shit,' I said. 'Candice, are there any other kinds of cognitive issues? Forgetting which day it is? Confusion, forgetfulness that's getting worse?'

'No. This doesn't look like dementia, Noah. He's sharp. Still playing chess and winning quite a lot.'

'Any car accidents? Fender benders? Lots of scratches on the paint job?'

'He hasn't driven since the macular degeneration set in.'

'Oh, right. Sorry.'

'And no. Nothing. It's not dementia, Noah, I've seen plenty of that. That's not it.'

'Well. Fuck.'

She looked at me. 'I was hoping for something a little more clinical. Is there any chance this is some kind of weird side effect? Of this Enlightenment Project?'

I could lie like most doctors do but Candice was a friend. 'Yes, that's very possible. Unfortunately. Candice, I'm going to have to talk to him about this. We'll need to have his eyes looked at. I'll go back over his MRIs, run—'

'Some tests. I know. Any chance you can do this without him knowing I'm the one who clued you in?'

I put a hand on her shoulder. 'I'll give it a shot, not telling him. Just asking him about side effects, see what he says. But if he doesn't tell me about it on his own, I'll have to bring it up.'

'He won't.' A tear trickled down her cheek. 'He's going to hate me when he finds out I told you this. But we have to do *something*, Noah.'

'You did what you had to do, Candice. So trust me. I'll look into this business with your dad.' I squeezed her shoulder. 'You did the right thing, telling me.'

And I couldn't help but wonder. Another victim of my project?

The boys were in bed by the time I got home, and I tried to kiss Moira, who gave me her cheek. She would not let me hug her, but I squeezed her hand and she squeezed back. Both Vaughn and Marcus were sound asleep. They looked peaceful, sweet. Worn out. Tash lay in the doorway of their bedroom, head on paws, keeping watch. She thumped her tail when I leaned down to give her pats.

Downstairs Moira was cleaning up the kitchen. I took the trash out. Shook my head at the dinner she had made.

'It looks good, truly.' Pork chops simmered in Marsala wine, balsamic vinegar, fried potatoes. Salad.

'You scared me earlier. On the phone.'

'I know.'

'How is Perry?'

'Broken arm. Cracked ribs. Concussion.'

She froze. Turned off the water. Took my hand and led me to the couch.

I told her everything.

'What the hell do you think you're doing with this, Noah?'

'My best.'

'I don't even . . . I don't even know what to think. I want you to leave this all . . . leave it all alone.'

'And if it doesn't leave me alone?'

'None of this makes sense to me.'

'That's OK, Moira. Make of it what you will. Just know I'm telling you everything. I'm not shutting you out of anything. Things are dangerous. They will get worse.'

'For real?'

'Oh yes, for real.'

She caught my hand. 'Should we . . . I don't know. Leave? Take a vacation for awhile?'

I shook my head. 'They'll find us wherever we are.'

'But we can't just do nothing.'

'We live our lives, we watch our backs. And I'll be talking to Perry. See if he has any ideas. He'll know what to do.' I hoped.

She grimaced. 'So much for the good old days. You know I don't believe in any of this? I know something weird is going on, but this demonic stuff?' She shook her head.

I nodded. 'That's fine.'

'So how worried should I be?'

'Well. If you don't believe in it—'

'I can worry my husband is losing his mind.'

I thought for a bit before I responded. Walking on eggshells, channeling Perry, considering every word I said. 'I'm sorry you think that.'

'I don't actually. Not you and Perry both at the same time. Can I see him?'

'Sure. I think that would be a good idea.'

She cocked her head to one side.

'What?' I asked.

'I just kind of expected you to tell me no. To shut me out.'

I shook my head. 'Never ever going to do that again.' And I meant it.

She looked away from me. 'What's the name of that patient you and Perry were treating today?'

'I can't tell you that.'

'Was he the one with the brain tumor? The one who thought he was possessed?'

'I can't tell you.'

'Not even to keep us safe?'

'I cannot tell you his name is Henry Mandeville even to keep us safe.'

Her eyes filled with tears. 'Thank you, Noah. Do you think he'll come after us? Do you think the red-haired man will be back?'

I put a hand on her shoulder and she didn't pull away. I nodded. 'He'll be back.'

TWELVE

Candice's father, Fielding, was in my office under duress, that was clear from the tension in his shoulders, and the set, unsmiling look he gave me when he shook my hand. He settled at the edge of the couch, feet flat on the floor, at an angle to my chair. The friendliness, the openness, had been sucked away.

His hands were rough, calloused, the kind of hands a man

earned spending his life farming, and he gave me a wary look. The usual smart-ass joking was gone. There was no prideful prodding for compliments on Candice.

He was trimmed and toned, but his color was high, a lot of red in his face, burnished in like sanded wood by years outdoors, and heightened by high blood pressure.

His shoulders were stooped and his hands were large. Like mine. He was intelligent and, it seemed today, weary of the world. He had spent a life working a family farm, hemmed in by the pressures of farming in a state that exports food grown locally and imports food from everywhere else in an insane system of agriculture that makes no sense to anybody but the middle men who skim the profit and the food pirate industry called agribusiness. He used to lecture me on this. He used to marvel with a certain hopeful pride that this latest generation preferred shopping at the Farmer's Market. That restaurants bought local as a point of pride. But that optimistic wonder was not here today.

He quit farming when Bonnet syndrome and macular degeneration, age and a lot of extra weight made it impossible for him to keep up the day-in and day-out labors of his farm work. But he put Candice through nursing school and had outlived two wives, grown tobacco and soybeans, raised lambs, and made a success of farming in a world that made farming a never-ending struggle to keep afloat.

'I do not want to be here,' he told me in a voice that was deep and strong. He was in his seventies and he had a gravitas that made you treat him with respect.

I nodded. 'You made that clear. The best I can do then, is get right to the point.'

That made him smile, just a little.

I held up my questionnaire. Ripped it in half and tossed it over my shoulder. 'I've got a list of questions that are supposed to reveal whether or not you are losing your grip, but let me just ask you right out. Are you?'

His laugh was more like the bark of an attack dog and just as cuddly. He leaned too close. 'I am not. What has that daughter of mine told you?'

I wished I could leave Candice out of this. But we were long past that.

'Candice says the little people are back, only now they're talking.'

Fielding frowned and looked away, and his hands, palms down on his knees, began to quake in a very slight tremor. 'That's my business and none of yours.'

'I'll take that as a yes. She also tells me you are talking back. Having conversations that stop when she comes into the room. Conversations that sound like arguments.'

He glared at me and rubbed the back of his neck. 'Look, I tell you that and you'll take me off the project, and I still got pounds I want to lose. Now, this could just be that Alzheimer's; everybody else seems to have it. Let me get the weight off and then you can boot me out.'

'You know I can't do that.'

He sighed and his shoulders sagged. 'I'm getting old, Dr Archer. It was bad enough when the vision started going, but when I got that Bonnet's syndrome, I thought I was losing my mind. I figure this is just another syndrome nobody knows about yet. So what if the little people talk to me? I'm just getting on with my life.'

I rubbed my forehead. 'What kind of things do they say?'

He didn't meet my eyes.

I was careful to keep my voice neutral. 'What do they want you to do?'

But he only shook his head. 'Look, I'll grant you it's not a good thing, me having them talking to me at all times of the day and night.'

'Fielding, do they tell you to hurt Candice?'

His cheeks went deep red. 'I *wouldn't* do it. I wouldn't ever hurt her.'

'Hurt her how?'

He put his hands on his knees and his shoulders sagged. 'They say . . . they say . . . *crush her*.'

I texted Candice and we set up an afternoon meet at the hospital Starbucks. It's my go-to place for a late afternoon caramel macchiato, and a chance to walk aimlessly through the hallways while I drank it. Candice was there ahead of me, sitting at a small, napkin-littered table while I waited in line. Her smile was grim and her eyes were swollen. Along with the caramel macchiato, I got a tall mocha peppermint with a caramel drizzle on the top. Her go-to comfort drink. Right now she was squeezing a cloudy plastic bottle of water. Her cheeks were very pink.

I sat her coffee in front of her and hooked a chair with my foot, dragging it out from under the table so I could settle in. My legs are long and the tiny round tables were cute but hideously uncomfortable. Maybe that was the point.

Candice had to work at a smile, and she took a sip of coffee. 'Thank you, Noah. For a neuro freak, you can be a nice guy.' She swallowed hard, choking a little.

'So. I talked to your dad.'

'*Oh, yeah.* I heard about that.'

I picked my cup up, put it back down. 'Look, it's pretty clear those little people he sees are after *you*, Candice. Which worries me a lot.'

'Don't sugar-coat it, Noah. And. They're imaginary.'

'Don't blow this off. My point is your dad is listening to them. I'm worried about you.'

She nodded and a tear spilled and trickled down her cheek. She scrubbed it away with a coarse brown napkin that made her pink cheek red. 'I'm your classic Daddy's girl. He has always . . . been gentle with me. Kept me safe. Sometimes, now, when he looks at me . . . it's not like my father. There's no feeling, no connection. He looks at me like I'm his enemy.'

'He sounds paranoid. Are you afraid of him?'

Candice rocked her cup on the table-top, but she did not drink. 'It scares me when I hear him arguing with them. It scares me when he starts pacing, in the night, outside of my room. I've been keeping my bedroom door locked.' She put her elbows on the table, made fists of her hands and tucked them beneath her chin. 'This is getting really fucked up, Noah.'

'It could be side effects from the treatments. So as of now they've stopped.'

'What about vascular dementia? Or Lewy body?'

'The hallucinations push me a little toward Lewy body, but it's rare. I'd like to follow this up if we can get him to agree.'

'Do you think once the treatments stop, the hallucinations will stop?'

Her eyes were so brown and soft and she looked at me with such hope, that it was all I could do not to tell her exactly what she wanted to hear. 'Look, Candice, the treatments have changed his brain. So the effects may fade or stay. We'll have to see. So answer me this, Candice. Do you feel safe with your father?'

She looked at the floor. 'He's still my dad. He's still in there, I know that. So mostly I do.'

'You've got my cell. You call me if things get scary.'

She smiled at me softly. 'Thanks, Noah.'

Another thing I couldn't fix.

THIRTEEN

I found Hilde stretched out on the celery green, microfiber couch she and I swiped from the dermatology lounge three years ago. It was coming apart on the arm rests and there was a diagonal rip down the center cushion. Since the couch conforms exactly to the contours of my back, shoulders and neck, I was annoyed that Hilde got to the neuro lounge ahead of me. My other option was a green floral antique nursing chair Hilde fell in love with at some antique flea market. She brought it here because it was too low to the ground to be of any real use. I was as comfortable as a basketball player on a tricycle in that chair.

'You locked the door,' Hilde said.

I nodded. We often did that. We didn't share the lounge, although we're supposed to. We're typical neurosurgeons. We don't work and play well with others.

I took the rolling chair from behind the desk where we keep a coffee maker that no one ever seems to wash. Placed the chair so I was facing Hilde.

She swung her legs to one side and sat up. 'You called the meeting, Noah. What do you want?'

'I'm giving you a heads-up. I'm filing another AE.' An AE is an Adverse Effect Report. Form 1572. Medical protocol for side effects in medical research.

'What, on Mandeville? We already did that.' Hilde stood up,

then sat back down again. She narrowed her eyes at me. Her hair was in a chignon today, or it had been when she left home this morning, about ten hours ago. She had been rubbing her eyes and the mascara was smeared.

'Fielding O'Brian.'

Hilde snorted. 'What are you telling me, because Fielding is doing great.'

'His Bonnet syndrome is back, except now he *hears* the little people. They have conversations. Conversations where they tell him to *crush his daughter.*'

'He told you that?'

I nodded. 'And Candice confirms.'

Hilde slid back on the couch, her legs sticking straight out. She had the mannerisms of a toddler. 'That's not good. Candice is . . . I mean if *she* says it, I believe her. But let's not jump into anything with the oversight committee.'

'We could wait till he kills her.'

'Noah, side effects in medical trials—'

'Hilde. He's not right, he's changed; combative, aggressive and secretive. That's my official opinion. With that, plus Mandeville's delusions – there's trouble here. We *are* creating spiritual experiences on demand.'

'Nobody ever said they'd all be good ones.'

I look at her. 'So you get it, then. You nailed it exactly, Hilde. We need to know the downside here. And be careful with our people.'

She didn't flinch. Many doctors would, trained not to think of the research subjects as actual human beings, which might result in adverse emotional impact. She wasn't like that. It was why I worked with her.

Hilde started pulling bits of fluff out of the slit in the center cushion and gathering it into a small, growing gray-white pile. 'Noah. You know that Maggie Horton just replaced Bill Barton on the committee. You know what she's like.'

'She's just one vote.' But I grimaced, because I was not being up-front with Hilde. Maggie was a godsend; Maggie would be just the ticket to get us shut down. I pictured Maggie's black little eyes behind the opaque oval lenses of her rimless glasses, the coldly clinical way she peered at people – all people, not just patients. The way she stood too close, crowding your space, making you feel like a smear under a microscope. Nobody liked her, least of all me. Hilde was intimidated, as she was by most professional women. And Candice refused to cooperate with her so often that Maggie had given up requesting her shifts.

'First do no harm,' I told her.

She fingered her pearls. Black ones today. 'OK, listen. Let's do this. You and I, we take four subjects each. Conduct one-on-one interviews *ourselves*, we don't leave it to any of the techs, students or neuro fellows. Our experience. Our brains, our instincts. See what we come up with and go from there. It's just a . . . an intermediate step. For information. We'll know it if we see it.'

'Define *it*, Hilde.'

'Trouble of any kind that seems out of the ordinary. Something developing after the treatments. Delusions, negative changes of any kind. Seriously bad spiritual experiences that started up after the treatments. But we chart the good ones too.'

'We've got two seriously bad ones already.'

She nodded. She knew as well as I did that half the patients would have to die for the committee really to care, and their concern would be lawsuits. This one would be hard to prove. If we shut down it would be us – me – doing it.

'Let's see if we get anymore. Don't file another AE until we're done. Will you agree to that?'

I nodded, trying not to think of Perry. 'It's a step.'

FOURTEEN

Abby Connors was third on my list of four patients. For the first two, so far so good, nothing to twang the antenna. Good results for one, OK for the other. So far I'd rate Abby's outcomes spectacular. I was nervous about talking to her.

I did not know if all doctors knew when patients lied to them. Abby Connors was lying to me now.

I liked her.

I don't like all of my patients, not by a long shot, but Abby, sitting across from me in a black pencil skirt, dark hose, and a loose, oversized sweater the color of oatmeal, was one of my favorites. She had tawny brown hair, stippled with blonde highlights, and it waved to her shoulders, shorter in the back, and tapered down the sides. She was wary about the interview. Studying me as I asked her questions.

Abby shoved rectangular red reading glasses to the top of her head. 'Nightmares? Obsessive thoughts? Why not ask me if I hear voices in my head?'

Evidently my attempts at subtlety had gone flat. I cocked my head to one side and glanced back through the notes. Depression, moderate. Occasional difficulty concentrating on work. I looked up. 'And the depression?'

'Better,' she said. 'The treatments, the meditations. It's making a difference. It's a good thing you're doing here. Know the value of your work, to people like me.'

'People like you?'

She put both feet flat on the floor, slid back into her shoes. She gave me a steady look. She was in her fifties – fifty-seven, to be precise. She was attractive. Smart. An artist. It was all right there in the file. I had been to her website. She painted street scenes, interiors of public places like train stations and restaurants and bars. Everything was in black-and-white, giving her art the feel of black-and-white photography. Her work was oddly haunting, always curiously absent of people. But even though the people weren't there, there were signs of them. Purses and briefcases left on benches. A sweater over the back of a chair. A table with the remains of a half-eaten meal. A cigar in an ashtray, smoke curling. The paintings had a curious tension, as if there were people nearby. Nearby, but missing.

'We done?'

I nodded.

She rose slowly. Looked at me over one shoulder on her way out. 'You should know that I'm painting again, like mad I am painting.' She laughed. 'I have a show in eight weeks.'

'Is it local? Can I come?'

She smiled at me. 'Love to see you there, if you're willing to fly to London. It's . . . it's a major gallery.' She took a breath.

'Dr Archer. When the project is over. Can I still get the treatments? I mean, look at me. My life is so good now. I can't . . . I won't, go back to the way it was. You can't just abandon me when the project is done.'

But that is what we do every day.

I frowned and leaned forward. 'Abby. What is it you aren't telling me?'

She looked away. Swallowed hard.

'Tell me what you lied about, Abby.'

She pushed hair out of her eyes. 'You know where it says depression, *serious*, *moderate*, *mild*?'

I nodded.

She laughed. It was not a happy sound. 'You don't have a category for my level of depression, Dr Archer. The way it was before.'

I put my hands together, trying not to sound pompous. 'Be specific, Abby. How does this chronic depression manifest?'

'Specifically? Before the treatments?'

I nodded.

She sat back down on the couch. 'Every single night I went to bed I would pray to die in my sleep.'

I swallowed. Abby Connors had delicate wrists and a silver bracelet with turquoise beads. I did not like this vision of her praying never to wake up.

'How did you feel in the morning when you did wake up? After a good night's sleep?'

She looked at me with a sort of pity. 'Disappointed,' she said. 'Someone like you. You're not going to get this. But I didn't just want to die at night. I thought of suicide – I could not get it out of my mind. Some days it would just pound pound pound. Psychiatrists call it a suicidal ideation. Or obsessive thoughts. Those are just labels, Dr Archer.'

'You're not a label, Abby.'

She smiled at me.

'And when you're happy? What is that on a scale of one to ten?'

'Off the charts. But not manic. If you have the capacity for great unhappiness, then you also have the capacity for great happiness.'

'Did you try antidepressants?' I asked.

She rolled her eyes. 'Yes, like everyone else on the planet. And they helped. *But*. It affected the quality of my work. I could show you paintings that were in progress when I took the medication, and pinpoint, pinpoint exactly, the day the antidepressants kicked in. And they made me gain weight. A lot of weight. It seemed to change my metabolism or something.'

She trailed off, but I was not surprised. Most antidepressants make people gain weight, no one ever warns them.

'The artistic temperament,' I said.

'It's not a joke, Dr Archer. And you know, I accepted it. A shitload of misery, mixed in with intense happiness and satisfaction. I would not trade my work for peace of heart. I was ready to just know it was my life. And then . . . your project. I was already doing yoga and meditation and that made a big difference, it did. But your treatments kicked that into overdrive. I started sleeping again. I sleep *well*. My nightmares are rare. I have dreams where I see visions of the things I need to paint.'

'You didn't have visions in dreams before? Can you tell me about the visions?'

'When I sleep, I see images, and they come with a feeling. Emotion. And it's not just in dreams. During the last three treatments – I saw images and I painted them. There's even music sometimes. Music I've never heard before. And when I hear the music and see the images, I *recognize* them. Like I'm remembering my future and I find the images and I think, oh yeah, there you are.'

'OK,' I said. I made some notes, but mainly I watched her. 'Any bad feelings with the paintings?'

'Well, bad how? Sometimes there is a bittersweet sort of grief.'

'Anything menacing? Anything scare you?'

She jerked back away from me. 'No. Nothing like that.'

I wondered if she was telling me the truth. I think she was.

'If you are looking for a downside here, there isn't one. The treatments help me be the true Abby Connors I always knew I could be. Abby Connors without the weight on her shoulders. I have it all now. My work. Energy. Peace of heart. Inspiration.' She stood suddenly. 'I have something for you. A painting. It's out in the waiting room, behind your assistant's desk. I was a little shy about giving it to you, but now I think I should.'

I stood up and opened the door for her, and she popped in and out, bringing an impressively worn and professional leather satchel. She had her back to me. 'This isn't my usual thing, to tell the truth, but I kept seeing it in my head, and thinking of you when I painted it. Which is very strange, but I've learned to go with that kind of thing.'

She unrolled the canvas on the top of my desk. It was about fourteen by sixteen inches – an odd size, I thought. And there was a person in it, unlike all the rest of her paintings.

A man, very young, early twenties. He was sitting on a wood rope swing hung over a black walnut tree, holding a kitten. A gray tiger-striped kitten with emerald-green eyes. The man was wearing a button-up gray sweater, and wool trousers and leather shoes and had a turn-of-the-century air I couldn't quite put my finger on. His face was broad, with prominent cheekbones, and his hair had been carefully combed and slicked to one side. He had dreamy brown eyes and a steady look, a knowing look. He was oddly charismatic.

Abby was looking at me, gauging my reaction. 'You like it.'

'I do,' I said. 'Very much.'

What I didn't tell her was that the man seemed familiar. I knew him, I just didn't know how.

FIFTEEN

So maybe I was stacking the deck, cherry-picking, working the spin. But when my interview with Nicholas Belker fell through a second time, due, he said, to caretaking obligations to his parents, I decided to make a house call. He had told me on the phone how much the treatments had helped him. He sounded calm, intelligent, his voice clear, confident, attractive. He was going to be another Abby, I decided. Another reason to keep the project going. Proof I was doing the right thing.

Belker had dropped out of the study about eight months ago, another fallen soldier in the dementia cul-de-sac – it seemed to me that half the population was red-eyed and exhausted, taking care of sick people in their family. I admired them. If I got dementia, I was going to kill myself fast, not suffer slow. Doctors are lucky enough to have access to easy options. Regular people are screwed.

Belker was a middle-school teacher, eighth grade. It would be a major event to make it to the grocery store, much less treatments.

I had looked at his scans. There were small but ongoing changes in the size of his brain . . . it was shrinking, with an imbalance of white and gray cells. Likely the effect of ongoing chronic stress – the stress of a caregiver with too much weight on his shoulders. I was not seeing this with any of the other patients, but none of them was giving care 24/7. If nothing else, it would be good to check on the guy to see if he was OK, emotionally. Kind of a wellness check.

I was on the road listening to Lavay Smith & Her Red Hot Skillet Lickers on *Everybody's Talkin' 'Bout Miss Thing*, wondering what kind of spiritual experience it would stimulate if I piped it into my test subjects while they were being zapped into spiritual enlightenment, courtesy of HORACE, the porcelain electrode hairnet. Wondering, as I often did, if I should have a go under the electrodes myself. I had always yearned to do it and been terrified. I knew the dark things were after me. It was a risk I wasn't going to take.

It was a strange thing, to be off the leash at 4.10 p.m. on a Tuesday, because business is usually humming this time of year. Spring for me means two things – one, the start of the suicide season, in what we like to call the Southern Suicide Sunbelt, which means an upswing in brain-damaged patients in the ER – suicides gone wrong – and two, new-car fever. But I bought the Audi last year. I planned to drive the wheels off this thing.

I turned left off Harrodsburg Road, heading into The Village At Rabbit Run, a planned condominium community geared to downsizing retirees who could afford to pay between $300K for a two-bedroom condo, and $500K for three. Pricey for a schoolteacher, but maybe his parents had a cushy retirement.

The rabbit village was made up of dark green, one-story condominiums with connecting walls, uniform architecture and layout, seriously manicured grounds with that deep-blue-green Kentucky Bluegrass, dogwood trees in full bloom, and hydrangeas snow-balling with flowers. At home in my yard the roses were blooming, and the peonies were heavy with showy blossoms the size of snow cones, and it would be a good two weeks before the petals dropped and turned brown. Late spring in Kentucky.

There were no children playing outside on the fresh black asphalt, and only one guy taking a walk, using one of those quick-release leashes that let his little dachshund roam into the street in front of my car.

The numbering system made no sense, and if a well-trained neurosurgeon couldn't figure it out, who could?

But I found the right little hutch in this village after circling around twice and annoying the guy with the dachshund. There was a car in the driveway, parked right in the middle in front of the two-and-a-half car garage. A battered old Mazda pickup, leaking oil. The driveway and the street out front were freckled with dried black stains and slippery-looking new ones. There were three bumper stickers. One said that children are our future, which, considering most of the children I know, is a fairly scary thought, and the second had a pink rabbit with a smirk and said CRAM IT. Another one let the world know LACROSSE STX.

The front door opened as soon as I headed up the small elbow of sidewalk, and Nicholas Belker opened the screen door and smiled. 'Well hey, Dr Archer. Come on in.'

I waited for the obvious joke about house calls, but he just smiled and put out a hand for me to shake. Belker looked good, like he had just stepped out of the shower, hair a little damp, thick brown-blond waves, a square tan face. He wore a spotless white tee shirt and loose khaki cargo shorts, yellow flip-flops on his hairy hobbit feet. Wholesome. Fraternity jock. Regular guy. The handshake was firm, the palms dry and rough, had a healthy set of blisters healing over. Gardening, woodworking. A dude with a hobby.

I followed him into the foyer, a small beige square, which opened into a great room, living and dining, that had all the usual bells and whistles – horseshoe granite counters, stainless-steel appliances, beige carpet, a gas fireplace, and a sunroom, with a tile floor and walls of windows. The couch looked almost new, pristine linen, three pillows perfectly spaced, but a battered brown recliner promised dude comfort in front of the big-screen television on the mantel that was tuned to a sports channel, with the sound off. Women's soccer.

'You checking up on me, Dr Archer? Oh, please, just move those pillows – my mom, you know, she obsesses about pillows. Have a seat. Cup of coffee or a beer?' he asked.

'Actually, coffee sounds great.'

'You're in luck. My dad is a Kona coffee nut, ever since he went to Hawaii. We get the beans from The Fresh Market. He has fits when they run out, and we have to go with . . . you know . . . Jamaican. Hard life.' He grinned at me and headed into the kitchen. 'Look, I'm sorry about dropping out of the program. Did I mess things up?'

'We factor that kind of thing in. I'm just doing some follow-up. It helps us if we know why you left the program—if it was connected to problems with the treatments or—'

'Oh, hell no. Those treatments were awesome. I wish I could have kept up with it. They really helped me cope. I just couldn't make the appointment schedule anymore. Didn't they tell you?'

'Tell me what?'

'Well, why I dropped out.'

The noise of the coffee grinder stopped our conversation, and the smell of coffee beans was welcome. I moved a pillow aside and sat carefully on the couch. Belker looked great, just like Abby.

'Yeah, they said your parents had health issues that made it hard for you to get out.'

'That's putting it mildly, they're like babies, you can't leave them alone for ten minutes,' Nick said, with a shrug and a grimace. 'As soon as the lease was up on my apartment, I moved in here. I could not keep up with the treatment program and teach full time and then come here after work every day. Parkinson's, my dad, and my mom – I've been hoping she's just tired from looking after my father, but I'm starting to face up to her Alzheimer's. She gets worse as the sun goes down, go figure.'

'Sundowner's syndrome,' I said.

He nodded. 'Yeah, so the Internet tells me. I guess that makes me feel better, that she can't help it. Her personality flips completely. In the morning she's my old mom, but in the evening, it's like she hates me.' He lifted his tee shirt and I saw bruises. 'She's tiny though. But she can pack a punch. I can't leave her alone with my dad when she gets that way. So, to be honest, it's been all I can do to teach my students, and come here after school every day. I barely made it to the last day of school. I don't know what I'm going to do when the summer break is over and the school year starts up again. It's getting so I'm afraid to leave them alone.'

'Have you looked into getting some help with things?'

He shook his head. 'I know what happens to people who get put in homes.' The coffeemaker sputtered and he took two mugs out of the cabinet. 'No offense, Dr Archer, but my great-aunt Hassie, she died in a nursing home. She starved to death and had rat bites on her toes. I was just a teenager then, but I wish I'd known. I'd have charged in and taken her out of there. She was a great lady. Used to make me popcorn and she came to all of my lacrosse games when I was at Sayre. If I had known what was going on, I would have made my mom and dad go get her. I would have gone and gotten her myself.' He gave me a second look. 'Nothing against you, OK.'

I didn't make the point that being a doctor does not make me responsible for the conditions of nursing homes; I am used to people lumping global medical care at my door. And he was right. Work Medicaid claims for a while and you'll lose your ability to pretend that a nursing home is humane, but there are people without options. So that's where they go.

'I understand,' I told him.

He looked up and studied me, then nodded.

I felt sorry for Nicholas Belker, and grateful, for his parents' sake, that they had him to take care of them. He didn't wear a wedding ring, and if he was in a relationship, she'd have to be compassionate. His future looked like rough going, but there was nothing I could do about it, so I would drink that cup of coffee and do my interview and go.

He filled two mugs, handed me one and headed for the recliner, then cocked his head. He heard it before I did, the whine of a muddy little Yorkie who stood outside the sliding glass doors in the sunroom. 'Oh, hey, Corky, I wondered where you were.' He grinned at me over his shoulder. 'You take cream in your coffee? Or sugar? I forgot to ask.'

'Cream, if you have it.'

'It's in the fridge – do you mind getting it?' He inclined a head toward the dog who had one very muddy paw up on the sliding glass door. 'If I let Corky in without cleaning those paws, my parents will obsess about the carpet. Just keeping this place clean is half my job.'

I nodded, wondering where his parents were. Maybe sleeping. It was quiet inside the home, just the hum of appliances.

I headed for the stainless-steel refrigerator, which had a pristine, freshly wiped surface.

'I am in official violation of the homeowners' rules here too because I let Corky out to pee on his own. All he does is circle the porch. You got to let a dog be a dog, even if it's a little fluff mutt like this one.'

He had Corky tucked under one arm like a football, and the little dog kissed him on the neck, while he gently wiped the dog's paws with a white towel. 'Corky, where the hell have you been, you little dude, you have mud all over your belly.'

'My dog Tash can find mud in a drought,' I said. I opened the fridge. Dropped my cup of coffee. The mug shattered, and the coffee splattered across my shoe and the white tile floor. I shut the refrigerator door with a slam, then opened it up again.

The inside of the refrigerator was smeared with dried brown blood. An elderly woman's decapitated head faced sideways on a meat platter that was smeared and stained with blood and spinal fluid, and her eyes, blue once, were now filmed over with decomposition and the cold. Her hair was white and yellowish, the skin on her cheeks brown and mottled and wrinkled like an old apple in a bin. I shut the refrigerator door and turned and faced Nicholas Belker.

He smiled at me, wiping the paws of the dog so very gently. There was a set of kitchen knives in a wooden block on the cabinet on my right. I inched closer to the knives, while keeping watch on Belker. My knees felt weak, like they might go out from under me, and I summoned up that surgical arrogance, the doctor warrior whose hands did not get shaky when wielding the knife. It wasn't exactly working.

'Sorry about spilling the coffee,' I said. 'My wife says she can't believe a klutz like me is a surgeon.' And it was true, Moira did say that. And my voice? It sounded iffy, to tell you the truth. A little high-pitched.

I waited for Belker to lunge for me, I waited to struggle for my life. But he just stared at me, friendly as ever.

My mouth was dry and cottony. 'So. I should go.'

He frowned. 'Oh, OK. I thought you wanted to ask me some questions, do the interview thing.'

'No, I've got all I need.' I didn't turn my back on him until I was at the door, and my hands were trembling hard when I pushed the door latch on the screen.

'Take care, man,' I heard him say, and then I was running to my car. Locking the doors. Dialing 911 on my cell phone, while watching the front of the house. Wishing, just for the sake of science, that I had gone through my interview with Belker before I'd opened that refrigerator door.

And I couldn't help thinking of power tools, and shovels, and ways that Belker might have gotten those blisters on his hands.

SIXTEEN

It was Corky the Yorkie, as he became known on YouTube, who led the police to the bodies. What was left of them, in the two-foot-deep graves where they were buried. Corky with his muddy feet and belly, who took the police right to the mound of recently churned earth. Belker had buried his parents lovingly, beneath a huge honeysuckle bush on the far side of a utility drainage ditch just over the property line at Rabbit Run. Corky had been spending his outdoor time curled up and grieving on the smoothly packed dirt. The bodies were wrapped in cotton blankets, face covered, hair smoothed on the father. The neck stump of the mother had been carefully washed. All of the fingers on the mother's hands had been removed. They were never found. When asked later where the fingers were, Nicholas Belker would always smile kindly and say he did not remember, in a tone that indicated he clearly did. The only person who found out what happened to his mother's fingers was me.

Nicholas Belker made a full and detailed confession with absolutely no coaxing or pressure whatsoever, then refused to sign the confession until he was allowed a private interview with me.

I had made my statement to the police, and it was clear that Belker's attorney had used Belker's treatments with the Enlightenment Project for some backroom trading leverage. I met Belker's attorney, Judith Van Hoose, at noon by the Phoenix Park fountain – about a thousand feet down from the police station where Belker was being held. Van Hoose was blonde, wearing a navy suit and a coral blouse, and her shoulders sagged.

'There wasn't a lot I could do for Nicky.'

I checked her out with a friend of mine, another attorney, and she was supposed to be pretty sharp. Years of experience, good negotiator. The gossip had her recently divorced, living now at a black-glass-and-steel condo on High Street. Her son, a biologist at UK, married with one son of his own, played lacrosse with Nicholas Belker when they were in high school.

Her eyes were sad. I knew that Nicholas Belker was going to be pro bono.

We stood away from the fountain so we could hear. The benches were filled, people having lunch, homeless catching some sleep. A man sat smoking on a bedroll under a tree, one hand on a sagging backpack. Two moms in yoga pants were one bench over in deep conversation, one of them pushing a sleeping baby in a stroller back and forth with her foot. At the edge of the park, customers stormed a boutique cafe for lunch.

'I read your statement to the police.' Van Hoose was frowning, looking into the water for answers she was not going to find. 'I've known Nicky since he was six. He and my son went to school together at Sayre all the way through – kindergarten to high school. I cannot believe this is happening. If he had not confessed . . . if the evidence was not so overwhelming.' She glanced up at me. 'Why? How could this happen?'

It was tempting to speculate but I knew better. This could blow up on me. Belker couldn't file a lawsuit – he signed those rights away, the usual protocol – but the publicity could flay me alive.

So I told her nothing. And there was not much I could say that would make her feel any better.

She tilted her head. 'He's confessed to everything; we've made the deal with the Commonwealth attorney. It's OK to talk to me, you know? That research study Nicholas was enrolled in—'

'Why are you asking?'

'I'm just trying to figure this out. Help me out here.'

'You're welcome to depose me on this, but you'll have to go through the usual channels.'

She sighed. 'OK. Just so you know, Nicholas thinks a lot of you.'

I had nothing to say. So far the hospital had not reacted in any way, though both Hilde and I – texting late into the night – were waiting for something.

'Look. Nicholas has already stated very clearly that he was well aware of the difference between right and wrong.'

I frowned. 'Surely you're having him evaluated?'

'Yes. It's set up.'

'Why are we talking, Ms Van Hoose?'

'So, I explained it to you last night. Nicholas will not sign the confession until he talks to you. It's part of the deal. The cops and the Commonwealth Attorney are anxious to announce a swift resolution to the press. We've got his plea bargain set. I just wanted to tell you to be careful.'

'Careful how?'

'The meeting will be conducted in an interview room. You need to understand that no matter what anybody tells you, there is no guarantee of privacy. Whatever you and Nicky talk about – it's going to be official knowledge as soon as it happens. One way or another, everything that passes between the two of you will be on a videotape, legal or not. They may not be able to use it in court, but they'll know.'

'I understand.' But I wanted to talk to Nicholas. And he wanted to talk to me.

'It seems odd to me,' she says. 'That you went to talk to him. At his home. A neurosurgeon. There has to be something you're not telling me. I'm sure the cops thought it was odd.'

And she was right about that. The cops did think it was odd. And there was a lot I wasn't telling her.

'I'm hoping . . . I am thinking we might have a shot at getting Nicky into a psychiatric facility. Which means he might get cured and someday get out. He has no history of any kind of violence, any kind of psychotic behavior.'

This I already knew. I pored over his medical records late last night and I could recite them to you right down to the last medical code.

'You'll stick with him then?'

She nodded. 'It's better than prison. And maybe later . . .'

I looked at her, feeling the slump in my shoulders. In a psychiatric facility, Nicholas Belker would spend the rest of his life on the latest, most expensive, antipsychotic snow cones. He wouldn't get better, but he might get worse. If he cooperated, he might someday be allowed to do therapeutic art with crayons.

Still. He did, after all, cut his mother's head off. There was that to factor in.

For me it came down to one question – did the treatments Belker received from the Enlightenment Project cause him to kill his ailing mother and father? This was something I had to know.

Judith offered to accompany me to the police department, and when I said no thanks, she gave me a manicured hand to shake and headed down the sidewalk to the high-rise building where she had an office on the sixteenth floor. I expected her to be there while I talked to Nicholas, but he had made it clear there would be no one else in the room – just him and just me. I wondered if I would be consulted, later, on Nicholas Belker's psychiatric evaluation. I was thinking not.

SEVENTEEN

Nicholas Belker was chained to a desk like a bear in a carnival sideshow. And yet he looked oddly gentle, in his prison jumpsuit, the blisters on his upturned hands still healing. He'd lost the robust air of well-being he'd had just two days ago when I arrived on the doorstep of his house. He seemed years older, his eyes shadowed, lines of stress on his face. They told me he was on suicide watch.

He grinned when he saw me and tried to rise, then the chains – locked around his wrists, his waist and his feet – brought him up short, reminding him he was a prisoner now and forever always.

'Please,' he raised a hand about three inches off the desk. 'Have a seat.'

I took a metal chair across from him. I admit I was wary. When I closed my eyes, I saw the severed head on the meat platter, the film of decomposition across his mother's eyes.

'Why did you do it, Nicholas?'

He gave me an odd sort of smile and swallowed hard. 'Can I start at the beginning?'

I shrugged. This man was the definitive end of the Enlightenment Project. I thought of Abby Connors, begging me not to kick her out. Of Hilde's slump of defeat. Had I created him? Did the blame go to me? Would Perry say that it did?

'Were you always like this?' I asked him. That was what I was hoping. That we'd simply snagged one completely fucked-up sociopath in our little project's net.

'Like what?' he said. The question was not what he expected.

'A killer,' I said. I had thought to approach him with compassion, and all I had was the urge to strangle him with those chains.

'Oh, I get you.' He shook his head. 'No, I never committed murder before. Never thought about it either, except, you know, like you say I'm going to kill you to people who piss you off. I mean, you say it, but you don't mean it.'

'What changed then? What made you a killer?'

'The treatments, of course, I thought that was obvious.'

I felt my stomach drop. 'I'm so sorry.' My voice was barely audible. The cops would have to strain to hear me.

'OK then,' I said, and started to rise.

'Please. Please, Dr Archer, I'm not saying this is your fault.' The chains rattled gently. 'I'm not, like, I'm not going to sue you or something. I mean I can't, right? I signed all that paperwork when I got into the trial. And I've told Judith we are not going to go to court and use this as a defense. That's what she wanted to do. But, you know, she's just doing her job.'

'Maybe you should let her, Mr Belker. The project will be on the hook for all of your medical care, which means you could go into a quality psychiatric facility instead of some place like Eastern State. I'll help your attorney get that sorted.' It would be the right thing to do.

He leaned across the table and gave me sad puppy-dog eyes. 'Listen, please. Just let me tell it. You need to know anyway, right? How the treatments affected me? I mean, I didn't quite tell you everything the other day.'

'You think? How could you do something like this? Were you tired and overwhelmed and you just snapped? Caretaking can bring enormous pressure. Were you drinking or—'

'There were two voices,' he said. 'Always two voices, right from the beginning when it started.'

I settled back into my seat.

'Not the kind of voices anyone else could hear. And not voices like I'm some kind of crazy guy.'

'Right,' I muttered under my breath. I knew better than this. I knew better. I need to be angry with *me*, not him.

'Listen up.' He sounded like an adult getting firm with a child. He scratched his unshaven chin. 'Look, I get it. I get how angry you are. But this is the end of the road for me, and I've gone to a lot of trouble to set things up so I can tell you stuff you *need to know*. You set up this whole project, you're . . . you're fucking brilliant, so why not shut up and listen to me, OK?'

I shut up. And listened. My heart thudding, my stomach cold, both fists clenched. Watching Nicholas Belker's blistered hands.

'Dr Archer. Look, what happened is that the treatments worked and I began having mystical experiences.'

'That's not what you reported. You said you had no spiritual experiences except a tingly feeling during the treatments, and a general feeling of well-being after. Other than that, you said they had no effect. I've read your file upside down and backwards.' Memorized it. I could recite it in my sleep. Maybe I did.

'I know. I lied.'

'Why?'

'Because it was personal and private. I am, I was, a pretty die-hard atheist. I fought my parents my whole life on not going to their precious Lutheran church, and my pride was not going to let me admit I started feeling the presence of something that you would call God.'

I did not tell him not to presume to know what I would call it. The clinician was taking over. I put my phone on record and laid it on the desk. He saw it and nodded but I was not asking permission. Just letting him know. Ever the ethical dude.

'Did God tell you to cut your mother's head off?'

'*Of course not.* Please, just don't interrupt. Let me say what I have to say and then you never have to see me again.'

'That sounds like a deal. I wish I believed it might work that way.' I would see him on the news. I would see him in my dreams.

'I don't blame you for being mad. But anyways. The experiences didn't happen there in the lab. But it was like they opened a sort of door. And, this sounds so weird, but the first one came at the Speedway on Harrodsburg Road, when I was pumping gas. There were all these noises – roadwork, jackhammers pounding the asphalt, traffic noise, a radio, and this woman laughing her ass off over something someone was telling her on the phone. And I overfilled my tank, and the gas spilled on my foot and I could smell it, and I started to see the smell, the vapors rising in the sun, and the wind was blowing and it was getting dark like there was going to be a storm, and instead of being annoyed by all the noise and the gas on my foot, and feeling like I was worried and needed to get home – I had to run out to get groceries, and meds for my parents and there was nobody there to look out for them. And I went from feeling all this stress and resentment and worry to . . . just a happy sort of peace.'

He looked at me.

'Go on,' I said.

'And there was a sort of voice, or feeling inside me and it said, they'll be fine. My parents would. So just be still. I am watching over them with you. You are not alone in this.'

I could not stop the classification system in my brain. Interior vision, theistic.

'And I felt so happy. Happier than I have ever felt in my entire life. And I just watched the people, and the jackhammers, and tuned in to the sound of the wind in my ears. And then I went home and I was happy to see them. The parents. My mom was going into that cranky phase, but then she stopped suddenly, and smiled at me, and just for a second there, it was my old mom, and I realized how much I'd missed her. How much I loved her.' He looked away and teared up. Wiped his cheeks with the back of his hand. 'And my dad, he was kind of sitting and staring and unable to move, like he was getting stuck, like he does, it's a Parkinson's thing. And I heard the voice again, telling me to go get the music box on my mom's dresser. She'd had it all her life, it belonged to her grandmother, and it played this old tune, "Let Me Call You Sweetheart", and when I was little, she and dad used to turn it on and dance around, you know, back when they were young and in love and happy just to be together. The three of us, you know, we were really happy when I was growing up. Other than me not going to church. I was a spoiled only child, went to private school, they bought me a cool restored muscle car when I was sixteen.

'So anyways. I cranked the music box and started the music up, and my dad, he smiled and he was back in the world again, it was like magic. And I knew this was a good thing, this voice in my head, and that somehow if I could just hang on, everything would be OK.'

I looked at him. Waiting. Trying to stay cold and sane, but in truth I could see them in that living room, the music box playing. It was probably the kind with a ballerina on top.

'Yeah, I know what you're thinking. If I was all full of peace and enlightenment, how did I get *here*? How could I do . . . such a terrible thing?

'So I can't tell you this deal with the parents was a picnic twenty-four seven. I had my epiphany or whatever you want to call it, and it changed me. I was more patient with them. But I can't say it wasn't hard. No matter how much you love people—'

'I understand.'

'I was hoping to have those feelings again. Like I did that afternoon at the Speedway. To get that feeling of peace and confidence, and to know everything was going to be OK. So I started meditating in the mornings. And nothing. Continuing treatments. And nothing. And then . . . my girlfriend and I broke up. She was great at first, but then when she realized that this was going to be forever, is how she put it, and that Mom and

Dad weren't heading for some kind of nursing home. She bailed.
Said the same thing everybody else said – that I needed to be
realistic and put them in a nursing home and get my life back.
And, you know, I get why she felt that way. Why she didn't want
to sign on for the kind of life that I had. At the time . . . at the
time I didn't much like it myself. Now . . . now I wish I could
have it all back. They always say it's a relief not to be a caretaker
anymore, but that's total bullshit. Because it means you lose the
people you love.'

I looked away from the pain in his eyes.

'And I started getting other thoughts. Like another voice in
my head, kind of egging me on. That it wasn't fair, that I should
have a life of my own, that my parents didn't have any kind of
life, they'd be better off dead, and if I didn't do something about
this, they'd suck me dry. All of that.'

I nodded. All of that.

'And I kept thinking about how it would be if they did die.
How it would be a relief. And the voice just kept on coming,
telling me how it would be better for all of us. Their life insurance money would pay off the condo, I could live there with no
mortgage and teach, and I could find a woman to share my life
with, that's how most people live, and I deserved to have my
own life too.

'But, Dr Archer. *I knew better.* An infant would know better.
It's one thing if it had been their choice. If they'd wanted to
die, asked me to do it. Or wanted to do it themselves. But they
didn't. Their lives kept getting smaller and smaller but
they were OK.' He smiled. 'Confused, maybe. But OK. So this
was different. This was *me*. I was just so . . . so tired. So I listened
to what I wanted to hear, I convinced myself, the more I thought
about it, that they'd be better off dead, they'd had a good life,
now it was time for me to have mine. Until I did it. I remember
drugging them, putting a pillow over their faces, it was so
easy, they were so gentle, so vulnerable. They didn't suffer. But
after that – it gets hazy. I remember the sound of a saw, being
in the garage, a lot of blood. A god-awful lot of blood. And I
looked down and there were my mother's fingers, laid out on
the workbench. And I could not remember how I even got there,
I don't want to talk about that. It's just – I saw her little wedding

band, just this thin little gold band with diamond chips on it that my dad got her when they got engaged. And I had this sudden rush of memories, of my mother's hands. Fixing me lunches for school. Scrubbing things. Writing in her plan book— she was a teacher too. She's the reason *I* became a teacher. I remembered all those construction paper projects she used to do with her students, and the glitter and the glue, and how she'd bring stuff home so I could do it too before I even started school. How exciting that was. I loved those projects. And I remembered the smell of the glue, and the paper, and then it happened to me again. That sudden feeling of presence and peace. There I was with my hands covered in blood, and . . . well, I'll spare you the details.'

But I could imagine them, the details.

'And that's when I really knew what I'd done. I messed up the plan. It wasn't going to be all bad, the way I had been dreading, the way everyone said it would be. These people . . . they're wrong. They don't get it. They don't understand it. It was going to be like this final journey with my parents. Not just good for them, but good for me too. That was the part I never got until it was way too late.

'I was an only child, and the three of us had been close all our lives, and I suddenly saw how it would have been. Tough times sure, but funny ones, and interesting changes in my mom and dad. Like they were the same as they had always been, but were going through something they had to do, so they were going to be changing, going on a journey, and they needed me to keep them safe on their way. It would be different. But not to be afraid of that. I could see how it would have been OK, how we were so connected, how there would be a love for me too, a woman in my life. And I missed all that. It was like an offer had been on the table and I just walked away.'

And I had to ask it though I knew I should not. 'And you don't think it would have happened this way, without the treatments?'

He shook his head at me. 'No, of course not. It would have been the usual tangled-up mess of resentment and duty and love and snarls, with me making the agonizing choice to put them in some kind of Medicaid nursing home, and regretting it but feeling I had no choice. I can see all of the outcomes now. I can see them.

'But you're missing the point, Dr Archer. I made a bad choice. But that was on me. The treatments opened up the world for me. That is *still with me*. I could have gone the other way, but it was me that made the choice, the *treatments* didn't make the choice. I am sorry for it. I miss them, my mom and dad, but I am still connected to them, to you, to everything. I am forgiven. I am just on my path. Being dead and being alive are not all that different, dude.'

I couldn't read him. I had no clue whether he was crazy, or wise, or psychotic or some weirdly awful mix of all three.

'So that's all I wanted to tell you. I appreciate you coming here and listening to me, and I hope that you will keep the project going, because you are doing important work. *Important work, Dr Archer.* And the main thing also, I wanted to just say . . . *thank you.*'

And I remembered Abby Connors, thanking me, and Henry Mandeville, thanking me. It was starting to creep me out. Perhaps they should curse me instead.

'There's one other thing.' Nicholas Belker wouldn't meet my eyes and that worried me. A minute ago he looked me in the eye to tell me about the mutilation of his parents. 'I just feel like I should warn you, OK?'

It was cold in the room. Very cold. The back of my neck felt oddly tingly. 'Warn me how, Nicholas?'

He looked down to his lap. 'I do my best to block out that dark voice. But it . . . your name came up.'

'My name came up?'

'Just. You should know. They're not happy with you. What they want? What they want is for you to shut it all down.'

'At this point Nicholas, I have no choice.'

'You're playing right into their hands, man. But. Could be the safest thing to do. Or not. To my way of thinking, it's going to be risky either way.'

'What did—'

He held up both hands, rattling the chains. 'That's all of it. I can't talk to them, OK. Things kind of . . . they seep through. But I've got to block them. So that's all I can tell you. That's all I can say. Stay strong, Dr Archer. Stay smart. And always watch your back.'

Nicholas Belker held out a hand to me, and I looked into his face, but did not shake his hand. Yesterday I pitied him for a future of caretaking elderly parents. And now that seems not to have been such a terrible thing.

Because now I pity Nicholas Belker for a future of being caged in the brutal American penal system, or the drugged-out psychiatric sewer. All with their greedy arms open wide. But the fact remained. He did not get here all on his own. I gave him a helping hand.

EIGHTEEN

And now it was over. The Enlightenment Project – shut down.

My interview with Nicholas Belker was exactly what I needed but did not want to hear.

Hilde and I sat on the patio of The Goose at a black metal table with a royal blue umbrella. The patio was fenced off, there was a large tree, all of this at the back of the restaurant on the Jefferson Street corridor downtown. We'd met here every night since the project shut down, three straight and counting, because both of us needed to sulk and it was easier to do it together. We had such hopes. Such hopes.

Hilde and I had decided to switch drinks, just for the hell of it, because we were empty, because nothing mattered, which meant I was sipping at a sweet Appletini and she was grimacing over a glass of Johnnie Walker Black.

'I can't believe it's over.'

'You've said that, Hilde. Like ten times in the last hour.'

'I get to say it twenty times before I have to stop.'

'Ten more to go.'

Hilde was wearing a sleeveless dress the color of French lavender and there was a sweater slung over the back of her chair. Her dress was cut low and her ample cleavage cradled a triple string of pink pearls. Her hair was wound into the usual mess that she informs me is a chignon. Summer was coming on a wave of sweaty humidity, and spring seemed to be over before it began, blurring right into a sultry hot, sticky mess.

The more I drank, the more I realized that I was fond of Hilde and her ridiculous nose, the pearls, the messy tortured hair. Hilde did not want to be alone at her house, but she did not want to leave her dog behind. So Miss February of the Golden Retriever Rescue Society lay at our feet. Chubby, smiling, easy-going, and continuously farting. We'd gotten looks from a couple with two children at another table, but they'd let their toddler bang a fork relentlessly for the last eight minutes. I figured we were about even on the annoyance scale.

A couple of hipsters – the guy with a man bun and pointy black shoes and a girl with a tattoo at the ankle – gave us a long pissed-off look. They both wore skinny jeans. The guy had little pursed lips.

Hilde leaned across the table, speaking in a loud whisper. 'I hope people know it's the dog.'

I patted Miss February on the head and she smiled up at me like I was the second coming. 'They think it's you.'

Hilde gave me a smoldering glare and blushed beet red.

The waiter dropped by and I ordered an Italian pizza and another round of Appletinis and Johnnie Walker Black.

'I'm not hungry,' Hilde said.

'Miss February and I can handle a pizza without your help.'

'Give me my Appletini back, this whisky tastes like dirty ass.'

'Well, exactly, Hilde. That's the sign of a very good whisky that's been properly aged. And, being a gentleman, I am not going to ask you how you know what—'

'Shut up, Noah.'

'Yes, ma'am.'

'Listen, Noah. Dr Merton came in to talk to me. She's going ahead with her own project and she wants to see our research notes before we publish.'

'Sure,' I said, and then Hilde and I burst out laughing, loud enough to get a long glance from the hipsters, and to startle the toddler into putting his fork down. He should not have a fork anyway. They should give him a spoon.

'Why do people bring toddlers to bars?' Hilde said.

'Because they need to go out for a drink like the rest of us and can't get a sitter. At least the kid's not farting.'

'Just shut *up*, Noah.'

'You didn't have brothers, did you?'

'You know I was an only child.' She picked the whisky up, then set it back down. 'We should go home.'

But instead we waited for the pizza to arrive and split it three ways. Miss February and I ate fast, we were hungry, but Hilde was delicate and slow, cutting bites with a knife and fork. She chewed and picked up her phone and took a picture of me.

'Drinking an Appletini, Noah. I'm going to show it to everybody at work.'

'You'll ruin my dude cred.'

'I know. That's the point.'

'Then I'm going to take a picture of you not drinking whisky.' But before I did, my phone rang. I put it back on the table.

'Answer it,' Hilde said.

I shook my head and hit decline. 'It's Moira. She wants me to come home. I don't want to go home.'

'Me neither.' When her phone rang she answered. 'Yes, Moira, he's here. He's drinking Appletinis. No, it's true, I've got a picture, I'll text it. OK, I'll tell him. No, he can't drive. No, I'm fine because he's been guzzling my drinks, so I'm unhappily sober. Yeah, he can walk. Probably.'

'I am not walking home.'

'It's not home. She says she's at a friend's place, at the Wellie.'

She meant Perry. Another person I didn't want to talk to. 'I'm not walking to the Wellie.'

'I'll drive you.'

'No way, I'm not going.'

I signaled the waiter and he brought us another Appletini and whisky, and I laughed when Hilde tried to take the Appletini, and gulped it down before she could get close to it. She glared at me and the whisky. 'Let's go. You're a mess, Noah, if you don't mind me saying.'

'I don't mind.'

NINETEEN

I t was after seven when I traipsed the marble floors of the lobby at 508 Main Street where Perry had a condo in the Wellie – the elegant and historic Wellington Arms. His unit was small, maybe 750 square feet. A one-bedroom condo on the second floor, right across from the elevator.

And I had the uneasy feeling that I had been too distracted by shutting down the project. I needed to pull myself together. Keep watch.

Moira had dropped by to deliver her homemade mushroom risotto, and to check in with Perry and see how he was healing, and if there was anything he might need. Evidently it was me he needed.

I had been expecting it. Perry had tried to get me over since I shut the project down.

I wished Moira was not there. I'd rather see Perry alone. So I could talk about her. Get some advice.

Because right now it felt like Moira was on the other side of a wall of glass. It seemed to me she lived in a dream world where evil was a concept, rather than a reality. Her world seemed to me to be entitled and naive. I used to like that. I used to want her to live in a world that made sense, that felt safe. Now I wondered how I could keep everyone safe, if she did not believe in the danger.

Her latest theory was that my view of the dark side and the demonic stemmed from the pressures of dealing with the never-ending stream of patients who dealt with catastrophic outcomes, because like all neurosurgeons, I had a heart-stopping share of patients languishing in nursing homes, on respirators, or shuffling into the ever-growing ranks of the permanently disabled. The lucky ones died. A small handful were healed. The rest fed that ravenous healthcare agony-gravy train, prolonging the pain and indignity of death. As if we could keep a person alive when time and the natural order of the world deemed otherwise. As if such a thing was heroic.

I had advance directives laid out years ago that demanded nothing but palliative care in case I go up against that particular wall. I kept copies in the top middle drawer of the desk in my office. And one folded tight in my wallet. I was considering a DNR tattoo.

Moira has been seeing Perry regularly. She did not tell me much about her meetings with him, even though sometimes I asked. My job was to watch over the fellas. And I think things were getting better. Vaughn had nightmares but not as often. I sat up late and watched the backyard. Vaughn knew I was on the job. I told him I would keep watch so he would not have to, and the look he gave me, the relief, made me feel strong and manly and oddly tearful. It had brought us closer but in a way that meant he is afraid like I was. And he was so little.

Moira had the door open as soon as I was off the elevator, and pretended not to see me lean in for a kiss. I squeezed her hand gently.

I loved this place and right now I envied Perry his lone-male solitude. He sat on a battered leather couch, his arm still in the cast, and his feet propped up on an ottoman that was a new and expensive cognac leather that had Moira's stamp all over it. The couch was propped against a bank of windows that opened to the dusky dark, downtown lights which were just starting to twinkle. The wood floors were polished, and there was black-and-white checkered tile in the kitchen and bathroom. I could smell the faint trace of the warmed-up risotto wafting in from the narrow, galley kitchen, and Moira was holding a glass of red wine. An open bottle sat on the kitchen counter, though Perry was drinking water.

Moira wore her favorite slouchy boyfriend jeans, cut in a straight leg at the ankle, and the heather-gray oversized sweater that used to be mine before she stole it. My favorite sweater became her favorite sweater. So we're compatible. And she looked better in it than I did. Dark curly hair tied carelessly back. Eyes so very blue. How beautiful she was. I wanted to touch her, pull her close to me, her head tucked under my chin. It was hard to be patient. To wait for her to come back to me. To wonder if she ever would.

She stepped back away from me but smiled and somehow I

felt better. She knew my heart. She'd remember that eventually.

The two of them looked happy enough together. I wasn't sure why they needed me. In truth I just wanted to hole up in my office at home, put my feet up and watch soccer. There was always a soccer game going, somewhere in the world, and I had the sports channels to prove it.

'Have you eaten?' Moira asked.

'Yep.'

'No risotto?' Perry waved a hand to the kitchen.

'Full of pizza and Appletinis, thanks.'

'My God, you've really lost your shit,' Moira said, and I had to laugh. We still have that connection, Moira and I.

'Where are the fellas?' I asked.

She cocked a hip. 'God knows. Roaming the streets maybe? Playing in traffic? It's hard to keep track of them every minute of the day.'

'Alec is with them,' Perry said.

Alec was Moira's younger brother. A newbie cop she adored and babied, and the boys were crazy about him. So was I. He's the little brother I always wanted, and though he clearly sensed the tension between Moira and me, he asked no questions and didn't take sides.

'So what's up, that you two have to call me away from drowning my sorrows with Hilde?'

They exchanged looks. They were worried about me. My project was dead, and I felt unmoored and disconnected. Like a ghost, haunting my life. I wanted to tell them not to worry about me. There were plenty of other things to worry about.

Moira curled up in a worn green armchair. None of Perry's furniture matched, but you couldn't beat it for comfort. Moira always told me furniture is not supposed to match unless it was a room in a Hampton Inn. I brought a straight-back chair in from the kitchen and sat and faced them.

I knew they wanted to know how I was feeling, but that was a private thing that I was holding tight to, trying to navigate. I knew I did the right thing, but it felt so wrong. I had failed me. No more hope that I could find a way for people, for myself maybe, to deal with the dark things, obsessions, depression, anxiety, the pressure of the whispers and the feelings that pulled you under, deeper and deeper. I had not realized how much that had fueled me until it was gone.

Perry looked at me and he reeked of sympathy, and I didn't want it. Didn't want to have to reassure everyone that I was peachy king and totally OK.

'You did the right thing, Noah, shutting it down.'

'There will be other studies,' Moira said. 'There are always setbacks.'

'You guys feel better now?' I checked my watch.

Perry leaned forward, and he looked tired. Feeling the ache in those ribs, no doubt. 'Henry's wife called me this afternoon. She and I talked quite a bit, before the exorcism.'

It seemed like years ago.

Moira took a sip of wine and looked away, frowning.

'How is she?' I asked.

'Wavering.' Perry winced and resettled his arm.

I stood up and headed into Perry's bedroom. Bed neatly made. Clothes put away, except one dark sock on the dresser. I took two pillows off the saggy queen-sized bed, headed back into the living room, put one pillow behind Perry's shoulder, the other as a prop to his arm. 'That better? How's your range of motion?'

'Improving, if I keep it slow. And yes, much better, thank you. I'll be fine so long as I don't sneeze.'

Moira worked steadily on her wine and I wondered who was going to drive who home. I sat opposite Perry on the couch and loosened my tie.

'OK. So Barbara Mandeville. What do you mean, wavering? I thought she took off. I thought she and Henry had a plan, if things went wrong.'

'Evidently she's in contact with Henry. She wants her husband back. Her daughter wants her daddy. You can't blame them. They were happy . . . before.'

I grimaced. 'He's not that guy anymore. Her husband is gone.'

'Noah, he's still her *husband*,' Moira said.

'You told her?' I asked Perry.

'He had to,' Moira said. 'She called the house, then came by, looking for you. Which while I don't appreciate, I do understand.

But I don't know what I'm supposed to do with her, and I don't like her showing up, or being around the kids.'

'She has a kid. A daughter.'

'Yes, I get that, Noah. That's why I'm here.'

Perry gave Moira a calming smile. 'She's found a new spiritual advisor, who has told her not to abandon her family. That she needs to talk to Henry, and work things out. He is recommending joint counseling so they can sort it.'

'Look, Perry. We've done all we can do, this is out of our hands. Everything this counselor has told her is logical. I mean, take the diabolical out of it and it makes perfect sense. We warned her. Henry warned her, when he was . . . lucid. She's going to do what she's going to do.'

Moira had looked away the minute 'diabolical' came up. She gave me a look. 'She wants to talk to you. She wants to meet with you and ask some questions.'

'Medical questions?'

'How would I know? But this business of the tumor being there and gone . . . I'd think she'd have questions.'

'And it's already been explained. So no. I'm not a marriage counselor.'

'I think you're right, Noah,' Perry said. 'But I am going to meet with her.'

'Yeah, priest stuff, counseling. Your job not mine. And what's going to happen if Henry shows up?'

Perry grimaced. 'I'm pretty sure he will. I think that's the whole point of this meeting. So be it. I'm not afraid of him.'

'You should be,' I said.

'Then go with him,' Moira said. 'You don't have to counsel her. That's Perry's job. But Perry's pretty vulnerable right now, Noah, so go and watch over him, and answer the medical questions. But guys – meet her in a public place, out in the open. That way you can end the meeting when you want to and it will be safer.'

I looked at Perry. Pain made you tired and he looked weary. He was better but no, I didn't want him facing off with Henry Mandeville & Company. 'Of course I'll go. You are absolutely right, Moira, and I'm glad you called me.'

Moira went a little pink. 'I was afraid you'd say no.'

I gave her a steady look. 'All you ever have to do, Moira, is ask.'

'Maybe they'll even be OK. Find a way to work it out,' Moira said.

Perry gave me a look. 'The goal is to help Henry's wife. She's going to have questions that you can answer better than anyone else. We can't fix it, but we can help her navigate. Since she asked for you, Noah, I'd like you to be there this one time. But after this, any more discussions she might need . . . she'll have to settle for me. These things never just end quickly. It's a process. Even if Henry is lost to her, she's going to have to see that on her own.'

My pager went off. My admin, Lil, who should have gone home by now. I frowned, rubbed my nose, and stepped into Perry's bedroom to take the call.

TWENTY

Lil spoke to me calmly and kindly, like she was gentling a horse, though I could tell she was shaken.

London was six hours ahead of us in the time zones of the universe. So while I drank Hilde's apple martinis and felt sorry for myself on the last evening of my marathon three-day sulk because the Enlightenment Project had gone to shit, Abby's sister was in a London morgue, struggling to identify a body mangled by being hit head-on by a double-decker bus.

It happened. American tourists looked the wrong way and stepped into oncoming traffic, that's why they printed LOOK RIGHT or LOOK LEFT on the sidewalks and street signs in London. But even without the note in her hotel room, the CCTV cameras that recorded every moment in the lives of Londoners showed Abby clearly waiting for the bus, and stepping out deliberately to get hit. The note was addressed to me. Her sister read it to Lil, who passed it on.

Not sleeping. Can't seem to do this on my own. And no more treatments to give me hope. It's unbearable to go back. I'm sorry.

We came close. The time I spent in the trials was glorious, and that's good enough for me. Thank you.

She'd drawn a little heart and signed her name.

I sat down hard on the bed. I wanted a do-over. I wanted to see her one more time. Beg her to hang on. We'd find a way to quiet that voice of despair.

Too late for that. Too late.

And that again. *Thank you.* Just like Nicholas Belker. They always said that and I didn't for the life of me understand why. I just wish to hell they wouldn't.

TWENTY-ONE

I stood at the edge of the living room, hand on the back of the chair I had brought in from the kitchen.

Moira had rinsed her wine glass and put it in the kitchen sink, and was gathering up her purse.

'What is it, Noah?' Perry said. 'An emergency? Do you need to get to the hospital?'

'He can't do that, he's been drinking all night, so he's not on call.' Moira looked at me. 'Whatever it is though, it's bad.' Not a question. For better or worse, she knew me. 'Honey?' she said. She reached out to touch me.

'Abby Connors. One of my . . . one of the project's successes.'

Moira tried to guide me onto the chair but I shook my head.

'She's dead. Suicide. And she was so . . .' I couldn't finish the sentence. How could I make it clear how she had resonance, a light, a beauty that was a culmination of her talent, her heart. 'I wish you could have seen her. During the treatments. How happy she was, so *busy*, engaged . . . she painted, she was in London, a showing, her first in years and . . . and she said in her note . . . She thanked me. For the treatments. They always thank me. Even Nicholas Belker thanked me.'

Moira drew a sudden sharp breath and Perry stood up, and tried to put a hand on my shoulder, but I backed away from both of them, gritting my teeth.

'I know this is hard,' Perry said. 'I know the project did a lot of good.'

'But you were right, Perry. It did a lot of bad too. It was risky. I just didn't know how risky. I want to apologize to both of you. I've been sulking. Making it about me. As if I'm in charge of the world. And, shocker, I'm not. But it's not about me. Sometimes you can help the Abbys in the world, and sometimes you can't. I just don't like it when I can't.

'And here's the thing. I did this. I put everyone at risk. My patients and . . . you, Moira. You and the boys. Everything that has happened. It's all on me.'

Moira took my hand. I kissed her palm and let it go.

'Don't take this wrong, either of you. I'm going to spend the night in a hotel. I just need a quiet place, by myself. I will come home tomorrow without fail, Moira, and I will straighten up and be a good husband and father. I will be present again. I will *pay attention.* I will keep you safe. But tonight . . . tonight I just need to go and breathe.'

I headed out the door, feeling sadly sober, and I headed down Main Street toward 21C, a boutique hotel downtown. I liked them because their icon was a penguin . . . they had penguin sculptures in every hotel, and each city had a different-colored penguin. Ours was Wildcat blue, of course.

I checked in and lay down in my room because, like it or not, tomorrow my schedule would be full of patients, and I absolutely had to get some sleep. The bed was ridiculously comfortable.

There was a cold sort of peace in the hotel room, the white noise and ease of impersonal space, no one to interrupt, to talk to me, to make demands. I loved my wife and I loved my children, but right then I had no room for the tension that was heavy in my house. Tomorrow I would apologize. Tomorrow I would make it right.

But right now, I had to assess my guilt. Decide where and how I had gone wrong. Decide how badly I had failed Abby. Abby and everyone else.

I took a deep breath, got out of the comfortable bed, and grabbed the complementary bottle of water. Pacing. The room, as always, was exquisite. Abby was in the morgue, and I had a hotel room with an espresso machine, chocolates on the pillow, and a cozy robe. The robe would keep me warm. Abby was stone cold, and nothing would ever keep her warm again.

I had dealt with the death of patients as a constant throughout my practice. I knew this was how it goes. It was not like me, this dark uncertainty. Still. It was not just arrogance but rank stupidity for a surgeon not to question, to think and weigh actions, outcomes, strategy. How long had it been since I'd done that?

The more patients I saw, the more outcomes, the older I got, the clearer it was that there were times I could do just as much good by backing away and keeping close watch. That there were times when the best medical care was patience and attention and abstinence from treatments that could do more harm than good. To face that. That medical care could be as much about stewardship as slash and burn.

A radical outlook for a surgeon.

But this . . . this dark uncertainty was deeper. So I paced, and I relived all the phases of the project, over and over in my head. I thought of Abby, the good and bad of how she functioned. The incandescent creative woman, painting feverishly. The bereft abandoned woman who would not go back to the dark abyss in her mind, who stepped in front of a bus instead. Fielding's face when I told him he was shut out of the program. And Nicholas Belker – his gentle acceptance after the shit-storm of blood and mutilation. Thanking me. All of them. Thank you, Dr Archer. Thank you so much.

I thought I had done my best. But now I was not so sure. How could I say I did my best when I failed to realize how very dangerous a spiritual treatment could be? Me, of all people. Me – who should have known.

In hindsight it made perfect sense. The outcome would be phenomenal – good and bad. Which made the treatment extra-ordinarily effective and extraordinarily dangerous. Even I, with my own experiences of being oppressed and possessed, had been so blinded by the power of possibility, I had underestimated how an effective treatment could take a patient in either direction. This was not about working to mitigate bad side effects. This was not a side effect. This was a desired outcome. The better the treatments worked, the more dangerous they were. Because

the outcome was determined by the spiritual strength and decisions of the patients. The outcome was literally offering a spiritual
choice to vulnerable patients who would be given up to the light,
and to the dark as well. I could not see a way around this. The
treatments came down to what it always comes down to. Free
will. How had I not seen this?

And I did fall asleep, in my boxers and undershirt and socks,
my shirt and dress pants and tie slung over a chair. My last
thoughts were a blur of memories. A falling domino of questions.
Mandeville. And Abby. Belker and Fielding.

   Now I knew why they always thanked me. The Enlightenment
Project had been a thunderous success.

TWENTY-TWO

Time to make amends. To mitigate the harm.
   Barbara Mandeville was suffering in a way that had
very little precedent for the average person. Who else
could she tell about this? Who could she discuss this with?
The things her husband did were no longer because of a tumor
in his head, but a demonic possession. How would she wrap
her mind around that? She would be safer if she believed Henry
was possessed, and gone from her forever. I was curious about
that. What she believed. This is the South, after all. We
specialize in denial. On the other hand, we're open to . . . the
unseen.

   So one meeting, and then I would be done, and any shepherding
and counseling and advising would be entirely left to Perry.
Barbara Mandeville would *not* be told that I had suffered as
Henry had, with a thankfully better outcome. That I would always
be at risk. But my presence would weigh on the side of belief
in the bizarre turn her marriage had taken. And I could answer
any medical questions she might have. After that, as far as I was
concerned, she was on her own.

*   *   *

We met at Josie's Diner, in Chevy Chase, halfway between my house and the Mandevilles' place. A noisy, family-oriented, cool-kids hangout that was a brunch tradition in the neighborhood.

We'd all ordered food, but Henry was the only one who was actually eating. He was having the ironic choice – Daddy's Omelet. We crowded together in a booth with a view of the parking lot, where nobody seemed to care about the buckling asphalt. They were there to pick up wine and bourbon at the Liquor Barn on the corner, to eat at Puccini's Italian restaurant two doors down, or the Mediterranean place right next door. To stop in at the drugstore, or Chevy Chase Hardware across the street.

Barbara, thinner than ever, very pale, had ordered orange juice and eggs and gluten-free toast. She had touched nothing.

It was not going well.

Henry wiped his mouth and his animosity was focused laser-like on me.

'You have a wife and two sons,' Henry said, and his look was hard, and he clenched and unclenched the mug of coffee in his left hand. I knew he was right-handed, but when he stirred sugar into his coffee, the spoon was in his left hand. As if in possession, he had gone from right to left-handedness, a mirror image of himself.

He leaned across the table, eyes narrow and tight. 'How would you feel if I kept your wife and child hidden? It is one thing for you to offer help, medical and otherwise,' he glanced at Perry, who was watching him like he would a rattle snake. 'But you have no right to interfere in my marriage. In my personal life.'

Perry shook his head at me and stopped me from answering.

'Enough of that,' Barbara said. 'I didn't set this up for you to be a jerk, you understand me, Henry? This is not about *you*, this is about our family. And I am making my own decisions based on what *you* asked me to do, Henry.'

Interesting. I admired her toughness and smarts. I worried about the deep shadows under her eyes, and the grief that I had long ago learned to read, etched deeply into her face.

Henry touched her shoulder. 'And now I am asking you to come home.'

'You missed the part where I said I am making my own decisions. Whatever it is you're going through, I'm sorry for it.

Sorry for you. But if I have to . . . I'm cutting you loose, Henry.
And keeping my daughter safe.'

'Our daughter.'

'Not legally.'

'I've been her father since she was three.'

'Not legally,' she said again, and I was careful not to let the
relief show on my face. Getting the legal system and the divorce
and child custody chainsaws in gear would chew them all
up, and just the thought of giving Henry visitation with Callie
made me grind my teeth. Barbara could divorce him or not, but
she had the power to keep her daughter safe. Legally anyway.

The biggest danger, of course, was her compassion and their
relationship history. If Henry said the right thing, if he apologized,
if he promised to do better, she might give him one more chance.
She loved him. She *wanted* him to come home.

She hadn't told any of us where she and Callie were staying.
My take was she had not quite given up, but she was close.

'You're the one who told me to go, Henry, remember that?'
she asked softly. 'This is what *you* told me to do.'

Perry looked at her and frowned. I could read his mind. She
was still in that other world where Henry was her husband, where
Henry loved her, and life had logic, and this was marriage and
maybe a medical issue. Like her husband was ill but rational,
and in need of her help. She had not quite realized that Henry
. . . *her Henry* . . . was gone. Never to return.

It was hard to keep my mouth shut and not tell her to run, get
away, and never look back. That she had a chance of happiness,
a child to protect, so cut him loose and go.

She looked at Henry with a calm but firm compassion. No
doubt thinking she was in control.

You're not, I thought. Not even close.

'What I'd like to do, Henry, is set up times where you and I
can meet, regularly, and if it is safe and if things work out, I can
come home and we can all be a family again. But it's going to
take time. We can't rush this.'

He took her hand across the table. 'I miss Callie. I miss you.
I miss Friday-night pizza. I just want us to be a family again.
Don't you see . . . didn't you learn anything? Life is short. Who
knows what time we have left together? Who knows what could

happen next? We need to hold each other tight. We need to be a family and be happy.'

It was good pitch, but something, some memory had been pinged, and Barbara pulled her hand away from his.

I looked at her steadily. 'Trust your instincts.'

'You shut up,' Henry said.

'Don't.' Barbara touched his sleeve, a gentle motion, and he clamped his hand tight on her wrist.

'Your place is with me. I've been ill. I've had a *brain tumor*. I'm cured now, by some kind of miracle I am cancer-free and, hard as this has been on both of us, it has been hardest on me. I almost died. You owe me. Your place is at home with me.'

'Let's not drop back into the dark ages,' Perry said. 'This isn't 1952.' And he peeled Henry's fingers away from Barbara's wrist, and there were red finger- and thumbprints on her pale pale flesh. 'She'll decide what is best.'

'Fair enough,' Henry said through clenched teeth. He took a breath. Gave Barbara a rueful, shaky smile. 'But why not come home with me for one night. There may be things at home you need, things you left behind in your . . . hurry.' He looked at her sideways. 'You know what I would love? I would love it if you would go get Callie, and we could all curl up with some popcorn, and binge-watch Netflix, just like we used to on Sunday nights. Just . . . just give me a chance.' He smiled, showing the dimples in his cheeks, but his eyes were glazed in the way I have seen in brain-compromised patients who were struggling with the loss of neural connection. They are in there, but not quite getting through. And then the glazing faded, as if it were never there, and Henry looked intense and alive and hopeful.

Barbara sat back in the booth, and gave him a steady look. 'So, you have to pass the test first,' and I saw the determination in her jaw, the intense way she watched him, though her voice was light, the tone almost flirty. Only I could see her hands, and how they shook and trembled in her lap. 'Do you remember, Henry, the tests you wrote down for me? We have to do those first.'

I had underestimated her. She had a plan.

Perry looked at Henry. Perry knew what the tests would be. I wondered if he and Henry had set them up together. Before.

Henry folded his arms, his eyes full of tears. 'Don't you love me?'

'I love Henry very much. My Henry. But I don't think you're my Henry anymore.'

He reached his hand out and they touched fingers. He nodded, jaw set hard. 'OK. I'll take all the tests you want. But first I want to see my daughter. Let's go get her, go home together, and I'll take every single test you can think of.'

'No, Henry. We'll take the tests right now. Right here. It won't take that long.'

'I *want* to *see* my *daughter*. Do you think I don't know where she is? Do you think I don't know she is one block away, on Sunset, at her old friend Mallory's house? Let's go get her, you and me, right now.'

I looked at Perry and he shook his head at me. I got it. Let it play out. My left leg was jiggling and I folded my arms.

'The Lord is my shepherd,' she said.

'The Lord is my shepherd.' Henry repeated it easily and with a smile. 'See? I'm still your Henry.'

Barbara looked at Perry, who shook his head. 'I'm afraid that does not prove anything, Barbara, now he is lost.'

Barbara looked back at Henry. 'Let's keep going. Just repeat it all after me. The Lord is my shepherd, I shall not want. He—'

Henry slammed his fist down on the table, bouncing silverware and drawing looks from other diners. 'Enough. No matter what I do, none of you will be satisfied. So look out into the parking lot, Barbara, my oh-so-darling wife.'

Barbara looked outside the window, and jumped up quickly, her coffee cup turning over, the creamy-brown liquid pooling and spreading and dripping into the booth.

It was her daughter. Callie. Out in the parking lot, no more than ten feet away. But she was not alone. The red-haired man had her, holding her left arm by the bicep, his grip tight and hard, and he was dragging her, and she was crying, crying hard, her face sheet-white, and there were fresh vomit stains on her shirt.

We were all scrambling out of the booth, and Barbara was screaming, *What did you do to her, what did he do to her . . .* and Henry smiled calmly.

'The Reverend Smallwood just went and got her so we can all go home.'

'But he was advising *me*.'

I looked at Perry, whose face was grim – the red-haired man, Reverend Smallwood, had been her advisor? Of course he had. Of course.

Everyone in the restaurant was staring, they had gone quiet, and I left Perry to deal with Henry and Barbara and I ran out of the restaurant and into the parking lot, and the red-haired man was smiling, smiling at me, showing the tips of his teeth, and I was only vaguely aware of a car door slamming and someone calling my name.

It was Moira, the driver's door open on the Mini Cooper Countryman Mommy Mobile, and both of my sons were seat-belted into the back, looking at me, puzzled, worried.

'What are you doing here?' I said.

'I got your text. You said get the boys and come.' But she is sharp, my Moira, and she saw the red-haired man and the little girl. 'You didn't send it,' she said, and then she was heading right toward Smallwood, not a hint of hesitation in her stride. She shuddered, smiled gently at Callie, and took Callie's hand and said, '*Let her go*. Come to me honey, come on.'

'A wife for a wife, Noah.' Smallwood smiled at me and let Callie go. He'd gotten what he wanted. My attention. 'Now Noah, you've been a very good boy. You shut the project down, just like we wanted. No more exorcisms with Henry. All good, Noah, all good. Just one more thing. Barbara Mandeville. And her sweet sweet child. We want them home with Henry.'

'Why? Never mind. No. You can't have them.'

'We gets what we wants, Noah. She'll listen to you. Send her home and I'll get out of your life.'

'You'll never get out of my life.'

He laughed. 'Think of it this way. Think what I can make happen in your life. Think of it as a trade. Two sons for a daughter. A wife for a wife. *Barbara needs to go home*.'

Smallwood looked behind me, and stiffened. 'Be a good boy, Noah,' he said, and walked away.

I turned to see Perry, moving toward us fast and strong, robes billowing.

TWENTY-THREE

Someone had called the police. Barbara and Callie had been hysterical, holding tight to Moira. When two cruisers pulled up, lights flashing, Henry and Smallwood were long gone.

Vaughn had gone still and quiet and Marcus was sobbing. I folded myself into the backseat of the Mini Cooper, and gathered both boys close, half in and half out of my lap. I talked them down in a slow, quiet voice. Vaughn's eyes were big and he nodded while I talked.

Yes, Mommy was making a police report, wasn't she smart and strong?

No, the little girl did not get hurt, but she was scared. The red-haired man scared her.

Yes, even bigger girls got scared of the red-haired man, but the grown-ups were taking care of it.

Yes, it was OK to be scared, that was your brain telling you to watch out and be careful.

Yes, Daddy got scared too. But we stood our ground and the red-haired man ran away.

Yes, Uncle Alec was a policeman too, and it was OK to tell him all about it. Yes, Uncle Alec was strong. But not as strong as Daddy.

Marcus giggled and Vaughn gave me a sideways look.

If anyone was a little bit hungry, we could go around the corner to Graeter's and get ice cream.

Yes, little boys who were so brave could definitely get two scoops.

Perry and I had ridden together, so after the promised stop at Graeter's, I drove him to the house, following Moira and the boys in the Mini. The three of us headed to the house and crammed into my study. The boys were watching their favorite Disney movie, *Moana*, enthralled with the ocean voyage and monsters and Moana herself. Both of them had a bit of a crush and Marcus liked to act out his favorite scenes.

Perry and Moira settled on the loveseat, and I had the leather chair behind my desk.

I turned it around to face them. 'So. That went well.'

Nobody laughed.

Moira pushed hair out of her eyes. 'Maybe it was for the best. I didn't like that husband of hers. Henry.'

'You were amazing,' I said. 'Grabbing Callie away from Smallwood like that.'

'I didn't feel brave.' She gave me a weak smile. 'Anyone want coffee? Fizzy water? Perry, do you need a pillow for your arm?'

I put a hand on her knee. 'Everyone is fine. Just sit for a minute. Breathe.'

She brushed tears out of her eyes. 'I don't even know why I'm crying. Everything is just so weird. I can't even imagine you dealing with this, Noah, when you were only eleven years old. I'm worried sick about the boys, but I don't know what to do. That guy made threats. I heard him. The boys did too.'

I looked at Perry, and told him what Smallwood said. 'But I'm not giving them Barbara. Not that it's up to me. I hope today scared her enough to stay away. I'm not sure what we do next.'

Perry shook his head. 'You cannot listen to their threats, and you cannot let them manipulate you. You do what you think is right and you stand in your truth. Do not give them a power they do not have.'

'We can't just ignore this.'

'We don't ignore it.' Perry shifted sideways, putting both palms on his knees. 'We kick it up a level and get some help.'

I leaned forward and so did Moira. 'Who can help us?' I asked.

'Bennington-Jones.'

Moira frowned. 'Is he some kind of detective or bodyguard?'

Perry gave her a small smile. 'Better than that. He's a priest.'

Moira slumped back. 'Another priest? Great. I'll leave you guys to it.'

'Stay,' Perry told her. 'You've talked to the police, and if they can help, well and good. Bennington-Jones is not just any priest, he's an expert on situations like Smallwood, and lost souls like

Henry Mandeville. He has . . . experience. And he is something of a legend.'

'With who?' Moira asked.

'With people who deal with these kinds of things. Look, it's a bit of a long shot. He's in huge demand. He travels a lot. He can sometimes be hard to find.'

'I'll track him down,' I said. 'Just tell me what to do.'

Perry held a hand up. 'I have contacts, Noah. Let me make enquiries.'

Moira put her hands over her face. 'What kind of a priest is this anyway?'

'The exorcist's exorcist.'

That night I woke up, alone in my bed, in the darkest part of the night. I wandered out of the bedroom, sitting on the top step of the staircase, looking down to the shadows below. Aware of the scent of our dinner, pork loin and carrots. The warmth of the oven cooling. Of our night-time routine: dinner, bath time, story time. Tucking in the boys, kissing them good night.

And I was thinking of the other things that I had brought to my family. The danger they were in. That they might be better off without me. That I was tainted. Somehow . . . *wrong*. They were everything I had ever needed, Moira and my boys. And what had I done, but bring darkness down upon them?

And I didn't know how to fix this. I didn't know what to do.

TWENTY-FOUR

Moira wouldn't talk to me. I understood. Her world was shaken and she had a lot to sort out. She was polite and distant and I dreaded going home. When I got my mom's call three days later, suggesting dinner, just the two of us, I was glad to agree.

And I could tell something was worrying her.

My mom was fond of Ramsey's, and the restaurant was only medium busy at seven p.m. on a Tuesday night. I was right on time but my mother was early, sitting in a booth near the bar. They had a fair selection of beer. A life-sized papier-mâché horse in a wooden stall beside the bar to let you know you were in horse country, if somehow you'd managed to find your way here without figuring that out.

My mother was watching for me and she smiled as I walked in, and it was good, so good to see her. My mama was a pretty lady. Her hair, usually a dark ash-blonde, was lighter, a butterscotch blonde that made her look younger, kind of sassy. She wore a silky rose blouse, chunky jewelry, khakis and ankle boots. A cashmere scarf was wound around her throat and draped with large black pearls. She stood up to give me a long, close hug.

She smiled over my shoulder at the waitress who magically appeared. Mama had the knack.

The waitress was college age, tight jeans, a tee shirt, dark blonde hair in a loose ponytail bun. Friendly. Most wait staff adored my mother, and were prone to telling her their troubles. Usually when I was trying to pay the bill and get out.

We ate here a lot and we gave our usual orders. I had a Kentucky Kolsh, my mother sweet tea.

'No wine tonight?' I asked. 'I can drive you home.'

She shook her head. She lived about three miles away, tucked onto a street called Shady Lane, our family home where I grew up. A red-brick, two-story, four-square house, with one bathroom upstairs. In those days, only having one bathroom was not seen as child abuse.

The house sat across from the back woods of the UK Arboretum. It had only been woods when I was growing up. There was a children's garden the boys liked.

Mama and her husband had done renovations on the house. A full bath downstairs. Replaced the old Kenmore electric range in the kitchen with a six-burner Bertazzoni gas stove. Put a pergola out back with a stone fireplace. And put in swings, a playhouse, and a jungle gym for the boys. Marcus and Vaughn would live there if they could.

The food arrived quickly and, as always, we both had the fried chicken. Her husband always ordered the yogurt chicken, which just goes to show he can't be trusted.

'You're clutching your pearls, Mom. Next thing you know

you'll be driving down the street at fifteen miles per hour with your turn indicator blinking the whole time.'

She gave me a tiny half-smile, but she had her *Steel Magnolia* face on. She was not going to be messed with tonight.

'How's Brent? He's not acting up, is he?' Invariably he treated her like a treasure. It was what she expected from the men in her life.

My mother salted her potatoes. 'If he was acting up, I'd take care of it, I wouldn't come crying to you.'

'Yes, ma'am. Now that you've put me in my place, you want to tell me what's going on?'

She smiled at me kindly, and tilted her head to one side. 'And I'm sorry, Noah. About the project.'

She is one of the few people who can say that without irritating me.

'I'm not going to lie and say I'm not basically crushed here. But this is life and I'm trying to roll with it and get my big fat ego under control.'

She set her fork down. 'You made the right decision, I think, Noah, but it's a close call. I can't help thinking that maybe you were *supposed* to follow this through. That it's your path. That it's why you had all that trouble, after your daddy died.'

I shrugged. 'What's on your mind, Mom?'

'I got a phone call from Marcus two nights ago. Two a.m.'

Our food arrived and my mother thanked the waitress, redirecting the plates so that I got my chicken with mashed potatoes, gravy, creamed corn and green beans, and she got hers with coleslaw, kale and beets.

'Beets are old lady food,' I said, and she smacked my hand.

The waitress refilled her sweet tea and asked if I'd like another beer.

'He most certainly needs one,' my mother said. After a moment of hesitation, the waitress took this as a yes.

I methodically cut a chunk of the chicken, but my stomach was tight. I shoveled the chicken into my mouth, followed by mashed potatoes, but it tasted like ashes and I put down my fork.

'That little rascal, Marcus, calling you at two a.m. We'll have a little talk. Sorry that he woke you up.'

My mother shook her head at me. 'No, you won't. I know

something is going on with you all. You can tell me to butt out, you can tell me to mind my own business, but don't lie to me like Moira did.'

'Moira?'

'I had lunch with *her* yesterday. Right here in this very booth.'

'Do they reserve it for you?' But she wasn't taking the bait. 'Moira didn't mention it.'

'I figured that much. It's starting up again, isn't it, Noah?'

'Yes, it's starting up again. I'm handling it.'

She added vinegar to her kale and cut it up into shreds. She was pretty fierce with the knife. 'Keep in mind, son, these are *my* grandbabies.'

'Did you ever stop to think I was trying to protect you, Mama?'

'Did you ever stop to think you might need me, Noah? Vaughn called me at two o'clock in the morning, don't you want to know what your son had to say?'

'Of course I do.'

'It was both of them, really, Marcus and Vaughn, huddled together over the phone. Vaughn would only whisper, he was scared. They stick together, those boys, and they are smart, just like their daddy.'

The lack of a biological connection to my sons had never slowed my mother's grandmother machine down one bit. She told Moira and me early on that you choose your children and they choose you before any of you are ever born, and 'it matters not' where you find them. Sometimes they were born to you, and sometimes you had to go and get them. Wherever they might be.

'They were scared?' I asked. 'Did they say why?'

'It took me a while to get it out of them. *Someone. It.* Told them not to tell their daddy or mommy or bad things would happen. But then they got the bright idea that they could call *me.* Because it didn't say not to tell their grandmother. So smart, those fellas.' She took her napkin and dabbed her eyes. 'There goes my mascara.'

I thought of my little boys, huddled in their bed. Hugging Tash and afraid to speak any louder than a whisper. And me . . . Unaware. How was it I did not know it? How was it I did not sense it? And I thought of the red-haired man and all of his threats. And wondered if Perry had tracked down Bennington-Jones.

'What else did they say?' I asked.

'I asked them what they were scared of. And they said there was something inside the walls, knocking. Really loud and really hard. They said sometimes it came from the floor. That when it happened, Tash jumped off the bed, went to the wall, and growled, with her head down low and her fur ruffed up.'

'Fuck,' I said softly. 'Why didn't they come and get me?'

'Moira told them you were working hard and had patients to take care of and to let you sleep.'

'*She said what?*' I put my fork down with a clatter.

'Does she know, Noah? About what happened before? I'm guessing she doesn't.'

'You'd guess wrong. She knows.'

My mother leaned back in the booth and folded her arms. 'I see. Well, I couldn't tell, yesterday at lunch. But it started up again with the boys and me on the phone. They held it up to the wall and I heard it and I heard Tash barking. And then Moira came in. She took the phone and apologized and told me not to worry and I told her I was *going* to worry, and I asked to talk to you and she said you were exhausted and had an early morning and maybe instead could the two of us have a late lunch after school tomorrow and I said OK.'

'So then what happened at lunch?'

'Moira danced around it. She said Marcus was having night-mares, you were stressed and working long hours and upset about losing the project, and for me not to worry, everything would be OK. That's all I could get out of her. And I didn't bring that old stuff up because I didn't know what she knew. But since you did tell her and she did not bring it up, or tell me – is she in denial or didn't she believe a word you said?'

'She thought it was likely a grief reaction to when Dad died.'

My mother shook her head, her mouth in a set straight line. 'I suppose that's an easier thing to think. I get that it's a hard thing to wrap your mind around. But Noah, you can't ignore this. You are going to have to get out ahead of this thing. Have you talked to Perry?'

I nodded. Mama idolized Perry. 'He's on it, both of us are.

I'm sorry to drag you into this, Mama, but you need to tell me immediately if Marcus calls you, or anything else comes up. You sidestep Moira, and you call me directly. Which is what I wish you'd done in the first place.'

'Well we're *here*, aren't we?'

'True. Sorry. I'm shook.'

'I know. Me too. The truth is, I was on my way over there, but Marcus got back on the phone and told me he was OK, that everything was all right again. He said he knew I would keep them safe and he could smell my perfume over the phone and it made him feel better.'

'Your perfume?

She held up her hands. '*I know*. I don't get it either. But he did sound calm, and Tash had settled down, and then Moira came back in.' My mother gave me a tense smile. 'I'm here when you need me, you know that, right?'

'I do.'

She took a long breath, and let it out slowly. 'Well good. Perry is a warrior.'

'So are you. And if I need you, I will call you.'

'Without fail,' she said. 'Or you are grounded.'

My mother tried to get me to order a slice of my favorite butterscotch pie, but I could not face pie tonight, and for once she did not argue, but she would not let me pick up the check.

'It's a mom thing,' she told me, and I walked her to her car, noticing that her walk was looking a little stiff. I hugged her extra hard. And I could smell her perfume. Like cool icy flowers. Jasmine? The scent was sweet but hard to put my finger on.

'Are you wearing a new perfume, Mama?'

She frowned at me. 'No. I'm not even wearing perfume tonight, I'm out. I need to run to Macy's and pick some up. Why?'

'I smell jasmine or something. Don't you?'

'*No.*' And the look she gave me let me know that she wasn't going to get any sleep tonight.

'Thank you,' I said. 'For being the kind of grandmother my little boys can call in the middle of the night.'

My mother gave me a soft smile and settled into her BMW SUV, rolled the window down and reached out to touch my arm. With my mama it was always the long good-bye.

'You haven't seen him, have you, Noah?'

I frowned. 'Who, Mama?'

'Him. You know. Oh, I don't even want to say it. *The red-haired man.*'

'You remember that, Mama?'

'I could never forget.'

'No, Mama. I haven't.'

I was a good liar, but she took a deep breath and smiled at me and I knew she didn't believe me.

It was only just starting to drizzle. I stood out of the way and watched her back the car out. One more person to protect.

TWENTY-FIVE

It was one of those nights when I was going to make it home on time. Not because the work wasn't piling up, but because I was just going home and the hell with it, and the parking garage was clogged with the slam of car doors and engine exhaust – staff going home, patients pouring in.

No parenting on autopilot right now. I had to be there. To have dinner with my family, see if Vaughn and Marcus were eating and light and playful. To sniff the air for that faint scent of trouble, for any trace of escalation, and then shut it down hard.

It was going to be a homemade mac-and-cheese night, one of Moira's specialties, and I was looking forward to it as much as the boys were. Moira was all about the comfort food these days. Her brother was coming over, Alec. He was off shift today and he'd be there already, building a fire in the outdoor fireplace, kicking a soccer ball around with the boys, sticking close to Moira. We were seeing a lot of him lately, and he made a nice buffer between Moira and me. I had not told her I'd talked to my mother. That I knew what had happened. I had not asked why the hell hadn't she told me. I was hoping she'd tell me on her own.

I wasn't sure what was going on in Moira's head. Sometimes I felt her drawing close to me, and then she would pull even further away. We were losing ground, the two of us. I was a model of full disclosure. She kept things to herself. I missed *us*.

I knew that the simplest – and often the best – solution was to focus on the most important thing. Which was keeping everybody safe. And right now it did not feel safe to me. It was out there, around the edges, seeping in like a relentless fog. I could feel it and I was walking that tightrope once again. Only this time I knew the rules.

Don't feed it. Don't call it. Stay on your path. And watch your back.

So when I saw Barbara Mandeville get out of a little green Fiat the minute I unlocked my Audi, I clenched my fist around my leather satchel, gave her a sympathetic nod, and opened the door of my car.

She'd been waiting for me.

'Dr Archer? *Please*.' She left the car door open on the Fiat, her little pink kitten heels clicking on the asphalt. I had the engine running by the time she tapped on the window, and I sighed, and turned it off.

She wore a blue cotton Oxford shirt, tails out, over Capri jeans; the weather was warming. Her face was drawn and tight, and she'd buttoned her shirt wrong ways, giving her an unsymmetrical look that triggered the compassionate streak I tried to keep in check. I rolled the window down.

The smell of oil and exhaust clouded the expensive leather and coffee smell of my car.

'I've been waiting for you,' she said. 'I hope that's OK.'

It wasn't. 'I've done everything I can do, Mrs Mandeville. You should talk to Perry though. He can guide you, if you need help.'

She put her hands on her hips. 'I can't just leave Henry hanging. You got us into this mess—'

'No, ma'am, I did not. And you need to take care of yourself and your daughter.'

'So what are you telling me? Abandon my husband?'

She bit her bottom lip. Watching me, hoping I'd tell her to stay with him. She was going to make me say it.

'Yes, I'm sorry, I think that's your only choice. Your husband had a brain tumor, but the man that came back . . . That's not the Henry you know. He prepared you for this, he told me that. Remember what he told you. Trust that.'

She lifted her chin. 'And would you do that? If it was your family, would you abandon your wife?'

I rubbed my nose. I admired her. I also wanted to throttle her. But most of all I just wanted her to go away. 'Your husband came to me for help, and I tried to . . . I truly did everything I knew how to do to help him. It did not work. I'm as sorry about that as I can be. I met with you. I answered your questions. But there is nothing more I can do. Other than tell you to give it up. He's lost, Mrs Mandeville. He is not safe for you or your daughter, he is a danger to both of you. Don't go back.'

'Don't go back? Because of his *complications*?' She put a hand to her throat, then laughed. 'You can't even say it.'

'Can you?'

'No. I don't even know how to say it.'

I opened my car door, got out, leaned up against the hood of my car, folding my arms. 'Well. That's honest.'

She held a hand up and laughed, an angry sputter really, and I could see her hand was shaking. 'Don't start being nice, OK, I am only just barely keeping it together.'

And I knew what she wanted. A safe haven. A shoulder to lean on. And a magic solution. Strike three and I was out.

'I want to show you something.' She held up a pink smart-phone, the big one. 'It's a video. It's short, I promise, just please. Just look, OK? I want you to see us. From before. How *pretty* we were. Just . . . just regular people with a life. Nothing special to anyone else, but to us.'

It was an odd word, pretty. But it was her word, so I took the phone after she pushed play.

Pizza night. Henry Mandeville coming through the front door with two Donatos pizza boxes held in front like an offering. The camera caught him right as he came through the door.

His daughter danced into view, seven, maybe eight; I'd say a year before Henry started into the project. Long straight brown hair, braces on her teeth. She shrieked. A pizza shriek, I guess. 'Just cheese, Daddy, did you get one that is just cheese?'

I heard Barbara's voice in the background, saying *Cassie, let your daddy get his tie off* and saw Henry grinning. He was a handsome man, that Henry Mandeville.

'Just cheese?' he said, with a puzzled look. 'Why surely you wanted little anchovy fishies on there to look up at you and glare at you while you eat them up. Yummy hummy anchovies.'

Cassie squealed.

He handed her the pizza boxes. 'Take them in the kitchen and get the plates.'

She dashed into the kitchen with an anxious mutter about anchovy fishies, because she *knew* he was joking, but it *wasn't fair*.

Henry leaned forward to give Barbara a hug, and the camera caught her laugh, and the dark buttons and searing blue of his shirt. He was so much taller than she was, and I glanced over at Barbara, realizing that the reason her shirt hung so loose right now was because it was one of his. I swallowed hard, thinking of how Moira took over my sweaters when they were broken in, soft, and worn.

'Netflix night,' he chanted. 'What's on for tonight? *Midsomer Murders* in the homicidal gardens of the English countryside?'

'Morse.'

'Ah, Inspector Sexy Morse. He's too old for you. You know he dies in episode—'

'You *hush*. Jealous man.'

Henry grinned at her and it was clear that this tall man with soft brown hair, a stubble of dark beard only just shading his cheeks, and eyes only for his wife, had no reason to be jealous. He was so different from how I had seen him. Confident, relaxed, a sort of glow about him. Healthy. Happy. She was right. They had been pretty then.

And then a blur as Cassie ran into the camera range, and handed Henry a bottle of beer that you just knew was cold and crisp. I recognized the blue and gold label.

Henry smiled down at his daughter. 'Did you find any little fishies?'

'Just cheese,' she said. And was gone again in a blur. 'I'm getting the plates. Mommy turn the TV on.'

Henry Mandeville would have had the tumor then. A tiny tiny malignancy. Growing in his head. Lying in wait.

I gave Barbara Mandeville back the phone.

'Did you see?' she asked me. 'Do you see us?'

'I saw you.' I squeezed her shoulder.

'So then you'll help? Father Perry, he is amazing, but he needs you too. *You* have to be there.'

'Be there for what?'

'Father Perry didn't tell you? He's agreed to another exorcism. *We can't just give up.* We have to keep trying. And *you* need to be there. Father Perry said he would not ask you, so I'm asking you. Please.'

'Because that's what *they* want?'

She looked away, and her voice was smaller. 'Henry thinks it won't work without you. He thinks it's his last shot and . . . I do too. Please be there. *Please.*'

I shook my head. 'Perry didn't ask me. He doesn't want me there. You have to trust him. He knows what he's doing.'

She grabbed hold of my hands. Her own hands were tiny, small boned. Moist and soft. 'You could talk to him. Convince him. My whole family is riding on this.'

'No,' I said. Simple, quiet, very firm. It was time for me to pull up the drawbridge. I had already given Henry a shot. No more Enlightenment Project. No more exorcisms. I might always walk a tightrope over that dark abyss, but for me it was over, as much as it could be. I would not willingly go to those dark places again.

She took a step backward. Grabbed a fistful of her hair.

I was a brick wall.

She caught her breath and narrowed her eyes. She was breathing hard and her mouth was set in a tight, narrow line. '*Why?*'

'Because I have a family too.'

'I see then. I guess . . .' She cocked her head to one side. 'I guess I understand.'

I gave her nothing. No discussion, no easing in the set of my jaw. No way in.

She dug in her purse, and pulled out a sticky note, purple, and I saw enough to know there was an address there. And a phone number. 'At least let me give you this. My daughter is in a safe place, and that is where I will go if this . . . if this doesn't work out. Yet again.' She tucked the note into the pocket of my shirt, her touch light, impersonal. 'It's my one last shot at getting my husband back. If this doesn't work out, I am taking Cassie away and never coming back. But I'd like you to be able to contact me. In case, in case maybe later, somehow, Henry is safe again. I don't know. But I would feel better if someone knew how to find me. Someone who understands.'

I took the note out of my pocket, folded it twice into a precise and tiny square, and put it in her palm, tucking her fingers around it. 'Give this to Perry.'

'Got it,' she said, and she said it hard. She clattered back to her little Fiat in her mincing kitten-heeled run, and I felt like a shit and got into my car. I slammed my fist on the steering wheel, waiting for her to drive away. She was either a terrible driver or too upset to be behind the wheel. She came within two inches of a concrete support beam, though she had yards of space. Saved only by the tiny footprint of her tiny car. I caught one final glimpse of her as she went by, dark hair whipping around her cheeks, both hands on the wheel.

I gave her plenty of time. Switched my engine back on, drove it stately and cold like the captain of a large, sleek yacht.

So Perry was going to give it another shot. They were both out of their minds. She, because she was desperate and didn't know what she wanted, just help. And Perry. Taking such a risk. Refusing to accept that Henry was lost. On the other hand, Perry was the expert. Maybe this was over my pay grade. I tried not to remember that last exorcism, the sickening thud when Perry fell so hard and so fast.

My stomach was a knot, and I wished I could walk into my home like a conquering hero, like Henry Mandeville had on that video, like I used to do.

Well hell, I could fake it.

I came through my front door with noise and a shout for my children and my beautiful wife. Greeted my brother-in-law with the usual exchange of dude insults, and Moira watched me with what was turning into a familiar tense set to her shoulders, backing away just slightly from my hug, giving me a cool cheek to kiss instead of her lips.

Her brother watched us with a frown and turned away to give Vaughn a piggyback ride. He was a good guy, Alec. So damn young, mid-twenties, hair a thick, wavy black like Moira's, the same intensely blue eyes. He was medium height and muscular, and only just now losing the intense shyness that had dogged him all his life.

But later. Later. With the fire dying down to the crack of embers and a hot red glow. The darkness lit by the string of patio lights Moira and I had hung together the first summer we moved in. Later the knot dissolved. Moira had fallen asleep after a second glass of wine, sprawled on the black wicker porch swing, Vaughn curled beside her. Marcus was sleepy but staying up to be one of the men.

Alec handed me another beer, opened one for himself. Added another log to the fire. It caught well, the embers were hot and hungry, and there was plenty more where that came from, a cord of wood stacked beneath the black walnut tree that made it a chore to keep the grass growing beneath. But it was an old tree, a couple hundred years, and it dropped fat, magnificent nuts that crunched underfoot and fed the squirrels.

Marcus eyed my beer. I offered it to him and he held it two-handed, and took a mighty swig without the smallest grimace.

'A historical moment, Marcus. Your first taste of beer.'

'Second,' he said matter-of-factly.

I glanced at my brother-in-law who gave me a wide-eyed look of innocence. 'Don't look at me.'

Marcus giggled.

'Seeing Candice again?' I asked Alec. Moira had set them up a couple of months ago.

Even in the firelight I could see the flush of red on his neck and cheeks. 'Tennis next Saturday, and then we're coming here, to grill steaks for the annual blow-out barbecue. Didn't Moira tell you?'

'No, but it sounds like fun. It's that time of year again.' I wondered about Candice. Her dad.

'She did too tell you, Daddy,' Marcus said. 'But Mommy says you don't listen.'

I smelled the wood smoke in my son's hair. Nudged Tash, who had fallen asleep on my feet to get close to the fire and to me. No doubt my clunky feet made a good pillow.

And I put Barbara Mandeville out of my head for good, as I had to do with all of the faces of patients and people I could not save. I knew I had done the right thing.

But Perry. Him I could not put out of my mind.

He'd be here for the cookout on Saturday. I'd wait until he was on the easy downside of a couple of Beefeater martinis, and I would talk to him then. I would change his mind. I had to.

TWENTY-SIX

I was up early the next Saturday, making coffee and drinking at the little countertop bar in our kitchen. It was the day of our annual cookout, and I was freshly showered, in khaki shorts, and a clean white cotton tee shirt. Faded flip-flops.

Moira padded in just after six thirty in panties and one of my oversized tee shirts.

'You're up early,' she said.

'Is that my favorite Ramsey's Pie shirt?' I poured her a half-cup of coconut milk, added a little cream, warmed it in the microwave for thirty seconds, then filled the cup the rest of the way up with coffee. Stirred it with an actual spoon and *not* my finger to impress her with how civilized I was. *Best. Husband. Ever.*

She took the cup, sipped, said thank you, then cocked her head to one side. 'You look . . . different.'

'I took a shower and shaved.'

She gave me a half-smile. 'That must be it.'

'Where's my list?' Moira always had a list. People would start arriving around three. So far it looked like we were going to have a good turnout. My mother and her husband. Candice and of course Moira's brother, Alec. Perry. Me, Moira, and the kids. Two families in the neighborhood and their various kids. Hilde could not make it, but everyone else had said yes.

We did this every year. Soon enough it would be the end of the school year, and Moira and the fellas would have the summer off. The summers got shorter and shorter, with the changes in school schedules. But I still got that excited feeling I had growing up, when school ended and you were free. Even though I would be working as usual.

'I didn't make you a list,' Moira said.

I picked my coffee cup up. Set it down. 'Why not?'

She shrugged. Looked away.

'Well, make it now. While you drink your coffee.' My stomach clenched. No need to pursue this. No need to look for trouble. Just get the list and things would be OK. No drama here. Normal. I wanted things to be normal.

Moira glanced over at me and I gave her a blazing smile. It was sure to dazzle her. Sweep her off her feet. 'At your service, madame. Your wish is my command. It's honey-do day. We are going to have fun, we are going—'

'Oh, don't try so hard, Noah.'

Or not. I looked away. OK, then. 'Would it be better if I went to the office awhile? Catch up on some admin stuff? Get out of your hair?'

'No. Hell, no.' She spun around and grabbed my shoulders. 'I'm *sorry*.'

'You don't have anything to be sorry for, Moira. You don't. Let it pass. Let's try and have a good day.'

'Don't you want to know what's on my mind?'

I knew better than to make a joke.

She laughed and if a laugh could be angry, that one was. 'It's a hostility thing. Because . . . oh, you know why. No point talking about it.'

I took both of her hands. 'Every point in talking about it.'

'Why? It's the same old thing. I just . . . I just wish you had trusted me and told me the truth.'

'I wish I had too.'

'Do you?'

'More than anything.'

'Then why didn't you?'

'Because it's so weird. How do you tell someone a thing like that without seeming crazy?'

'You managed. Finally.'

'I *wish* I'd told you. So much I wish that. I was wrong, and I am sorry, and if I had it to do over, I would tell you every-thing, I would have trusted you to know this. About me.'

'I honestly don't know how I would have reacted, Noah.'

I put a gentle finger on her lips. 'The point is not what you would have done. Neither one of us knows that for sure. The point is I should have told you. Do what you will. Given you a choice to trust who I am.'

She frowned. 'I like how you framed that. Because I know your heart, Noah. I always have.'

'Do you know it now?'

'Part of me wants to say no because you *didn't* tell me. That's what my logical brain says. But in my gut? I never stopped trusting you and I trust you now. I know our connection.'

'Thank you, Moira Bee. I know it's a leap.'

She laughed. 'How long has it been since you called me that?'

'Too long. Moira. I want to talk to you about something but I am afraid to bring it up.'

She kind of smiled, but her shoulders tensed. 'Do it anyway and get used to it.'

'I talked to my mother.'

She tried to take a step back, but I held on to her.

'Oh hell, Noah. Do we have to go into that now? I'm just trying to navigate all this.'

'Yes. I get that. All I ask is that you come to me and let me know what is going on. Is that fair?'

'Yes. More than fair.'

She pulled me close, her lips soft on mine. We held on to each other really tight. She tucked her head into my chest. I put my arm around her and she relaxed into me and I felt the tension in both of us melt away. 'I've missed you, Noah.'

'I've missed you too, my wife.'

She smiled up at me, pulled away, picked up her coffee but forgot to sip, drifting away deep in thought. I've seen her do it a million times. She was now in full-on hostess mode, planning things in her head. She frowned at me. 'Where are you going?'

'To get my notepad so we can make the list. But keep it short, OK? I've got beer to drink.'

It was a magical day. Unlike most women I know, for example my own mother, once the guests started arriving, Moira relaxed, let go of perfection, and just had a good time. No tense hostess face while the rest of us drank and ate. She was a happy general giving orders, drafting everyone, and I do mean everyone, into helping, and somehow also managing to be sure that we were all fed, the beer was cold, and no one was on the fringes feeling left out.

It helped that we were a small, close group, we knew each other well, and everyone settled into their familiar roles. Me at the grill. Alec keeping the cooler stocked with beer, Perry in charge of bourbon shots and martinis, and my mother and her husband ensuring that the fellas and their buddies got piggyback rides, time in the inflatable kiddie pool, and as many chocolate brownies as they could hold. Candice, new to these parties, found her niche organizing croquet and that old southern standby, the Corn Hole Game. It's not what it sounds like, OK? All of us the troops under Moira's slightly tipsy supervision.

We were doing frozen margaritas and Moira was sipping them slowly but steadily, and she looked sun-warmed and pretty in a red cotton dress, her bare arms going a pinkish brown in the sun. Low eighties, no humidity, a perfect day. Her lush dark hair was pulled back loosely, caught up in some wispy complex arrangement that left corkscrew curls drifting around her face. She had kicked off the black velvet flip-flops, her feet tiny, the skin tan against the white-tipped French pedicure. The red of her lipstick was smeared on the edge of the margarita glass, and on the side of my cheek where she had branded me earlier.

Perry brought me a Jack Black over two ice cubes, though I had already had a lot to drink. Enough to feel the glow, not enough to fall into the grill. Always a tightrope. He hefted his own freshly made Beefeater martini – with onions and olives, he was going hog wild. He flicked the smear of lipstick on my cheek. 'Things going better with you two?'

I shrugged. 'She only kisses me when she's drunk.'

'But she kisses you. That's progress.'

'It annoys me beyond belief, Perry, how relentlessly upbeat you are.'

He laughed.

We both looked over at Moira, who was curled up in the porch swing with Candice, their heads close, their conversation intense. Both of them looked over at me and my brother-in-law often enough for even the most oblivious man to realize he was a hot topic. Alec gave Candice a look over his shoulder and she froze and smiled, and they both looked loopy with new love. I felt happy for them, with the envy of the long married.

I took a sip of my drink. 'I saw you sitting and talking to the fellas while they were in the pool.'

'They were complaining about the water wings Moira strapped to their arms.'

'They have a point. The water is about six inches deep.'

'So are Candice and your brother-in-law a thing?'

'They are. She's vegan and he's a hard-core carnivore, but we think they can work it out.'

'She's a nurse, right? I think I remember her.'

'Yeah, I asked her to look in on you that day in the ER.'

Perry grimaced. But his bruises were a memory and, though I saw the occasional hitch of pain, he was moving easily now. Fluid.

'How do you think the boys are doing?' I asked him.

Perry was the ruffle-your-hair-how-are-you-doing sort with children, so I know he had not been over there with them just to hang out. I'd watched him sitting by the pool, talking casually, admiring the plastic boats and battleships the boys went to war with. I noticed too that he'd put the squirt guns out of reach before he'd pulled his chair close to their little plastic pool. He was watching them. Wary like me.

His eyes narrowed. 'I'd stay watchful, Noah.'

'Shit. Not what I want to hear. Did Moira tell you about the phone call? That Marcus called my mother in the middle of the night because he and Vaughn were scared?'

'Yes, she called me the next morning.'

'She didn't tell me that.'

He raised an eyebrow. 'She should have. These are things you need to know and, to be frank, she has no clue what she is dealing with. She's pretty much in total denial.'

'I think we're lucky she still trusts *you*, Perry.'

He set his drink down. 'You need to keep watch, Noah. We already know the red-haired man is . . . present. Watching them. Now we've got knocks on the wall. Muffled voices coming out of nowhere. That's how it started with you, remember?'

Oh how I did remember. Me frozen in my bed, hearing that heavy beat against my bedroom door. Expecting the wood to splinter at any moment and *it* to come thundering in. To get me. Get me how? I could not even imagine what it wanted, which made it all the worse.

'How did you find out then?' Perry asked, looking at Moira with narrowed eyes.

'My mother told me.'

He nodded. 'Moira should have seen that coming.'

I shrugged. 'Probably she did. I'm kind of on the sidelines right now.'

'She's protecting you.'

'That would be idiotic since I'm the resident expert. We talked this morning. She said she trusted me, she was sorry, and she'd tell me the next time something happened.' I gave Perry a loopy grin.

Perry nodded and smiled. 'Just what you wanted to hear. Please tell me you were rock solid and didn't give her a hard time.'

'I was and I didn't. I can't blame her all that much. I don't think she knows what she feels or why. I think she's scared for the boys, angry at me for bringing this home, and so far out of her depth she is just going on impulse and instinct. It's not about me as much as the kids. She's going to protect them and figure this out.'

Perry nodded. 'She's protecting you too. Which is a mistake. Nobody knows this better than you. Not even me.'

I looked at him.

'That surprises you, that I think that? They're in *your* head, Noah. They were. They look for opportunities to get back in. Marcus and Vaughn are obvious targets to get to you.'

'Yeah, about that. I need to fight back. *Do* something.'

'Noah, you live your life, you hold your ground, and you deal with what comes up. There's nothing else you can do.'

I drained my drink and looked away. Perry gave me a puzzled look. But my feelings were hurt. It was that old shameful feeling. I was different. They singled me out and they had me. For a while, they had me. What was it about me that attracted them? What did it say about me that they got in?

'I'm surprised your mother didn't call me,' Perry said.

'She thought she'd talk to me first and I asked her to let me deal with it.' I glanced at my boys and caught Marcus looking at me. He seemed worried and I gave him a thumbs-up, and saw the relief on his face, the broad, slowly spreading smile that was so very sweet. Would he lose that as he grew up? Became a surly teenager? And I knew that *he* trusted me.

'So then. The boys were told not to go get you or Moira, and like a brilliant future litigator, Vaughn called your mother.'

I nodded. 'That's right. She talked to them till they felt better. Told them she would come right over. But Vaughn said, no, they were OK. That he could smell her perfume and he was OK.'

Perry frowned and set his drink down beside the grill.

'I know. It's odd. I asked him about it. He told me that right before he called my mom he could smell her perfume, and he knew then that he would be safe. He said he almost didn't call her till he smelled that smell. It made him think of her, so that's why he knew to call. Perry? Why are you looking like that?'

'He smelled her perfume. What kind of perfume does she wear? It's . . . would you say it's flowery? Would that be right?'

'Something with gardenias, I think. Or jasmine. I can never remember. Why?'

Perry gave me a strange, small smile and he paced back and forth in a little rectangle. He would not be still but he did not want anyone to hear us, that was clear. He took my elbow and nudged me away from the group. I saw Moira notice, frown a little, then look away when her brother brought her two frosted salt-rimmed margaritas, one for Candice, one for herself. Mere husbands cannot compete with margaritas. Alec put a hand on Candice's shoulder, and she turned her head and kissed it. Open PDAs. Serious progress. I saw Moira get a smug little smile. I remembered falling for Moira, how easy that was, how new. How fun. And to see Candice this way. To see her light and happy . . . she was different. Glowing. It struck me how the care and worry for her father had weighed her down. She did not look worried now. She looked happy. Her hair, thick, long and shiny. Dangling gold hoops that you could see when she tossed the hair over her shoulder.

Perry tugged my arm. He was looking over his shoulder at nothing, eyes narrow, a small half-smile. There was a snap of energy about him I had not seen in a long time. It reminded me of the day I met him. How confident he had been. I did not realize, until this moment, how the years of exorcism and dancing with the demons had made him slower, more careful, a man carrying weight in his heart.

'What the hell is it, Perry?'

He was smiling like a man who was trying not to. 'I've heard of this, of course. It's just . . . such a rare thing. A miracle. A blessing. I would never have expected to see it. If it really is—'

'*Perry*. What?'

'The perfume, Noah. Vaughn smelled flowers and knew he was safe.'

'It happens. Like when you think you hear your mother's voice and she's not there. It's a neuron firing, nudging a sensory memory. Happens all the time.'

'Or.'

'Or?'

'Or he smelled them because they were there.' He took my elbow. 'Let's walk.'

He opened the little white gate, and Tash, lying next to the little pool and the boys, lumbered up and followed. Perry held the gate for her and she padded along beside me as we walked. My dog. She loved and protected the whole family, but I knew she was mine.

'Noah. Have you ever heard of a *good* possession? An . . . angelic possession or presence?'

I frowned.

'We are talking about a heavenly entity. A good angel, not a *fallen* angel. One who comes as needed, almost like a vision, only it is a possession. For guidance. For protection. For good.'

Tash nudged and leaned against my leg, and I reached down absently and scratched her ears. 'No. I've never heard of such a thing.'

'It's rare. So rare, Noah. And one of the signs is the sweet sweet smell of flowers.'

'So then not perfume.'

'And the thing that really strikes me is that Vaughn said as soon as he smelled the perfume, he *knew* he was safe. It would . . . it would make sense.'

I gave him a sideways smirk. As if *any* of this made sense.

'Perry. What if Elliot was real? What if he *is* a fallen angel who wants to go home?' I waited for the explosion of anger. The look of annoyed frustration. For Perry to shut me down cold.

He looked away. 'Actually, I've been giving that a lot of thought. I can't get it out of my head. I've been having . . . dreams.'

'Really?'

'*A* dream, actually. The same one, over and over. It makes no sense to me, really. A man on a swing holding a cat. It feels random but it comes over and over.'

'Shit,' I said. 'Come with me.'

We went in through the front door, unlocked for the party, Tash chugging close to my leg. The house was cool and silent, the echoes of party drifting in from the back.

I led Perry to my study. He sat on the tufted leather club chair and Tash settled noisily beside him.

'Something I want to show you.' I dug into the closet and brought out the painting Abby had given me. I had forgotten about it.

I set it up against the side of my desk facing Perry and pulled the sheet off.

Tash sat up. Then settled back down.

Perry stood up and lifted the painting. 'That's him, Noah.' He smiled. 'The man in the swing with the cat. This is my dream.' He peered down in the corner. 'Do you have a magnifying glass?'

I rummaged one out of the center desk drawer. 'It's just the author's signature. Abby Connors.'

Perry looked up when I said her name and looked at me hard. 'Abby? The one who died?'

'Committed suicide, Perry. Go on and say it. The note said she simply could not bear to go back to the way life was before the treatments.'

Perry took the magnifying glass out of my hands and peered at the bottom right corner of the canvas. 'Take a look.'

He handed me the magnifying glass and I bent close. I saw *Abby Connors* in a practiced, rounded swirl. And below, in impossibly tiny gold letters. *Portrait Of Elliot.*

'Elliot,' Perry said in a soft voice.

I put the glass down on the desk, and sat deep into my chair, feeling like I was held in by centrifugal force. I did not think I could get up if I wanted to. Tash whimpered and put her head on my feet, and I only just managed to scratch the soft white-blonde fur on her head. She looked up at me, worried, and I noticed how gray her muzzle was, my aging dog.

Perry was on his feet and full of fiery pacing, back and forth, running his hands through his thick, gray-streaked blonde hair. Tash and I watched him pace.

Perry picked the canvas up, propped it up on my desk, and stepped back, absorbing it, studying it, head tilted to one side.

Elliot. Hair slicked down hard, a severe side part, black eyebrows. The cheekbones were sharp, a heart-shaped face, something about him utterly compelling. His skin was tanned, a shade of flush in the cheeks, and the tiger-striped cat, eyes as green as emeralds, curled next to his chest. The bond between them was palpable, as if they had truly been together always. Like me and Tash.

Even sitting in the swing, you could tell Elliot was tall, solid, broad shouldered. Big square hands. Eyes, black. Creases down the side of his face, like someone who'd lived a life, one that had not been all that easy.

The longer I looked, the more I saw it. Something about that sideways smile invited you in.

Perry was full of questions now. About Abby. About her art. About her reactions to the treatments. Her expression on canvas. Her joy. And was it pure joy? Had she experienced anything at all . . . dark?

I held up a hand. 'Perry, please. Be still.'

He leaned back up against the desk.

'I can't tell you what was in her mind. Or in her heart. What she told me was that the treatments brought her peace from the constant weight of depression, the onslaught of constant suicidal thoughts that ran like an endless loop through her mind. That she was energized. Painting. Happy. More herself than she'd ever been. And afraid to go back to how she'd been before the treatments.'

'What did she say when she brought you the painting?'

I thought back. 'She said it wasn't her usual thing. But that she had dreamed about it over and over, been compelled to paint it. And then she knew, after it was done, that she wanted to give it to me.'

'It was a vision then.'

I shrugged. 'She's an artist. They get away with saying stuff like that and you just don't question it.'

Perry nodded. As if that was what he expected me to say.

'I hear Barbara Mandeville ambushed you after work yesterday.'

I looked away. 'She tell you about that?'

'She did. She said you blew her off.'

'I did. I was sorry to hear you're planning another exorcism, which I think is seriously fucked up. If you don't mind me saying.'

'I've been talking to both of them,' he told me, clasping his hands together. 'Barbara first, when she came to me. Then Henry. About a second exorcism. I've agreed.'

I rested my hand on top of Tash's head. If he asked me to be there, I was going to say no. 'I thought you said Henry Mandeville was lost.'

'He is.'

'Then why?'

'I could be wrong.'

I cocked my head to one side. 'You want to talk to Elliot. This isn't about Henry at all. This Elliot – the fallen angel thing – has hooked you in.'

Perry paced to the window, looked at me over his shoulder. 'You're right. It has. To tell you the truth, Noah, it's very unusual that Henry has agreed to go through with this. Unusual enough to intrigue me. So if Henry wants to try again, I'll do it. If his wife has not lost hope, neither will I. But my main reason is that I am giving Elliot a chance to come back. To get free. I've never seen anything like this, so I'm only going on instinct.'

'It's a terrible risk and you know it.'

'Which is why *you* can't be there. That's what Henry wants. You.'

'I don't know, Perry. I'm beginning to think I'm not the target. I'm beginning to think you are.'

He shrugged. 'Does it matter? You and I, we do what we do.

We don't let them dictate any more than we'd take direction from a cockroach.'

'The last time you did an exorcism on Henry, it almost killed you, Perry. Sometimes even you have to back away.'

'This is what I do, Noah. I don't back away. And maybe there is something to resolve with Elliot.'

'And maybe he's the bait. Hubris, Perry?'

'Ever possible.' But he smiled. 'I've been thinking.'

'About?'

Perry was properly sober and serious but a current of excitement ran through him so strongly he looked plugged in. 'Noah. I want you to give me a treatment. Like you did for Henry and Abby. It made Henry strong; honestly I've never seen anything like it. It could give me the edge I need to bring Elliot through. If that is where this is going.'

I felt a sick knot in my stomach. Why had I not seen this coming?

'The exorcism is slated for ten days from now. That's when I've got my team ready to go.'

His team. I didn't even feel excluded.

'Noah? Will you do it? I thought you'd be—'

'Surprised?'

'That too.'

In Perry's place, I do not think I could resist the lure.

'Perry, you know the risks. It hasn't gone so well, even for the people it helped.'

'I'm not just anyone.'

'So you want a level playing field.'

He nodded.

'This is the part where I talk you out of this.'

He raised an eyebrow.

'Perry, you've spent the last few weeks trying to convince me I was playing with fire here. You were right. It can take you to places you can't navigate. It's not just about strength of will. It's about being human and vulnerable and in over your head.'

'Exactly,' Perry said. He sat on the edge of my desk. 'The difference is I think I am uniquely qualified to navigate the dark places. And the flip side as well. The light ones.'

'You're chasing angels, Perry.' I had to grin. 'How cool is that?'

His smile was rapturous. 'Let's try *one* treatment. See how it goes. You take care of the medical side. I take care of the spiritual side. It's a lot to ask, but I do ask it.' Again that smile. 'You said you wanted to fight back. This is how we do it.'

I took a deep breath. I had only just busted loose from this whole business and it had taken a weight off me. A weight I no longer wanted to carry.

Perry was dragging me back.

But was he? Vaughn and Marcus were still at risk. The red-haired man was a shadow that threatened my family. And to cut to the chase, I owed Perry. I would not turn him down.

'OK, Perry. I'll do it.'

'If it goes well . . . how many treatments could we fit in, during the next ten days? Say eight days, so I can prep.'

'How *many*? Let's do one and see.'

'How often did you do them with Henry?'

'Once a week.'

'So, theoretically we could do two.'

'Perry. The project is dead. I don't have an MRI in my garage and things will have to be arranged.'

'Of course.' He grinned. 'I don't see my health insurance covering this, so I'll pay for the use of the MRI.'

'That you won't.' I held up a hand. 'I'll get it figured out. I'll tell you when. You start with one. Then we see. Don't push your luck.'

He grinned at me, perched on the edge of my desk, swinging one leg, and he looked like a kid getting away with something. 'You going to hang that painting up? I could take it off your hands.'

TWENTY-SEVEN

I was in my study, legs stretched out, going over tomorrow's surgeries step by step in my head. Imagining the outcome that I wanted. In my very private patient notebook, the one that no one – and I do mean no one – saw except me, I went to the next step. Just random thoughts on the patient. Odd quirks I had observed, their experiences with their meds, worries about their specific surgery. There was no rhyme or reason to it, and yet . . . I blundered into crucial insights often enough that it felt worthwhile, and it had become a pre-surgery ritual, as if it gave me control. I kept the little red leather-bound book locked in a desk drawer and there were no names or identifying patient numbers, just a nickname and a date. It was private, unofficial, for my eyes only.

But it took concentration, and the teeth-gritting annoyance of Tash barking was freezing my brain. I called out for Moira, waited for her to handle it. But the barking got louder and sharper and I slammed the notebook onto the side of my desk and stuck my head out the door.

'Somebody get that dog in out of the rain.'

It was pouring like hell and Tash would be drenched, and she was already slowing down with arthritis.

I headed to the back door, but no Tash, and I stared out the open door, puzzled. The water was literally coming down in sheets. The rubber strip on the edge of the door jamb had a chunk missing and the water was seeping in, making a small puddle next to the rug.

I could still hear Tash barking. I realized it was coming from upstairs. I headed up just as I heard the bedroom door open and Moira, fresh from a shower, came out wrapped in a worn pink terrycloth bathrobe, her hair drenched and dripping.

'Dammit, Noah, why can't you let the dog in? She'll be drenched.'

'The dog *is* in,' I said, and I was a step ahead of her on my way into the boys' room.

Marcus and Vaughn were huddled together on their bed and Tash was up there with them, up on all fours, fur in a ruff from neck to tail, barking, snarling, all of them staring at the wall.

'Tash. Hush.'

She acknowledged me with a hysterical broken-off bark, and went right back to it. Her head was low. She was in the red zone.

Before either Moira or I could even ask what was going on, the knock came again, this time on the wall under the window.

Shave and a haircut, two bits.

That universal staccato anyone would recognize. That made a point – *nothing random here*. Something . . . purposeful. Something aware. It could not be explained away.

Vaughn covered his face in his hands and burst into tears, and Moira's teeth were chattering. I scooped both boys up in my arms – how warm and tiny they were. And the knocking came again. Behind us. On the wall next to the bedroom door.

Vaughn shrieked and Marcus, too silent, went very white.

'What is that?' Moira whispered.

'Not sure, darling, but I'll sort it. Tash. *Tash, come.* Come on, guys, let's curl up in Mama and Daddy's bed.'

Tash snarled, and jumped and clawed at the window, and Moira was right beside her, looking out.

'There's someone out there, Noah.' Moira's voice was hard and too tight. 'I think it's him.'

'The red-haired man?'

She nodded. 'I'm going out there.'

'No, you're not dressed. Take the boys in the bedroom with the dog. I'll handle it.'

Moira gave me a look, nodded, and I knew she'd be getting her Glock out of the gun safe. 'Should I call nine-one-one?'

I shook my head. 'They can't help us with this. Let me deal with it.'

She took Vaughn out of my arms, and I set Marcus down and she hurried them out of the bedroom and down the hall. 'Come on, Tash,' she said.

But Tash had other ideas. She stormed ahead of me out to the landing and scrambled down the stairs. The hunt was on.

By the time I got down the stairs, Tash was scrabbling at the front door, not the back, and I opened the door to stick my head out. The red-haired man had been nothing more than a blur in the rain when I'd looked out the boys' window, but I didn't see him now. But Tash was beside herself so I knew he was out there.

I grabbed a leash, and clipped it to her worn leather collar, though, as Tash had aged and slowed down, a leash had become nothing more than a formality, a guard against the slim possibility that a particularly snotty squirrel would get her juices up.

But the minute I opened the door, Tash was out ahead of me with a snarl and a war hoop I hadn't heard since the night a couple of high-schoolers from down the road tried to amuse themselves by peering into our French doors. Tash had only paused long enough for Moira to open the doors, which gave the kids just enough time to high-tail it over the fence. Just.

The rain fell hard; fat, warm drops that drenched me immediately. My tee shirt and sweats were clinging to my body like a second skin, and water squelched into my Reeboks and thick white cotton socks. It was gray out. Bleary. Hard to see.

Tash raced to the side of the house, nose to the ground, following a scent. The gate to the backyard hung open. She zigzagged across the yard, working the area in a series of angles, then stopped for a second in the middle of the yard and sniffed hard, her sides going in and out like bellows. It made sense. In that spot there would be a line of vision right into the boys' bedroom upstairs. I looked up at the window, lit but empty. For a moment I thought I saw a flicker of movement, but it was gone so fast I could not be sure.

Tash was on the move again, and I followed her out of the yard and to the sidewalk. She was pulling hard and I had to jog to keep up. A black Suburban went by too fast, sending a spray of water slopping all the way up to my knees.

'Thanks a lot, you fuck. *Tash*. Easy girl. Let me catch up.'

A nuclear bomb could have gone off and she would not have wavered, or lifted her nose from the ground.

I was proud that the old girl still had it in her. I took pride in my ragged blonde brute of a dog. There were times I missed the energy of her more maniacal days.

She darted ahead and I followed, stumbling to keep up. She picked up speed and barked and I saw him. The red-haired man, drenched, head down, moving steadily, seemingly unaware of Tash bounding toward him.

I sprinted and held the leash hard, keeping Tash close just as the red-haired man crossed East High Street, plunging right into the middle of a stream of cars, lights bright and blinding as they sped through the rain, leaving a plume of water in their wake.

And it hit me again, that fear I knew so well, that fear that was ingrained into my soul.

The traffic cleared, and Tash quivered, circling my legs.

'Good girl,' I said softly.

Lean into it. Keep breathing. I thought of my boys, scared, so little, so vulnerable.

Tash whined and strained toward the street. I could not see the red-haired man but I knew he was close.

'Hell, yeah,' I told her.

She seemed to know where she was going and we headed down the sidewalk past Starbucks, navigated the hellish intersection on Euclid. We passed the building where the Morris Book Shop used to be, and Bella Cafe & Grille. Tash hesitated at the corner of Sunset, but kept going, confident, nose working, to Melrose, where she turned right.

I was aware of the stares from people in cars. I wound my way around a woman with a high ponytail in yoga pants, pushing a double stroller that had twin girls tucked safely away from the weather, but it was too wet and rainy for many people to be out. I saw no one on the sidewalk ahead of me.

Halfway down Melrose, Tash faltered, but it was no coincidence we were a half-block from the Chapel of Disciples. And I wanted him, the red-haired man, the Reverend Fucking Smallwood. Enough of this crappy little do-si-do. I was going to make him sorry, and I was going to make him bleed, and there was no more little-boy fear, and no Moira to pull me off, though I knew she'd only do that so she could shoot him. I love my wife.

Tash sniffed, lifted her head and looked behind me, and growled. I looked over my shoulder.

He had gotten behind us somehow. But it was him. In drowned-rat mode, with his hair plastered around his pasty white face, and his jeans slick as sealskin in the rain.

Tash lowered her head, absolutely silent, which in dog language means *I'm going to kill you, Motherfucker*, and she went right for him, and I was right behind her. She lunged and knocked him down and I said *good dog* and kicked him brutally in the ribs, then dropped to my knees and smashed my fist into his face, again and again.

'Son. Of. A bitch.' I liked it. The feel of my fist smashing into his face. 'You son of a bitch, you son of a bitch.'

My gentle sweet Tash, who had never even snapped, much less bitten anyone, sank her teeth into the red-haired man's shoulder, just grazing his throat, and shook him hard, and blood spurted and flowered over her muzzle.

He screamed and I hit him again, but it was laughter I heard, not pain, not fear, and his mouth opened wide to show blood-flecked teeth, and his eyes were black, the pupils huge, and he laughed and egged us on, and I knew in the back of my mind that I *could* stop this if I wanted to, but I did not want to. Between the two of us, Tash and I were going to kill him.

I thought fleetingly of the surgeries I had scheduled for later this week, and I knew I should protect my hands, but it did not matter. None of it mattered except the sweet, pure satisfaction of breaking the bones in his face.

He had threatened and terrorized my boys and my wife, and I was going to end him. I slammed a fist into the side of his head and grabbed him around the neck and squeezed, waiting for him to lose consciousness, choking him harder and tighter, willing him to die.

I still don't know how it happened. How he was up on his feet, Tash rolling off him with a whimper and me slammed hard to the ground, and then it was his hands around my throat. I heard a snarl from Tash, and the blare of a car horn, and I blacked out.

I don't think I was out for more than a second. I took a huge, deep, gaspy breath, grateful to be sucking in air. Tash stood over me, licking my face and whining.

The red-haired man was up on his feet, leaning over me, his eyes shiny with the thrill of it all. Blood trickled down his lips, his chin. Some of it was washed away by the rain. I scrambled to my feet.

He waved a hand toward the church. 'Come on in out of the weather, why don't you, and keep a hand on the dog. Leave her outside.'

'She stays with me and I'm not going in there.'

A pickup truck had slowed, the driver watching us.

'We don't want other people around,' he said, licking blood off his lips. 'It wouldn't be safe for them.'

Tash growled, and I put a hand on her head. She leaned against my leg, panting. It was catching up with her. The good reverend was lucky she was older and slower and it gave me pleasure to see the shredded shirt and the deep, ripping bite wounds of Tash's attack. 'If you've got something to say, say it.'

'OK then.' He cocked his hip to one side. 'You stopped the project, Noah, you shut it down like a *good little fella*, and we left you alone.'

'You call this leaving me alone? Lurking in my yard, bothering my boys?'

He wagged a finger at me. 'You can't lie to something like me, Noah. I thought you'd know that. Don't do those treatments with the priest.'

Interesting how he would not say Perry's name.

'You're afraid of him,' I said.

The red-haired man took a step closer. Tash lunged at him, and I held her tight, thinking *good dog, good girl. Brave dog.*

'Back away from me, or I'll let her go.' I wasn't going to give any ground. I was going to make him do it.

'For her sake, don't.' His voice was flat, eyes black and oddly reflective.

My fingers tightened on Tash's collar.

'Noah, you know what to do, and you know what *not* to do. And you have only had a *tiny taste*, Noah. Noah. Noah.'

My name seemed to echo, and I felt dizzy for a second, and took a wobbly step backward.

The pickup truck pulled to the side of the street, and the driver cut the engine off. There was a squeak and a thud as the driver's door opened and closed. The red-haired man looked over my shoulder. His shoulders tightened even as he gave the man a wide, rubbery smile.

I was aware of the driver of the truck, though I had my back to him. I was not taking my eyes off the red-haired man.

'Everything OK over here? Either of you want me to call the police?' Very southern of him. Tactful. If it was a private matter, he'd leave us be. He had a deep voice, confident, I'd have put him in his forties.

'Just a family squabble that got out of hand,' the red-haired man said.

'He's not family and if he does not walk away, then yeah I'd be happy for you to call nine-one-one.'

The red-haired man opened his arms wide. 'I am the minister of this church,' he said, pointing.

'I do a lot of contracting work for a lot of the people here in this neighborhood, and I haven't heard one good thing about you or your church, but I have heard plenty of bad.' The guy from the truck took a step closer, so he was beside me now on the other side of Tash. Well-worn, loose Levi's, a worn green barn coat, heavy shoes. He had blond hair, cut short, brown eyes, high cheekbones and an air of confidence. When the red-haired man stared hard at him he stopped hard, but he did not look away.

The red-haired man turned to me. 'You know what you need to know. And the next time I see that dog of yours—'

'You'll what?' I said. 'I'll get you first.'

He smiled, just a little. 'If only you could. All these years, Noah, and you still haven't figured it out.'

Tash and I staggered into the house, both of us limping.

Moira and the boys were in the kitchen, making quesadillas, and the three of them looked surprisingly calm and OK. Everything seemed . . . normal. The only thing out of place was the Glock that Moira had laid carefully on the top of the refrigerator, out of reach of the boys. She'd have to stand on tiptoe to get hold of it herself.

'Noah? Jesus Christ. Oh my god, *Tash.*'

I stood to one side, bleeding sluggishly, while Moira and the boys swarmed the dog and toweled her dry. 'She looks like she's hurting,' Moira said.

'There's Tramadol in the cabinet. Give her four.'

'How about you? Looks like you could use a dose of something.'

'No opioids in my system, thanks just the same. I'll tank up on Advil.'

I filled a bowl with warm soapy water, and plunged my hands in carefully, wincing and cursing.

Marcus looked at Vaughn. 'Daddy words,' he whispered.

Once we had Tash dry and full of salami-wrapped Tramadol and a big bowl of kibble, Moira got me settled on the couch with pillows and a bowl of ice. She sat up close to me, talking in a low voice while the boys watched television, the two of them stretched out on the floor by Tash's bed. She had a bed down here and one up in the boys' room, orthopedic memory foam beds with a little ledge of pillows where she liked to prop her head. She lay quietly, drifting off to sleep, but whimpering now and then in her dreams.

'That was him out in the yard, wasn't it? That Reverend Smallwood,' Moira said.

She was shivering. I tried to put an arm around her, but she guided my hand back into the bowl of ice.

I nodded. 'Yeah. It was him.'

She touched my swollen knuckles. 'What happened?'

'It was weird. I lost sight of him, but Tash picked up the scent. Moira, she was amazing. She took off toward High Street, she was going so fast I could barely keep up, and she tracked him over to Melrose, about half a block from that hellish little church, and then Tash suddenly whipped around and lowered her head, and he was behind us.'

'Jesus,' Moira said. 'I wish I'd been there with the Glock. Did he attack you?'

'Other way around. Tash and I went after him.' I looked at the world's best dog. 'Not the shoulder, next time, Tash. Always go for the throat.'

'Shush, don't wake her up,' Moira said. 'I am so proud of her.'

'World's best dog.'

'Then what happened?'

I spoke low in her ear, so the boys could not hear me. 'I tried to kill him. I would have, if I could have.'

Her chin got firm. 'And you are the most fabulous husband.'

'You think?' Things felt good between us. Like before.

'My only regret is he is not dead. Is he?'

I shook my head. 'I have no idea what he is.'

I told her all of it. The laughter. The insane strength. The confusing moment when the red-haired man suddenly and effort-lessly slammed me to the ground and tried to break my neck. Moira shuddered.

We sat snuggled together. Just being still. Watching the boys and Tash.

'Nothing makes any sense anymore, Noah,' Moira whispered. 'It's starting to feel real. Everything you told me. I don't feel safe anymore.'

'I'll keep you safe. What happened after I left? Anything . . . else?'

'No.' She shook her head, thoughtful. 'It was fine. As soon as you and Tash were out the door, things felt . . . normal. No more noises. No more knocks. I brought the boys down to make dinner and get them distracted with the TV.'

'It's me. I bring it here.'

'And maybe you chased it away. There is no point in looking at things like that, Noah. We're a family. We're a team. We stick together no matter what.'

'I will do everything I can to protect you guys. To get this out of our lives.'

'Perry says he was there, when it started up. You were what, ten? Eleven? Perry says it's all real. So . . . how worried do I need to be? On a scale of one to ten?'

'Eleven.'

She put a finger to my lips. Closed her eyes and laid her head on my shoulder.

I held her tight. 'Listen, Moira. We need to make a decision. Together.' And I told her about Perry, and the big question . . . whether or not I should go forward with Perry's treatments when the red-haired man had warned me not to.

Moira chewed her bottom lip. 'What are our options, Noah?'

'I can tell Perry I am out of the exorcism business in every possible way, including the treatments. Because it is dangerous to our family. He won't push it. But if I go along with the dark side, turning tail like a coward, giving them control, *obeying* their threats. Is that the smart way to go? It is even a viable option? It's not about ego, not now. It's about survival. I know . . . I *know* . . . that I am being led by the nose and following where they take me. I want to get smarter, be a proactive step ahead rather than a reactive step behind.'

Moira looked toward the boys. 'Look, Henry Mandeville demanded that you tell him where his wife and daughter were and you didn't. And that was the right thing to do, obviously.

It's the same thing here. Better *with* Perry, than against. Go forward with the treatments, and make him stronger.'

'Maybe I have to. Just so we can hold our own. But it's something we have to be all in on. You and me both.'

'I'm all in, Noah. For better or worse. And this feels right to me.'

I moved my hands out of the ice and winced, setting the bowl on the coffee table. The Advil was kicking in and the ice was pulling the swelling down. Tash was sleeping hard now, and I felt the fatigue taking me under. I would be asleep soon if I just let go. I wondered if I would have to postpone this week's surgeries or hand them off to Hilde. I could not let the patients down, not when they had spent the weekend in anxious agony.

I felt Moira putting a blanket over me as I fell hard asleep.

TWENTY-EIGHT

Perry would be looking for angels today.

His treatment was easier to set up than I imagined because we were going around the system rather than through it. Hilde would not know. But I had a lot of confidence in Carl, the tech. Carl was just the right kind of guy for this sort of thing.

His first concern, and mine, was the paper trail. Nothing that could get me snarled up in fraudulent hospital billing – the hospital's, not mine.

And Carl, good man, came up with a brilliant solution and seemed happy with the bottle of Old Town bourbon that I handed him that afternoon. Just a little thank you, man to man.

'I get it now,' Perry told me, when I unlocked the door of the MRI lab and let him in. It was three p.m. and we'd have the lab unit until six. I had not told Perry about the latest visitation from the red-haired man. I didn't want him to back down. To protect me. Because yes, all right, I wanted to know. To see how the treatments would affect a spiritual warrior like Perry, a man descended from the Magdalene. To see if Elliot really was an angel, trying to find his way home.

'What do you get now?' I asked him.

He was bouncy and excited, a little half smile lurking at the side of his mouth. 'I get how you felt about the project. That's how I feel right now. About this. It's . . . *possibilities*, isn't it, Noah?'

He was definitely feeling the thrill.

'And do you feel guilty now for pressuring me to shut it down?'

'Not at all. Just saying I get it. And you'd have shut it down anyway, on your own. Right?'

I hesitated. 'Right.' I scrambled around for a pen. 'OK, Perry, I have papers for you to sign.'

He took them, put on a pair of reading glasses, and frowned, gave me a quick look. 'I don't think this is my paperwork.'

'Actually, it is. You, Perry, are a nine-year-old, one-hundred-fifty-eight-pound Great Pyrenees named *Elliot*, with suspected severe spinal stenosis. You're a candidate for orthopedic surgery, and you need an MRI so the surgeon can see exactly what, and most particularly *where* the issues are. Your x-rays show spinal fusion and narrowing due to arthritis and suspected disc bulges.'

He had a funny sort of smile. 'I'm not really following, Noah.'

'The canine ortho uses our facility when the equine hospital is booked. Usually he goes to the children's hospital in Cincinnati, but a one-hundred-fifty-eight-pound dog needs a big-boy machine. Will you sign off?'

He scribbled his signature in three places. 'Who do I pay?'

'Nobody – you don't want to submit this to your insurance company, trust me.' The vet would bill me and I would pay out of pocket. It would cost me $1,500. A bargain, these days. And that was with the friends and family discount. 'Come on, Perry. Get your shoes off, put whatever crap you have in your pockets in this little plastic vomit tray, and hop up on that metal bed.'

'Shelf, you mean.'

He climbed up and I got him settled in. He was wearing gray sweats and a long-sleeved tee shirt. 'OK, Perry, this thing that looks like the hairnet from hell is what Hilde and I like to call HORACE.'

'It has a name?'

'It does.' I settled it over Perry's head. He fingered one of the ceramic discs that would send electric pulses into his brain.

'Perry?' I pointed to the metal cross that swung from his neck.
'Right.' He hesitated, took it off, and I closed it in my fist
then put it into the tray, with his keys, wallet, and phone. Which
I powered down. I noticed that Perry wore thick white socks that
were fuzzy and clean.

He took a breath. 'Let's get on with it, Dr Frankenstein.'

The spiritual impulse is coded into the biology of our
brains. The very mechanics of neurology that allow us to be
flexible in a capricious world, that give us the ability to create
art, write poetry, novels, paint a picture, sculpt the angel from
the stone. We don't just have ideas. We don't just make sense of
our world. We create it . . . our reality.

I knew that going into the Enlightenment Project. I knew that
going forward with that first treatment with Perry.

I knew how powerful, how utterly dangerous it could be. I
was well aware that what made Perry so strong, also made Perry
vulnerable.

But I trusted Perry. He wanted a treatment. He knew the risks.
And even then, in spite of everything, I believed in it. I believed
in my work, stripped of ego, humbled by outcomes that had hurt
the very people I longed to heal . . . I felt compelled to go
forward. Something deep inside of me urged me on.

I saw it, the beautiful mystery of our neurological processes.
We knew so little of what we were capable of. The very good,
the very bad, beautiful and ugly things. What makes one create
beauty, and another relish dark havoc, was ingrained in the
neurons of the brain.

My awareness of Perry, still and tense on the gurney, faded.
In some part of my mind I was aware. Watchful. The good doctor.
I wore headphones so I would hear him if he called out, and
they were sensitive enough for me to be aware of his steady
meditative breathing. This was a man of formidable intelligence,
a warrior's compassion, a man whose very life was an exercise
in meditation and prayer.

I was more confident than I should have been. I knew that if
anybody could benefit and make use of this, it was Perry. That
a man like Perry was capable of great, mysterious things.

Our test was being recorded not just by the images on that

MRI, but on a camera we had set up. I looked at the computer screen, and smiled just a little, with something like awe.

Perry's frontal lobes, controlling focus and concentration, were highly developed, and lighting up. Which made sense, meditation was concentration. As his frontal lobes fired up, his parietal lobe was going dark. Perry was deep in meditation almost instantly, his brain blocking all sensory and cognitive input. A mystical state.

The electric impulses were firing gently and Perry's brain seemed hyper-reactive. It was like watering a rose bush and seeing a rose grow and bloom instantly, right before your eyes. It was like seeing the presence of God, there in the firing of the neurotransmitters of Perry's brain.

How would this change him? Where might it take him? I was almost envious. On the verge of great things.

I heard a noise from Perry, something small.

'Perry?' I said.

He did not answer. He was not there. The lab, the machine. Me. We were all screened out.

And that was the moment things got odd.

That striatum of the hippocampus, the part of his brain that filtered, organized, created order in the world, was on fire. Like nothing I had ever seen. Picture it this way – your brain keeps emotions, thoughts, impulses in their safe and organized corrals. It keeps the onslaught of information categorized so things can be made sense of. What was going on in Perry's mind was like a stampede. As if someone had thrown all the gates open, and created a panic. It was as if Perry was in a small raft in the ocean in a hurricane – overwhelmed with sensory overload.

'Perry,' I said. Firm, confident, my voice would be something for him to hang on to. To come back to.

No answer. But . . . something. A sob?

I did not hesitate. I stopped the treatment, in that zone of cold control that allowed me to compartmentalize panic, allowed me to think analytically, to function and concentrate.

Perry began to hiss. I did not like the sound of it. The activity in his frontal lobes went dark, and yet Perry began to mutter, speaking in tongues. He was panting like a dog.

'Perry? Can you hear me?' *Shit, shit, shit.*

I remembered a study of Pentecostal Christians, the drop of

activity in their frontal lobes as they danced and writhed and spoke in tongues, with no control of what was happening to them.

I made the decision quickly – stimulate the frontal lobes, so Perry could regain control, and find his way back.

It did not happen instantly but once the frontal lobes began firing, Perry stopped panting, and breathed hard but steady. He was not chanting anymore. He was crying, softly, like a very small child.

I kept talking to him, telling him to focus on my voice, to come back to me, that he was safe, that he would be all right, that everything would be OK. The voice is a powerful tool, it is why the OR nurse says your name as you come out of deep anesthetic.

And I could see it. Perry was taking hold. His frontal lobes were buzzing like a colony of bees and I eased back on the stimulation, gradually, very gradually as his hippocampus striatum took hold, and the frenetic activity dropped away.

'Perry?' I said. 'Can you hear me? Can you just say *OK*?'

Silence, but the crying had stopped, his breath was steady. Time to get him out of the machine.

My hands shook slightly as I stood by the gurney, the brutal clack of the machine reduced now to a simple hydraulic whine as Perry was brought out of the white metallic doughnut of the MRI.

His left hand clenched, unclenched. He had bitten his lower lip, drawing blood. His head was to one side, turned away from me.

'Perry?' I said.

He would not look at me. His eyes were red rimmed, tracks of tears drying on his cheeks which were flushed and swollen. I helped him sit up. Gently and carefully removed HORACE from around his head. He stayed still, not resisting, and I helped him swing his legs over the side. He made no move to get up and off the gurney, and I stood close. I used my pen light to check the reaction of his eyes. Normal. I listened to the thump of his heart, checked his pulse. If I were him I would have found my fussing annoying but Perry said nothing, and did not bat my hand away or call me a brat, though I wished very much that he would.

TWENTY-NINE

We ended up in Perry's small condo, because Perry refused to come and stay at my house with a simple, quiet shake of his head. So I'd taken him home.

His favorite place was the battered leather couch that sat in front of the window. He could stretch out there, with a side table for a drink, and in direct line of the TV. Perry would have none of it. He had settled instead in the chair I usually take. It sat at an angle and he could see the window, the darkness pressing in.

Perry looked around his apartment, immaculate but for a coffee cup with dregs of cream and coffee. He seemed to be looking *for* something.

'What is it, Perry?' I said. 'Are you hungry? We can go out . . . order a pizza. I can cook us a steak.'

He glanced at me over his shoulder, as if surprised that I was still there.

'Perry, I know you were fasting before the treatment. You should have something to eat.'

He cleared his throat. 'A glass of water would be good.' His voice sounded rusty, clogged.

I didn't know if he was thirsty or if he was humoring me. I didn't know what to do. He was intensely distracted, as if he were somewhere else and had to be reminded that I was there in the room.

He got up suddenly and went into the bathroom. I heard the water running, and his face and hands were damp when he came out. I handed him a glass of tap water, feeling helpless. Feeling lame. He took it from me gently, put it on a side table, then opened the blinds. He pulled the cord tight, so that the whole window was open and clear. An unimpeded view. He headed for the chair, facing out the window, and I realized that it was a good defensive position. In that chair he could keep his back to the wall. Watch out the window, keep an eye on the front door, and see Abby's painting of Elliot that he had hung on the wall.

He lowered himself into the chair slowly, like he was sinking to the bottom of a well.

I settled at the edge of the couch. 'Perry. Please talk to me. I saw strange . . . unusual reactions on the MRI. I know it was a hell of a ride. I know you're shook up. But you need to eat. You need—'

He looked at me. Somehow I trailed off, unsure what to say. He was not smiling. He was not angry. He looked old. The excited energy was long gone. He was watchful, and his shoulders sagged.

'You don't know what I need. You can't.' He spoke softly, as if it did not matter what he said, or what I understood. 'You can go now, Noah.'

'I'm not going anywhere. I'm worried about you, Perry. You're not right, you know it, and I know it, so what are we supposed to do? I'm kind of out of my depth here.'

He looked at me and shook his head, as if he had only just tuned in to what I said. 'You and me both.'

It took a while for me to give up.

I ordered a pizza. He shook his head at me when it arrived and said no thanks. I sat on the couch and ate two slices methodically, while he stared over my head and out the window. As if I were not there.

'You should leave, Noah,' he told me at regular intervals, when he suddenly remembered I was there.

'I am not leaving.' I went into the kitchen to wash pizza off my hands. I stood in the doorway. 'Perry. For God's sake, tell me what happened.'

He took a deep shuddering breath and gave me a quick look, then was back to staring out the window. 'Noah, I don't even think I have the words to tell you.'

'Try.'

I paced the living room and he pointed to the couch, and like a good boy, I sat. 'Please talk to me, Perry.'

He shook his head, looked away, frowned gently. 'There were so many . . . it was like being swarmed. It was so fast and they almost . . . they almost had me.'

'Had you? How?'

'I don't know how to say it. But it made me realize. You and I, Noah. We're so . . . small. It's going to wear me down eventually, and it's going to take me. Because whatever happened with that treatment. It let the drawbridge down, and they're *in*. I don't know how long I can keep them away. Sooner or later . . . I'm toast. I don't mind dying, Noah. But I don't want to lose my way to God.'

'You can't lose that, Perry. You know that.'

'I don't think I know anything anymore.'

'Was Elliot there?'

He shook his head. 'I don't think so.'

'We need help, Perry.'

He nodded.

'How's it going with that guy you told me about? The exorcist's exorcist.'

'I've been working on it. Made a lot of calls, called in favors. He may be too old now. He's certainly a legend. But evidently . . . he retired. He doesn't do exorcisms anymore, but he will sometimes work with exorcists who get in trouble. Mostly he advises. Does research. Sets policy and protocol. But it's like no one can find him. There are layers of bureaucratic protection, it's hard to get through. I've been trying to get in touch since . . . since Elliot showed up. I've been told he is unavailable. Traveling.'

'Expected back when?'

'They won't say.'

'Let me work on it, Perry. I'll find him or I'll find someone better.'

'There's no one better, Noah.'

I handed him a plate with a cold slice of pizza. 'Your job is to eat this slice of pizza. My job is to find Bennington-Jones.'

He almost smiled. Almost. Waved to the small writing desk against the wall. 'My notebook is right there, top drawer . . . contact information, everyone I've talked too. I don't see how you can do it if I can't.'

'Come on, Perry, damn it, don't roll over and give in to this. I will find him if I have to get on a plane and track him down.'

He looked over my shoulder, out the window.

'I'm going to get you a beer to go with this pizza.'

'*No.*'

I looked back at him over my shoulder.

'No alcohol. I cannot lose control. You focus on Bennington-Jones, and let me take care of me.'

'I *will* find him.'

Perry closed his eyes just for a moment, then sat up straight, like a man afraid to sleep.

THIRTY

I was in that phase of exhaustion that was so overwhelming that just lying in a bed felt delicious and sweet. Moira was settled next to me, propped up against the black metal curlicue of our headboard, supported by three fussy pillows I would like to chuck into the garbage. We were sleeping together again. She could have all the pillows she wanted. Moira had taken in the whole story of Perry's exorcism fairly calmly, and was going through Perry's notebook on Bennington-Jones.

I closed my eyes. Aware of Moira tapping on the keyboard, the glow of the computer. There was no way I could sleep but I was not going to slow her down.

She snapped the laptop shut. 'Done.'

'You found him?'

'Not yet. But I am closing in. Is Perry . . . I mean, is he OK by himself? Shouldn't he come here?'

'He wouldn't, I tried.'

'Stubborn.'

'No. Protecting us.'

She rolled to her side and propped up on her elbow.

I ran a hand over my face, feeling the rough growth of beard. 'He's not OK, Moira. I appreciate you taking this on.'

'I'm only teaching one class this summer; let me give this everything I've got, and if I need you I'll tell you.'

'I never should have given him that treatment.'

She frowned. 'I would have thought it would have been a good thing for him. Him more than anybody.'

I rolled over to face her.

'Noah, in spite of the . . . the issues with the project. You do good work. *Brilliant work.* I *know* you do.'

I took her hand. It was soft and warm. 'Thank you.' I had to clear my throat to make the words come out. 'I would have thought so too, that it would be perfect for Perry, of all people. But he was . . .' I trailed off. 'I thought he would handle it better than anybody.'

'Or be more vulnerable. But Noah, it was his decision. He's the expert. He always seems so invincible. I'd have done the same thing you did, and gone along with it.' She traced a finger on my chin. 'I will hound everybody listed in that notebook and not go away. I will be relentless and I will find this Bennington-Jones. He's an Oxford don, did Perry tell you that?'

I shook my head. But if anybody could pull this off, it was Moira. I frowned.

'What is it, Noah?' She put a hand on my chest.

'If Perry is protecting us, then the danger is very real.'

'That we already know.'

'Yes, but . . . so maybe . . . maybe it's not a good idea for you to pursue this. If I can't see what's coming, how can I keep you safe?'

Moira closed her eyes tight for a moment. 'Noah. Whatever is happening, I am already involved, and so are the boys. You can't compartmentalize us in some kind of mythical safety zone. We already know that doesn't work. This is how life works. You can't shut me out and you *can't* keep me safe.'

'I can too. I have superpowers.'

She smiled. 'Ever and always the surgeon. And speaking of which. You have patients in the morning, go to sleep.'

'You sure? You need to sleep too.'

'Well done, husband. Very considerate.' I heard her chuckle, pleased that I was excelling in my husband training. 'I've got this, Noah. It's a relief that there is something I can do. I've been in way over my head lately.

'You and me both.'

She blew me a kiss and padded barefoot out of the bedroom, wearing one of my soccer jerseys, laptop tucked under one arm. I knew she'd be up very late, scouring the Internet, researching, plotting and planning. She headed down to my office, and I listened to her soft footsteps as she went down the stairs.

THIRTY-ONE

As I strode down the hospital corridors, Dr Hot-Shit Surgeon, I checked my phone. Moira had texted me early that morning with the good news that she'd had a lead on Bennington-Jones and to stand by. Nothing since, and it was two fifteen. Moira's summer-school class on Shakespeare's Comedies started at two, so best not to bother her now. The fellas were with my mom, roaring through her house like wild animals.

The call came through before I had time to tuck my phone into my pocket. I frowned. The call was coming from Artie, Moira's teaching partner, a horn-rimmed poet who might be wounded by the things students said about him if he ever paid attention. Students were no more than a distraction to his inner life.

'Noah,' he said. He sounded different. Voice high, breath coming fast. He was married to an Amazonian brunette who managed a restaurant downtown, and it occurred to me that Moira and I had not been there in a while.

'Hey, Artie. How's—'

'*Noah.*' Artie sounded oddly out of breath. 'Today is the first day of Shakespeare. Moira didn't show.' I could hear the murmur of students in the background.

I stopped walking.

'*People.* You are supposed to be writing a sonnet. *Sorry,*' Artie said. 'I heard the rustle of clothing, and pictured Artie heading out into the hall. 'Have you heard from her in the last little while?'

'Not since early, just after eight.'

'OK, Mrs Lancaster was here, she just came in to find . . . to find Moira. Her car is in the parking lot. The driver's door was wide open, the keys were still in the ignition, and her purse was on the ground right under the car.'

'Let me talk to Mrs Lancaster,' I said, breathing hard. Mrs Lancaster was the principal. I felt odd. Like I was walking on the bottom of the ocean. I turned and headed toward the parking garage. Walking fast. Almost running.

'She's gone already. She's . . . she's running down the hall. She never runs.'

'Artie. Grab a pen. I'm going to give you a number – this is for Moira's brother, Alec. He's a cop. Call him. Tell him what's going on.'

'OK. OK.'

I reeled off the numbers, had him repeat them back. 'Good man, Artie. I'm on my way.'

My car keys were in my office, and that slowed me down. There was the usual traffic jam at the elevator as a fragile-looking woman on a stretcher was orchestrated through the doors.

I burst through the exit door to the stairs, and galloped down. I was a tall man and I overtook two women in pink scrubs who were already fishing out cigarettes on their way to the smoking huddle on the side of the building.

My phone rang.

'Dr Archer?' Aly Lancaster was using her calm voice, but it was clearly an effort and she sounded shaky.

I was out of the stairwell, heading through the glass doors that opened into the parking garage, where a snarl of confused patients clustered at the door. My white coat swung out behind me as I ran for my car, which was right around the corner in reserved parking. I smelled oil, and damp concrete, heard the echo of engines on the floors above.

'Where's Moira?' I said. 'Is she OK?' That's all she needed to tell me. That Moira was OK.

'I think there's a problem,' Aly Lancaster said.

I stopped by the car. My hands were shaking. Mr Hot-Shit Surgeon had abandoned me now.

'Dr Archer—'

'I talked to Artie. I know about the car and not showing up to class. Have you called nine-one-one?'

Mrs Lancaster was nothing if not patient. 'Yes, Dr Archer, they are on their way and Artie wanted you to know he's called Moira's brother.'

I took a hard breath. 'Good. That's . . . good.'

'One of the students, a boy who was in her Poetry Through the Ages section last term . . . he says he saw her with a man. They were walking but it looked weird, his words. The man was wearing camo. Heavy work shoes. And he thought . . . he thought that Moira was crying.'

'Shit.' Shit shit shit. 'I'm on my way, Mrs Lancaster.'

'I'll be waiting for you on the front steps.'

THIRTY-TWO

B y the time I got to the school, there were police cars, the pulse of emergency lights, and clusters of students on the lawn. In the thick of it all, I saw Mrs Lancaster, waiting and waving me in, perched on the front steps as promised. As soon as she saw me, she headed my way. There were no parking spaces. I parked on the lawn.

Mrs Lancaster ran pretty fast, for a wide woman in a tweedy skirt, nylons and sensible heels. Her reddish-brown hair was bound tightly in a bun but was starting to come loose, one strand hanging like a tail.

'They found her,' she said and she grabbed my forearm. When I take people by the forearm like that it is because the patient is dead and I am breaking the news to the family. This is the instinctive gesture of tragedy. Of death. 'They need you over here, come with me.'

She led me like a child and I heard someone call my name. I glanced over my shoulder as I went. It was Alec, Moira's little brother, grim-faced and pale.

He ran toward me out of the school, the equipment on his belt heavy, clacking, slowing him down. It was more than good to see him. He wiped the sleeve of his uniform across his eyes and we hugged. Brothers.

'What do you know?' I asked him.

'She's a hostage,' Alec said. 'And the prick that's got her is asking for you. And listen, do you know anything about the Chapel of Disciples? Because he says he's from there.

And if you ask me a religious nut is the worst kind of nut.
This sucks.'
  'Oh, fuck,' I said.
The red-haired man had warned me.

THIRTY-THREE

It was so beautiful here. An utterly beautiful place to die.
    Patchen Wilkes Magnet High School, Moira's school, was
brand new, adjacent to an upscale housing development butting
up next to Patchen Wilkes Farm, named for a Standard bred
trotter called, naturally, Patchen Wilkes. The farm got sold to a
car dealer in the 1930s who went into the thoroughbred side of
the horse business, and then the farm distinguished itself by
becoming the birthplace of White Beauty, a pure white, non-
albino thoroughbred filly – the first ever recorded by the Jockey
Club.
    Patchen Wilkes Farm was everything that is good and bad about
Kentucky. The good – pastures of rich bluegrass, bordered by black
four-board fences, a working broodmare farm, still home to the
occasional miracle of rare white thoroughbred horses, Patchen
Beauty, for one, and her colt, The White Fox. The bad – the farm
had been whittled down by the Interstate highway, schools, like
the one where Moira teaches, a park, and the ever-growing suburban
sprawl of houses that slowly eat away at the land.
    The farm was split down the middle by a seven-acre lake, and
standing at the end of the dock on that lake was a man I had
never met before. He had a gun. He had my wife. But what he
wanted, the police said, was me.
    Police cars, EMTs, SWAT – they came with equipment and
what looked like organized chaos, and I was grateful.
    But sidelined.
    I had been told to keep my distance. I couldn't see much detail,
the police had called in the SWAT team, and Moira's little brother
Alec was guarding me, to keep me from running down that dock
and *escalating*.

Alec and I stood together, under a black walnut tree that had been invaded by insects that the tree wrapped up in galls that bubbled up on the leaves like tiny prisons. The green and black hulls of tiny new walnuts littered the ground and crunched under our feet.

We could see her. Moira. So far away, her face nothing more than a blur, but the man was burly, overweight, and he wore the green, black and white splotched camo they sold at Cabalas. For hunters. His head had been shaved and now showed what looked from here like a three-day stubble. I didn't know him, but he sure as hell knew me.

He stood behind my wife, with one burly muscled arm holding her tight to his chest, and her arms were clamped to her side, and her dress fluttered gently around her knees. It was the yellow dress I loved; I was with her when she bought it: high waisted, with a thin yellow sash, little covered buttons that went up the top. Her black curly hair was tied in the back in that way she had, tied at the bottom, so it was somehow long and loose but still gathered back in pretend and sexy severity, and the small breeze blew dark curls into her face. And his.

How I wanted to hold her, to gently push that hair out of her face, to shield her, put my body between hers and the burly man, to let him take me in her place.

Alec kept a grip on my shoulder. But he himself was quivering like a dog who wanted to be let off the leash. The question was: who was going to hold *him*?

'Is she crying?' Alec asked.

'I think she is, but I can't tell.' I couldn't hear her either, I wasn't close enough, and worse she couldn't see me. 'She doesn't know we're here. She's so scared.'

'She knows us, so she knows we're here,' Alec said. 'Noah. No.' He pulled me back.

'Look, dude, he wants me, not Moira. She's all alone out there, dammit, let me go, or better still, come with me.'

'We have to be smart.' Alec was sweating, though it was cool out, the leaves from that walnut tree leafing out in the warmth of the sun. 'Trust the SWAT team, Noah, I know those guys. They know their stuff.'

I shook my head, and Alec put a hand on my shoulder.

'Here's what happens, Noah. You go out there, he gets what he wants, which is you *watching* his little drama unfold, and then he shoots my sister in the head to show off and get your full attention.'

'Maybe he shoots *me* in the head, Alec. I can live with that. I can be a distraction and talk to him, and you guys can shoot *him* in the head, which sounds like the best option to me.'

Head shots. I don't like to think about them. They pour into the ER every week. Gun shots to the head are the second leading cause of head injury. They have a 90 per cent fatality rate. Two-thirds of the victims die before they ever get to the ER. They account for a slim 10 per cent of Traumatic Brain Injury patients who survive.

I have seen the damage a bullet does inside the human skull. Not Moira, *never Moira*. I would not allow it.

Alec said, 'Give them time to do their thing.'

As if I had a choice. 'Why don't they just shoot this fucker; they have snipers, right?'

'His gun will go off, he has the muzzle tight to the side of her head. Trust me, they're looking for a shot.'

Alec's radio, mounted on his shoulder, was muttering with static and urgent voices, and he tucked his chin sideways and listened.

'OK, Noah, the SWAT team is in place. They'll try to talk him in, but if that doesn't work, you may get your chance.'

We waited and we sweated and we heard voices on a bullhorn, and the man at the dock backed closer to the water, shaking his head. He was getting tired and Moira was sagging; he had to hold her up. Alec's radio crackled and he listened and affirmed and looked over at me.

'They're not happy, they don't think they can talk him in. Things are escalating. Time for Plan B.'

'Plan B? Is that me?'

'Yeah, that's you.'

'Good. I'm ready.' And I was. My heart was racing, my hands were trembling.

Alec shook my hand, his own slick with sweat. He clapped a

hand on my shoulder and herded me toward the knot of detect-
ives, uniforms, police cars, and flashing lights.

Showtime, Moira would tell me. And then she'd say *break a
leg* for luck.

THIRTY-FOUR

I stood at the edge of the lake behind an armored truck. A
police detective with a face like a shovel was giving me advice.
He was an ugly man, but ugly in the way of a bulldog, and
confident, and I liked what I saw in his eyes. I was glad he was
in charge, and I had no doubt women found him attractive and
men scrambled to follow his lead.

Detective Orrin gave me a headset so we could communicate,
and held a bulletproof vest up in the air. Beige, and it wasn't
like the ones I'd seen on TV. It had coverage for groin and neck.
It looked awkward, but I took off my white coat and Orrin
strapped me into the vest.

'If I go in the water—'

'It's not quite eight pounds, and my people will have you out
of the water, you won't drown.'

'How deep is the lake?' I asked.

'Deep. A mile at center.'

I wished I hadn't asked.

'And when we pull you out, you'll have a bruised chest, not
a shredded one. You've seen gunshot wounds in the ER?'

I nodded.

'Looks like he's got a Taurus 85. Five rounds, easy to use.
You need to wear that vest.'

'I'm thinking of Moira. If *she* gets shot, I'm going in the water
and pulling her out. I don't want a vest weighing me down.'

'Sir, if she gets shot at close range in the temple, she's dead.
You're a neurosurgeon, and you know it better than I do.'

I did know. How important the trajectory of the bullet was.
The brain damage that came from a compound fracture to the
skull. How the brain suffered two separate hits – the first at

the point of impact, the second as the shockwaves threw the brain against the back of the skull. The infection when the brain tissue was exposed to the outside air, or, God forbid, the bacterial soup of that lake water. The secondary damage to brain tissue, blood vessels, and nerves when the brain began to swell inside a hard skull, compressing tissue against bone. Compression of the brain stem, which shut every vital function down.

Detective Orrin gave me a look. 'Your job, Dr Archer, is to keep him talking, and to angle your body to the right, your right, as you face him. His arm is tired. We've been watching him; his muscles are starting to tremble just a little. That's good and it's bad. If you distract him, it will be normal for him to shift for comfort; he may do it without thinking about it, and if he does my guy will take the shot. The best angle is going to be him turning left, your right. That's all you've got to do, is turn him a little and keep him talking and distracted. If we're lucky he'll shift that arm, the muzzle of his gun will be deflected, and then we'll take him out. Any questions? This make sense to you?'

'I'm good.' It wasn't much of a plan, but it was a plan.

He shook my hand.

I looked at Alec, who nodded.

The grass and the ground were dry beneath my feet, we had not had rain in the last five days. I stepped up onto the wooden dock, heard the thump of my heels. I paused for a moment, getting my balance. The dock was steady enough, dipping gently with my weight.

The man who held my wife clamped in his arms saw me, that was clear, and I could not tell if he was surprised or gratified to get what he wanted. I had looked at his face in binoculars and confirmed that I did not know him. He had the neck of a bull and the stubble of hair on his head was salt and pepper. He was clean shaven. He had an unhealthy, bloated look.

Law-enforcement wheels were in motion. I heard a voice in my ear. They'd gotten results on the prints they found in Moira's car.

'We've ID'd the guy.' It was Detective Orrin's voice in my ear. 'Gustav Melosa – you know him?'

'No,' I said. 'Who is he?' They had his prints in the system. He must be somebody.

And he was. It was worse than even I expected.

'Currently he is supposed to be in lockdown in Ward Five at Eastern State Hospital.' Orrin paused, to see if I got the significance.

I did. I felt the hope drain out of me. My knees were shaky but there was nothing to hold onto. No railing on the sides of this dock, which floated, ever so gently, with the undulation of the water.

Ward Five at Eastern State Hospital was reserved for the criminally insane, the worst of the worst. The men in Ward Five were sometimes inventive, sometimes mundane, all times brutal. Cannibals, men fond of dismembering their victims, men who would do terrible things and then disassociate, with no memory of why they were covered in blood that was not their own.

'You ever work Ward Five, doctor?'

'Never.'

'Any other wards out there?'

'No, detective, I've never set foot in Eastern State. And neither has Moira. This man has *no* connection to my family.'

Orrin sighed, I heard him in my earbud. 'OK, Doctor Archer. Best of luck.'

I glanced over my shoulder, but no one could be seen from behind the truck. I knew Alec was watching, though. Still young enough to have hope, to think both Moira and I could come back alive. Which was very young indeed.

I walked down the dock. Toward Moira.

I saw little hope of reasoning with a guy from Ward Five. His reality was not one that was going to make any sense to me. If I was lucky, it would be me he wanted. All I needed, was for Moira to be OK.

THIRTY-FIVE

My wife, my Moira, was never more beautiful than she was today. As I walked down the dock, I was steady, no more shaking hands and wobbling knees. Mr Hot-Shit Surgeon was right here when I needed him. Was I afraid?

Somewhere I was. Somewhere I was really afraid, but I had disconnected that fear the same way I do when I walk into the OR. My footsteps echoed and set up vibrations in the wooden planks.

Moira saw me and I sensed her relief. She knew I would come, in my inevitable khaki slacks and blue button-down, a yellow silk tie, my white coat exchanged for a bulletproof vest. I walked steadily toward her. We were connected as if there was no one else in the world, and I felt the weight of it, her life, my sons, our future in my hands. I welcomed it. This weight belonged to me.

And I saw her. Really saw her. Like I ought to see her every day, but don't. The woman who knew when her brother was over his head in debt, and quietly paid down his bills. The woman who saw two boys alone, sitting on the same chair in a police station awaiting Child Protective Services, and recognized them as her own. The woman who gave theatre roles to students who needed them, lifting them out of the ranks of the unpopular. The woman who loved me but wouldn't let me step out of line. Who loved Regency romances, and peppermint ice cream, and drove me insane singing made-up songs to the dog, who watched her like she was God's gift to the animal kingdom.

This woman was everything to me. Her eyes were swollen with tears, but she smiled at me, and I was smiling back, and just for a moment, between us, there was no one else in the world.

I began angling toward the right side of the dock, and studied this Gustav Melosa, this killer, this man labeled criminally insane, who had one arm wrapped around my wife, holding her too tight, too hard, he was hurting her, and he still had that gun to her head. At this range and that entry point, if Gustav Melosa pulled the trigger, Moira would be dead before she fell.

I cursed him. In my heart, and in my soul. I would kill him. Whatever happened, Moira and I would go down fighting, and Gustav Melosa would not get off this dock alive.

I was fifteen feet away, and full on the right side of the dock, and as I turned Melosa turned too, like we were dancing and I was leading, and I checked one job off the list. He was in position for the sniper to blow off his head. If only he would move that gun away from Moira's temple.

Ten feet away.

Melosa took on an air of satisfaction, as if he had gotten exactly what he wanted. I was eight feet away and crowding him, but he did not take a step backward, like I wanted. He actually moved in closer, but that was fine too. I should have expected that. An alpha male. It didn't matter, all I wanted was his attention on me.

'Archer?'

'Yep. That's me.'

'Good. Because the Reverend Smallwood of the Chapel of Disciples wants to know he's got your attention. He says to tell you that the first treatment you did for the priest will cost you a wife. Do another one? That's going to cost you double . . . two sons.' His voice was cold, no emotion, no satisfaction, a soldier doing his job.

And I knew this was it. This was all he wanted, all he was waiting for, all he needed from me. Moira and I were out of time.

And Moira, with a sixth sense of her own, bit his arm, then dropped, her weight knocking him off balance, and he lost his aim, the handgun drifted up, and there was a blur of movement as he spun sideways. His head was an exploding pink mist and I registered the crack of the sniper shot as I saw the kick of the gun in Melosa's hand, and the blood streamed like black oil across my wife's forehead.

Water shot up in a geyser as Moira then Melosa tumbled off the dock.

I was in the water a split second after Moira, who was sinking sinking, her dress swirling yellow and rising up as she went down, and a fan of blood streamed from the top of her head. I could not see exactly where the bullet entered her skull, but I was already calculating, tracing possible pathways in my imagination, and working out detailed scenarios for treatment.

There were shouts, the thunder of heavy footsteps on the dock, and I was sinking fast, the vest was awkward and I could barely maneuver, but I kicked my feet and managed to catch Moira up in my arms. I was aware of a splash and motion in the water, and Alec was swimming toward us, and he managed to get Moira's head up and out of the water. Our feet scissoring, the murk of algae in a swirl around us, and Moira limp, heavy, not quite lifeless, hair black and trailing, blood streaming from her scalp.

Behind me, Gustav Melosa had disappeared under the water. There were two men and one woman diving, trying to retrieve him, but I paid no attention. It was Detective Orrin who reached down to take Moira, and Alec, right beside me, helped me up, and I would like to say we were gentle getting Moira up on the dock, but she was a dead weight, trailing water, and getting her and me up and out of the lake meant rough handling. Alec helped me out of the vest, and I crouched next to Moira, cradling her head.

I was vaguely aware of Alec, gripping my shoulder, asking me questions, but I couldn't make sense of anything he was saying. Like me, he was soaking wet and shivering.

The ambulance was already in place, and I heard the hydraulics of a stretcher barreling down the dock. I crouched beside Moira, and parted her hair to find the wound and hope hope hoped that it was nothing more than a graze.

But the bullet had entered her skull.

THIRTY-SIX

Moira was unconscious, but breathing, no water in her lungs or mouth. I pulled her into a sitting position and clamped her close to my chest. An EMT tried to put a bandage to the side of her head, but I grabbed his wrist and pushed it away. The bullet wound was two inches above her right temple, but the bleed was slow enough that she was better without compression, the bullet hole could work for her now to relieve the pressure I knew was building inside her skull.

'Sir?'

'I'm a neurosurgeon. Noah Archer.'

He nodded. He and two other paramedics got Moira up and on the stretcher and I ran beside it and climbed into the ambulance and was aware of Alec, shouting, being bundled into a police car by one of his buddies, and I knew he would be right behind the ambulance. He'd be making phone calls, alerting family. Things I could not even think about.

Because there were other things making noise in my head. I could not look at my wife as only a husband, the neurosurgeon was making calculations while the husband cringed, and I was obsessed with scenarios of midline shift, obliteration of the mesencephalic cisterns, the build of subarachnoid blood, intraventricular hemorrhage, and the possibility of hyper-dense or mixed-density lesions, bilateral or unilateral. And the bottom line, basically, was that it was not looking good.

I wouldn't know anything without a CT scan.

I sat beside Moira in the ambulance, and I was wrapped in a blanket but didn't remember anyone placing it around my shoulders.

'When you call it in,' I told the EMT. 'I want my partner, Dr Hilde Sweetwater, standing by.'

The tech nodded but his attention was on Moira. He checked Moira's vitals. Her blood pressure steadily plummeting, her pupils nonreactive. No response to pinprick. No deep tendon reflex. Respiration dropping, her brain function falling away, and he made the decision a split second before I did, and put Moira on a ventilator.

I held Moira's hand in mine, saying her name and squeezing gently, but her fingers were slack, there was no response. I didn't need a CT scan to tell me that Moira's survival rates were less than 1 per cent. I sobbed softly while begging my wife in muffled whispers to live.

And what I was thinking – brain damage. Coma. Moira in a hopeless helpless PST vegetative state.

THIRTY-SEVEN

My clothes were drying, and wrinkling tightly around my body.

Hilde had both hands on my shoulders, a steady comfort, and I was grateful, and I sat and she stood and we both studied the results of Moira's CT scan, which had made me nearly catatonic.

The bullet had pierced Moira's skull, then mushroomed to nearly twice its size, fragmenting in the right parietal region of Moira's brain. It then traversed to the right temporal lobe, and the rear of the right frontal lobe. At that point it crossed the midline and penetrated the left frontal lobe, where it sat, awaiting Hilde's attention.

The mid-brain structures, the brain stem, the basal ganglia, are what controlled Moira's body temperature, her hormones, heart rate, breathing. All compromised.

'We've got her down, for now,' Hilde said.

Moira was in an induced medical coma to quiet her battered brain, but when the swelling started, and it would, any time now, Hilde would remove half of Moira's skull to relieve the pressure, the tissue destroying thrust of fragile brain cells jammed against hard human bone, and she would put the skull section in a sterile freezer. If Moira were a soldier, in battle, the skull section would be sewn into her abdominal cavity where the blood supply to the bone would keep it healthy and sterile, and quite frankly, prevent it from being lost.

'I'll be right here, Noah. I'll do the surgery myself, I'll watch over her every second. I'm not sure about removing that bullet. But—'

'Should we even do it?' I asked softly.

'Surgery? Let's make the decision when we get there.' When the swelling began, she meant.

'No, Hilde, let's get there now. Nobody survives a bullet crossing both hemispheres of the brain. If Moira's lucky, she'll die fast. If not, she'll die slow. But you know and I know that Moira is gone. She died on that dock. She died this afternoon.' I had not noted the time when it happened and that bothered me. A good doctor always noted the time. For the record. The death certificate. The family. It was part of what a good doctor did.

'We have to do *something*,' Hilde said. 'We have to try.'

'If Moira were not my wife, we would not do a surgery. You know that. We've made this call before.' And we have. Gunshot wounds poured into the ER at a steady rate. Hilde and I faced these decisions every day.

'Miracles happen, you *know that*, Noah. Give Moira her chance at a miracle.'

'Hey, Hilde, do you know why they have to nail the lid of a coffin shut?'

She already knew the answer. 'To keep the oncologists from administering more chemotherapy.'

Her voice was soft and I heard the fatigue, the shock. Moira was like a big sister to Hilde. Hilde's face was etched with grief. Just like my own.

THIRTY-EIGHT

On day three after the shooting, Moira was as deeply comatose as anyone could be and still be alive. A fatal outcome was almost certain. She exhibited no purposeful motor activity. Her Glasgow Coma Scale was three – her blood pressure low. I checked her pupils. Again. Dilated, nonreactive. Her eyes were open but they did not track. She had the eyes of a corpse. She was in PVS, persistent vegetative state, the medical term for the living dead.

The rise and fall of the respirator was something I barely noticed anymore. It was as familiar to me as the hum of the heat compressor in my home.

Brain swelling, like any damage to the muscles of the body, usually came on day one or day two, peaked during days three to five, and though Hilde was standing by to do the decompressing craniotomy, it had not been necessary yet. Maybe tomorrow, surely by day five. Moira's beautiful mahogany curls were tied back and swept away from her face, a patch shaved away and bandaged where Hilde stopped the bleeding, evacuated a handful of small clots, did the surgical debridement, removing the dead brain tissue which took out a healthy chunk of Moira's right temporal lobe.

Moira had not had seizures, not unusual, and we would stop the anti-seizure medication at the end of the week. We were pumping her full of high-powered antibiotics, fighting the bacteria in that lake.

Pointless. All of this.

DAI, diffuse axonal injury, did not show up on a CT scan, but I knew that in the first six hours post injury, the concussive impact of this gunshot wound caused her axons to stretch and shear. This was the most common cause of injury from high-velocity trauma.

Brain neurons did regenerate. They did heal. But Moira was too far gone.

Perry sat beside me. Shell-shocked and thin, wearing worn jeans and an old charcoal gray sweater with a hole in the sleeve. But he was here. He said nothing while I held Moira's hand, squeezing her fingers gently then hard, willing her to squeeze back, but her fingers slid lifelessly out of mine if I let them go. No response, still no response, none of Hilde's miracles for me today. And I knew, of course, what I needed to do.

Moira has always been very clear. Respirators, life support, a living will, a DNR . . . *If I've got a festering hangnail,* she would tell me, *take me off the damn machines. Promise me, Noah. Promise.* And I did. I promised. She made the same promise to me. I thought of my mother, making this same decision when my father died. How strong she had been, my mother.

I kissed Moira's fingers. I looked over at Perry. 'It's time to let her go.'

He nodded at me. 'I agree. And I am utterly sorry, Noah.'

'I know.'

He took my hand, and Moira's hand, and we just sat that way for a while. Sometimes you just need to be still.

THIRTY-NINE

Everyone gathered quickly. Alec, eyes shadowed and puffy, sat on one side of Moira, and Perry and I on the other. Candice stood near the head of the bed, close enough to Alec to hold his hand.

My mother and my sons had come and gone, kissed Moira good-bye, and my mother, eyes flooded with tears, was taking the boys home. I thought of my sons, how alike they looked, round, wounded faces, and flyaway fine blond hair, blue eyes, and an unnatural stillness you rarely saw in children of any age. Their ability to stay quiet was clearly an ingrained survival mechanism they had no doubt learned the hard way, in that life before they came to Moira and me. When they cried, as they did by their mother's side, they did it silently and intensely, with welling red eyes and the gush of tears across their cheeks.

I would have a long road ahead with my boys. I didn't know how to do it without Moira. I wanted the life I used to have, before all this craziness started. I wanted my wife back. I wanted to lie in this hospital bed beside Moira and go to sleep for a hundred years.

Perry touched Moira's forehead, quoting William Penn. 'They that love beyond the world cannot be separated by it. Death cannot kill what never dies.'

Candice gave me a look. I shook my head. I would do this last thing myself.

I started with the needle, disconnecting the IV drip. The respirator tube popped and cracked and there was no truly gentle method of disengagement, but I did my best. I didn't bother watching the monitors, I watched Moira, waiting for that first telltale sign of death, when the pink flesh of her lips would turn white, the blood draining away as her heart stopped beating.

I held Moira's hand, and Alec caught his breath, sobbing.

But it did not happen like I expected. Moira took a gurgling raspy gasp, and breathed on her own for the first time since she was shot. I listened to her heart with the stethoscope slung around my neck. Her heart was sludgy but beating.

I looked at Candice, then Alec. 'It happens this way sometimes. Moira will go when she is ready. It looks like we're going to do this dance in stages.'

'How will we know when it's close?' Alec said.

'It's close now,' I told him. 'Her organs are going to start shutting down. It won't be long, Alec.'

'No hope?' Alec said, looking from me to Candice.

Candice shook her head. 'No. Sometimes the body has to play this out.'

'So what do we do?' Alec asked.

'Put her in neuropalliative care. That's comfort care, Alec. Hospice. She'll be comfortable, peaceful, she'll have no pain. And then she'll slip away from us. And then she'll be gone.'

FORTY

I was too tired to eat. Too tired to be hungry. Too alone. But I needed to go home. I needed a shower. A change of clothes. Some time away just to breathe.

We were suddenly scattered, my family and I, and from the street our house looked large and empty, silent and dark. No lights on, no one inside. The boys and Tash were tucked safely in with my mother at her house. I didn't know where Alec was. Moira was alone in her hospital bed, her body catching up with the reality of her death, while Perry sat at her side. How long would it take, I wondered.

Hospitals were lonely places. Full of bustle, activity, the dark energy of fear and pain. Was Moira lonely? Was Moira aware? I did not think she was. She had left me already. She was gone.

I got out of the car, parking in the driveway for some reason I did not even analyze. I did not want to spend even a few moments in the cloying darkness of the garage. I didn't want to enter that space of darkness, smell the scent of oil, the earthy smell of potting soil, the faint fumes that came from the separate little bags of fertilizer that Moira had on the shelves – roses, tomatoes, they all seem to need their own little bag, each with their own specially made concoction. I could not face the final slam of the automatic garage door leaving me in that dark vacuum.

So I left my car locked up tight, halfway up the driveway, outside where I could breathe. I was home. It was just as bad as I thought it would be.

I opened the front door, thinking of how Tash would usually be right there, warm and soft, tail wagging. There would be the scent of dinner. The feel of them, my family.

I paused in the doorway and considered getting back in the car, driving back to the hospital I had only just left, back to Moira's bed where I kissed her still-warm cheek less than an hour ago. And in my mind's eye I picked her up, gathered her up in my arms, carried her to the car and took her home. Why

not? She was going to die. Why not let her die here? At home.
With me.

I hesitated. Thinking of logistics, paperwork, the reality of
minute-to-minute care. Wary of sudden impulses.

I walked in, distracted, stooping down to retrieve the mail that
had been dropped through the slot in the door . . . and I felt
them. Oh how I felt them. Filling up my house like a fog, and
I imagined that I heard that faint drone of vibration, the dark
chorus they brought in their wake.

I remembered this well. How the press of their presence would
seep into my bedroom like a fog. I was a little boy adrift and
lost in the pressing miasma, but I was not that little boy now.

I turned on the porch light. The light in the hallway. I left the
front door wide open, as if it would let the fog of them out. I
turned on the office light, the bathroom light, the lamps in the
living room, I set the kitchen ablaze. I snapped the television on,
opened the white plantation shutters to the dark of the night.

I poured Jack Daniel's Black over two cubes of ice and held
my glass high in the air.

'I am here,' I said. 'So get the fuck out.'

I walked from room to room, waving my glass, challenging, and
the fog slowly began to slip away. I went to the kitchen,
and cooked an egg, just to see the butter melt in the pan, to fill
my home with cooking smells, to bring the normal back.

And slowly the fog dispersed, and it was just me now, alone
in my house, every light blazing. An egg growing cold in a pan
on the stove. And the darkness pressing in against the light shining
out of the windows.

I took a breath and sat on the couch, massaging the knot in
my left shoulder. I didn't have the energy to go upstairs. I didn't
have the energy to shower and change.

But the fog, at least, was gone. I really was alone. But I knew
how this worked. It would come back again when I was gone,
and the house was empty again, and there was no one, and
nothing, to keep them away.

I knew what they brought. Torment. They brought torment.

Well, fuck that. I was hungry.

I headed for the kitchen, because my mother had tucked a

mushroom risotto in the fridge and I was going to warm that up, and I was going to eat it, and I was going to drink Jack Daniel's.

I was pulling the casserole dish off the shelf when I caught sight of Moira, out of the corner of my eye.

The refrigerator door slammed into my elbow and the dish crashed to the floor. It was Le Creuset, and it did not break, but fell on one side, the lid popping open, spilling risotto into sticky little mounds on the floor.

Moira was walking past me down the hallway, toward the front door. But she was there. She was definitively there.

'Moira?'

I headed around the counter, stepping over the mess on the floor, and caught sight of her. She was checking the lock on the front door, and I heard the click and fumble. She wore a long oversized gray tee shirt, worn and soft, her favorite, one she wore to bed more often than not, and she headed into my office.

I'd seen her do this a million times. Check the kids, check the front door, come into my office to kiss me good night. Her hair was wild and curly, down around her shoulders. I wanted to touch it.

I called her name again, as she trailed through my office doorway. She did not turn, or answer, or give any indication she knew I was there. From the side I could see her face, the dark black arch of her eyebrows, the azure blue of her eyes. The bandage over the gunshot wound. She was different. Her eyes were flat, inward, and she had that gone, glazed-over look that I sometimes see in my dementia patients, my Parkinson's people, as they fall deeper and deeper into the mysterious, mist-strewn abyss of cognitive decline. She moved as if in a trance.

'Moira?' My voice automatically took on the firm but gentle cadences of the tone I used with frightened patients.

I knew she could not be there, I knew it was physically impossible for her to be on her feet, and when I turned the corner into the doorway of my office, she was gone. But my Italian blood-red leather chair rocked gently, then was still, as if she had touched it, looking for her husband to kiss good night.

'Moira,' I said softly. 'I'm right here.'

But she was gone. I scoured the house, inside and out. There was no trace of her.

I went back to my office, grabbed the edge of my desk, feeling a wave of nausea so strong I sat suddenly in my chair, feeling it creak and rock beneath my weight. I took slow steady breaths, battling the viselike grip of panic in my chest.

What had I seen? She looked real. Flesh and solid. I rubbed my forehead, thinking of the disturbing emptiness of her gaze.

I knew how the ghost stories played out. I remained neutral on that topic. Tolerant of Moira's intrigued speculation, I knew too much about dark energies, I knew their risk. Hauntings came under the heading of things I did not have to deal with, so I shut it out of my life.

But I could not help but wonder. About sightings, loved ones appearing at the moment of death, to bid a final good-bye.

My phone was on the charger, and my fingers shook as I made the call. It took a while for them to track Candice down, and when she came to the phone, she was breathless. So was I.

'What's going on, Candice?'

'Noah—'

'You sound stressed.'

'*Noah.*' Her voice settled into a professional tone, calm and kind, the voice she used on patients coming out of anesthesia, families stretched tight with emotion and ready to break. 'She's comfortable, Noah. No change. I just checked her, and Father Perry is there in her room. He'll be with her tonight. He told you that, remember?'

I sagged back into my chair. Perry refused to leave Moira's side. He was so oddly shattered now, but he had told me, whispering in the hallway outside of Moira's room, that he felt safe there, with Moira. He and Moira together. Both of them broken.

'Noah?'

'You're sure?'

'Yes, of course I'm sure. When they told me it was you on the line, I was coming out of the stroke guy's room, and I stopped to check on Moira, because I knew you'd want to know. Are you OK, Noah? Are you taking time to eat? You need to get some sleep, if you can, you know that, right?'

'Yes. I'm fine. Thank you, Candice.'

'Of course. Whenever you're worried, Noah. You call.'

I laughed, more of a sputter. 'I can't believe I'm *that guy.*'

'You know what? When it's somebody we love, we're all that guy.'

I shut the call down, put my head in my hands. No drinking tonight. Clearly I was losing my mind. I *had* to sleep.

Still, I did not go up to my bed, where I would once again sleep alone, in a bedroom that was too too quiet, as if all of the life and energy had been sucked away. Instead, I sat for a long time in my chair, rocking gently, wondering what it all meant. Coming to the conclusion that I knew absolutely fuck all about what it all meant.

I was a brain guy. I knew better than anyone that this was likely a shift of shadow in my kitchen that triggered a memory. I had seen Moira check that door and tell me goodnight, her nightly routine, just exactly that way, so many times before. I was tired. I was worried. There was a heavy weight of dread upon my shoulders every minute of every day. I had had no food, just coffee infusions. If I were a patient, I would tell myself to get some sleep. To stop skipping meals and eat. I would give myself the kind of safe, common sense, possibly useless drivel we confidently tell patients when we have no actual fuck all of an idea what they should do. Advice their mother could give them, though she'd likely do it better.

It was imagination and memory, a brain trigger that would feel completely real. It wasn't Moira.

But in my gut, I was convinced that it was. That she had been there, edging past me in the kitchen, trailing down that hall.

I rocked gently in my chair and watched the doorway of my office into the hallway, where the light was burning bright.

'Come back, my love,' I whispered. 'I'm right here.'

But the hall stayed empty, and though I sat and waited until I fell asleep in my chair, Moira did not come back.

FORTY-ONE

I had finally gone up for a shower, and slid, damp and exhausted into bed, and was deep asleep when the call came through from hospital security. Asking me if I'd authorized clergy from the Chapel of Disciples to visit my wife. The Reverend

Smallwood had tried to get into Moira's room while Perry had gone down to the cafeteria for something to eat, and security had not liked the looks of him. Especially as he was there at three thirty a.m.

At four in the morning, the streets were empty, and I made good time under the glare of streetlights. I got off the elevator, barreling past the huddled families packed together in the ICU waiting room. A security guard was talking to Candice just outside the swing doors.

Candice saw me over the guard's shoulder, took one look at my face, and grabbed my arm. 'She's OK, Noah. Perry is in there with her.'

I stopped. Took a breath. Turned to the security guard so it was a three-way huddle. This was a guy I knew, this guard. Tyson Morgan. I was breathing easier already. 'What's going on, Ty?'

Ty was youngish, ex-military, refused to carry a gun, which was an alarming new hospital trend he did not agree with. He wore his dark hair in a buzz cut, had old acne scars fading on his cheeks. He had a firm confident air and a trustworthy feel about him, and I'd seen him diffuse mental patients in the ER more than once. He was known as the Tin Foil Hat Whisperer, but it wasn't a nickname you repeated to his face. He and I had talked several times. He was married, had a couple of little girls around the same age as the fellas, worked nights, and took care of the kids while his wife worked shifts as a medical resident. She'd shadowed me a couple of times, years ago, when she was applying to med schools. Smart woman, looked younger than young, with fine blonde hair, freckles, and a baby face that made her a target. She had no problem putting the male residents in their place, and had once punched an old-fart anesthesiologist in the stomach when he'd dragged her into a stockroom. Twice she had raised holy hell with colleagues dissing the patients. She was fearless. I'd gone to her rescue in the dust-up with the old fart, but I worried that politics would slay her. I felt like she was a tiny wildcat I had to walk behind and protect, though I knew that the very idea would piss her off. The more she realized what she was up against, the more she stirred things up, and I was not sure whether she or the hospital board would survive her residency. She had once stood up on a chair in a meeting when she felt she was being ignored and interrupted too much. She would be a good doctor, though, if she and the hospital survived her training and the legion of misogynists, male and female, in medicine.

'What's going on, Ty?'

'Noah. I saw somebody I didn't like the looks of standing outside your wife's room. In the middle of the damn night, no less. Father Perry came up from the cafeteria and called me, but I was already on my way up. I'd seen him on the security cameras.'

'In ICU? How'd he get in?' I turned to go find Moira, but Ty held his hand up.

'He's not there now. I checked, so did Candice. Your wife is OK and I'm going to keep close watch over her.'

Candice nodded. 'We both will. And Father Perry is guarding her.' She looked pretty tonight, hair shiny and soft; there was a lightness about her, like people got when they fell in love. The same glow my brother-in-law had.

'Red-haired guy, right?' I asked.

Candice folded her arms and nodded. 'He said he was clergy. There at the request of family.'

I clenched my fists. 'Bullshit.'

Ty put his hands on his hips and I saw him methodically scan the corridor behind me. He'd been an MP during two tours in Afghanistan. 'Take a look at the security video.' He took his phone out of his pocket, took a moment to pull up the link and then handed the phone to me. I could feel Candice's warm breath as she stood on tiptoe and looked over my shoulder.

It was him all right. The red-haired man, in creased and ironed blue jeans, a black shirt, and white collar. The image was blurry then sharp as he moved in and out of range of the camera. He stood outside Moira's room, hand on the door.

'You know him,' Ty said, when I handed him the phone.

'I do. He's trouble. I don't want him anywhere near my wife. The guy that shot Moira was from his congregation.' I gave Ty a quick rundown on what the cops said, and the creepy church set-up that the red-haired man had. The intrigued look on Ty's face worried me. He was young. He did not know what he was dealing with, and I didn't want anything to happen to him.

Ty rubbed his chin. 'I'll make a police report. I can't say I'm surprised to hear any of this. I've been watching him a while. Caught him on the camera a few times. Usually very late at night. Glimpses of him sometimes, going down the stairwells, then the cameras seem to blip out. Always with him. It's weird. I never see much of him. Mainly it's a flash and a blur. But I'll keep him away from your wife. In fact, I'll toss his ass out.'

'I appreciate the help.' We shook hands, and I got the pity look that demoted me from hot-shit surgeon to sad sack with a dying wife. Ty headed off to the stairs. I'd never seen him take an elevator. Elevators were for patients, hospital staff, and wimps.

Moira's door was closed and I pushed it open gently. Perry was sitting stiffly in the recliner, hands clamped on the armrests, waiting for me.

'You knew this would happen. You've been guarding her, haven't you Perry?'

He shrugged. 'Not well enough, evidently.'

'You stopped him. You have to eat and you have to sleep.'

I sat down on the edge of Moira's bed, leaned down to kiss her warm cheek, and held her hand. The room was sweet with the scent of icy flowers, which was peculiar. There were no flowers in the room.

'Do you smell them?' Perry asked. 'Flowers?'

I looked at him. 'Definitely. Very strong. So what does it mean, exactly? It's some kind of sign.'

Perry nodded. 'It is. And honestly, I'm still figuring this out. But it's a good thing. Still. I'm going to stay with her, Noah. And I managed to get something to eat earlier. How about you?'

I thought of the mushroom risotto on the kitchen floor. 'Not exactly.'

He waved a hand at me. 'Go. I'll text if there's . . . a change.'

'If she starts breathing hard, Perry. Deep gaspy breaths. Text, OK?'

'OK.'

'There's no telling how long this will go on, Perry. It could take a couple weeks or a few days. No food, no water, system shutting down, but she's . . . young. Was healthy.'

'I know,' he said.

'Maybe we'll both stay.'

FORTY-TWO

It didn't take long for me to wolf down a cheeseburger, fries and Dr Pepper, and I was awash in the satisfaction of sugar, caffeine and carbs as I headed down the hallway toward Moira's room. I'd brought doughnuts in a white paper bag, and two coffees, and was just about to head inside when I caught a blur of movement from the corner of my eye, and I knew. It was more of an impression really, the chill in the air, the waves of uneasiness that seemed to emanate from nowhere, that curious feeling of pressure in my ears. The red-haired man was close.

I set the doughnuts and coffee right outside Moira's door and rounded the corner, looking for him. The stairwell door was closing and I got a glimpse of a nurse – Candice, it looked like Candice to me. And close behind her, the red-haired man, catching the door just before it shut. *Shit.*

I ran.

Two strides from the door I heard Candice scream, the echo and clatter of someone falling, tumbling down the unforgiving concrete of the stairs.

The first thing I saw as I barged through the door was a white shoe, scuffed and bent in half, three steps down. I ran, breathless, down the gray and steep stairs, and found Candice two floors down, upside down on the steps, legs splayed, back arched, head and neck jammed hard at an angle I did not like the looks of. It was bad. And she was conscious, her left pupil a pinpoint, the right wide and blown.

Shit shit shit.

Her eyes were full of awareness and brought to mind the conversations she and I had during late nights on breaks after dealing with comatose, intubated patients. Knowing, both of us knowing that, like all neurosurgeons, I had left a brutal trail of neuro patients who might never walk, or breathe or even think on their own again. She always told me she'd rather die. A personal choice. The same one I sure as hell would make. The same one I'd made for Moira.

And now she could only look at me. Unable to talk. Unable to breathe. The panic of air hunger in her eyes.

I took the pen out of my pocket. 'I've got you, Candice. I'm going to help you breathe, OK?'

I slid my finger down her larynx to the cricothyroid membrane, and used the ballpoint pen in my pocket to open the airway. Saw the suck of air in and out, the look of panic fade from her eyes.

The door above swung open, and I looked over my shoulder. It was Moira, barefooted, in a hospital gown. The sweet scent of icy jasmine flooded the stairwell and I scrambled to my feet.

'*Moira?* Good God, how—'

She put a hand on my shoulder, not for balance, but to steady *me*, and I felt a jolt at her touch, like a surge of electricity. 'Be still.' It was Moira's voice – but not her voice. And her eyes were not blue. They were yellow.

Moira crouched down beside me. 'Sweet Candice,' she said, putting a hand on Candice's forehead.

And Candice . . . changed. Her eyes were knowing, and she tracked Moira. She saw her.

'It is time, Sweet Candice. Don't be afraid.'

I would look at her autopsy results later. Her neck was broken, nerve tracks in the spinal cord severed. But her blood work would show a flood of endorphins that carried Sweet Candice out on a wave of bliss that our best pharmaceutical pain management could not approach.

The light went out of her eyes, and Candice was gone. And I looked in wonder to Moira, but she was not there. And I was alone, there in the stairwell, holding tight to Candice's limp, moist hand, still so very warm, and the smell of flowers trailed away. I headed back up the stairs to get the crash team who would be too late. It did not take long for the stairwell door to boom open, and the team of medics arrived after Candice was long gone.

I went to Moira's room, expecting her bed to be empty. But she was there, still and quiet, and I wondered if I had been hallucinating. Perry was so deeply asleep that he stirred but did not wake when I came through the door.

I went to the foot of the bed, peeled up the cotton blanket and tucked-in sheet and looked at the soles of Moira's feet.

They did not have the waxy, clean, shrunken look of a comatose woman. I saw smudges of dirt on the bottoms of her feet, the kind of dirt you would find on a woman who had walked barefoot down a hospital corridor, and down three flights of concrete stairs.

I touched her hand. Her eyes were closed. But she was breathing.

'Moira?'

She did not respond.

I went back to the stairwell. Hunting for him. The red-haired man. I found the detritus of medicine, sterile wrappers, and I heard a rustle and a sigh. Fielding O'Brian sat in the middle of the stairwell, just below the spot where his daughter died, holding a shoe that she lost in the fall, his head on his knees, one arm folded over the back of his neck, as if he was protecting himself from God knows what.

He gasped and sobbed and I touched his shoulder.

'Fielding? It's Doctor Archer.'

He looked up at me and I saw it in his face. The glazed eyes, the outraged puzzlement, the dread of the days to come. Grief. This was grief. I sat down beside him.

'I couldn't stop them.' He clutched my arm. 'I knew they were after her. They tried to get me to hurt her, but she was my Candice. My little girl. *I wouldn't.*' He looked at me, hard.

'Of course you wouldn't. I know how close you two were.'

'She's dead now, isn't she?'

'I'm sorry. She fell down the staircase.'

He shook his head. 'No. She did not fall. This was no accident. You know that, don't you, Dr Archer? They pushed her. They hurt her. They killed her. Where is she now? Is she OK?' He frowned at me, tears streaking the lines in his face, and his cheeks had a sunken look, bristled with gray whiskers. His trousers and shirt were wrinkled and stained, and he had the oily, dirty-sock smell of a man who had not bathed.

'She's . . . gone now, Fielding. I'm so very sorry.'

'But where is she now?'

'They've taken her away.'

'That . . . that place in the basement?'

'Yes. In the basement.' I pictured Candice growing pale and stiff in the cold chill morgue.

'I need to see her. Is she OK?'

I took his elbow. 'Let's go sit down and let me get you a cup of coffee. You take it black, don't you?' I would put sugar in it, though. I was going to load it with sugar.

He rose slowly, and clutched my shoulder, and he was trembling and so fragile I kept a firm grip on him as I guided him up the stairs. He had to concentrate hard, and I steeled myself to go slow.

He looked at me and he was vague, his eyes dull. 'I wouldn't hurt her. My little girl. They wanted me to. But I wouldn't.'

'I know. Up the steps, OK, go slow.'

'They're gone now.' He stopped, and peered behind us, down the stairwell. 'I don't hear them anymore. I don't . . . feel them. You can feel them in the room behind you, did you know that, Dr Archer?'

'Yes. I do know. One more step. Come on, let's head on up.'

'They were always there, watching me. I tried to make Candice go away but she wouldn't leave me. I was going to leave because she wouldn't.' He looked up at me, eyes red rimmed, swollen, dull. 'Is that why they left, because they got what they wanted? Do they have her? Do they have Candice?'

'Who is they, Fielding?'

'The Little People. We talked about it. *You knew*, even when I told you it wasn't true. Candice told you.'

'Candice is safe from them now, I promise. Why did they want you to hurt her?'

'Because she was getting in the way. They've been after your wife, don't you know that? But Candice was always watching over her. She was working double shifts. They wanted to get to her before *She* came. They're afraid of Her. She's a Warrior.' He took a deep breath. 'And I can have coffee?'

'Yes. You can have coffee. When is the last time you ate, Fielding? Do you remember?'

'Oh Candice, she is always trying to get me to eat. She says I forget to eat. Now what kind of dang fool forgets to eat? That girl fusses over me. But she's a good girl. You know that? And that young man she's seeing. He comes over and we have dinner, all three of us. I like that. He'll keep her safe. She's a good girl, my Candice.'

'She's the best.'

He frowned. 'There's something I'm supposed to tell you. *Protect Moira.* But who is Moira? I don't even know who she is. Do you know her? Is Candice going to be all right?'

FORTY-THREE

After three days nonstop at Moira's bedside, I needed a break, I needed to see my boys. Perry had refused to leave, and he was looking worse than Moira was. Alec was in shock and grieving, and was checking in on Fielding, and spending time at my mom's with the boys. He saw Moira regularly but could not bear to stay at her bedside. It was all he could do to set foot in the hospital. He had to go back to work tomorrow. We would bury Candice next week.

I drove through the city as if I were trying to find my way home, but didn't know where home was. I ended up at my mother's house, engine idling. It was late, but the porch light blazed, and a dim glow came from the back of the house. My mom left the light on over the stove at night, and the porch light on for me. I drove past slowly, knowing my mother and her husband and my boys and my dog were safe and snug, asleep inside. It would be cruel to rouse the house, to wake them. The boys had bunk beds there. Marcus would be curled on the top, Vaughn tucked in the lower bunk, and Tash would be stretched out in front of the doorway, keeping them company and keeping guard. I would see them tomorrow. I would go over in the morning.

I headed downtown past the Wellie. Perry's windows were dark, and I wondered if he would ever go back.

Where was I headed? Truly, I did not know. I drove in a pattern that took me past my mother's house, Perry's condo, the

Mandevilles' little bungalow, and finally home. I was keeping watch.

I sat in the driveway, engine off, and looked at my house, just like I did so many nights ago when all this began. The little wicker chairs in a semi-circle on the porch. Two big, two little. The giant pots that held dwarf hydrangeas, bursting with heavy cones of white flowers, lush hanging baskets of now dead geraniums. A pot that held St John's wort, a plant that Moira took a fancy to at Redmond's Garden Center. Orange and red berries, fuzzy yellow flowers, dried and brown right now. Moira fell in love at garden centers with unlikely things, unplanned things, things that should not thrive in our yard but sometimes did. Practical gardening eluded her.

I locked the car. Left it in the driveway and not the garage because I could not bear to see Moira's little red Mini Cooper gathering dust on the other side.

There were no lights on in the house. Even the front porch light was dark. How was it that one minute you can have a family waiting at home every night, and the next, somehow, you don't?

There was food in the fridge. My mother stopped in regularly with casseroles, and packets of thin-sliced salami, brie, cashews; she stocked the kitchen with anything she thought might tempt me.

I had French fries around lunch time yesterday, which is the last memory I have of food. I was hungry, but too tired to eat. I poured a short portion of Jack Daniel's Black over two ice cubes, and trudged slowly up the stairs with my drink.

I was keeping a tight watch on my alcohol consumption. It would be easy, too easy, to get lost in an extra drink or two every night, so I followed my usual patterns, no more, no less.

The bedroom was clean, hardwood floors gleaming and fresh sheets turned down. It was Thursday, the cleaning service had come and gone, leaving fresh linens and a welcome order in their wake.

I sat on the edge of the bed in my boxer shorts, sipping my whiskey and contemplating Moira's Glock, which I laid with great care on the bed.

Moira would be annoyed. No one was allowed to touch this gun but my lovely wife. But my lovely wife was not coming back. The Glock belonged to me now.

I wanted it to all be over. I wanted this panicked dread to go away. I was losing my wife, I had lost her, there was nothing I could do.

It was the limbo of uncertainty that threw me. Moira off the machines, no snaking tubes taxing a digestive system that was shutting down with unneeded and frankly unkind nutrition that would cause fluid buildup in her lungs and tissues. She felt no pain, no hunger. I'd made sure of that, keeping her on a low and steady dosage of Ativan and morphine. What I did not understand was why she was still breathing, still alive. Why her hands did not curl in the way of a coma patient, why her cheeks were flushed, not that gray-yellow pallor of impending death.

Did I really see her . . . on the staircase comforting Candice? Walking the halls of the house checking the locks? Did grief come with hallucinations?

I knew I could not take hope from this. I knew Moira was not coming back.

And I wanted it over with. Moira was neither dead or alive; Perry was alive, but not really there, and I was fucking lost.

I had two sons to raise. And I would have to do that alone. How would they cope without their mother? Could I be the mom and the dad and do it right and not screw them the hell up?

I would just have to be there. Cut my work schedule back, and take the daddy track on my career. The world was full of single parents. I'd just be one of the crowd.

I locked the Glock away, telling myself I was only just looking at it, sat the drink on the bedside table, and turned the television on. Somewhere in the world, someone was playing soccer, and I aimed the remote and found a game. Soccer, sons, a good old dog. This was my future life.

I woke to pounding, violent pounding on the front door of the house. The soccer game was not even a memory, the ice cubes in my drink long since melted away. I had been dead asleep, drooling on the pillow, sprawled on top of the bed.

I was up and on my feet when the pounding stopped, and I looked out the window, into the dark. The neighborhood was deep asleep at two a.m., I didn't see anything moving in the stillness, not even a car drifting by.

I grabbed a worn pair of jeans and the pounding started again, only this time, it was on the bedroom door, and a chill swept through me, raising goose bumps in a thrill of nerve endings up and down my back.

I froze. Listened. Afraid. I tried to remember if I set the house alarm, and I couldn't remember, and I wished I'd kept Moira's gun out. I headed to the closet to get it out of the box, and the bedroom door opened. Slowly. I caught my breath. Everything was odd. Off. Wrong. Nothing made sense.

All night long my only thought was that Moira would not come home. And yet . . . there she stood. In the doorway. Feet bare and dirty, wearing the sweatpants and tee shirt I'd left in her hospital room days ago – nobody wanted to die in a hospital gown. I made a noise, deep in my throat, and stumbled backward. I could not seem to get my breath.

Her hair was wild, her face tear-streaked, and she looked at me with wide eyes, pupils huge and black.

'Noah?' She sounded uncertain. As if she was not sure it was me. She touched the bandage on her head as if it puzzled her.

I crossed the room to sweep her into my arms, but she took a step backward, and I made myself slow down.

'Moira? It's OK, my love. I'm right here. Everything is all right. You're safe.'

She tottered sideways and I caught her before she fell. She was warm. Her cheeks were hot.

'I can't find the boys. Where are the boys?'

'They're at my mother's house. They're OK. They're safe.'

My hands were shaking, and I laid her gently on the bed, tucked her under the covers, and she shivered, and I lay down beside her, under the blanket, and took her in my arms. She was real. She was solid. She was . . . Moira. How could this be?

'Noah, what happened? I don't remember. Nothing is making sense. Where have all of you been? Why did you leave me alone like that?'

She sobbed and hiccupped, and she was crying so hard I could not make out much of what she said. Just two words. Lonely. Alone.

I stroked her hair, telling her over and over that she was OK, she was safe, I was right there. The boys were safe, Tash was safe, everything was going to be OK. I looked over at my phone on the bedside table, but nobody had called. No panicked notice from the hospital that my wife was . . . missing. Maybe I was losing my mind. Maybe I didn't care.

The crying faded, as Moira relaxed in my arms, the tension melting away, and then Moira looked up at me and smiled. Sweet. Uncertain. 'I've missed you. And the boys, and Tash. I've missed you so much.'

'I've missed you too, sweet love.'

'Did we have a fight? Did you leave me and take the boys?'

'Never. I would never leave you, my beautiful wife.'

She frowned. 'But you did that one night. In the hotel.'

'But only one night. I told you I was coming back. I just needed to sulk for awhile.'

It made her laugh. Something I thought I would never hear again.

'But why did you go?' The trembling started up again, and I stroked her soft pale cheek. 'I don't . . . I can't *remember*. What is happening, Noah? Please. Tell me what is going on. Have . . . have I been sick? Was there an accident? I have this bad feeling that something terrible happened.'

'Yes, my sweet, there was an accident.'

'But I'm OK?'

'Can you remember anything, Moira?'

She frowned. 'The man.'

'The man with the gun?'

'*No*. No, was there a gun?'

'Just tell me what you remember.'

'The boys are OK?'

'The boys are fine. Tell me about the man.'

She bit her lip, and took a long slow breath. 'He was sitting in a swing. A big rope swing, hanging from the biggest tree. A beautiful tree. It was so tall that tree, really thick. It must be five hundred years old, a tree that big.'

I thought of Abby's portrait. Elliot? I frowned and held Moira tighter. 'Do you remember anything else?'

'Yes. The man had this sweet little kitten.'

Definitely Elliot. The fallen angel with the cat.

'And the man, he told me, I would be safe if I stayed where I was.'

'And where were you?'

She frowned. 'It was like a paddock for horses. It's really pretty. You know, like that one we see when we're out driving that I love so much, on Delong Road. You know the one?'

I nodded. 'I do.'

'And it was bordered by a stone wall. But there weren't any horses, and there was a section that was really overgrown with bushes and shrubs, thick and snarled, and I found another fence, a wrought-iron fence, rusted, and kind of sagging, and it had a gate. The fence was really . . . tall. You couldn't climb it. And the gate was always closed. I tried once to open it but the man told me no, not to open the gate, or go through the gate, not to even go near the gate. To stay away from the fence. To stay in the paddock where I would be safe. That's what I was supposed to do.

'But then . . . then I heard you calling me, and the boys were crying. I heard Vaughn crying in his sleep, like he does when he has nightmares. And when I went to the gate . . . it was open. So I went out. But then I was afraid. There was something watching me. Something bad, it was after me, I heard it rustling and coming fast. So I ran and I ran, and I wanted *you* Noah. I wanted to come home and then, I saw the house. It was all dark and I almost missed it. And I beat on the door and I ran up the steps and the boys were gone and I thought you would be gone too, and I was so sad, I missed you, but I opened the bedroom door and . . . you were here. *You're here.*'

She was laughing or crying I couldn't tell which. She looked up at me and touched the growth of stubble on my chin. 'Oh, Noah. You look so *tired.* You look . . . thin. What happened to you? Have you been ill?' She paused and shook her head and her voice changed. It grew deeper. With an awareness, a sudden awareness. 'That doesn't make sense.' She sat up suddenly and looked at me. 'I got shot?'

'Yes. You got shot.'

'That awful man in camouflage. He was so strong. So . . . rough. He shot me and you dove into the lake and you pulled me out.'

I nodded, my throat constricted, voice thick. 'And then what?'

'I remember you holding me up in the ambulance when I wanted to just sleep. And then—'

'And then?'

'After that it gets weird.'

It was already weird. 'Tell me,' I said.

'I don't . . . I don't remember.'

'You remember the man? In the paddock?'

'Yes. The man and the cat and the swing. And the gate.' She sat up. 'Did I die?' Her voice was tight. Her eyes were bright, and she bit the back of her hand.

'You were in a coma.'

'Were?'

'I just left you. At the hospital.'

She gave me a look I knew well. A look that told me I was in big trouble.

'Did you have me on life support? I told you never to do that.'

'I took you off.'

'And then I died?'

'I thought you would. But you didn't. I touched the bandage on the shaved part of her scalp. 'Does your head hurt, Moira?'

'No.'

'Are you in any pain? Are you thirsty? Hungry?'

'No. And no. Am I dead?'

'Your heart is beating. You go from warm to cold. You are breathing.' I sat up but she pulled me back. 'Hold me, Noah. Just hold me for awhile. And don't let me fall asleep.'

'Why don't you want to sleep?'

'Because if I sleep, I'm afraid that when I wake up, you'll be gone. Noah, I *love* you.'

'I love you too.'

'Just know it. I love you and I love the boys. So much. So much.'

I was afraid. Afraid of the joy that simmered inside of me. So aware of Moira in my arms. How impossible it was. The soft intake of her breath, the softness of her skin on my skin. All I wanted was to hold her, to keep her safe, to never let her go.

'The geraniums are dead.'

I laughed. 'Sorry, my love.'

'I'm afraid to go to sleep,' she said, and I felt her clinging tighter.

'Me too.'

She pressed close to me, and I kissed her gently, then hard, and she held me so tight. And there were other things to do than sleep.

Eventually, inevitably, we did sleep. Something woke me, some noise, a dream. The memory of an unmuffled car, speeding well over the limit, roaring past the house.

I sat up, and even as I reached for Moira, I knew she was gone. I pulled the blanket back, found a strand of her rich brunette curly hair on one corner of my pillow.

A pounding on the bedroom door sent a zing of adrenalin that had me up on my feet, stumbling toward the door.

'Moira?'

The pounding was hard, aggressive, and the door slammed open.

It was Moira, it was *not* Moira. I could not seem to move or talk, but my mind was moving fast, noticing everything, marking every detail. That hyper-aware brain activity one gets just before a car accident, a crisis, where the neurons fire and the mind works so swiftly that the body seems to follow like moving through thick mud.

The scent of icy sweet flowers flooded the room. Moira/not Moira seemed taller, her eyes yellow and hyper-aware. Knowing.

'Be still,' she said. Her voice was confident. Strong. Warm and safe . . . but compelling. The kind of voice you obeyed.

'You are not Moira.' I took a step toward her and she held up a hand. I stopped. 'Who are you?'

'Somersly.'

The voice was different, the stance was different. The eyes, intense, on fire.

'Help is coming,' she said.

'Who? What do you mean?'

'*Listen*, Noah-son. Just listen. Help is coming, do not give up. You will know it when you see it. The hospital is a bad place for Moira and for Perry. I will guard them but you should arrange to bring both of them home. Take Moira to your mother and your sons. You will not be able to care for her. You will have things you must do.'

'Is she . . . is she going to . . . be OK?'

'There are worse things than death, Noah-son. She must be away from the hospital and it must be tonight.'

'Who are you? How are you . . . here?'

'You know of possession, Noah-son.'

'You possess her?'

'I do.'

I took a gulp of air. 'You're a demon?'

'Not as you know demons. I am an angel. Not fallen.'

'You're here to help us?'

'Elliot. I am here for Elliot. To bring him home.'

'So it's true then?'

'Elliot did not want to fall. He followed to bring me back. To keep me from falling. He saved me and got . . . caught. You will help me bring him home, Noah-son.'

'How?'

'You will know. You must not retreat. The ones you love are snarled up. There is only one way forward. To set Elliot free.'

'That was you, wasn't it? In the stairwell. With Candice. And you are the *She* they are afraid of.'

'They should be afraid.'

'Candice—'

'They are dangerous, Noah-son. It was Moira they wanted. Candice was brave and heroic.'

'But you let her die.'

'There are consequences. I have told you this. Candice did not suffer, Noah-son. I helped her home.'

'What will happen to her father, to Fielding? To Perry? To my family?'

'That will depend on you, Noah-son. You will have choices to make. Perry is a chosen one. As are you.'

'If I do everything I can. Everything that is asked of me. Will you keep them safe? Moira, Perry, the boys?'

'There is a consequence to every outcome, Noah-son. You know this.'

'I just need to them to be safe. That's all I ask.'

She tilted her head. 'But they are always cared for, Noah-son. Always.'

She turned and walked away. I ran out into the hallway, and she was gone. I searched the house from top to bottom, but there was no one there, and the scent of flowers slowly faded and was gone.

And I needed to get to the hospital, tonight.

FORTY-FOUR

The roads were empty, and I was making good time.
My reality had shifted, and the world was draped in mysterious shadow. My confident, centered logic, my *context* had been shaken. The pressure of dark things breathed against the back of my neck. And I could never go back to that crystal clear, sun-drenched life of normal expectations . . . of what was real, and what was not.

And yet. I was excited, I admit it. I was still in the fight.

Perry was dozing but uneasy in the recliner next to Moira's bed. His feet were up and he was still in the same old sweater and worn-out jeans. I could see the weight loss in his face and his neck, how pale he was; skin waxy and white without the usual healthy ruddy flush that used to make me worry over his blood pressure.

I shut the door and sat on the edge of Moira's bed, and took her hand.

It was damp and cold. She had the posed look of a patient tucked in by hospital staff, hair brushed back against the pillow, loose sweats, while she drifted, unaware, so far away.

And yet, earlier tonight . . . she was awake and aware and curled up with me in our bed. It made no sense that I had held her in my arms a short time ago.

'You're back.' Perry. Awake and watching me from his chair. He pushed the recliner footrest down, so his feet were on the floor. He cocked his head sideways. 'What is it, Noah? Something happened, didn't it?'

I nodded. 'I'm here to take Moira home. You were right. I saw Moira, but not Moira – this is what you thought it was.'

'An angelic possession?' he said. Something in his eyes, that reminded me of the old Perry.

I nodded. 'Well, either that, or I have totally lost my mind. I can't tell the difference.' And I told him about Somersly, and he had questions, but he latched on to the part about getting Moira out and away.

'*Good*,' he said, getting to his feet. 'I want her out of here. I want me out of here too. How do we do this?'

'I've snagged a wheelchair, it folds up so we can put it in the car. It's right out in the hall. We'll have to prop her up with pillows but it will do the job. I need you to help me stop her falling out of the chair, and to get her in the car.'

'You don't want a stretcher?'

'Hard to manage. Let's not overthink it, let's just do it.'

'Got you.' He took a breath, and put his shoes on. Quickly. 'Let's do this fast, OK?' He trailed off, then looked at me. 'You're sure it's safe . . . medically?'

'Medically? I think we're long past medically.'

FORTY-FIVE

I t went better than I expected, getting Moira out, and while I had the calm look of a sad, brave grieving husband, inside my heart was slamming, though my surgeon's hands were steady. I wasn't sure what I was afraid of. Just that I was afraid.

I was exasperated but understanding and I kept my temper when it was clear that there had been a holy hell of an administrative breakdown between the hospital admin and home-care hospice, and Moira's paperwork was nowhere to be found. I'd made the hard decision to put her in hospice care at home, instead of one floor up with the in-hospital hospice care staff, and with a shorthanded, overworked staff, and my position at the hospital, it was shockingly easy for us to cut loose.

I managed to be charming in spite of my grief and frustration. The staff appreciates that sort of thing.

*   *   *

My mother, meeting us at the door in a pair of black yoga pants and an oversized white shirt and black ballet slippers, had clearly not been to bed.

'Well I knew it was going to be something,' she told me, as soon as she saw Perry and me on the doorstep. 'I had one of those feelings.'

'Shit. I should have called you,' I said.

Like any good Steel Magnolia, my mother took my decision to bring a comatose Moira to her home in the middle of the night in stride, concerned only with the practicalities. 'Brent couldn't sleep, so he went to Kroger's to pick some things up for the boys for breakfast.'

I didn't comment but I felt ashamed. Why was I always so stiff and difficult about my mother's husband? I didn't want my mother to be alone. And now that I worried every minute about losing Moira . . . I found I could no longer look with hostility on Brent.

'Perry. It is so good to see you.' She gave him a hug, and he embraced her tightly.

She knelt down beside Moira, who was sliding sideways, eyes closed, propped with pillows and looking pretty damn precarious. 'My sweet girl. Come on, I'll tuck you right into my bed. You're going to love the thread count on those sheets.'

When I protested that my mother should not give up her own bed, she put her hands on her hips and cocked her head to one side. 'Noah, now you listen. I could explain to you that it will be a lot easier to take care of Moira downstairs, where I can keep tabs on her, but what I want you to do is put her where I tell you and don't interfere.'

Perry and I got Moira into the bed with just a little more trouble than we'd had wrestling her out. We were in a sweat as we watched my mother tuck Moira into the king-sized bed, the linen sheets, and the white ruffled duvet. Not practical but I kept my mouth shut.

'You'll need help,' Perry said to my mother.

Evidently Perry was allowed to have opinions.

'Brent will help. And Alec is here quite a bit. But Noah, I am not sure what I am supposed to do for her. I'll need you to tell me all that.'

'I'll make arrangements first thing in the morning, and I'll have someone with her 24/7. You won't have to do any caretaking, OK?'

'No sir, that is not OK. I don't want strangers doing this. I took care of my mama, so I sort of know what I'm getting into here. I'll send Brent out later for supplies, but I don't know about medicine and dosages and things like that.'

'I have her meds, enough for the next few hours, and I'll call in and have what she needs delivered, OK? You'll have to sign for the morphine. It's not an injection, just a tiny bit of liquid, you can use a syringe to drip it into the side of her mouth, right into the flesh of her cheek, she won't have to swallow. I'll show you. Any kind of emergency – you call me and only me,' I said. 'Not nine-one-one, and do not take her to the ER.'

She bit her lip and nodded. 'So she's home . . . to die.'

I didn't answer. 'If she starts breathing hard or seems distressed, just let me know. Do you want me to get a hospital bed in? It might be more practical.'

My mother shook her head. 'Let it be like it is; if I change my mind I'll let you know.' She took another look at Moira, and plumped another pillow under her head. 'All right then. She seems peaceful right now, so let me make us some coffee. Are you hungry? And while I make us some eggs you can tell me why you decided to do this in the middle of the night.' She stopped and looked at me over her shoulder. 'What about the boys? They're sound asleep right now. So is Alec. I think he should be around people right now, if that makes it easier for him. And he is so good with those boys. Should I wake them up? What do I tell them?'

'Let them sleep. I'll stay till they wake up, and I'll talk to them myself.'

She took a deep breath. 'Yes. That's a good idea. And I think it's better this way, Noah. Better to have her home.'

'Mom?'

'Yes, honey?'

I gave her a long hug. She smelled like vanilla lotion, a familiar, comforting scent. 'Thank you.'

'Of course, Noah. You did the right thing, bringing her here to me. I'll keep her safe.'

Perry and I exchanged looks over my mother's shoulder.

Sitting in the kitchen, with the smell of coffee brewing, my boys and Moira's brother upstairs, Moira in the next room, and Perry at the table, I felt a weight of worry lift. Moira was home, out of the hospital, where we could keep watch and protect her. Whatever happened would happen, but this is where she needed to be. I should have done this days ago. I flashed on Candice, neck broken, eyes wide, crumpled in the hospital stairwell. I should never have left Moira there after that, I should never have left her behind.

I heard the click of Tash's toenails on the stairs, and she made her way slowly across the kitchen and put her head in my lap. Her tail wagged wearily, and she snuffled my hand as I stroked her shoulder, pulled gently on her silky ears. I was as glad to see her as she was to see me.

I was well aware this might be the last time I had all of my family together, rounded up in one place. It was a good feeling. Almost happy. Something to hang on to.

FORTY-SIX

He came into our lives so quietly, Dr Lucian Bennington-Jones. He was there that morning when Perry and I left my mother's place and headed to my house for showers, a change of clothes. Neither one of us had any idea what we should do next, and we had been debating our next step on the drive over.

I had set Bennington-Jones aside as mostly a legend at this point, almost a rumor. Until he appeared that morning on my front porch.

'Who is that?' I said, as we drove up in the driveway.

Perry squinted, then leaned forward. He smiled, just a small one. 'It's him,' Perry said, with a note of wonder in his voice. 'Bennington-Jones. He came.'

Bennington-Jones smiled at us gently as we scrambled out of the car, shook each of our hands. 'I'm Lucian Bennington-Jones.

Are you Father Perry Cavanaugh? And you're Dr Noah Archer, correct?'

We both nodded.

'Just the fellows I wanted to see.' His eyes squinted as he gave us a big smile and he seemed oddly relieved to see us. 'I am so glad to meet you, both of you. And my abject apologies for taking so long to get to you. There were certain . . . distractions, and I had a long journey here.'

His presence was like an anchor in a world that had been spinning, and he had a gravitas that made me feel safe.

His credentials were the kind that can only be called impeccable, with a strong dose of impressive. An Oxford don, retired. A learned man with strong opinions, and the kind of reputation that made academic and church bureaucrats nervous. An Anglican priest. Until his life took a turn and he became an exorcist. He told us later that it was a simple thing. He saw what needed to be done, and he did it.

Born in a small English village, a firebrand exorcist who worked relentlessly, until he had grown tired. He stopped doing exorcisms. He stopped teaching. He needed intense solitude and to look out his front door and see a garden, to walk in beautiful places. He settled quietly in the South of France, with frequent visits to London. He could only take people in small measured doses, and needed to be left mostly alone. He often wandered restlessly, relentlessly driven by the search for something that felt like home, flooded with a sort of nostalgic grief as he traveled and stood in towns he'd lived in, houses he'd lived in, like a ghost haunting his past.

He called himself a shepherd. But his days of bringing the possessed out of the dark and into the light were long gone. Eventually, Dr Lucian Bennington-Jones realized that he had nowhere to go but to duty. He took on the more difficult calling, one that maybe only he could do – that of bringing priests lost to the fallout of exorcisms back into the light. Priests who had taken the path down into the dark places, priests who could not find their way back.

Priests like Perry.

Bennington-Jones was a cypher. He moved like an elderly man who was used to gauging every move with the knowledge of how much pain it would involve. He walked slowly and with great care, with a hitchy limp that clearly sourced in his right hip. He was tallish and thin, bony and angular and, as painful as his movements seemed, this man moved with a confidence and an emanation of strength. His hair was fine, a sort of dirty blond-gray hay, cut short, side parted, and prone to random cowlicks.

His eyes were cerulean blue, his paper-thin skin brown and crisscrossed with the imprint of age and sun. When he looked at you, he *saw* you. As if he knew the good of you and the bad of you and was watching to see which way you would go. A confident man, oddly gentle, like a worn-out warrior, highly intelligent, highly detached. He would have made a formidable surgeon.

He wore creased tan khakis and a nubby gray sweater, and expensive, worn loafers, Italian, handmade.

And he sat down with Perry and me, that first morning he arrived, opened the plantation shutters to let the sunlight in, and talked of easy things. Places he had been. People he had met. He loved architecture and he told us of favorite rooms and homes he had had. It was interesting enough to pass the time, dull enough so Perry could simply listen and be still. There was a hypnotic, lyrical flow to his voice, and I could see the tension easing in Perry's shoulders, the muscles in his jaw.

He talked until Perry began to slacken, and then sleep, then he held a finger to his lips and walked me to the kitchen.

'Should we get him to bed?' I asked. 'I have plenty of room upstairs, for both of you.'

Bennington-Jones shook his head. 'Let him stay right where he is. He feels safe right there, tucked into that lovely leather couch.'

'He doesn't sleep much anymore.'

'Yes. That's to be expected. He had to keep watch. He did not feel safe enough to sleep.' He put a hand to my shoulder. 'I'll be staying here with both of you, now is not a time for either of you to be alone.'

'I can't stay here. I'll be sleeping at my mom's house, I'll be sitting beside my wife.'

He nodded. 'Understood. You've been keeping watch over Perry, like the good friend you are. I'll do that now. But for now, go upstairs and get a short nap, if you can. Later we will have things to discuss and planning to do.'

'I'm OK. Can I fix you some breakfast? Let me take your things upstairs, we have a guest room.'

He smiled, but it was a stern kind of smile, bracing, like a commanding officer sending you off on a suicide mission. 'I want you to sleep. You had a rough night.'

'You know that?'

'It shows. And it makes sense, considering what you've been up against. It's crucial for you to pace yourself, Noah. I have everything in hand, but you're very much needed here.'

'My wife—'

'Yes, your wife. Once you've had your sleep, Noah, I want you to come back downstairs and tell me all about that.'

'You may not believe me.'

'I think, Noah, you will find that I very much will.'

It was late afternoon, and I'd gone out for subs, and we'd eaten, and were gathered on the bar stools in my kitchen, drinking Guinness and Cougar Bait beer. Perry and I had filled Bennington-Jones in on everything, start to finish, and he had listened, and nodded, and not ever seemed shocked or surprised. I was clearing away the mess, and Perry looked up, and frowned.

'I feel as if I have spent a lifetime doing my work blindfolded. And now that I have the chance to do something extraordinary, to help Elliot – I can't. And I don't even know if I should. If this is my ego.' He looked to me. 'I know what Somersly said. But what if she is . . . what if she is dark too?'

I sat down across from him.

Bennington-Jones put a hand on his arm. 'I understand, Perry. You are weary and you see dark in such depths and layers now. Where before you only understood it intellectually, you now know it on a gut, visceral level, and it has shaken you to the core.

'I wish you could feel how joyous this is. What a milestone. Because it's useful. It's better to know, to really know. What do your instincts tell you, Perry? About Somersly? About Elliot?' Jones cocked his head to one side, studying Perry.

'Logic tells me I cannot listen to what Elliot says. You cannot listen to the voices of the demons. Anything said is by definition untrue. But in my gut . . . I believe him. I want to get him home.'

Bennington-Jones nodded. 'These are words. Angels. Demons. Dark angels. We will set words and definitions and dogma aside, Perry, and we will follow your instinct.'

Perry looked away. 'Another thing. My gut does not want to leave Mandeville lost like he is. I don't want to abandon him. And I feel like he is the way to helping Elliot. But I have tried so hard with him and failed. My fear is it could go very wrong.' Perry laughed. 'Even more wrong, I mean. Still. I have never felt easy with the notion of no return, for angels – or humans – cast out with no hope of redemption. I am not talking about free will. I am talking about no hope if the will is there.

'I admit I want the happy ending. Something other than this *weight*, this heavy sense of despair. I don't believe it – that anyone or anything is eternally lost. That I could never help someone like Henry Mandeville find his way back, if he came to change his mind. I get that his change of mind is the essential point here. That there are times of . . . of no hope. But if we are being shown a way . . . And Somersly has come. She has said this is what we must do. So . . . is she to be trusted? Or is she leading us into trouble?'

I grimaced. 'Both, don't you think?'

Bennington-Jones smiled at me. 'Let's see where this takes us. You, Perry, and you Noah. Me. We are the tools Somersly uses to help Elliot find the way. Have you not considered, Perry, that it was no coincidence that you and Noah should meet? That Noah should have first-hand the exact experiences that kept him from falling into the abyss, but allowed him to glimpse what is there, experiences that drove him to find the scientific side of the solution? That he should be taken up by you, a direct descendant of the Magdalene, wife of Jesus—'

'So that's true?' I said.

'That Perry is descended from one of the most powerful exorcists in history? Do you think this is coincidence?'

'So that's us?' I gave them a lopsided smile. 'The three of us? A perfect storm of exorcism?'

Bennington-Jones nodded at me. 'Perry is the wary warrior. Noah, you are the healer.'

'And you are the mentor,' I said.

'Nothing is random in the universe, Noah.'

'What if we don't win? What if we go under? What happens to my wife? My boys?'

Bennington-Jones looked at me and he did not smile. 'There are no guarantees, Noah, and always consequences. We are three now, and it is going to take everything we've got. Now we don't have a great deal of time. We move fast, and we move smart, but we strike.'

'Elliot told us to hurry,' I said.

'But what precisely are we going to do?' Perry asked.

'Bring Elliot home,' Bennington-Jones said. 'And to do that . . . you must be prepared. Both of you. Physical preparation, and mental preparation. Mandeville will be the conduit, as he was before. He has a heightened ability, brought on by Noah's treatments. So you must match him with the same strength, *and more.*'

'That's what got me into trouble in the first place,' Perry said.

'Yes. The one treatment. And you were overwhelmed, I understand that. *It's why I am here.* Noah will get you there physically. And I will be there to guide you both and be a spiritual safety net. But you are the exorcist, Perry, and I am afraid the hard work is on you. You went to the dark places, you got into trouble. This time you will be ready.

'And you are right, both of you, to worry and be wary. It very well might go wrong. There are questions in this life, quite a few of them actually, where we don't get to know the answers. The decisions are really quite simple, Perry. You see what needs to be done, and you do it. And you don't get to ask if it will work. So there is only one question here, Perry.'

Perry took a breath, rubbed his temple. 'Yes. I'll do it.'

'And you?' Bennington-Jones gave me a steady look.

'I will. And I can probably get things set up for a treatment tomorrow night. With some luck.'

'Not yet. There are things to do before we begin the treatments for Perry. Leave this to me.'

FORTY-SEVEN

The delivery truck came early. It arrived at my house the next morning, a Saturday, as I sat alone in my kitchen drinking coffee. Thinking how quiet the house was. I had spent the night sleeping with my comatose wife, glad my mother had said no to a hospital bed, taking comfort in Moira's physical presence, wondering, like I did now, if this would be the very last time I would see her alive.

Bennington-Jones had asked me to be here. He didn't say why. He and Perry were gone, who knew where. I could see signs of their presence. Perry's sweater draped over the back of the couch. Two old leather books I had never seen before on the coffee table. Food in the kitchen that I did not buy.

The doorbell rang, followed up by a meaty fist on the door, which I opened warily to a stocky, gray-haired man in a ball cap, work boots, and a crisp white Hanes crew-neck tee shirt. He had a permanent ruddiness and a nose full of broken veins that bespoke high blood pressure, plenty of alcohol in the off hours, and physical labor outdoors.

He held a clipboard in calloused mitts, and I noticed a white scar at the edge of his left eye. He was a smoker, the scent of tobacco clung to him like a second skin, and his voice was deep and rough.

'Morning,' he said, glancing down at the paperwork on his clipboard. 'Archer, Noah? Fincastle Road.'

'That's me.'

'Where do you want your pallets?'

'Pallets of what?'

The man frowned and shifted his weight, giving me a sideways look in case I was some kind of smart ass. 'Stone. Fieldstone. I can put it right here on the side of the driveway, leave you space to get in and out, and have it off the lawn so it doesn't kill the grass. Where are you building? I could get it closer to that back-yard, on the side there, depends on where you're putting the wall.'

'I'm not building a wall.'

He thought about that. We both did.

'If I have to haul this back, you're going to have to pay a delivery and restocking charge.'

'Who ordered this?'

'You did. Didn't you?'

'Nope.'

He studied the paperwork. Nodded. 'OK, I see. Delivered to you, but bought and paid for by L. Bennington-Jones.'

When Perry and Bennington-Jones arrived an hour and a half later, the stone, beautiful, gray fieldstone, sat in pallets on the left-hand side of the driveway, blocking Moira's car in. Bags of mortar were stacked inside the garage where my car usually sat, and I was now parked on the overcrowded street.

Perry and Bennington-Jones arrived in Perry's dinged-up old Volvo sedan and Bennington-Jones waved at me and grinned. 'Excellent, excellent, I didn't think we'd get this delivery so quickly. Give us a hand, can you, Noah?'

Perry's trunk was full of tools. Trowels. Buckets. Work gloves. A new blue wheelbarrow. Perry wore a faded and loose pair of jeans, and Bennington-Jones was in khaki work pants with boxy pockets and loops on the side. He clapped me on the shoulder.

'Where do you want your wall, Noah?'

'Would it be disingenuous of me to ask what wall?' I looked at Perry over my shoulder, expecting a smile or a chuckle or even a smirk, but he was looking off into the distance with that otherworldly air he now had. I looked back at Bennington-Jones and he gave me a grim nod.

'Let's take a walk around the property here, Noah, and see what works best.'

Perry followed us, hands clasped behind his back, and I saw the beginnings of a smile.

We headed through the gate of my short white picket fence, onto my pergola, and Bennington-Jones tramped around my backyard, hands on his hips sometimes, arms folded sometimes, frowning and rubbing his chin.

'If you really want to build something out here, I'd like short little walls around the pergola, to enclose it. Kind of like a gazebo,' I told him. 'That's what this is all about, right? Getting

Perry out of his head, wearing him out with physical labor. I can see how that could help.'

Bennington-Jones gave me a small half-smile. 'By all means, do build yourself a gazebo, I do think it would be a lovely thing, but that's not what I'm here for. Perry needs to build a serious wall. As do you. I'll be helping, but this is crucial for both of you. Time permits?' He asked gently, and I knew he was talking about whether or not I was willing to leave my wife.

'How long will it take?'

'Two days tops. Quit when you're tired or need to get back to your wife.'

I looked out over my yard. 'Look, let's replace that little picket fence there with a short stone fence. Two feet maybe?'

'No, Noah, we're not building a *little* stone fence. We're building a strong, sturdy wall. Six feet tall.'

'I don't get it.'

He gave me a broad smile, and pointed to the back of the yard where my neighbor had already erected a six-foot privacy fence around his in-ground pool. 'We'll build it there. No one should be worried by it there. And we'll do a good job, my father was a stonemason and I spent my summers as a boy doing this kind of work. You can hang flowers on it and make a little garden around it later on. I think you'll be pleased.'

That was a politeness, because I knew this this was not about me. Perry had already lost interest, and stood very still, with that off stare that grew ever familiar. 'I don't need to be pleased. You build however and how many walls you want.'

What did it matter, after all? My life could not get any more weird.

I liked working with my hands. I was a surgeon, though my hands were big and unwieldy, not the slim tapering things some of my colleagues had. And once Perry and I got started, under Bennington-Jones's focused but gentle supervision, I began to enjoy the work. The weather was cool but sunny. There was no time to think, to worry; all of my concentration was on that wall. We dug a trench. We lined it with overlapping landscape fabric. We used string and stakes for markers. Bennington-Jones knew how to build walls. He spread the mortar evenly on the run of stones, after Perry and

I set them, and used the trowel edge to cut the mortar even with the wall face. This was no dry-stack wall. This wall was going to be solid. This wall was going to be forever.

Perry seemed distant as we began, with the distracted weighty look he carried now. But gradually, as we sweated, our skin layered in the grime you accumulate moving stone and laying mortar, he began to focus completely on the job at hand. So did I. I could see a look of satisfaction in Bennington-Jones's small smile. He worked beside us, but he was slow, measured, careful of his hip, and Perry and I, in silent agreement, shielded him from the heavy work. We set the stone. He mixed the mortar and used the trowel. Once we set up a rhythm, Bennington-Jones began to talk in a slow, steady, reassuring tone. Hypnotic.

'You are safe, Perry. And Noah. You are safe and it is OK to rest. Know that you are enough, just as you are. And you are more powerful than you know. You have a unique journey and purpose in this life. Everything is happening just as it should. You are exactly where you are meant to be.'

I took a breath and set the wheelbarrow down. The words resonated.

Because I had felt guilty all of my life. That I'd been weak, that I'd brought it on myself, the possession. I had always felt marked. Other. And now I felt something ease up inside me. Something that had been holding me hard, and holding me down.

I looked up see Bennington-Jones watching me with that gentle intensity he had.

'And now, gentlemen, I want you to focus on the feel of the stones as you set them along the wall.' He picked his trowel up, slapped mortar on the next level of the wall. 'Imagine this wall is going up in your mind.'

He told us that the wall could not be breached. If we doubted that, all we had to do was feel the weight of the stone, the texture of it beneath our fingertips, to see it go up, stone by stone. To imagine the mortar dry and hard and impenetrable.

The wall would keep things out. We were to build it in our minds, as we built it with our hands.

'There are dark things that have come close to both of you. Dark energies that have infiltrated your thoughts. You, Noah, as a child – your father always protected you. He had a strange sense of something he did not even speak about. Just an instinct, to keep you safe. He shielded you. And when he died, you became vulnerable. You were fair game, then, but that is no longer the case. You are grown now, a strong, confident man. You have driven them out and away. I know they plague you. I know they watch you and they always will. I know the effort it takes to keep a mental barrier up, but that is going to get easier for you now. You have a wall now, reach out, touch it, it is here, right here beneath your hands. It is going to be easier for you from this day forward. You will always have this wall to protect you.'

And somehow, the wall beneath my fingertips and the wall forming in my mind became one and the same. When I closed my eyes, I could see it. When I reached out, I could touch it.

There were times when Perry stopped working. He would not move, he did not speak, sometimes I think he barely drew breath. Bennington-Jones would nod at me and incline his head and I knew I was to keep working steadily. So I did.

'Perry, my son, everything you have seen and felt have been things that I have seen and felt, and others before you, other exorcists. Many of us have found our way back. Many of us have survived.

'There is something inside you that knows what to do. You will find this knowledge, you will gather this strength, and you won't just survive. You will grow stronger. And you will *thrive.*' Perry faltered, and Bennington-Jones gently guided Perry's hands and Perry did not resist, but he was barely there, his mind in some dark and terrible place. 'So now you have seen the full measure of their malevolence. Now you *know* things you have only seen in glimpses before, you know things very few people ever do; and that feels like a curse, a weight, Perry, like something you wish to unknow. But I will tell you to be brave and hold the line and stay in the fight. It is safer and wiser to *know*. To go eyes open, not blindly forward. Remember that you are only the vessel, the conduit, and that you are protected always. That you will never be sent forward alone.'

Perry picked a stone up out of the wheelbarrow, set it down. 'Sometimes I have a . . . a future memory. And I see what will happen to Elliot if I cannot get to him. If I leave him behind.' He rubbed a hand over his face. 'I see it at night. At night when I try to sleep.'

'And now you will sleep behind the wall,' Bennington-Jones said. 'It makes sense to worry. It makes sense to be afraid. To wrestle a fallen angel out of their hands – it is a formidable thing. This wall is your protection, but you'll have to come out from behind the wall, and face them, and whatever you saw or felt that first time will be nothing compared to what comes next. It will be infinitely worse. This time though. This time you will be ready.'

'Comforting, that,' I said.

Perry gave me a look over his shoulder and it was the old Perry, and it was good to see that ironic half-smile.

Bennington-Jones waved a hand and dismissed us. 'I don't know about the two of you, but I am starved.'

We washed up, and headed out for a tiny, homey Salvadorian buffet on Versailles Road, and blended in nicely with the workmen who frequented the place, and we loaded our plates under the satisfied eyes of the owners, who liked men who were hungry and ready to eat.

That night I made it to my mother's house in time to give my boys a bath, read them a story, and tuck them in. They asked me if we would always live with their grandmother, because they thought it would be a good idea. They asked me if since I was a doctor, could I please help Mommy wake up.

Afterwards I drank coffee in my mother's kitchen, Tash curled up at my feet. And I felt again the sense of weight lifted off me, and a moment where I was almost . . . joyous. Right here, right now, my whole family was gathered together, and Perry and I had Bennington-Jones to lead us and we had a plan.

My mother had put a big leather chair and ottoman beside Moira's bed. That is where I slept. Fitfully. Exhausted. Always listening to every breath Moira took.

When I looked in the mirror the next morning, I saw a man I barely recognized. A man who looked tired, his face etched with grief. It surprised me, to see what a physical thing grief could be. I knew what it looked like now. I wondered that I had never realized this before.

But I was still in the fight. And that felt good.

*   *   *

I did not like going home to my house. Leaving Moira behind. And at the same time, I yearned to get away. Truly I was restless, no matter where I was. I avoided the puzzled looks of my neighbors when they saw me come and go. Pretended not to hear their greetings, or see their hesitant waves. By the second day, the wall was done, as promised. I went home to Moira that afternoon, but at seven p.m., Bennington-Jones called me and told me to come back. It was time for phase two.

I heard the two of them laughing when I came through the front door, smelled garlic, tomatoes and onions and bacon sautéing in olive oil, and found the both of them in the kitchen. They were drinking Guinness and Perry gave me a salute when he saw me. They had showered. Bennington-Jones in clean khakis and a white tee shirt, Perry in his favorite old jeans and gray sweater.

'Noah.' Perry gave me the smile that crinkled his eyes up and handed me a bottle of Guinness.

It was good to see the old Perry. More relaxed. Less . . . hunted.

Bennington-Jones turned and looked at me over one shoulder. 'Perfect timing. Perry, grab the shrimp out of the refrigerator there, won't you?' He gave me his small, lopsided smile. 'I have to say I'm getting quite comfortable in this brilliant kitchen of yours, I hope you don't mind? Hungry?'

'Is that shrimp scampi?' I asked. I took a long swallow of beer. I was starving.

'It is.'

'Look at these big boys,' Perry said, holding up a fist-sized shrimp, tail off and deveined.

'Et voilà,' Bennington-Jones said, snatching the shrimp out of Perry's hand and adding it into the giant cast-iron skillet that Moira had inherited from her mother. The shrimp popped in olive oil, simmering with garlic, hot sauce, tomatoes, peppers and onion, and Bennington-Jones poured Marsala wine in slowly, stirring and concentrating. He'd found Moira's tarragon and basil growing in pots on the pergola, and he took the pepper grinder and used it liberally, then sprinkled in ground Ancho chilies.

'This is heaven here, Noah, everything right at your fingertips, mise en place. Who is the cook here, you or your wife?'

'Both of us.'

Perry laughed. '*Moira.*'

'I would cook more if I had time.'

Perry nodded. 'And he's the man for deboning the chicken.'

'That goes without saying.' I settled onto one of the bar stools.

Perry put Camembert and small sweet black grapes within my reach.

'We're celebrating, gentlemen,' Bennington-Jones said, with a quick steady look at me over his shoulder. 'It's time.'

'Time for what?' I asked. I ate a chunk of cheese, and Perry leaned across the counter and grabbed a handful of grapes. But I knew what he meant. I knew what it was time for.

'Perry is ready for you now,' Bennington-Jones said. 'For his treatments.'

Perry chugged his beer, and put the bottle down on the counter with an audible thump. He gave me a lopsided smile. 'Enlightenment on demand.'

I swallowed hard. Carefully set my beer down.

Bennington-Jones put the shrimp on simmer and turned to look at me. 'Come now, Noah, it's time to do your part. You're needed. As dangerous as the treatments can be to the unwary, that's the measure of their power. And that power will give Perry the spiritual strength to deal with Mandeville's obsessors, and to bring Elliot across. The first treatment will be very short. Minutes only. One small step at a time.'

The shrimp simmered gently, the rice, ready, off the burner, under a tight steamed-up lid. No one moved to eat. Perry stood with his feet apart, face rosy with a touch of sun, streaky blond hair combed back. He gripped the edges of the kitchen counter and I watched him, while sipping steadily at my beer.

Bennington-Jones was oddly serene, energetic, like a coach easing the team through pre-game jitters. He wiped his hands on a striped red dish cloth and smiled at me.

'Now, to business.' Bennington-Jones clapped his hands. 'I have arranged the facility. Somewhere safe, somewhere private, you tell me what you need, Noah, and I'll take care of that end of things.'

'But the hospital—'

'*No*,' Bennington-Jones said. 'Out of the public eye. *Private*. We cannot have interference and we cannot have interruptions.

It must be in secret and it must be safe. I have people who will set this up.'

I stood up, heading for my office. 'Look, I'll write it down, what we need. Basically an MRI set up. I have my own equipment specific to the treatments here at the house.'

HORACE, wrapped tenderly and carefully boxed away in my office. Even Hilde didn't know I had it.

'You can tell me all about it in the morning, Noah. Tonight, my boys, we eat shrimp.'

FORTY-EIGHT

P erry's treatment we scheduled early the next evening, around six. We arrived at 5:45 p.m., everyone tucked into my sleek black Audi, the engine idling after I parked in the lot of a boxy concrete facility at the edge of the University of Kentucky Med Center. Flying under the radar of a massive facility was brilliance. When no one knows everything, no one knows anything.

The squat box of a building looked more industrial than medical. It looked like a place for equipment storage, building maintenance.

'You OK?' I asked Perry.

In truth, he was not.

'Do you mean, am I scared?' He gave me the lopsided half-smile that I had not seen much of late. His hands were trembling.

Bennington-Jones was out of the car and we followed him. He kept tabs on us, but in the way of a mama cat whose ears flick when she is distracted. He approached the building sideways, gaze focused, as if he were smelling the place out. He froze for a moment, tilted his head to one side. Then nodded, and gave me a look.

'Open the door for us, Noah, the lock code is 48792776.'

I punched in the number, lifted the hasp of the lock. It was a heavy door, but it opened like silk.

The inside surprised me. Clean. Light and rather beautiful. Whitewashed plaster walls, Italian tile floors, a couple of couches, both new, expensive. It smelled clean. Antiseptic. Like Clorox and a lemon.

No windows though. I tried to think in terms of secrecy rather than escape. Airplanes have windows so passengers don't go insane.

I looked over my shoulder into a dark hallway. 'No torturous stackable vinyl chairs, so this can't be a medical facility.'

Bennington-Jones waved me forward. 'Straight down the hall, bear left, room at the very end.'

I went first, Perry following, Bennington-Jones bringing up the rear.

The treatment room had clearly just been set up. Boxy, the floors here old linoleum, but the equipment was state of the art, and so new it might as well have dangled a price tag. Once I started getting things ready, I was focused and breathing easy. I was in my comfort zone. My job was medical staff. Bennington-Jones would handle the demonic.

Once Perry was inside the machine, the ceramic net of Horace lighting up his brain, I squinted, peering closely at the results on my monitor. Perry's concentration was intense. His heart rate was high, his blood pressure up, but very quickly both slowly and steadily eased back.

I saw flashes of light in the room that made me look up. No one else seemed to notice. I double checked the equipment, but everything was fine. Bennington-Jones stood at Perry's feet, deep in concentration and began to speak.

'What then is enlightenment, but a remembering. Who you are. Why you're here. It is not a state of being. It is a place you find, again and again. It is not set in stone, it never ends, it is a circle. A path you follow, spiraling inward and outward, to your very best self. It is nothing more and nothing less than a remembrance of who you are, and the sure steady knowledge of who you are meant to be.'

I thought suddenly of Moira and me bringing our boys home for the first time. We showed them their rooms and ordered pizza. Everyone was shy and awkward, but the energy was good . . . a family being born. I smiled.

The lights flashed again.

And it started. What felt like a stray thought, soft. Lethal.

You are the problem, Noah.

I looked up. Bennington-Jones had not moved. And Perry's vitals were good. He was calm. My monitor showed him in a deep dive state of meditation. I was envious. In awe of Perry's ability. I wondered if he felt the kind of quiet joy my patients had described. Or the creative euphoria of an artist like Abby.

And I thought of how happy Abby had been the last time I'd seen her. Relieved and ecstatic at feeling like her own true self. And so afraid that feeling would disappear.

Had she died instantly when she was decimated by that bus in London? Had she lived long enough to feel the pain and trauma of being crushed?

You are the problem, Noah.

The despair came over me in waves, and I slumped down low in my chair. I kept an eye on the screen but my mind was elsewhere. In trying to do something good, I had brought nothing but misery. And danger to Moira and the boys.

They are better off without you, Noah.

I nodded. Because as soon as the thought hit, I knew it to be true.

You have come here to die, Noah. It is time to let go. You are tired. Tired of struggling. Come home to us, where you will no longer be Other. You will be one. This was always meant to be. You know this.

I took a deep breath. Became aware of a soft, steady dripping. A thin stream of water was running down the wall across the room. Some kind of leak, slow and steady.

I had forgotten the monitor, and watched the water instead, as another stream began to run beside the other, merging with the first one, water pooling out on the floor, spreading slowly toward my feet. The water was like my despair, running softly but gathering momentum.

A hand on my shoulder made me jump.

'*Noah*.' Bennington-Jones was beside me; I had not heard him approach. He looked down at me. I expected anger, judgment maybe. But he gave me a gentle and encouraging smile. 'Noah, you are a surgeon. Your powers of concentration are formidable. Do not let yourself be distracted. You built a wall. Think of the wall and let it shield you while you do your work. You are exactly where you need to be, doing exactly what you need to do, and you are powerful, Noah. Powerful.'

Something slammed against the metal door, the thick metal door that we had locked behind us. And there were no windows in the room.

I looked up at Bennington-Jones. 'We're trapped in here.'

'Look at the screen, please, Noah. Look there at your monitor and give me an update on Perry.'

I took a slow breath. Looked at the monitor, then at Perry himself, on that ridiculously uncomfortable table. And I wondered why every medical procedure seemed perversely engineered to make patients nervous, uncomfortable. To cause them unnecessary pain. Was this my life's work, bringing pain to my patients who looked to me for help? Who trusted me?

'*Noah.*' A hand on my shoulder, squeezing. 'The update, please. Tell me how Perry is doing.'

I looked at the monitor again. 'He is calm. In a deep meditative state. Focused. Concentrating. At peace, I would say. In a place . . . a place that I envy.'

Another hard slam against the door.

'Did Perry react to that, Noah? It sounds like someone trying to kick the door in; can you tell me if that registered with him?'

I shook my head. 'I don't think so. I'm not seeing any uptick in reaction. Everything is still steady.'

Thunder cracked, followed by a rolling cascade of rumbles. I frowned. We weren't expecting rain, no storms in the forecast.

The air pressure changed, the temperature of the room went up and thunder cracked again, a sonic shock wave. And whatever it was in the hallway was slamming into the door again, slamming hard, making the door bow inward.

The water seeped under my feet, and the thunder began a low rolling rumble that got louder and louder. Thunder has acoustic energy. Shock waves from thunder can actually cause internal contusions and hearing loss. Rare yes. But it happens.

I had always loved the sound of it.

'Noah, it's time to bring Perry down from the treatment.'

I nodded. I cut my fears loose, and walled them away, and took a breath. And it was back. My focus. Mr Hot-Shit Surgeon was here again and, while he might be a bit of a prick sometimes, I welcomed him home.

The pounding at the door got louder but I had myself in check. I was under control. I looked at Bennington-Jones. 'The door will hold, don't worry. They can't get in.'

He shook his head. 'Oh, no, Noah. They are already in.'

We worked quickly. Got Perry out of the machine, and as soon as he sat up on the table, I could see that the tension had gone out of Perry's shoulders, his eyes were clear and focused.

'You're better,' I said.

He thought about it, and nodded.

He came off the table slowly, ignoring the hand I held out, and walked carefully, like a man who was reorienting himself to the world. Recalibrating.

Still. As the three of us came out of the treatment room, it was Perry who seemed the steadiest on his feet.

The water had seeped into the hallway, and we made our way carefully on the slippery linoleum. Bennington-Jones and Perry, a few feet ahead, stopped at the edge of the lobby.

I caught up with them and caught my breath. The couches were overturned. One upside down, the other upended and crooked against the wall. The front door, with the bolt and digital locking system, was wide open, the light from inside a beacon to the darkness that had settled while we'd been inside.

Bennington-Jones headed out into the parking lot without a backward look. He clapped his hands together as he herded us toward the car. 'Well done, gentlemen. And now, I think, some dinner. Hamburgers, don't you think? And beer?'

We wound up at a round wood table in the corner of Ranada's Kitchen, dark navy walls, wood floors, a newly rebuilt bar, and large storefront windows. We could see the street, the glare of headlights from the cars that streamed by.

The beer was cold and we were on our second pitcher. I was having the Havana Nights burger and both Perry and Bennington-Jones had gone for the Bourbon Jam burger, and we all had the hand-cut fries. I had my eye on the Bananas Foster Panna Cotta for dessert.

Bennington-Jones was smiling. 'Hamburgers. My very favorite thing about America.' He took a sip of beer, set his pint glass down and looked over his shoulder at the cars in the street, ever watchful tonight. Then he looked from me to Perry.

'A couple of things to discuss.'

'Am I a problem?' I asked. Because those words still echoed inside me.

Perry looked at me, head cocked sideways.

Bennington-Jones shook his head. 'Just the opposite. You may well be the reason any of this is possible. You and Perry together. To go after them like we are going to.'

I shrugged. I admit it appealed to my ego.

'This thought, Noah. That you are the problem. Did it come to you, perhaps in the middle of Perry's treatment?'

And I remembered his hand on my shoulder, how he'd guided me through. 'How did you know?'

Perry and Bennington-Jones exchanged looks.

'It's called a psychic attack, Noah.' Perry leaned forward. 'We talked about this. Years ago, when we first met. You don't remember?'

'I don't, actually.' But I thought of the young boy that I was all those years ago, looking over High Bridge into the abyss, the red-haired man very close. I had been suicidal that day, and it was a close-run thing. And I had felt tonight exactly the way I'd felt that day.

'So,' Bennington-Jones said. 'To you then, Perry. How do *you* think the treatment went?'

Perry smiled just a little. 'Honestly, it took some time for me to catch hold. I had to go through a sort of fog, very thick, and I could barely see a way forward. And I felt . . . felt pretty shaky about it, to tell the truth. And then, it was OK. I could focus. I had a sort of concentration that brought me . . . relief. And so many things suddenly made sense to me, and connected up in my thoughts. I was aware of a sort of pressure, and loud cracking noises, but I was on the other side of the wall. It was . . . I could detach from the noise and the changes in the energy that was all around me. Like feeling exhilarated in the middle of a tornado. Not logical, but still. What was it like for you guys?'

I gave a harsh laugh, and Bennington-Jones nodded at both of us. 'Good, Perry. I'd say it went better than expected. So. Change of plan then. I know we had thought to do four treatments.'

Perry nodded, as if he welcomed them, but I felt a thread of chill in my stomach.

'But this stops tonight. No more treatments. It's time.'

'Is it because of me? I choked. 'I know that.'

'Yes, Noah, it is because of what happened to you. Not because you failed. You actually did quite well.'

'I can handle more treatments,' I said.

Perry nodded. 'Me too.'

'I don't doubt that. But every treatment we do puts a target on your backs and gives them a way, an opportunity to come after you. This is a risk-cost-benefit analysis. It's time to go forward.'

I looked out the window. The streetlights, the cars, the people on the sidewalk.

'And so. It is time now, Perry. You did well, both of you, but this tonight was your last treatment. Tomorrow, Perry, you will sleep and meditate, and the day after . . . we will do this. We will bring Elliot across.'

I felt a sick feeling in the pit of my stomach. 'Across,' I echoed. That seemed guaranteed to stir up trouble. 'So Perry's ready now, and we have a level playing field.'

'Oh no,' Bennington-Jones smiled. 'We don't want a *level* playing field. I have no intention of playing fair.'

FORTY-NINE

The night before Mandeville's last exorcism, I sat beside Moira and watched her breathe. She seemed far away and gone. I had been instructed by Bennington-Jones to get as much sleep as I could, and eat a solid steak dinner. But I could not eat. And I could not sleep. I could hold Moira's hand, so that is what I did.

And the next morning, so early it was still dark, I showered and shaved and put on loose jeans, an old worn tee shirt and a black pullover sweater, laced up my running shoes, and kissed my sleeping family good-bye. Tash walked me to the door, tail wagging, and I crouched down close to her, and she gave me doggie kisses, and I stroked her ears. 'Don't give me all of your kisses now, puppy dog. Save some of them for later.'

It was five a.m. when I got to the paddock – encircled by black, tarry four-plank horse fencing, lush with thick bluegrass, bounded by a creek. Bennington-Jones had arranged it. He assured us the owner was happy to let us make use of the land. Bennington-Jones had shaken his head in horror when Perry had suggested doing the exorcism indoors. 'Outside, it will be safer,' Bennington-Jones said. He did not explain why. He simply gave me an address and told me to be there by sun-up.

And yet, Perry and Bennington-Jones were there before me. Perry was leaning against the hood of his old navy blue Volvo, head low, wearing the robe and the stole with the cross around his neck. Bennington-Jones approached as soon as I stopped my car. He himself was in khakis and a sweater, and he embraced me when I got out of the car.

'It's time,' he said. 'We will start when Mandeville gets here.' He pointed to a tree, a good twenty feet away. 'You go there, Noah, and you stay there, until everything is over, and I give you the all-clear. Until then, you stay right there, *no matter what*. Promise me you'll comply.'

I nodded. Caught a movement over his shoulder. The sun was just coming up, and I saw a man in the darkness and pre-dawn shadow, standing several feet away. Mandeville.

'He's here,' I said.

Bennington-Jones nodded. 'I know.'

He watched me until I was in place, hunched close to the rough bark of a large ash tree. Then he went to Perry, embraced him. Perry nodded, straightened up, and turned his back on both of us. His focus entirely on Henry Mandeville. They would do this dance again.

It was frustrating not to really be able to hear what was being said, but as the sun came up, I could see Perry standing no more than two feet from Mandeville, and he seemed calm, strong, almost serene. Mandeville stood his ground, facing Perry, challenge and malevolence in the way he planted his feet and held his arms.

The wind began to blow.

232 of Lynn Hightower

The limbs of the tree beside me began to sway and shed leaves, and the wind blew harder, whipping up dirt and rippling across the grass. I smelled smoke, and looked over my shoulder.

It was a fire like no other, and it ran along the fence line of the paddock, sweeping closer, eating up the ground. It happened like a formless, dancing, mysterious dream. I felt the heat and I felt the cold. It was a fire that lived, that had spirit, that could sweep us all away. It obeyed no natural laws that I knew; it was alive, it mesmerized, and when I looked into the flames I trembled and my breath came out in a cold fog of air. I wanted to run but I was hypnotized by the heat and drawn to the flame.

Perry held his ground. He was shouting now, though I could not make out the words. But I could hear the power in his voice, the confidence, the calm.

And as I watched, the fire whipped across the field and we were circled in tongues of flames. There was nowhere to run now.

The fire swept toward Perry and he raised his arms and I knew that he was seconds from death and I called his name, but my cry was lost in the living roar and crackle of flames.

I started toward him, but Bennington-Jones was there beside me, coming out of nowhere, it seemed, and he grabbed my shoulder and held me back.

'*No*. Be still.'

He was stronger than I would have thought possible, and I called Perry's name as the fire swept toward him. Mandeville lunched forward, screaming, arms raised, shaking his fists at Perry, the flames igniting his hair.

And then the fire parted and began to take form and in the flames I saw the churning hooves and shadows of horses that were not horses.

Mandeville bellowed, but this was not anger, this was fear. And then I saw her.

Moira.

Moira, but not Moira. Somersly, a warrior, arms raised, and I heard her scream of rage. It was like a dream, a kaleidoscope of images behind a wavering wall of shimmering heat. Mandeville ran, but she was behind him in three swift strides. She called his name and he froze She pointed at him, said his name again, and a cold blue light pulsed and swept through him, and he was in flame from his neck to his waist. A hot dark wind blew through the flames, pelting us with dirt and rock and hot, gritty embers, and I shielded my eyes. Mandeville screamed, staggered and fell, steaming and smoking, and his hair, his clothes sizzled in the flame, billowing black oily smoke.

And then I saw Elliot.

The man in Abby's paintings, the man on the swing. But he was tall, so tall, and somehow beautiful. Strong and sturdy, his arms open wide, his face joyous as he was bathed in a light that was not the fire.

I heard the scream of horses, the fire flared impossibly high, and Elliot and Somersly embraced like long-lost lovers, in the shimmer of light and heat.

And they were gone. It had happened so quickly.

'It is done. At last. He is home.' Bennington-Jones looked oddly lonely, as the tears ran down his face.

FIFTY

The heart of the fire collapsed and a soft rain began to fall. I ran to Perry, who stood there in the paddock looking off to the right, and I knew he saw things I could not see. His hands slowly fell to his sides. I was aware of Bennington-Jones struggling along behind me, limping, canted sideways with the pain from his hip.

Perry was dazed, his face reddening with burn.

'Don't touch him,' Bennington-Jones called out.

Perry staggered sideways and I reached out to steady him, but Bennington-Jones, panting and sweating, grabbed my arm and stopped me. I took a step back.

'Where is Moira,' I asked him. 'Is she gone? Is she dead? That wasn't her, that was Somersly. What happens to her now?'

Perry lurched forward, heading toward Mandeville, and I was right behind him. Like Perry, I needed to see.

Henry Mandeville had literally roasted in the fire, his skin a blackened carapace, the rictus smile showing the white of his teeth. He was curled sideways, arms drawn close, hands a ball of charcoal fists. Agony. I felt no pity. I felt nothing at all.

Perry slumped forward and this time I caught him. He did not smell of smoke and soot. He smelled of flowers. Cold, sweet flowers, and touching him made my skin burn with cold like I had clutched a chunk of chemical ice. I jerked away, felt the sting of skin peeling away from my hands, the ripping of my sweater as the fabric pulled away.

Perry looked down at Mandeville. 'Lost,' he whispered.

Bennington-Jones clucked over my hands, and patted my shoulder as he turned to Perry. 'You are the vessel, Perry. The instrument. It is not yours to decide the outcome.'

My voice sounded harsh and it surprised me how angry I was. 'What happens now? To Moira?'

The both of them looked at me, and I felt like a child, making unreasonable demands. I did not like the pity in their eyes.

Bennington-Jones had his hands full with the pair of us, as rain pattered gently into the blackened, scorched ground. Perry was stumbly, in shock, not quite lucid, and I was sulking and tense, emanating anger that hid my fear and the chilling conviction that now Somersly was gone, Moira would die, and soon. I knew in my heart that when I walked back into my mother's home, Moira would be dead. It was all over now. For all of us.

'Can you help me get him to the car?' Bennington-Jones asked me. 'It's safe now. You can touch him.' The icy-sweet scent of flowers had dissipated, leaving the scent of black oily smoke and roasted flesh.

Bennington-Jones was struggling, and I took Perry and shored him up, my shoulder under his, my arm wrapped around his waist. Perry seemed too distracted to keep his feet. I looked into his face, the skin burnt red like a sunburn, already starting to blister, but could not catch his eye; he was distant and absorbed, and I wondered, in a twinge of despair, if, like Moira, Perry would be lost to me too.

Between us, we got him hustled to the car, and Bennington-Jones smiled at me, an old man renewed and looking oddly young, though his body betrayed him, and his twisted sideways walk spoke of a man engulfed in pain.

The pragmatic side of me took over and I was competent, strong and in cold control as I helped Perry into the car. The keys were in the ignition and I looked hard at Bennington-Jones.

'Can you drive?' I kept my voice gentle and it was a good question. Eventually the religious exultation would wear off and he was already in a lot of pain. I was not sure how long he could stay on his feet.

'I can if I must . . . are you hurt then?'

I did not answer.

'Of course, Noah, I can manage. Climb on into the back there and I'll get everyone home. We'll pick your car up later.'

Ah the practicalities of the exorcism. Not the least of which ought to be a designated driver.

And I felt as if everyone was going home, except me. Without Moira I had no home.

I shook my head. 'No, I am not hurt, but if you can manage Perry, I'd rather find my own way back.'

Bennington-Jones put a hand on my shoulder. 'Whatever happens with Moira, you are going to be OK.'

'So she's gone then?'

'We both know she should have died that day, there by the lake.'

Perry looked at me with a thread of worry and said something I could not catch. Bennington-Jones nodded, and turned toward me, but I waved them on.

'Go. Really. I'm fine. Go on ahead, I'll be right behind you.'

Bennington-Jones opened the car door, then turned back again to look at me. 'You'll be OK, Noah,' he said. A statement. Not a question. A gust of wind ruffled his hair and he raised a hand and gave me a smile. 'I'll be in touch.'

I watched them go, Bennington-Jones driving, Perry slumped in the back seat, slowly bumping over the burned-out paddock, and then settling gently onto the pavement as Bennington-Jones guided the car onto the narrow ribbon of country road that would wind past horse farms and stone walls, built by Irish laborers in the 1800s. Grassy paddocks, black walnut trees, horses nose to ground snatching up mouthfuls of grass. The car slowed, then moved forward and trailed away out of sight.

And now it was just me. I looked to my car, but I was heavy now, a fatigue that slowed my walk, and shortened my breath.

In truth, it was an odd feeling, as if I had literally had all I could take, and there was nothing left to draw on. I did not think I could make it to the car. I had never felt anything like this before. And I knew what this was. This was grief. And it was taking me down into darkness.

I came to a halt beneath the ash tree, reached out to brace myself against the rough dark bark, and stumbled, the trunk of the tree breaking my fall as I slid against it, onto the ground.

I had nothing left. I settled slowly, legs out, back to the tree, the bark rough but solidly comforting. I would just sit here, and not move, because I knew I could not get to my feet if I wanted to.

In truth, I did not.

I did not want to go home to the empty echo of my house. To face the teary-eyed, uncomprehending grief of my young sons. Where was Mommy? Gone. Just . . . gone. I would have to go home sometime. I knew that. But not now. Not now.

I took a deep breath. It was cool out, and there was a mist gathering in the air, turning into a slight sprinkle, and I was damp, but protected, beneath my tree. I clutched a dead leaf in my hand and crumbled it in my fist. I liked the solid comfort of this tree against my back. I thought about the trees I climbed when I was a boy. I thought about a tree house. I always wanted a tree house growing up, but we never had the right kind of tree. My boys and I, we could have a tree house. The black walnut in my backyard that shaded the side yard and kept the grass from thriving, that was exactly the right kind of tree. I wondered why I had never thought of it before.

The boys and I, we would build a tree house. And none of your skeletal platforms on a branch. It would be a phenomenal tree house. With walls, and built-in shelves, a roof. We'd have a battery lamp so we could be up there at night. We could sleep up there. I could put up hammocks. Even build bunks.

I closed my eyes, picturing myself, Marcus and Vaughn, curled up together as darkness fell. I could see them in my mind's eye, huddled close.

There was a rock under my right thigh and I wanted to move it, or at least move my leg, but I could not find the strength.

My last thought, as I feel asleep, was of Bennington-Jones, the gentle smile as he raised his hand and told me I'd be OK. I heard the echo of his voice. *I'll be in touch.* It seemed an odd thing to say.

The rain picked up, and I was wet, and I was cold, but it seemed a reality that was incidental and of no consequence. I folded my arms tight, turned my back to the rain. Even the shivering did not keep me conscious. I slept and slept hard.

I am dreaming of Moira. She is wearing strappy red high heels, a dress that billows and twists as she spins. Someone, I can't see . . . someone is holding her hand, up high, and they are dancing. I do not hear the music but I see the delicious sway of her hips as she steps, then turns. In perfect harmony, in this dance.

And there it is, the music. I can hear it now, piano, the sweet sound that is specific to a baby grand.

I have her hand. It is me she dances with, and she smiles at me over her shoulder, eyes so blue, brows so dark, lips red and shiny with crimson lipstick, and I want to kiss her and gather her up, but she pulls me along, she wants to dance. I feel the warmth of her hand in mine as she spins. I hold her hand firmly. Keep her steady. Keep her safe.

She squeezes my hand and laughs at me. She squeezes harder, too hard, and calls my name.

The first thing I noticed was a soft pawing on my cheek, and the peculiar and unexpected hum of purring, and a welcome warm spot against my side. I opened my eyes and frowned. The cat was tucked up next to me, folded up like a little cat loaf, purring softly, content, blinking when he saw me open my eyes, watching me as cats do.

'What the fuck,' I said. My voice sounded odd. Slurred.

I knew that cat. Elliot's cat. The one in the painting. Tiger-striped . . . emerald eyes.

The cat was unperturbed and not inclined to move, and the light shifted suddenly, and I realized someone was standing over me.

I scrambled up on my side, muscles slow, cramped and achy, and she bent down and sank to her knees and smiled at me. Beautiful Moira. Hair wild and damp. She was wrapped in my big gray sweater, just like the other night, jeans, her hiking boots. Her tough terrain outfit.

I touched her cheek. It felt very real. 'No high heels?'

'Really? Even for you, Noah, that's an odd thing to say.'

'I was dreaming.'

'You aren't dreaming now. Wife in boots, not high heels. Welcome to reality, my love.'

Such a Moira thing to say. I laughed, took her hand, then was up on my knees, gathering her up, and holding her close, and it was *her*, Moira, not Moira Other. Soft. Flesh. Human. She felt right, she smelled right. She had a crumpled leaf caught in her hair.

'You're home,' I said. 'Am I dead?'

She chuckled. 'Good question. Maybe we both are.'

I looked at her.

She shook her head. 'You look like hell, Noah, and you smell like smoke and soot, but I don't think you're dead.' She glanced over her shoulder at the burned-out paddock. 'What happened here? Did you start a fire?'

She started to stand up, but I grabbed her and pulled her down, and wrapped my arms around her, holding her tight.

'You don't remember?' I asked.

'Remember what? The last thing I remember is you. When I came to you last night.'

'A week ago, Moira.'

'A week?' She frowned. 'It feels like just a few moments, really. I went back and got my kitty.'

'Your kitty?'

The cat was ignoring us, intent on something minuscule moving in a thread of grass beneath a leaf, and Moira stroked his head, and he twitched his ears, annoyed. 'Yes, my cat. The man on the swing gave him to me. It's Mister Timothy. You know, I told you about him, the cat I lost when we moved here from Atlanta, when I was a little girl? Elliot said they'd been keeping him safe, and it was time Mister Timothy came home to me. And I said thank you, and I cried, and I said I wanted to take the cat and go home. And Elliot said . . . he said, *and so you shall*. And then I was here and I saw *you*, Noah, under the tree. You looked so tired. I called your name, I squeezed your hand, but you didn't wake up. So I watched you sleep.'

'And that's all you remember?'

'That's all.' And then she burst into tears and tucked her head into my chest.

I stroked her hair. How much did she know? How much did she remember? How much should I tell her?

'I don't even know why I'm crying. It's . . . confusing. It's just that I missed you. And I missed the boys. I feel like something . . . bad things . . . have been happening, but I can't really sort them out, just that I have been so worried sometimes, so afraid. And sometimes my head, it really aches.' She touched the side of her head, and I parted her hair and saw the red welt of the scar where the bullet had entered her head. Impossible. All of this. Impossible.

'Noah, that hurts, stop messing with my hair. I'm glad, so glad, to be home. I just want to be safe. I want all of us just to be safe.'

I held her until the sobbing stopped. And I eased her sideways, so that when she lifted her head, she would not see that blackened obscenity in the field.

The kitty stood up and butted my arm and wormed his way into our laps.

Moira laughed and lifted her head. 'Can we go home, Noah? Please?'

'We can.'

'And the boys are there? At home?'

'They're at my mother's. So is Tash. We'll pick them up on the way. I wonder what Tash will think of Mister Timothy.'

'Oh, Noah, you are clueless about cats. It's more a question of what Mr Timothy will think of Tash.'

FIFTY-ONE

Hours after Moira and I gathered up our little family, and made it home safe and sound, the sun set and dusk filtered down on a day we would forever remember . . . and the little church in Hollywood burned. Just past two a.m., the neighbors saw flames flickering high and fierce, lighting up the stained-glass windows that had been painted over and covered with a dark alphabet no one understood. The fire that seemed to come out of nowhere, and had no clear-cut origin, shattered those windows, and plumes of black, oily smoke came roiling out.

The neighbors first on the scene saw a man moving around in the sanctuary, and one of them kicked the front doors open. The fire roared out, and the heat drove them back, singeing their hair, turning their faces raw and red. But several of them saw him, the Reverend Travis Smallwood, of the Chapel of Disciples, standing several feet back from the door. He did not come out. He turned abruptly and disappeared, as if he'd been called away.

A team of firefighters was there in minutes and went in after him. One broke her leg when the floor gave way, one broke a shoulder when he was hit by ceiling debris. Two suffered massive burns trying to find him, trying to bring him out.

But he could not be found, in the flames and the smoke, and no remains were found in the investigation. There were no definitive signs anyone had been living there, though he had been seen coming and going at all hours, and his congregation swore he lived right there, in a little office studio at the back of the church.

I wish I could tell you that the red-haired man is gone. But what I know is that Perry calls him the Inciter. And that he looked exactly the same that night in my backyard, as he did that day years ago on High Bridge. The name was different, but he was not. I think of him now as a harbinger of trouble. Like the howl of a wolf in the night. But I am no longer that terrified boy. If I hear it again, I'll be ready.

And Moira . . . she is different, now . . . my beautiful, my beloved, my wife.

She is here, and she is not.

She is the same.

She is Other.

It comes like a patina on a copper pot. Her eyes blaze then turn yellow, lion eyes; she seems taller somehow, and that scent of jasmine and white roses mingles in a frosty, sweet essence that is like crushed flowers in snow.

Things will never be the same, our lives, our marriage, our family . . . it cannot go back to what it was – fallible man, fallible woman – because the Other comes at inexplicable times. Does it watch us? Does it *lurk*?

'Is it always there, Moira?'

She looked away, but she did not pretend she didn't understand; she did not pretend not to hear. She frowned and brushed hair away with a gesture that was so familiar, so much the Moira of before.

It is moments like this that I cling to. Moments where we are the *us* we used to be. And I know, with a clench of my stomach, that I could have lost her entirely. That to all the parameters of medical science that *I* know, I did lose her. I know I should be grateful, and I feel like a sulky child, but I want only Moira, not that Other presence. Just Moira and me, as we always were, as we've always been. My wife is here, and yet not here. A familiar. A stranger.

'I shut her out,' Moira said.

'You can control it?'

'No. She will come if she wants to. But there are times where I feel her at the edges, if that makes sense.'

'What about this makes sense?'

She laughed. She pushed me down on my back, and sprawled across my chest. Her hair draped over my shoulders, us on the couch, the boys in bed, guarded by Tash.

She peered down at me. 'Here's how it feels, Noah. Like I am mostly . . . just me. But that she is around, sometimes; not like she is me, but that she is in the same room. And sometimes she comes into the room and when she does that . . . I go out.'

I closed my eyes and swallowed. 'Always come back, Moira.'

'Always,' she said. Holding tight to my hand, nestling her head into my shoulder.

And with that, I must be content.

And what I know, is this. That life brings many things, some of them good and some of them terrible. And the only thing that is important, is who you love when it all plays out.

FIFTY-TWO

Perry and I were lucky to find space at the bar, and we sat side by side right in the middle. Harry's was thick with customers, intent on bar food, beer, and the football game. We were no different.

Perry had something on his mind, but he was working his way into it. 'Boys OK?' he asked, drumming a finger on the bar.

I nodded. I was drinking a local draft, and Perry was on his second martini. He wore the gray sweater with the hole and the same battered, loose pair of jeans he'd worn out while building the wall with Bennington-Jones.

My boys loved that wall, Marcus perching on the top, legs dangling, Vaughn finding tiny toe-holds to climb, with my steady hand on his back. Moira was debating on how to cover the top with flowers. Wandering through garden centers with her head cocked to one side.

Our food came – sliders and shrimp cocktails. The sliders had cheese and crispy bacon on tiny burgers. The shrimp, boiled pinkish white, came on a bed of ice with a blue LED light beneath.

'Excellent presentation,' I said to the waiter, who smiled but didn't much care. He suggested a third round of drinks, an idea we met with enthusiasm.

Perry rubbed at a ring of water that had gathered at the edge of his martini glass. I dipped a shrimp in cocktail sauce and took a bite, my eyes watering at the generous dollop of horseradish swirled through the sauce. Perry frowned at the burgers, and did not eat.

'Have you spoken with . . . Henry Mandeville's wife? Did you go to the funeral?' I thought about going. But I wrote her a letter of condolence instead.

He nodded.

'How is she?'

'She's . . . sad, Noah. Incredibly, unbearably sad. We have regular counseling sessions. She's resilient. I have hope that she'll find her way. How is Alec?'

I took a big, long swallow of beer. 'Inconsolable. Spends time with Candice's father. Is with us a lot. The spare bedroom is his now. The boys love it.'

Perry nodded. 'I like the sound of that.' He looked away for a moment. 'So. Bennington-Jones and I. We did a lot of talking. After.'

I pushed my beer away. 'Where is he? I haven't seen him since that day.' I'd been curious about the things they'd discussed, imagining dark secrets and wisdom and feeling excluded. I hoped Perry was going to let me into the cool kids' club and dish.

'He wants us to work together to offer treatments. Your treatments. But only to experienced exorcists. To help train them, to give them guidance, strength. An enlightenment edge, he called it. Obviously, Noah, I can't do it without you. It would not be connected to a hospital, but you could continue your research. And of course, your medical practice.'

I took a bite of shrimp, swallowed, took a pull of my beer. 'You really think this is a good idea, Perry?' There was no need for us to go into the pros and cons, we knew the good and bad of it. 'Considering the risks?'

Perry nodded. 'I've given it a lot of thought. It's got serious dangers, we both know that. But it's like . . . a new form of knowledge. It can't be used without ethics. So we'd tread carefully. I don't think these treatments are safe for just anyone. You do the treatments, and I'll be there, to guide them through. But.' He picked up a slider, then set it back down.

I cocked my head sideways. 'What?'

'I'm very conflicted about asking you to do this. I had thought there, for a while, you were thinking to cut loose from all of this once and for all. Have a normal life.'

'It's what I want, Perry. A plain, normal life.'

He narrowed his eyes and his shoulders tensed but he smiled gently and nodded. 'Of course. It's the wise choice.'

I wiped my hands on a black cloth napkin. Nodded at the waiter when our drinks came. Perry clutched the stem of his martini but did not drink.

I thought of Moira, who was and was not my wife. Of the pressure in the room, the shift in the air currents, the rise of tension, when *they* were close. And they *were* close, much too often, drifting in like a fog. Closer than ever. I had to work to keep them out. I had to sleep behind the wall.

I would never take a treatment myself. I would never risk it. I don't think I would find my way back.

I noted Perry looking subtly and quickly over my shoulder, in that sudden furtive tense way he had now, and I knew he had seen *something*. A bit of darkness on the back of our necks.

'Look, I'll admit it. Part of me would be thrilled to have the chance to get back to my research. To find a treatment protocol, maybe to dovetail with an exorcism, to bring people back from possession.' I leaned close to Perry and lowered my voice. 'I've looked at the MRI I did while you were giving Henry Mandeville that exorcism. The changes in his frontal lobe were massive.' I rubbed my chin. 'Perry, if I thought I had a choice, I'd ditch all of it. But I don't think either of us has a choice.' I thought of myself at eleven, afraid in my bed at night. Full of dread and exhaustion. 'I'm not sure I've ever had a choice.'

Perry sighed. 'There is that. Yeah. I'm sorry, Noah. I think it's chosen us. For you and me, there's no going back, and Bennington-Jones was right, it is better to face it head-on than to run and hide. Better to stay in the fight.'

I took a huge bite of burger. 'Stay in the fight. *Fuck those guys.*'

Perry grinned at me. 'Sounds like a mandate. *Fuck those guys.*'

'You know what's worse than the creepy stuff, is the paperwork – admin and detail stuff. It will take some time to get this up and running. Just getting it funded—'

Perry put a hand on my arm. 'That's part of what I was going to tell you. It seems Bennington-Jones has been a step ahead. He envisioned this . . . years ago. He's got the bones of the organization sketched out and the seed money committed.'

'I don't want to be tied up to religious dudes,' I said, shoulders tense.

'I'm a religious dude.'

'That's different. I don't want to be under their thumb, Perry. I don't. They're always going to have a twisty agenda. That's a serious deal breaker for me.'

'We'll be working with the International Association of Exorcists, though, yes, the Vatican and a lot of religious dudes will certainly be a part. But they are the people we need.

Experienced exorcists. They bring the money and the resources, Noah. But. We won't be giving up our autonomy.'

'Money is power, you know that.'

'Of course I do. But we already have the funding, and if we don't like the strings they attach, we take our treatment and go home.'

'And this is all set up already?'

'Bennington-Jones has been working on this for years. Putting it all together. Remember when we met him. He said: *Just the fellows I've been looking for*. He wasn't kidding.'

I frowned. 'Maybe it's the beer but I am having a hard time wrapping my mind around that. I thought *we* called *him*.'

'Yes. We did. I did. So did Moira. But.' Perry put a strong, heavy hand on my arm. 'Noah, I had a strange call this morning. From a church administrator in Oxford. The one I talked to when I was trying to track down Bennington-Jones. He apologized for leaving me hanging with my request, said he understood that I was in serious distress, and said that Bennington-Jones was not available, but he was looking for another candidate to send, and hoped to hear back with a confirmation within the week.'

'Wait, what? Not *available*? What a bureaucracy. These guys could not find their asses without a vote and a committee. I hope you told him Bennington-Jones was right here and to fuck on off. Or fuck all y'all, as we say in the south.'

Perry looked at me for a long moment. 'I said something of the sort, more politely. It shook him up.'

I set my drink down.

Perry leaned close and spoke in a low voice. 'He told me that they had not been in touch because Bennington-Jones had disappeared. At first, they thought he was off on travels. He'd done that before, without a lot of notice. But he did not show up to teach. Someone went out to check on him and they found him slumped over his desk. They say that evidently he died suddenly. Likely a massive stroke.'

'What? When?'

'Once they pieced it together – who had seen him last, who had talked to him. They said he died sometime, very late, on the evening of the sixth of June.'

'But—'

Perry grabbed my arm. 'June sixth, Noah. And then he showed up here on—'

'June eleventh.'

Perry looked at me and I concentrated on my breathing. My appetite vanished. I picked up my beer, wondering if I should keep drinking or stop drinking. Perry took the glass out of my loose grip and set it gently on the bar.

'Yes, Noah, I know how you feel.'

'When?' I choked, cleared my throat. 'When was the last time you talked to him, Perry?'

'After he took me home, that day in the paddock when all hell broke loose. Literally.'

I almost laughed.

'I was . . . shook up. Elated. Triumphant and scared shitless. And he spoke to me, in that way he has. Calmed me down. I have wracked my brains, but I cannot remember what he actually said to me, just that he spoke calmly, and repetitively, and I remember thinking how everything he said made such good sense. And it . . . it comforted me. But still I knew that what he was saying was crucial, that I had to pay attention, but I don't remember the specifics. Just that – it felt right. I felt hopeful. I felt safe. I felt . . . peace.

'And he told me this. That it is the job of the elder to guide, to protect, and to carry the weight and not despair. It is the job of the younger to have warrior energy, and to wage the fight.

'And then he looked at me very steadily, and he asked me to think hard and long about the work that you and I could do with the foundation.'

'The foundation?'

'The Enlightenment Foundation.'

'He named it after my project?'

'He named it years ago, you'd have still been in med school. I told you, he's been putting it together for a long time.'

'Holy fuck, Perry.'

'Exactly. And then he said that he was leaving for now. But that I . . . that you . . . would be OK. I remember that word for word. And then . . . then he gripped my shoulder, gave me the gentlest smile, and said . . . I'll be in touch.'